MW01064734

water dreams

water dreams

Jeanne McDonald

University Press of Mississippi / *Jackson*

Water Dreams is a work of fiction. Names, characters, incidents, and places are fictitious or are used fictitiously. The characters are products of the author's imagination and do not represent any actual persons.

www.upress.state.ms.us

Designed by Todd Lape

The University Press of Mississippi is a member of the Association of American University Presses.

Manufactured in the United States of America

11 10 09 08 07 06 05 04 03 4 3 2 1
∞
Library of Congress Cataloging-in-Publication Data
McDonald, Jeanne, 1935–
Water dreams / Jeanne McDonald.
p. cm.
ISBN 1-57806-548-8 (alk. paper)
1. Men—Southern States—Fiction. 2. Drowning victims—Fiction. 3. Southern States—Fiction. 4. Midlife crisis—Fiction. I. Title.
PS3613.C387W38 2003
813'.6—dc21 2002154350

British Library Cataloging-in-Publication Data available

The heart of another
is a dark forest, always,
no matter how close
it has been to one's own.

—Willa Cather

1

He wasn't that far gone yet, but as he waded into the water he thought how it might be easy, peaceful even, to keep going, to let the lake take him in its cold dark arms and hold him for a while. But it was a momentary notion, one he entertained only a few long seconds at the most, and then he was all right again.

His legs began to sting from the chill of the water, and, over his shoulder, the climbing sun was beginning to warm his back. His feet were cold and he couldn't remember why he was standing there. His mind had been wandering, something that happened more and more often lately. He brought himself back to the business at hand. Secure the boat. Park the car and trailer. Move.

Move.

Once he was in the boat, he drifted for a while, listening. As the sun hit the shoreline, dim forms along the bank shaped themselves into hickories and locusts and dogwoods, and beneath them emerged a few low, weedy shrubs and fallen trees. Nurse trees, his father had called them. A fish leapt a few yards away and the sunrise illuminated gleaming droplets where the surface of the water was broken. It seemed strange that the moon still floated in the sky opposite the sun, caught in an eerie collision of time.

Tires popped on the gravel road above the marina and he realized he was no longer alone. He yanked the starter cord. The roar of the motor ripped through the stillness and the sound trailed him across the water. By the time he turned into his favorite fishing cove, the sun had sailed halfway overhead, scouring the sky white. The few patches of blue that had survived the heat of the sun's rays were so pale they were almost silver. It would be a hot day, but at this hour the water was still cool enough for fishing. Besides, it didn't matter whether he caught anything. It was good to be alone, good to be away from the house.

He shut down the throttle and let the boat float. There in the tree-lined cove off from the main channel, the absence of sound was stunning. Eyes closed, he let the current carry him until the boat bumped against the bank. When he stood up to push off again, he mistook his reflection in the water for the image of his father. It unnerved him. Sometimes the pain was sharper than at others—when he woke from a dream, for instance, because in his dreams, his father, Hollis, seemed so much *there*, so fully realized, smiling at him from the other end of the boat or treading water in the lake and calling to that boy Miller had been a long time ago. "Come on, son, come on in. It's not so cold once you're in." But when Miller jumped in, Hollis was gone. There was no one there to catch him.

He looked down at the water and thought how innocent it seemed, how clear it was this morning in the shallows, pale green, like celadon. But he remembered as a very young child jumping off a pier as his father tied up the boat, and the water had closed around him in a shocking embrace which then had become a determined pull. He had struggled, cried out for help, but when he did that, the water had invaded his throat as well. It must have been only seconds until his father pulled him out, but it seemed forever, a panicky time measured by his physical struggles and the sense of being alone in a green, alien world.

His grief was like a wound no longer fresh but not quite closed. It had been six months now since Hollis's death. That evening the winter before, when Miller had opened the door and called out his father's name, he'd felt the emptiness of the place blow against him like a gust of wind. Except that he *was* there—his father—asleep in his armchair, yet not asleep. *Your father expired about six this morning,* the doctor said. And now, sometimes, on the lake where they had spent so much time together, Miller actually felt his father's presence. Occasionally the boat tipped as if with a shifted weight, and Miller knew what caused it, because it changed the very texture of the atmosphere.

When Miller ran his hand across his face and leaned over to open his lunch box, the sun struck the glass bottle under the plastic-wrapped sandwiches. Not yet. He should wait a while. Not on this now bright and perfect morning. And if things went well, he might not need it all day.

He cast his line near the bank, where rotting stumps from trees that had once stood tall on valley farmland spawned a rich underwater life that for some reason attracted bass. He began to feel better, smelling the ripe vegetation, feeling sun on his shoulders, watching the water for movement. Then voices fractured the silence, echoing from the lower end of the cove like a pebble skipped across the smooth surface of the lake. At first the sounds were low, and then they grew louder and sharper, peppered with coarse laughter.

Miller picked up an oar and pushed against the bank. At the mouth of the cove he stood up in the boat and shaded his eyes. They were fifty or sixty yards up the shoreline in the shade of a grove of hackberry trees—kids, two girls and three boys, diving from a dock probably not their own. There was no sign of a boat. They must have parked their car on the road above and walked down through the woods. Miller guessed them to be in their early twenties—only a few years older than his son, Judd.

Older, yes, because one girl balanced a baby on her hip. But you never knew these days. Miller noticed the girl because of her pale skin—it had the sheen of alabaster—and her hair was so black it glinted blue in the sun. She was looking his way, but with the light in his eyes he could not tell if she was staring at him or simply facing downstream.

Nothing, he thought. *Let it go, they're up to no harm, just a day in the sun.* One of the boys had lassoed the limb of a tree with a rope knotted thickly at the end to make a foothold. He grabbed it midway, closed his knees together, and spun out over the water. His shrieks bounced across the lake and then he let go and plunged into the water while his voice still echoed above in the shimmering air. *That does it,* Miller thought, *they've spooked the fish,* but he continued to watch while the rope swung back and a red-haired girl grabbed it. She climbed onto the bank, leaned into space and swept out over the lake, her long laugh tumbling into the air behind her. At the highest point of the arc she released the rope and her body hung for a second suspended in sunlight, as if time had stopped. *It used to be like that,* Miller thought. *Time used to stand still sometimes, and now it won't stop for anything.*

He blinked. His eyes swam with sunspots. He was lifting the anchor when another of the boys stood up and grabbed the rope. He was skinny and pale, with long blonde hair plastered against his shoulders and dripping with water. The dark-haired girl seemed somehow connected to him. She shifted the weight of the baby in her arms and pointed. "Look, Sister," she said, "your daddy's gonna fly. He's gonna fly right out over that water, just like Peter Pan."

The boy laughed and moved as if to kiss the girl, but he seemed unwilling to go beyond the length of the rope he held. She, too, looked to be estimating the empty space of dock between them and remained fixed where she was, as if she had judged it too far to go, though in fact it was only a couple of yards. The boy flexed his bony shoulders, stared deliberately at the girl for a few seconds, then turned his head and spat into the water. He shook his head and tucked his long hair behind his ears, then pushed one foot against the bank and started running down the length of the dock. When he released the rope, his feet were still churning the air.

After the splash, the rope swung back empty, a lazy length of gold drifting in the sunlight. It bumped against the tree trunk a few times and finally hung motionless. The girl sauntered to the end of the dock and peered into the water.

"Je-*sus*. You see that run?" said one of the boys, laughing. "Jimmy Duane coulda gone to the Olympics."

The others laughed, too. A broad concentric circle spread on the surface of the water. The redhead stared down into the lake and said something, but Miller could not make out the words. The girl holding the baby shook her head and said, as if for her own validation, "He's playacting. He's just down there trying to scare us. He'll be up in a minute." Her voice was deep and throaty, like a country singer's. She repeated her assumption. "He'll be up in a minute." She hoisted the baby higher on her shoulder and sat down by the ladder, her long feet dangling in the water. She wore faded blue jeans cut off at the thighs and a sleeveless tee shirt the color of a pale green apple. Her breasts were high and round and her hips were straight as a boy's.

The red-haired girl started to chant in a singsong voice, "Jimmy Duane is drown-ded, Jimmy Duane is drown-ded," and then her reedy voice broke off in midsentence, as if she had thought better of it.

"I'll bet he swam underwater to the other side," said one of the boys. He hunkered down and peered into the water. "Shit. Reckon where *is* he."

The dark-haired girl leaned forward, addressing the water where the boy had jumped in. "Jimmy Duane," she called, "you get the hell out of that lake and get on up here. Get on up here right this minute, you hear?"

Silence expanded. The swells generated by the boy's plunge had moved downstream, nudging Miller's boat. He felt a little dizzy, and he realized he had been holding his breath, forgetting to breathe.

"The way they do it in the movies," said one of the boys, "is they get them hollow reeds and stay underwater and breathe through 'em?" He phrased his observation like a question, lifting his voice at the end of it. Nobody answered him. Nobody else was talking anymore. Miller, watching, held the anchor rope so tightly his knuckles were white. Finally the girl said something soft, something that seemed more contemplative than communicative. It sounded like *Oh sweet Jesus*. "Get on in there, somebody," she ordered then. "Jesse. Bobby. What? Are you scared? Go on, now, I mean it. I'd go myself if I could swim." Her voice grew louder, but quavered. "Maybe he *is* drowned. Maybe he hit his head." She leaned out over the water again. "Jimmy Duane, this is not funny. Get back on up here, damn you."

The boys were arguing about who should go down first. "What if he pulls us under?" asked one.

In Miller's head a small vein began to throb. Slowly, deliberately, so as not to make a sound or a false move—something seemed to depend on it—he laid his fly rod down in the bottom of the boat and waited. Upstream, they waited, too. Then the boys eased themselves into the water and swam in slow circles around the area in front of the dock. One went under briefly and then reappeared, blowing water. The girls hunched together, watching, and the one with the baby began to keen. Miller had never heard such a sound. The hairs on his neck stood up, and a long chill raveled down his spine. Abruptly, he jerked the starter. The girls snapped their heads in his direction and began to wave him toward them, as if they could pull him closer with their frantic gestures. Oh, Jesus. Miller's heart pounded as the boat sliced across the water toward the dock. All the time he kept thinking that he did not want to get involved, it was none of his business. Why should he do anything? Why? Because, he told himself, that is the way you were brought up. To do the right thing. That's what Hollis would have said, that's what Hollis himself would have done.

He kept scanning the water, hoping the boy would pop up, laughing. *Got you that time, didn't I?* he would say.

Son of a bitch.

A long minute had gone by since the boy had gone under, maybe two. Miller killed the motor, and when the stern of the boat swung toward the dock, he heaved the anchor into the lake. The dark-haired girl shifted her baby to the other hip and leaned forward, offering Miller a hand; her wrist was circled by a dark bracelet. Once he reached for it, though, Miller realized that it was not a bracelet at all, but bruises. The skin was stained green and purple, as if someone had twisted it. He stared, transfixed, until one of the boys suddenly yelped and scrambled up onto the ladder. "Shit, oh Christ, he's down there. He grabbed me," he gasped. "He tried to pull me under." His mouth gaped at the horror of it.

"Where?" Miller yelled. "Let's go." He ripped off his sneakers and dived in. The shock of the cold water stunned him for a second, but he lowered his head and began to kick. Under the surface, the lake was murky and foreboding. His own heartbeat thundered in his ears and his breath gathered in his chest like a clenched fist, but he pulled hard against the water until his lungs began to burn. When he came up, they were all screaming. "Over there. His hand came up."

Miller took a long breath of air and went down again. His head pounded in the roaring silence. He swam with blind, awkward strokes and suddenly a weight fell against his back with such force that in his panic he opened his mouth to protest and swallowed a throatful of water. Someone—something—grabbed his hair and jerked his head back, and Miller realized that the drowning boy had fallen against his body and was riding his frame as if to climb to safety on his shoulders.

A hand grabbed at his face, covering his mouth and nose, and from that moment, it was all reflexive response. Miller flailed his arms, straining against the pressure of the water and the weight across his back. He hadn't realized he would do it, but he sank his teeth into the hand and then he was suddenly free, thrust upward as if propelled by his own adrenalin. When he broke through the surface, a net of water blurred his vision like a cataract and the air seemed solid with screaming.

Jesus God. He was up, he was alive. He sputtered and grabbed the first step of the ladder and drank in long rough drafts of air. The girl pushed her baby into someone else's arms and leaned over the edge of the dock. Her black hair fell around her face. But Miller could see the dark circles under her eyes and the transparent blue of her lids. "Did you find him?" she shrieked. "Did you see him?"

Water rained from Miller's hair and rolled down his face, and the metallic taste of the lake was on his tongue. He looked back at the water and shook his head.

"How could you *not* see him?" the girl screamed. "How could you *not?*"

Miller kept picturing something he was not even sure he had actually witnessed—the boy's face—ghostly in the eerie light, mouth open, eyes rolling. Long blonde hair floating around his head like the transparent tentacles of a jellyfish.

The girl screamed at him again and Miller released the rung of the ladder and fell backward into the lake. He calculated the place below where the boy had fallen against him, and for a few seconds he hung suspended in the dark golden water, moving his arms slowly, letting himself sink and rise.

He was biding time.

Sink and rise. Sink and rise. Below him in the dusky labyrinth of the lake he could make out a ghastly form rocking in the current. *Wait,* he told himself, *wait. I could die here. I could die for a stranger who climbed up my body to save himself.* From somewhere far off he heard a chambered sound that he recognized as his own internal moaning. He was tired now, and confused. The filtered light was hypnotic and the silence compelling and unrelenting. Why not just go up, tell them he couldn't find the boy?

Still. Imagine his own child, imagine Judd. Hollis seemed to be at his shoulder, prodding. "Go on," his father was urging. "He's only a boy. He has his life before him. He has a wife. He has a child. Go, go. Hurry. Go."

Stroking downward, Miller touched flesh—this time a flat plane—the back, maybe, or the shoulders. His first impulse was to jerk his hand away, but suddenly he understood that the boy was face down now, bobbing gently on the floor of the lake, unconscious, probably, and no longer a threat. Miller pushed against the weight of the water and moved his hand along the length of the body, searching for a handhold. He found the belt loop of the jeans and pulled, but the body was incredibly heavy, filled with water. Waterlogged.

Oh Jesus, forgive me, Miller prayed. *I waited too long.* He pulled again, but the body would not be lifted. Miller pushed away from the boy and burst to the surface—into the flood of sunlight and the cacophony of screaming and weeping. "I found him," he sputtered. "I found him, but I need some help to bring him up." They stared at him, stupefied. "Will you for Christ's sake help me?" He coughed and something bitter pushed up in his throat.

One of the boys slid into the water, shuddering, and followed Miller down into the gloomy depths of the water. At the bottom, Miller motioned for him to take one of the boy's wrists, and he took the other, and then, with their cumbersome burden, they struggled up toward the light.

The girls were hysterical as they reached out to help drag the boy onto the dock. His body was awkward, heavy, arms flapping limp as a doll's. "Turn him over," Miller yelled. His chest hurt as he pulled himself up the ladder. "Get the water out of him." His own body now felt as heavy as the boy's. For a second that he hoped was imperceptible, he looked for the bite mark. It was there—an unmistakable ragged crescent just below the thumb, bright pink against the pale gray color of the skin. The others were pulling at the boy's arms, trying to shake him back to life. "Jimmy Duane. Jimmy Duane."

Miller scrambled across the dock and rolled the boy over on his side. When the last of the water had drained from his throat, Miller pinched the boy's nose and put his mouth to the cold blue lips. It was almost impossible to establish a rhythm with the others pulling and crying. He tried to wave them away with his arms. And when he paused between breaths, he could not keep from looking. To him, the mark seemed enormous and the flesh around it dark and discolored, but there was no blood.

He made himself concentrate on the work at hand. Occasionally he felt the throat for a pulse. Nothing. The young wife squatted beside him, moaning, so close that Miller felt her breath against his shoulder. The baby was screaming now, too. Miller nudged the girl away with his elbow and rolled the boy on his side once more. Another thin trickle of water drained from the pale lips. *So much water,* Miller thought. *So much water.* For a second he felt frozen with exhaustion, and then he forced himself back to the business of pushing his breath into the boy's lungs. *Breathe, rest. Breathe, rest.* He swallowed the bile that rose in his throat and tried not to look at the boy's face. For a while he lost track of time, and the motions became automatic. The noise around him became white noise, the faces negative images. He was lost in a vacuum of rhythm. *Breathe for three seconds, wait for two, breathe for three, wait for two.* He must have worked at it for ten, fifteen minutes. Finally he looked up at the others. "Can somebody take over for a while?" he asked.

They backed away, horrified.

"Jesus Christ almighty," Miller yelled. "I thought this guy was your friend, for God's sake. What are you afraid of? You worthless shitheads." He turned back to the drowned boy and laid his palms on his chest. Again and again he pushed his weight against the skinny ribs. But even as he worked to coax out even a spark of life, he couldn't help feeling revulsion when he looked at the boy's dripping goatee, the death's head earring in the left earlobe, the yellow, broken teeth. After a few minutes he leaned his weight for a last time against the boy's chest and shuddered. "I can't raise him," he whispered. "I can't. He's gone."

"Liar. *Liar. You're lying.*" The girl struck out at him, and when she came close, there was something like hatred in her eyes. It was the same kind of look Miller had seen in his own eyes in the mirror that night. *Your father expired about six this morning.*

The girl pounded her fist against Miller's arm. "He's not dead, I know he ain't. Do you hear me? You keep on trying." She struck out again, and when Miller grabbed her wrist to deflect the blow, he was amazed at how small she was, how fragile her bones.

He stared at her for a moment, then shook his head. "I'm sorry. He's gone." The girl howled and Miller hunched his shoulders and waited for his punishment. *I deserve it*, he thought. *She knows what happened.* Her fist glanced off his ear and shoulder, but the blow was not nearly so painful as it should have been, he told himself. And in the moment before he closed his eyes, he saw again the bruises circling her wrist.

"Adra, stop it." One of the boys pulled the girl away and held her tight against his chest. When Miller got to his feet, his knees shook, and he was suddenly cold. He didn't look at any of them, couldn't. He couldn't meet their eyes, especially not the girl's. Through the planks of the dock the green water below was lit obliquely by the sun, as if it were an ordinary day like any other, and for a moment he felt dizzy. He made his way around the body and spoke over his shoulder. "I'll send somebody to help. Somebody from the marina. They'll call an ambulance."

He jumped down into his boat, striking his shin so hard against the oarlock that he almost wept. And when he started the engine, he swung about so sharply that he nearly swamped. All he could think of was escaping. He cranked the throttle to *full* and careened across the cove, glad for the deafening noise of the engine because it covered the unearthly sound he let loose from his throat as the boat rushed away from the dock and into the open lake.

2

At the marina he blurted out the location of the drowning and when the manager went inside the bait shop to call for an ambulance, Miller hurried away. That was it. He hurried away. He had risked his life, what else did he owe them? He stumbled toward his car, his knees wobbling, backed the boat trailer down the ramp and jumped out to secure the boat. As he drove away the manager ran out of the bait shop and motioned for him to come back, but he kept going, flying down the dirt road with a tower of dust behind him.

As soon as he reached the highway, he pulled over and went back to the boat for his lunch box. He carried it to the car, took out the bottle, and drank a deep swallow. The warmth routed some of the chill that had been shaking his body. The second swallow calmed him enough to think about the girl, to wonder if she had noticed the bite mark. Adra. What kind of name was that? *A-dra.* She was a mystery if there ever was one. Where did those bruises come from, and what about her anger, the way she had struck out at him? She knew what he had done, he was certain she knew. He took another couple of swallows, stashed the bottle under the seat, and pulled out onto the highway. He pushed his foot against the accelerator until the speedometer reached eighty. It was almost a disappointment that no policeman appeared to arrest him, because he could not remember ever having done anything so cowardly. Everybody tells you to save yourself first, but the ones who save themselves first are the ones who never get to be heroes. They survive, but at what cost? The whiskey rose in his throat and for a minute he thought he might be sick. He knew what his father would have done. The right thing. It was the test Miller had lived by all his life, and this time, he had failed.

When he got home he was relieved to find the house empty. It was Saturday afternoon. Judd would be at the country club pool, lifeguarding, and Katie, as usual, would be at the club, too, playing tennis or golf. Miller closed the shutters in the front window and stood in the dim light of the living room. He shivered a little, but the dark, cool house felt safe. The air conditioner hummed predictably and the ice maker knocked out a few cubes periodically, but other than that there was silence.

In the kitchen he stripped off his damp shirt and shorts, and, naked, poured himself a tumbler of whiskey. He stood there in the pool of his clothing and swallowed the drink all in one gulp. Then he walked naked through the house and up the stairs.

In the bathroom he adjusted the showerhead to the hardest stream and let the hot water stab his flesh. His throat felt swollen, knotted with tears that could neither be swallowed nor released. Finally he turned off the water and, still dripping, stumbled into the bedroom and fell across the bed. He didn't wake up until Katie came home a couple of hours later. She must have called his name because when he opened his eyes he saw her standing in the doorway, holding his wet clothes. It was the way she held them, almost accusingly, that bothered him. "What's going on?" she asked Miller.

He rolled over on his side and pulled the sheet across himself. It was the first time in their marriage he had ever hidden his nakedness from her.

"Miller?" Katie dropped the clothes in a pile on the floor and sat down on the edge of the bed. "My God," she said. "These sheets are wet. Did something happen?"

Then his tears exploded in a torrent. It was the way Judd had always cried as a child when, after suffering some minor disaster away from home, he had saved up his weeping for the moment his parents arrived to save him.

"What, Miller?" Katie cried. "Oh, God, is it Judd? Is Judd all right?"

Miller waved his hand to dismiss her fear. "A boy drowned," he managed. "At the lake."

Her hand flew to her mouth. "Oh Miller. You saw it?"

He pulled the sheet tighter across his chest. "No," he said. "I went down after him. I pulled him up."

"You pulled him up? You? Oh my God. How old was he?"

"For Christ's sake, Katie, what does it matter how old he was? He was twenty, I guess, around twenty. Jesus, what kind of question is that? I just told you, he *died.* He *drowned*. What does it matter how old he was? He was a kid. He was only a boy." He rolled over so that his back was to her.

Katie shook his shoulder. "Miller, look at me. Talk. You went after him? You risked your life for a stranger?"

"What? Are you *blaming* me now?"

"Blaming? Of course not, honey. But the risk . . ."

Miller spoke into the pillow, his voice muffled. "You don't understand," he said. "He died. He fucking *died*."

Katie moved around to the other side of the bed and put her hand on his cheek. "Yes, but Miller, you tried. You *tried* to save him, that's the important thing, sweetheart."

Miller pushed himself up on his elbow and slammed his fist against the headboard. "Goddamn it, Katie, are you listening to me? It wasn't a happy ending. Did you hear me? The kid died. I didn't save him. I didn't get him up in time."

Katie flinched. "Miller, what's the matter with you? I was only trying to say that if you jumped in after him . . ."

"Don't say anything," he said. He wiped his eyes with the hem of the sheet and pulled his knees up to his chest. "Just let me sleep for a while, will you? I don't want to talk anymore."

"No, I won't let you sleep, Miller, not until I know you're okay. Look, it wasn't your fault. You risked your own life to save another human being, and—all right—he didn't make it. But you did the right thing." She sat there on the edge of the bed, her hands fluttering over him, and then she repeated it, her voice almost a whisper. "You did the right thing."

"Did I?" he said. "How do you know? How in the *hell* do you know? You weren't there. Were you there?"

"Miller, you're scaring me." She clasped her hands between her knees and stared at him.

Miller squeezed his eyes shut. He was shaking again. "If the police come," he said, "tell them . . ."

"The police? Why would the police come?"

"Because I was the one who went in after him. What if they think I'm culpable?"

"Culpable? *Culpable*? Miller, this is crazy. I mean, for God's sake. Honey, please calm down and explain how it happened, and how you got involved."

So finally he told her most of it, how he had heard the low conversation, then the laughter, and how he had watched them swing out over the lake. He told her about the boy jumping in and not coming up. He told her most of it except for what really happened there underneath the water. Not yet. He would tell her later, after he had rested, when it was all clearer in his mind.

Katie leaned forward, crooning to him the way she had the night his father had died. "It's all right, honey, you did your best. Sleep now, sweetheart, it's all right." Usually Miller liked the touch of her hand, but not now. He pushed against the pillow again and shrugged her off.

Downstairs, the front door opened and Judd came bounding up the stairs, skipping three steps at a time, as usual. He stopped at the bedroom door and looked in. "What's wrong with Dad?" he asked Katie, talking around Miller as if he were deaf or retarded or invisible. "Is he sick?"

"Something happened," Katie said. "I'll explain later. Let your daddy get some sleep."

"What happened, Mom?" Judd asked. "Is Dad okay?"

"Yes, I promise you, honey. I'll be with you in a minute." She waved him away.

"Shit," Judd muttered. "You always treat me like a kid."

"Dammit," Miller yelled, pushing himself up to a sitting position, "you *are* a kid. Do what you're told for once. Do you always have to mouth off about everything?"

"Shhh, shhh." Katie motioned Judd away. "Please, honey. I promise, I'll be right there." She glared at Miller. "He's only concerned about you, that's all," she said. "He's not used to seeing you in bed in the middle of the day."

The thing was, Miller hadn't wanted to face Judd, not yet. He was too ashamed. He closed his eyes and heard Katie moving around the room, closing shutters, picking up the damp clothes. "Throw those things away," Miller muttered. Katie paused for a minute, watching him, and then went out, closing the door behind her.

He slept for twelve hours. At four in the morning he climbed out of bed, careful to avoid waking Katie. He pulled on his robe and went downstairs in the dark, feeling his way in the long-familiar rooms. For a while he stood at the kitchen window and then he opened the back door and walked out into the yard. The lawn was wet with dew, and the heat that had lingered from the previous day cast a milky glow to the sky, but Miller could still make out a few stars. He sat down in the grass and looked up, but his thoughts were still out there under the dark waters of the lake. He saw again the flat plane of a bare back, blonde hair waving like pale seaweed. The neighborhood was absolutely still, but suddenly, something moved in the shrubbery, and he jumped.

The night had never spooked him before. He had always liked sitting in the dark, beginning in his childhood, when he would set up camp in the backyard and his father would come out of the brightly lighted house to make sure he was safe and comfortable. Later, when Miller's mother had left home, Hollis slept outside, too. Why not? With no woman in the house, they could do whatever they wanted. His father taught at the junior high school and had the summers off, so they didn't need to worry about getting up early.

Once, on a night when they lay together side by side on a quilt in the grass, Miller mentioned his mother's name, and for a long time, his father was silent. "I never knew," Hollis said finally, "that she was capable of doing a thing like that." The words cracked and blurred and there was silence again. Other than that, they had talked little about Miller's absent mother. The truth that she had not loved either of them enough to stay, Miller thought, was far too painful even to consider.

Now Miller stared into the vast open sky and managed to convince himself that if his father had been in his place, he would have died trying to save that boy. Then he waited for something to happen. What? A comet to streak across the horizon? Some sort of sign or message? But the sky remained calm and the only sound he heard was the metallic song of the cicadas and occasionally the hum of traffic far off on the interstate.

Lying back on the damp grass, he felt a ripple of shame working up from his belly and an overwhelming sense of loneliness. Christ, he needed the old man. He needed him to tell him how to get out of this situation. Until this moment, he hadn't realized how much he had depended on his guidance or how thoroughly his life had been shaped by him. Why couldn't he be that kind of father for his own son? Judd was drifting away from him. He was maturing, yes, but fitfully, with false starts and long lapses, as if his approaching manhood were an ill-fitting skin he could slip into and out of at will. Once, seated by a window at a beachside restaurant, Miller had watched a chameleon shed its skin outside on a bayberry branch. It had been a long and tedious process, much like Judd's growing up, with quick, productive spurts of activity and then long, protracted lapses—even backsliding. Katie was more patient, but, damn it, here was this kid facing graduation in a year and he hadn't the slightest idea what he wanted to do with his life. He was jaded at seventeen, had lost his boyhood curiosity. Everything was *boring*. Miller mourned the loss of Judd's excitement about life, but Katie was more optimistic. "He'll be fine," she kept telling Miller. "He's a good boy. You'll see. He'll grow up and one day you'll be friends again."

There was something more, though. Miller was scared. He couldn't explain it, even to himself, but there was something threatening about Judd's new musculature, the hard line of his jaw. Sometimes at the country club, Miller watched the girls looking at him with something akin to hunger. Part of it was Miller's fault. He had given Judd a much more affluent life than he had at that age. If anyone were to ask him what kind of wife he wanted for his son, Miller would say a plain but intelligent girl who knew the date of the Spanish Civil War and could list all of the United States in alphabetical order. A girl who knew where Kathmandu was. And *what* it was. She'd be creative and brilliant, but kind, too, a girl who eschewed makeup and grew organic foods and wore long skirts and sensible shoes. Judd would love her more than she loved him, because of her independent spirit, but she'd be morally responsible and they'd marry and have children who would all graduate from Harvard and become doctors or diplomats and ambassadors in foreign countries. But who would ask Miller, anyway? Certainly not Judd, who wanted one of those girls whose father had already given her a convertible for her sixteenth birthday. One of those girls who wore bikinis to the pool at the club, who had perfect teeth and immaculately applied makeup, and who believed she was the center of the universe. Only the best for Judd. He had a self-assurance that Miller as a grown-up lacked. He walked among both friends and strangers with an easy confidence, completely at home in the privileged world that Miller abhorred. But more disturbing was this attitude that Judd and most of his friends displayed—that the world owed them a living.

Anyway, what did Miller know? He was forty-three years old and for months now, he had wanted out of his own life—there—right there at the halfway point. Halfway if he was lucky. He was a mechanical engineer for an aircraft company, he made a better-than-average salary, he had a nice house and three acres of prime property in the best part of town. Big deal. What did it really mean? It meant that, clipped to his pocket, he wore a laminated card imprinted with his photograph and ID number and that he sat at his computer all day and looked at renderings of aircraft parts and tried to make airplanes better and safer and more efficient. Yes, it was a good job. He knew that. It had given his family a comfortable life. Yet more and more he dreaded going to work. He made excuses, he went in late, he couldn't get out of bed, he was sick. And when he finally did make it to the office, he found himself daydreaming about walking away from it, going somewhere new, living alone, maybe even somehow connecting with a less demanding family, a simpler lifestyle.

Ahhh, God. It was a dream. Of course it was all impossible.

Those dreams were what kept a man going, and the thing was, they were never attainable. As he pushed himself up from the grass, he remembered something that had happened to him a few years before. He had fallen in love with another woman, but not in the usual way. On a business trip in New Hampshire, while riding to dinner one evening with some colleagues, he had seen a girl standing in the middle of the town square in full riding regalia—hat, breeches, jacket—practicing her cast with a fly rod across the perfectly trimmed and clipped green grass. The sun setting behind her made her line gleam like the thin silver stroke of a comet across the low evening sky. That bizarre, romantic image—the whole unlikely scenario—had stayed with him for five years, as vivid as the moment it had happened—maybe more so. Now he wasn't sure any more just how much he had embellished it. Things like that had a way of getting away from you.

But the incident had made him restless. Sometimes he woke in the middle of the night to the strange sensation that something had been stolen from him, and always, always, he would think of the girl fly-casting on the village green and he would see again the fine bright scribe of her line looping across the glowing horizon.

She was the ideal. She was the substance of the dream.

Miller rubbed his eyes and sat up. Finally he went back into the house and stepped into the dark kitchen. He opened the refrigerator door for light and rummaged in the cabinet until he found what he wanted. He poured himself half a glass and stood sipping it in the cool, eerie illumination. The knot in his throat, burned by the whiskey, dissolved for a minute and then gathered again. Suddenly he felt the weight of the drowned boy's body—hooked under his finger, in the belt loop—the way an amputee imagines he can feel his absent limb. An unbearable weight.

He closed the refrigerator door and finished off the bottle in the cool, humming dark. When he took the last sip he noticed that the sky to the east was softening. He shuffled into the living room and walked over to the window. Katie had opened the shutters that he had closed the afternoon before. Miller looked out at the familiar street of perfectly kept lawns and well-appointed houses. The neighborhood slept in its usual Sunday morning tranquility, but Miller tensed as a pair of headlights scoured the dim street. It was a white car, the kind policemen often drive. Miller pulled his bathrobe across his chest and cupped his hands over his mouth to see how strong his breath was. The car stopped momentarily and moved on. It was only the paper boy, slowing down to toss the Sunday edition up onto the sidewalk.

Six twenty-one A.M. The sun was rising over the rooftops of the houses across the street. When Miller went outside to get the paper, he found the story in the local news section. It was written from a police report. Too soon for an obituary notice. He stood on the front steps and read the column. It was a simple, straightforward account of the events that had led to the death of Jimmy Duane Goodfriend.

The newspaper reported that an unidentified fisherman had pulled the drowned man from the lake and worked valiantly to revive him. He'd been right about the girl. "Mr. Goodfriend is survived by wife Adra and daughter Selda." They lived in Blue Creek and Jimmy Duane had worked for an awning company. Miller felt shame washing over his body. He went back inside and sat down on the sofa to read the story again. Twenty. The boy was only twenty. Now what would happen to the wife, that girl who almost certainly knew what Miller had done? Why else had she hit him, cursed him? He remembered her dark eyes, that fragile wrist, the long dark hair flying across her face. He made a decision then. He folded up the paper and went upstairs to change clothes.

By the time he had found the road to Jimmy Duane's house, it was half past noon. He had been driving around for hours and every time he stopped for a light or a stop sign, he looked down at the paper and read the notice again. Finally he saw the turnoff he had been directed to back at the gas station. It was an overgrown dirt lane at the edge of the secondary road. A rusty mailbox was scrawled with the hand-painted name: *Goodfriend.*

He stopped the car at the entrance to the driveway and hesitated. At the opposite end of the long rutted lane, the foliage of a dozen or so crooked dogwoods and crusty old locusts obscured the view of the house. The red dirt road was powdery from the heat, ground to the consistency of talcum. The weather was so hot that the day seemed to be smoldering, kindled by the early summer drought. The air smelled sulfurous, dangerous almost. Miller's heart began to race as he started down the drive. The rhythm of his breathing had been erratic ever since the day before, ever since the first moment he had jumped into the lake after Jimmy Duane Goodfriend.

He drove slowly, staying within the grooves patterned with fresh tire tracks. A bee flew through the open window and he fanned it away with his hand. Along the lane, wildflowers bloomed—honeysuckle, daisies, cornflowers, Queen Anne's lace, and passionflower. When he passed the low-hanging branches of the locusts, the house came into view. It was a shotgun structure, painted in a bright blue, with rooms arranged in a long row along a narrow hall and a porch at the front and side. The foundation was raised by crumbling brick pillars, and a few chickens pecked the bare dirt in the shade beneath the porch. Everything about the place was in disrepair. The corrugated tin roof was patterned with map-shaped configurations of rust, the paint was peeling. A yellow shutter on the front window hung on a single broken hinge, and behind the house, in an overgrown lot sprinkled with patches of wildflowers, a rusty car, its tires gone, balanced on a jack.

When he inched the car past the second stand of trees, he could see people walking around in the side yard, an area of smooth, grassless red clay. They must have been holding some sort of a wake. Two sawhorses had been set up, with boards laid across them to fashion a makeshift table. The top, covered with a sheet, was laden with pitchers, plates, and bowls of food. A few men in rolled-up shirtsleeves stood talking and smoking and occasionally lifting the lids of pots or casseroles. The coats of their dark suits had been hung over the backs of folding chairs that looked as if they might have been borrowed from a church. Children ran among the adults, chasing each other, laughing and shrieking.

The door of the house opened and three women came down the steps carrying platters of food. Behind them was Jimmy Duane's wife—the girl they had called Adra. Her long hair was tied back with a narrow blue ribbon. In her cotton print dress, she looked different from the way she had looked at the lake—softer, prettier, even though the dress hung loose from her thin shoulders. Framed in the doorway, she hesitated, shaded her eyes with her hand, and looked down the road toward Miller's car. She stared for a long time, showing neither interest nor surprise. It was as if she had expected to find him there. And then, just as casually, she turned away and went back inside.

Miller's heart bounced wildly. He wasn't sure what he had expected from her, what he had planned to say, but now he was frightened. The girl had seen him; he was sure of that. Maybe she was still watching from somewhere inside the house. His scalp tingled with apprehension. Impulsively, he threw the car into reverse and gunned the motor to back up. In the process he nearly ran into the ditch alongside the road. When he looked back, he thought he saw a face at the window of the house, but he could not be sure it was a face at all or merely a reflection. It might have been a trick of the heat.

Katie had been making blueberry pies for the country club bake sale. She glanced up at him when he walked into the kitchen but did not speak. He noticed the little crease that always appeared between her brows when she was annoyed. Her hands fluttered over a pastry lining, fluting the edge with an intricate pattern she sculpted by pushing the dough against the groove she made with the tips of her forefinger and thumb. Miller watched with fascination. He had always loved her hands. They were small and dainty and her nails were oval and pink and shiny. For a moment he felt a deep affection for his wife and penitence for his behavior toward her. "Baby?" he ventured, but Katie refused to recognize his presence. So he asked her a direct question she would have to respond to. "Where's Judd?"

"Upstairs." That was all she would give him.

Miller tossed the newspaper down on the counter and Katie leaned forward, her shiny blond hair swinging against her cheek. She squinted to read the type. It was annoying that she could never find her reading glasses when she needed them. She stared at him in amazement. "That's where you've been since six-thirty this morning? Oh Miller, why did you have to go there? That wasn't necessary. Didn't you do enough yesterday? I've been worried sick. What if they tried to sue you for some reason? They don't know your name, let it go."

He shrugged and pushed his finger through a sprinkling of flour on the marble countertop. "I was driving around." He glanced at her to measure her mood, then looked away. "I couldn't sleep this morning, and then the paper came and I saw this." He tapped the paper with his forefinger.

"I heard you leave." She spoke pointedly, as if with this privileged information she could reestablish her role in his life, reclaim her rightful place. Then she added, speaking deliberately. "And I saw the empty bottle in the kitchen."

"I needed it," he said. "Do I have to justify everything to you?"

Katie's head snapped up and her hair swung forward again. At that moment Miller observed her as if for the first time. She was short, stocky, and muscular from playing tennis and swimming, a small but formidable woman of middle age. Tough, even, but still pretty. Her blue eyes, creased at the corners from being so much in the sun, lit up her small, expressive face. "Explain this to me," she said. "You try to save a boy's life—which is, by the way, Miller, an act of mercy—and you spend the next twenty-four hours agonizing over it."

"He died."

She slammed the wooden rolling pin against the counter and rolled her eyes toward the ceiling. "I *know* he died, Miller. I *know* he died.

Don't you think I know that by now? And I say—*again*, Miller—it wasn't your *fault*."

"What if it was? No, Katie, I'm serious. Listen. Will you just please shut up and listen to me for once, please?" This was the moment to tell her the whole truth, but then he hesitated and lost his momentum. "What if I tried to save him, but I did a half-assed job of it? I mean, what if I didn't try hard enough?"

Katie's laugh was clipped and hard. "Is that the trouble? You feel guilty because he died? Well, what if you *didn't* try hard enough? Isn't the number-one rule of rescuing someone to save yourself first? Don't look at me like that, Miller. I know. I took CPR and lifeguard training, too." She dusted the flour from her hands and counted off three fingers. "One. *Listen* to me, Miller. One. You pulled him up. Two, you brought him out. Three, you gave him CPR. What more could anyone do?" Her face darkened. "Miller, you're not yourself. You're scaring me a little. You've made this . . . incident . . . into a monumental event, when in fact it's only . . . what do you call it? . . . a random, natural occurrence. Something that just happens. Something unexplainable. A boy went under. You jumped in after him. It was too late. He drowned. And yes, it's traumatic. I can understand that."

"No, I don't think you can. I don't think anybody but me knows how it feels."

"Well, let me try, why don't you? Stop pushing me away. You could have told me where you were going this morning. You could have let me help you. God, Miller, I would have gone with you."

"No," he said. It was an involuntary utterance. But he was horrified. He couldn't imagine letting Katie be a part of the nightmare.

"Oh, God, Miller." Her voice shook. The air seemed to have gone out of her. "Talk to me."

His hands waved in the empty air. "Katie. I have things on my mind. *Things*. Can't I have any thoughts of my own that I don't have to share with you?"

A long silence played out between them, and finally it was too much for Katie. Her mouth peeled down at the corners and she began to cry. She laid her hands flat on the counter, as if for balance, her fingers splayed in the flour.

At that moment Miller's heart felt as cold and hard as a chunk of ice. He was aware of an empty space inside himself, a place where something should have been pumping, but had somehow shut down. A sense of injustice boiled up in him and erupted as anger. "Oh Jesus," he said, "give me a break. What in the hell are *you* crying about?" He shoved his stool back with such force that it fell against the counter, scraping a long gash in the pine cabinet beneath it and then crashing to the floor.

Once he had left the house, there was nowhere to retreat to but his car. He headed south, to the mountains, and turned the radio up full volume to keep from having to think. Close to Gatlinburg, the traffic backed up and Miller pulled off the road at a country market. He had forgotten about the Sunday tourists. He sat in the car for a while and then went inside the little store. He stood immobilized, studying the contents of the candy counter. Katie had told him once that chocolate was a mood elevator. Women were full of weird little bits of information like that. He bought a candy bar and a soft drink and, outside, walked around behind the store, where a path led down an embankment to a swift mountain stream. Miller took off his loafers and socks and stepped out onto a large flat rock. Cool air rushed up around his ankles. Then he made a long leap, and another and another, until he was sitting on a boulder in the middle of the streambed. When he landed on the boulder, a piercing pain stabbed the knee that the oarlock had injured the day before. Water swirled beneath him, rushing around his rocky perch with a swift, deafening thunder. He dipped first one foot and then the other into the icy stream. The cold and the noise helped to clear his head. He had traveled much in the past twenty-four hours and everything he had learned about himself reinforced his conviction that he was cruel and cowardly. Cruel to a desperate drowning boy, then cowardly in running away. Cruel to Katie, and why? Had he actually wanted her to *agree* with him that he had been responsible for the boy's death? Or had her commiserations only emphasized the excuses he had fabricated for himself and made him see how thoroughly dishonest he had been?

Now he had compounded a lie of commission with a lie of omission.

He needed someone to talk to, someone who could be objective. He thought about finding a phone so that he could call his friend Jack, but then he decided that he might not be willing to tell Jack the whole truth, either. Maybe it wasn't fair to burden him in that way. Jack's wife was having an affair, and she had defiantly pledged to continue it, even after Jack confronted her about it. But Jack hesitated to give her up because, he told Miller, she had such a beautiful name. Nadia. Where, Jack had asked, could he ever find another woman with such a beautiful name? That, of course, was bullshit—Jack's way of protecting himself against the truth by making it into a joke. The truth was that Nadia was drop-dead gorgeous and Jack was crazy in love with her. Everybody else knew that it was only a matter of time before Nadia dropped him. That was her pattern. The marriage was Jack's first, but Nadia's fourth. She just kept moving on, or moving up to something better. She was too beautiful for her own good, or anybody else's. Especially Jack's. The man was losing his sanity. He'd been desperate one moment, sad the next, angry the next. Maybe he would find comfort in knowing that Miller was having problems, too, because Jack was always envying Miller's perfect life, perfect family, perfect everything.

Stop thinking about it, stop thinking.

Miller unwrapped the candy bar, pushed the crumpled paper into his pocket, and wedged his drink can between two submerged rocks in the stream to chill it. He took a bite of the candy and let the smooth chocolate melt against his tongue. As he watched the cold water swirl around the aluminum can, something caught his eye and he gasped, but when he peered down into the clear rushing water he realized that he had seen a wavering clump of pale grass that resembled human hair.

Don't think about Jimmy Duane Goodfriend. Don't think about what you did or what you could have done or what you should have done. Forget about it. Put it behind you.

Miller hugged his arms close to his body and looked up into the trees—black oak, ash, beech, birch. You could actually smell them growing. You could smell the age of the mountains, too, which were centuries old and redolent of the wild scent of fresh growth mixed with the smell of moldering. Death fed the life and life fattened things up for death. The process kept on like that, and the layers of the earth slid silently beneath the surface. Over time, rocks swelled up and disintegrated and the land went on breathing and heaving. From an airplane you could see the ancient, wrinkled visage of the mountains, their hoariness, the soft green bristle of treetops in summer. Folded, is the way his father had described this terrain. There were two ways mountains could be formed, he told Miller—by volcanic explosion or by parts of the land breaking off and then slamming together again. Miller liked that expression. Folded. It was like his life—

pushed up by an implosion that had erupted on the floor of a lake. What had Katie called it? Random. A random natural occurrence.

He willed himself to stop thinking about it. It was too pleasant there on the rock, with the water making a white noise that drowned out all other sounds. He felt at home in the mountains, had been taught to be. He remembered his father talking about mountains as reverently as another man might speak of a woman he loved, his voice lazy and seductive, his descriptions metaphorical and mysterious, almost mystical. *Crystalline, volcanic, granitic, metamorphic.* Miller could still call up the words his father had used. He could hear them echoing behind the wild noisy rush of mountain streams and the silken sleeves of rivers they had fished, just as he could sense his father's calming presence in the lake's shady coves and in the buoyant swelling light that rode the surface of the water. He longed for those endless summer days that thickened with heat and anticipation, for the late afternoons when the light became golden and the descending quiet was so palpable even the sound of a mosquito was audible across yards and yards of glassy water.

He'd been six years old the first time his father had taken him fishing. "In the old days," Hollis told him, "when they taught you to fly-fish, they made you hold a book under your arm to keep the cast controlled. Now, hell, you can use your arm, your shoulder, whatever. The thing to remember is that you don't cast the fly, you cast the line. Concentrate on the line and remember that it creates wind resistance. You have to factor that into your cast, too. See? Control it, that's the trick. There's a feel to it. It's a forward, stop motion until the line straightens itself out. You'll learn to recognize when that happens. It's intuitive. When you feel the slack, sharpen your pull to get line speed. Aim it high, about eight feet above the water, so it has time to straighten out by the time it hits the surface." It wasn't what his father had said so much as the setting—the surrounding forest, the wild stream, and the feel of the rod in his small hands, the thing that connected him to the stream. So much had happened since then. So much had changed.

He was suddenly overwhelmed with fatigue and, despite the heat, his perch on the rock all at once seemed too chilly. He retrieved his drink can from the water and started back toward shore, but on the last rock he slipped and struck his already injured knee. It was a simple, almost negligible wound, but the pain jolted him. He limped to the bank, picked up his shoes, and got to his car.

Driving home through the late afternoon traffic, he held the cold aluminum can against his knee to lessen the swelling. The mountain air seemed weighted with coolness. Haze was circling the mountaintops, and the sky to the west was turning pink. It would be a good day tomorrow, weatherwise, but he dreaded going to work. And now, he dreaded going home.

When he got there, though, Katie was out, and Judd, smelling of Miller's cologne and some sort of coconut shampoo, was just leaving, but he hesitated with his hand on the doorknob and looked at Miller. "Hey, Dad, what's going on? Mom's been crying all day and then she just blew out of here without saying where she was going."

Miller limped toward the stairs. "Sorry, son," he said. "We had an argument. These things happen in a marriage. Some day you'll understand."

"Why, though? And why did you peel out like that before? Why did you get so pissed?"

Miller shrugged and leaned against the banister. "Look, son, this is all pretty complicated, okay?" He struggled for an explanation but couldn't think of one. "Just give me a break here. I've been up since four A.M."

"And what's that?" Judd asked.

"What's what?"

"Your leg. You're limping."

"Oh. That." Miller laughed. "I had a confrontation with a rock."
He grinned at Judd. "The rock won."

Judd didn't smile. "Why can't you give me a straight answer, Dad? I'm not a kid anymore."

Miller started up the stairs, leaning on the good leg. "Yeah, well, you could have fooled me."

He was sorry, sorry as soon as he said it, but when he turned to apologize, Judd was gone, slamming the door behind him.

Miller waited for Katie until midnight. It was a Sunday night. Where in the hell could she be on a Sunday night? The club closed at eleven. He sat in the wing chair in the living room, a book in his hand. He had read the last few pages a dozen times and still hadn't absorbed the words. He leaned forward when he heard Katie's footsteps on the porch. She swept in and started up the stairs without speaking.

"Have you eaten dinner, honey?" Miller asked. "Come on, sit down and talk." His voice was too loud, too cheerful and hollow. Just speaking seemed awkward and fatuous.

Katie kept walking up the stairs. "I ate at the club."

"Katie."

She stopped, her hand on the stair rail, and looked down at him. "What?" The light from the lamp on the table below the stairs distorted her features and Miller could see nothing in her face that pleased him. *This too shall pass,* he prayed.

He walked out into the hallway, trying to ignore the twinge in his knee, trying to arrange his features into a pleasant composure. "I'm sorry," he said. He still wasn't sure for what, but it seemed imperative to get that out and let her apply it to her most pressing grievance.

"You should be," Katie said. "You damn well should be. Crashing out of here without telling me where you were going or why. Staying away for hours this morning and then again this afternoon, even when you knew how upset I was." There was a dangerous snag in her voice. "There's another part to this equation, Miller, besides you and that boy. There's me, too, and Judd. Don't you care anything about *our* feelings?" She continued up the stairs without waiting for his answer.

Miller stood there in the hall for a while and then sat back down in the chair, staring at the book in his hand until his eyes watered. He had wanted to ask Katie where she'd been, what she'd been doing, but he was afraid to. On the edge of his consciousness, he heard water running in the upstairs bathroom and then a long silence. Katie would be in bed, waiting for him to come up and comfort her, but he couldn't summon the energy to walk up the stairs or to put himself in jeopardy if she decided to unleash her anger on him. He snapped off the lamp and stretched out on the sofa, letting his book slide to the floor.

He tried to remember what he had been reading, but though he lay wide awake for a long time, staring into the dark, he could not summon up enough curiosity or energy to turn on the light and look at the title.

3

When Miller looked at his watch, it was after ten A.M. Katie had left for her job at the university without bothering to wake him. That was a pretty good measure of her hurt, Miller thought. When he stood up, the pain in the bad knee gave him a good excuse to call in sick. Hobbling, he spent the day cleaning the garage, a chore Katie had been begging him to perform since early spring. He was ruthless in what he threw out—dozens of family treasures they had kept for sentimental reasons—Judd's old sled and wading pool, Katie's antique Singer sewing machine, canvasses he had painted in college, bird cages, a pet carrier for a cat long since gone, a barn door he had salvaged when one of the old neighborhood lots was bulldozed. He didn't touch Katie's recycling bins, though, which were spilling over with glass jars, cans, and papers, but straightened them the best he could and pushed them into a cleanly swept corner. When he was finished he called a number he found in the newspaper and had everything hauled away for fifty dollars. That way it would all be irretrievable. He paid in cash so there would be no record of the man's name in the check stubs, no way to get anything back. He showered and dressed and sat down to wait for his wife to come home from work.

By six-thirty the ice had melted in the drink he had mixed for her, and at seven he began to worry that she might not show up at all, but half an hour later she pulled into the driveway. From the living room window Miller saw her stare into the open garage and shake her head.

When she came in she glanced at him briefly. "You did a number on the garage," she said curtly, ignoring the glass in his outstretched hand.

He thought maybe he could joke his way around her anger. "I thought I'd get into practice for odd jobbing, since nobody woke me up for work today."

"You're a grown man." She plopped her briefcase down on the hall table. "You can get yourself up."

"You don't want your drink? I made it with fresh oranges."

She shook her head and riffled through the mail. "I had a drink at the club."

"Oh, really? A drink? Who with?"

She opened an envelope, glanced at the letter inside, and put it down. "Jim," she said.

"Jim Skinner? Our accountant?" He laughed. "Oh, great. That's just great. He probably charged us for the time." He watched her face, but her expression was impenetrable. "So what did you talk about? Did you tell him anything?"

Katie laughed. "About you, you mean? Don't be so self-absorbed. We didn't talk about you. We didn't even mention your name."

"So since when do you stop by the club for a drink on the way home from work?"

"Since this weekend. Since you went crazy and started excluding me from your life."

He snorted. "For God's sake, Katie. Aren't you blowing this thing a little out of proportion?"

She turned on him, eyes flashing. "What am I supposed to do? You've been acting as if I'm your enemy."

"Katie." He put the drink down and reached for her. She started up the stairs but he circled her from behind with his arms and then turned her around to face him. Tears were streaming down her face.

She pushed her hands against his chest. "I feel so damned betrayed," she said. "All I did was try to comfort you and you turned on me."

He murmured into her hair. "I know, I know, honey. I'm sorry, I'm so sorry." There was a smell about her like bronze—sweet and slightly metallic, valuable.

He lifted her face and kissed her on the mouth, but she pulled back quickly. "Stop," she said. "I can't breathe for crying." They both burst into laughter.

Miller slid his hands along her waist and hips. He knew her body by heart, every gentle swell and soft slope of flesh. It was an easy, familiar comfort. When he held her, he felt at home again.

Katie leaned into him with her eyes closed, waiting. He could hear her ragged breathing. "Come with me," he whispered. "Come upstairs with me and we'll straighten all this out. This time we'll really talk, okay?"

She tightened her arms around him and pressed her face into his neck.

Miller leaned over and scooped her up in his arms. Her face was still pressed against him as he carried her upstairs. On the first step he caught his breath sharply. His injured knee pinched every time he moved. At the landing, Katie tensed. Her weight shifted suddenly. "Where's Judd?"

"Out," said Miller. "I gave him money to take his girl to dinner."

She laughed and put her mouth against his ear.

In the bedroom Miller laid her on the bed and turned around to lock the door. Just in case. When he turned back, Katie was arching her back in order to slip off her skirt and stockings.

"Wait. Let me do that."

And then he noticed the clock. It was seven forty-four. Miller stopped, frozen, his hand on the zipper of Katie's skirt.

"What?" Katie said.

He shook his head. "Nothing."

She looked toward the table and suddenly grabbed his wrist. "It's that boy again, isn't it? You were thinking about him."

"I can't help it," Miller said, shaking his hand free from her grasp. "The viewing is tonight at the funeral home. I just happened to remember that when I saw the clock . . ."

Katie sat up. "My God, Miller. You were actually thinking about going to the funeral home?"

Miller spread his hands in a gesture of surrender and Katie swung her legs over the side of the bed. Miller reached for her but she pushed his hand away. "It was just . . . ," he began. "I was thinking I should go there to pay my respects."

"For God's sake, Miller. Didn't you read the obituary in this morning's paper? He was a member of the Church of God. He worked for an awning company. No mention of any kind of education. He was probably a dropout. Those people are nothing but *rednecks*. You owe them nothing. You pulled that boy up from the bottom of the lake when nobody else would do it, and that's *enough*. Let it rest, Miller. Let it *be*."

"Katie." He was going to tell her then. That would have been the time to tell her. He *had* to, eventually, regardless of what she might think of him, but she ran into the bathroom and turned the lock. Miller followed and tried the doorknob, then leaned his forehead against the door. "You're right, Katie. I need to put it behind me, but I need some kind of closure on it. Maybe I should see a shrink. Do you think I should see a shrink?"

"Go to hell," Katie choked out, her voice muffled. He could hear her opening cabinets, slamming things around.

"Katie, that girl—his wife—she has a baby. How's she going to manage? I feel responsible." He hesitated, listening. Nothing. Miller fell backward onto the bed and stared at the ceiling.

When the door finally opened, Katie's blue eyes were dry and flinty. "There's something I want you to understand, Miller." Her words were spaced out and emphatic. "I do not give a *damn* about those people. You hear, Miller? I do not give a damn about the wife or the baby or the drowned man. All I give a damn about is *this* family, ours—you and me and Judd. Remember *your* family, Miller? You have a child. You also have a wife, in case you've forgotten. Those people don't even know your name, and that's good, because there's no sense in getting involved with that sort of trash. I want you to stop letting this thing interfere with our lives."

Miller's stood up and grabbed her arm. "And our having sex? Isn't that the real issue? Just because a man died, we can't let that interfere with our sex?"

Her hand seemed to come out of nowhere, slamming against his cheek, and he stumbled backward. When he tripped, his elbow hit the dresser and Katie's antique Delft pitcher came crashing down onto the hardwood floor. Katie gasped and dropped to her knees on the floor. "This was my grandmother's," she kept saying. "This was my grandmother's." She picked up the broken pieces and threw them at Miller. "Get yourself together," she said. "I don't care what it takes. Yes, for God's sake go see a therapist. But do *something.*" She ran out of the room and down the stairs.

Miller made his way to the bed, sat down, and rubbed his cheek. Katie was right, of course. He had to get himself together. And he would. Really, he would. But it was difficult to take even the first step, to get from one minute to the next, to get through the rest of the evening, and the next day and the next. Especially the next day, because it was the day of the funeral. After a long while, he stood up, tucked his shirttails in, hobbled down the front stairs, and stepped outside. It was dusk, and lamps were coming on in the houses along the block. Everything looked peaceful and calm. Everyone else's lives seemed ordinary. For all he knew, they thought things were ordinary at his house, too. Normal. He went back inside and turned on the television set.

Katie ate a solitary supper and went to bed early. Miller waited up for Judd, but dozed off, and when he woke at two A.M., Judd's car was already parked safely in the driveway and the porch light was off. Miller limped upstairs and undressed in the hallway bathroom. His knee was stiffer now, and his elbow ached from the encounter with the dresser. When he brushed his teeth he saw the pale shadow of a bruise under his eye where Katie had hit him. He had to laugh. His first shiner, and it had come from his wife. He must have led a sheltered childhood.

In the dark bedroom he edged into bed, keeping well to his own side. He could tell from her breathing that Katie was awake, but she lay rigid and silent. Miller turned on his side, away from her, and waited to fall asleep.

In the morning when Katie went into the bathroom, Miller reached for the telephone to call his office. Funeral, he said. Death of a friend. When he looked up, Katie was standing in the doorway, pale and oddly regal in her white satin nightgown. "I heard you," she said. "If you go to that funeral today, don't bother to come back home. Do you understand? If you go there, you can just stay gone."

Miller's hand went to his cheek. "What about this shiner? I can't show up at work with this."

"I mean it," she whispered fiercely. "Don't go."

Miller turned his face to the wall and pulled the sheet over his head. When Katie left the house he fell asleep again. At eleven o'clock the telephone woke him, but when he answered, the caller hung up. It must have been Katie. It had to be Katie, checking up on him.

During the next week he felt like a man on the edge of a precipice, teetering and unbalanced. Everything seemed disproportionate and strangely distorted. He was always off balance. On street corners he stepped back from the curb, fearing he would be pushed or sucked into the traffic. On escalators he closed his eyes and held onto the handrail for dear life, afraid that gravity might fail and he would suddenly be thrown into space. In his car, he imagined that he was rolling backward, even when his foot was pressed firmly on the brake. Strange things happened. One day on the interstate he saw a church bus ahead of him with a painted sign that read "The Redeemed." He was tempted to follow it when it turned off at the next exit. Perhaps he could have learned something, he thought.

The source of his fears was elusive. The best he could determine was that they seemed to center around a sense of loss for some part of himself—or worse, that he would lose something and not realize it.

A few days later at lunch he tried to explain it all to Jack.

"I've sensed that *something* was wrong," Jack said, "but I didn't want to pry. It's nothing to do with Katie, I hope? I've always thought you two were the last perfect couple."

"Yeah, right, Jack. The last perfect couple." Miller took a sip of his coffee. "No, it's not Katie," he said. "Well, yeah, it is, sort of. She's part of it, I mean. A big part, actually. But the real trouble is with me."

Jack leaned forward. "I get it. You're still obsessing about the death of your father. Katie feels neglected. She wants you to get over it."

Miller raised his eyebrows. "Give me a break, Jack," he said. "It's a lot worse than that." He leaned across the table and whispered. "You notice this shiner?"

"How could anybody miss it? I heard you telling the secretaries that Judd jabbed you in the eye while you were playing one-on-one, but who's going to buy that?"

"You're right. That was a lie. Katie did it."

Jack's eyes widened. "Little Katie? *Your* little Katie? You shitting me?"

"Yeah, my little Katie. Yeah, that's the one."

"Wait a minute, bud. Let me get this straight. Katie gave you a black eye? On purpose?"

Miller glanced around the restaurant. "For God's sake, Jack, keep it down."

Jack inched forward in his chair. "So what in the hell did you do to deserve that?"

"It's complicated."

"Isn't everything? Come on. What happened?" Jack reached for the salt shaker. "But I'll tell you what's the truth, Miller. It's hard for me to feel sorry for you when Nadia and I are right on the brink—I mean right on the fucking *brink* of divorce." He shook the salt across his plate, set the shaker down, then picked it up and went through the same routine again. "What does that word mean, anyway, Miller? *Brink*. Who in the hell uses a fucking word like *brink*?"

Miller laughed. "You do. You just did."

"So where does it come from? Is it Dutch? It sounds Dutch. Hans Brinker. Remember that story? Hans fucking Brinker." He picked up his fork and then laid it back down on his plate. "Where was I, anyway? I was trying to make a point."

"Yeah, about how you don't feel sorry for me."

"Right. Okay, I remember now. Look, you and Katie have it all. The great house, the great kid, the great marriage—at least I thought so up until two minutes ago. And man, you're moving up in the company."

"I'm sick of that, too," Miller said.

"Sick of what?"

"The job. Haven't you noticed? I don't give a damn any more. God, I thought everybody would have noticed. I've been slacking off, and I mean shamelessly. Me, Miller Sharp, the responsible guy, the faithful employee, the eager kid whose father taught him to respect the great American work ethic. I couldn't care less anymore, Jack."

Jack looked over his shoulder. "Take it easy, Miller. You're talking too loud. Hanson from Planning and Estimating is sitting over there by the window."

Miller looked, then leaned across the table and whispered. "I'm serious. I couldn't care less. Hell, Jack, how many times have we talked about this? The company is more concerned with meeting deadlines and constructing paper trails than it is with building safe airplanes. You know as well as I do. The quality assurance program is a sham. I feel either scared or guilty all the time about what's going on there, and I'm a part of it. So are you, Jack. Jesus, don't you worry? Doesn't it bother you that every day we work there implicates us that much more in the wrongdoing? I mean, Jack, we are making airplanes that may not be safe."

"Oh, Jesus Christ, Miller. It's not that bad. Look at the ratio of plane accidents to automobile accidents. Look at the records. Anyway, hell, you're making great money."

"Would you believe I don't care about that, either?"

"Oh, yeah? Well, you'd sure as hell miss it if you didn't have it anymore." He glanced over at Hanson again. "And you're whispering, aren't you? You're still worried enough to whisper."

Miller put his head in his hands.

"Is it your dad, some sort of delayed reaction to his death?"

"Maybe it's part of it, but no, Jack. Listen. On the way to work this morning, I kept feeling like I was going to lose control of the car, like I might suddenly swerve into oncoming traffic. Or, on the parkway, I thought I just might fly straight over the side of the bridge. When I ride on escalators I feel like I'm going to be catapulted into space. Jesus, Jack, do you think I'm going crazy?"

Jack lifted his fork again, took a bite, and a tomato seed squished out and landed on his tie. He dipped his napkin into his water glass and swiped at the stain. "Okay, Miller. Why don't you just give me the goddamned bottom line, okay?"

Miller could have told Jack the truth. Jack, of all people, would understand, but it was the same as with Katie. He told only half of the story. He was amazed, because it was even easier lying to Jack than to Katie. He was becoming practiced at it, skilled even.

"I'm going to have to side with Katie on this one," Jack said. "You need to put this whole experience behind you. Forget about those people. You did what you could. It's over. Christ, man, you're a hero." He reached across the table and clapped Miller on the shoulder.

Miller shrugged the hand away. "Katie thinks I should see a shrink."

"Jesus, I don't know about a shrink. Pay me and I'll throw out the requisite phraseology: *I hear your pain, Miller. Tell me how you feel about that.* No. Nadia and I tried a marriage counselor. This guy would always touch his chest and say, 'How do you *feel* about that? I mean how do you feel about that *here*?' The only positive things that came out of our sessions was that when we got mad at each other and expressed our innermost feelings, we'd always be horny as hell afterwards. We'd come home and have passionate sex, and then the next day things were frigid between us again, until the next session." He grinned. "Hell, I actually started looking forward to the appointments."

Miller laughed. "Strange. That happened to us last week, too, or almost happened, anyway. It's almost like trying to conquer each other through sex. Or to connect on some primal level."

Jack chuckled. "So tell me how you feel about this, Miller. How do you feel about that *here*?" He touched his chest and feigned an expectant expression.

Miller didn't want to play games. He was worried about his state of mind. And he was inordinately bothered that he found Jack's salad so interesting. He saw everything as if it were skinned or peeled back to its essence. The carrots were a spectacular orange and the seeds of the tomatoes a viscous and vivid green. Miller stared for a minute, then forced himself to concentrate on Jack's question. "What? Oh. Good question. What's on my mind. The family, I guess. His family, I mean. He had a wife—the guy who drowned. She's really young—nineteen, twenty, I don't know. And she has a baby."

"Pretty?"

"Who?"

"The wife."

"Jack, come on, will you? I didn't notice. So much was going on. She was screaming. They were all screaming. She tried to hit me when I stopped CPR. That's not the point, though. I'm worried about how she's going to survive. She lives in a dump."

"Jesus. You went to her house?"

"Not exactly. I drove by there to see where she lives."

"Oh, I get it now. She's pretty, she's alone, you and Katie aren't hitting it off, you're having a midlife crisis, the job sucks . . ."

"For God's sake, Jack. I drove by her house to see if she needed help. I didn't even talk to her. I think she saw me, but I didn't go all the way up the driveway. There were people there. They were having a wake or something."

He watched as Jack pierced a satiny slice of red pepper with his fork. "What's her name?" Jack asked.

Miller leaned forward and lowered his voice. "Christ, Jack, stay with me on this, will you? The girl's not the issue. I mean, not how I feel or do not feel about her. I don't even *know* her."

Jack bit into a crisp slice of cucumber. The crunch of his bite echoed across the table. "Come on, Miller. What's her name?"

"Jack, Jack. Who cares? Okay, Adra. Does that satisfy your twisted curiosity? Her name is Adra Goodfriend."

Jack smiled. "Adra. What kind of name is that? Adra? Did you realize that rhymes with Phaedra? Isn't there some kind of symbolism there?"

Miller shook his head. "Jack, get serious, will you? Phaedra was the woman who killed herself because her stepson wouldn't sleep with her. Jesus Christ, are you even listening to me?" But he couldn't help thinking about the day he had driven out to her house. That straight, unflagging stare, those tough, bony shoulders. She had none of the soft or feminine features or the sophistication that usually appealed to him in a woman. He had to laugh at Jack, though. "I know what you're thinking, but this doesn't substantiate your theory about interesting women having exotic names, Jack. Adra Goodfriend is no Nadia."

Jack pushed his salad away and put down his fork. Just like that, he seemed to have lost his appetite. Miller had a sudden intimation that everything in life had to do with hunger—not just for food, but for breath, sex, excitement. The hunger was at once a need and a fulfillment, a reason to live. Jimmy Duane Goodfriend had hungered for a last breath, and to get it he would have done anything. He would have pulled Miller down with him to the bottom of the lake.

Miller drifted off into his own thoughts, but then he realized that Jack was talking to him about Nadia. "What? Sorry. I was distracted."

"I *asked* you," Jack said pointedly, "if you know what she's doing lately. She's calling up this boyfriend of hers at night, when I'm in bed. She goes downstairs to the kitchen telephone when she thinks I'm asleep. Except I'm not sleeping, see? Haven't been for months. Sometimes I lift the receiver and hear them whispering to each other. Last night when I picked up the phone they stopped talking for a second and then Nadia ordered me to get off the line. Voice hard as nails. *Get off the line, Jack. This is a private conversation.* My *wife* says this to me—her husband—for Christ's sake."

"What'd you do?"

"Shit. I obeyed. I got off the line." Tears welled up in his eyes. "I don't know, Miller. I don't know how to deal with it. What the hell? I love her."

Miller felt blood rush to his cheeks. He was embarrassed at Jack's distress. He was confused, too, about how the conversation had turned around to Jack's troubles. If Jack had only given him an opening, he might have been able to tell him the rest of his own story. But it was too late now. They had gone past the point where he might have confessed, at least for that afternoon. He stared down at his untouched sandwich. It was only lunchtime and already the rest of the day stretched out before him like a vast, dangerous battlefield. The prospect of going home that evening was even worse, especially with the weekend coming up. But at least on Saturday he could escape the house, go fishing, clear his head, commune with nature, maybe even somehow communicate with his father. Miller felt helpless about what was happening with Katie, with himself. Worse, he felt powerless to change things. Sometimes he couldn't decide whether staying married was a sign of cowardice or a show of courage.

Jack blew his nose on his linen napkin and picked up his fork again. By the time they walked out of the restaurant he had regained his composure. He slapped Miller on the shoulder and laughed. "What did I tell you, buddy? It's that exotic name. Adra." He rolled the name around in his mouth as if he were tasting it, measuring its value.

Once back at his desk, Miller returned to the papers he'd been working on before lunch. Aeroelasticity. Flutter. Panel response. Now, in some ways, it made sense. The study he was reading was related to the events occurring in his life. *Due to structural nonlinearities, panel flutter or aeroelastic instability does not often lead to immediate catastrophic failure. Instead it causes a sustained constant amplitude oscillation that may eventually cause long-time fatigue failure.*

A sustained constant amplitude oscillation. That was it. That explained it. One thing after another, wearing him down. Instability. Long-time fatigue failure.

He read further. *Shock-induced separation can be used to capture the onset of vortex shedding during dynamic stall.* Should he make a clean break with Katie? Start over? What about Judd? What would his father think?

Now he was excited. It was like working a crossword puzzle. Looking for the parallels between his work and his personal life erased the tedium of the job, at least temporarily. *In the case of pressure differential and thermal stresses, the sensitivity of the models to environmental factors must be determined, especially static pressure loadings and thermal stresses caused by temperature differentials between model and support. When conditions are favorable, turbulence can actually increase the stability of a linear structure of more than one degree of freedom by means of providing a conduit that feeds energy from the least stable mode to the more stable modes. However, the effect is probably very small.*

The effect is probably very small. He sighed and pushed the document across his desk. The steely-smelling air conditioning belied the stifling summer heat of the outside world. Miller's desk was piled with neat stacks of papers—proposals, studies, reports, memos. In the past he had treated such documents with reverence, but now he could read through their faults and pretensions, and—worst of all—their occasional errors and inefficiencies. Hell, maybe he knew too much for his own good.

He walked over to the window and looked at the sky. It was a brilliant blue, cloudless. It would be too hot for fishing, but it was a good day to be in the mountains. He sighed again and went back to the desk.

It is often difficult to distinguish between forced and self-excited response, as in the case of structural response due to forced excitation by atmospheric turbulence or flutter of lifting surfaces.

He looked back over his shoulder at the clock on the wall. One forty-five. He laid his head down on his desk, thinking, "Just for a few minutes." When he woke up, it was after five, and then he had to go home to Katie.

4

On Saturday Miller got up early and drove to the mountains. Just as the sun was coming up, he turned into the Lynn Camp road, parked, and walked the half mile along the trail to the stream where he and his father had often fished for brookies. For the next few hours, he tried all kinds of flies—a green drake, a royal coachman, a little sulfur dun. Nothing he tied on the line tempted the fish.

When he left home that morning, Katie had burrowed under the sheet, pretending to be asleep. Miller stood by the bed and looked at her, loving the way her blonde hair curved against her cheek. Her small hand, resting on Miller's empty pillow, was smooth and delicate. Miller whispered her name, but she never moved. It used to be that when he got up early to go fishing, she would roll over and wind her warm, solid legs around his waist and whisper, "Stay a while longer, stay."

"Sugar?" he whispered. He had not called her that in a long, long time. His chest ached for something he had lost. Whether it was Katie or something else, he didn't know. He hadn't slept well, either. He had dreamed about the drowning again, except that this time when he turned over the body at the bottom of the lake, he saw that the face belonged to his father. He woke himself by crying out, and Katie had turned to him in the dark, but then she must have remembered her anger, because just as quickly, she turned away again. That might have saved them, that moment, if either of them had followed through on it, but they didn't. And that morning he might have knelt by the side of the bed and asked her forgiveness, but he didn't do that, either.

The sun rose higher and Miller cast his line again, but his heart wasn't in the fishing. Something hovered around his shoulders, a weight but not exactly a weight, something worrying. Then he realized that it had been exactly two weeks since the boy had drowned, the longest two weeks of his life. He retrieved his line and started picking up his gear. He ought to go home. He ought to make it up with Katie once and for all, crawl back into bed with her, hold her, tell her the rest of the story and accept whatever shame and disapproval she would heap on him.

But when he hiked out to the car and started the engine he knew that home was not where he was heading.

This time he found the road easily. This time he knew what was ahead. Dust flew up from the road. It had not rained in weeks, maybe a month. The flowers in the adjacent field were blanched from the heat and coated with a layer of clay-colored dust. Miller was sweating freely, having driven down from the mountains with the window open, craving fresh air. His pant legs had dried stiff from where he had stepped into the stream, and his shirt stuck to his chest.

He was glad that only the one truck was parked by the barn. Hers, probably—Adra Goodfriend's. So this time she was alone. Miller pulled the Saab up next to the truck and turned off the engine. There was an echoing silence that was almost voluminous after the deafening rush of the stream in the mountains and then the roar of the hot, windy ride coming back. He didn't know why he had come nor even what he wanted to tell the girl. He knew only that something irresistible had drawn him there. He opened the car door and got out, pulling his damp shirt away from his chest. All that time, he had been watching the house, but there was no movement there at all, no sound of any kind. He walked slowly, his feet crunching on the rough gravel driveway. Next to the porch, three tires with peeling white paint were laid in a flat row and filled with red dirt to create makeshift flower beds. A few straggly petunias wilted in the cracked clay soil. *You have to pinch petunias back to keep them blooming,* he thought. Even he knew that. But the girl was young. So young.

When he put his foot on the first step of the porch, it gave a little under his weight. He peered underneath the porch and saw that most of the steps were half rotted. The decay was overwhelming—crumbling foundation, rotting windows, rusting roof. When he stepped onto the porch the whole house seemed to shake. He put up his hand to knock, but the girl was already standing behind the screen door, watching him. He stepped back, surprised. "Hello," he said.

She said nothing.

"Do you remember me?" he asked. His own voice sounded foreign to him, theatrical and false. Behind the screen the girl's face was blurred and mysterious in the dim hallway, sectioned off by the mesh into small, dusty grids. Her hair was pulled back from her face and plaited in a single skinny braid, making her cheekbones gleam in sharp relief. Her skin was so fair that it had a greenish cast where it pulled tight over her bones. She wore a loose cotton housecoat, colorless, it seemed, and her feet were bare.

While Miller struggled to think of something to say, she finally spoke. "You were here before," she said. "You sat in your car and looked. But at the dock that day you never said your name."

To have something to do with his hands, he pushed them into the pockets of his jeans. "Miller Sharp."

The shadows beneath Adra's eyes seemed to have been scorched there by the heat of her stare. "There's lots of Sharps in this part of the county," she said. Her tone was accusatory. "You kin to any around here?"

"No. No relation," he said. "Just my father and me in our branch of the family, from North Carolina originally. We're not—I'm not—related to anybody around here. Not that I know of, anyway." He kept wishing she would push open the screen and come out so he could see her better, but he was afraid to ask.

The girl's arms were lightly freckled. The way she held them folded across her chest lifted her shoulders and made her seem impatient. "Well," she said, "I'm not surprised. You don't look like nobody around here."

"No," he said, and then he felt foolish. What had he meant by that?

She stood perfectly still, waiting. Her nails were bitten to the quick, but her fingers were long and graceful, what Miller's mother would have called a pianist's fingers.

Neither of them spoke for a minute. A hornet buzzed, and out on the highway, a truck rumbled by. Miller cleared his throat. "I was thinking," he said, "that maybe you need some help. I know you have a baby. That is, I noticed at the dock that you were holding a baby. It's yours, right? Yes, well, of course. It was in the paper. I mean, I was just wondering if there was anything I could do to help."

She tilted her head but said nothing.

"Anything," Miller said. "Just let me know what you need." It was maddening, her silence, her cold stare. "I mean, I just thought . . ." Miller's voice tumbled on. "My father died last winter. Six months ago. I know what it's like."

"You know what it's like," the girl said flatly, without emotion. The declaration was spoken not as an affirmation, but more in the way of a confrontation. Her mouth pulled up at one corner and then went slack again, as if she had meant to smile and then thought better of it.

"I loved my father very much," he said. "He was a good man. My mother left home when I was young. Well, what I mean is, my father brought me up, mostly."

"Ever'body has their cross to bear," she said.

"Well, yes. And you," Miller stumbled on. "I'm sorry."

She waited, watching him.

Miller shifted his feet. "What about money?"

The girl laughed abruptly and turned her shoulder to glance back down the dim hallway, as if in that one brief glance she could assess her entire situation, count all the failures and disappointments of her brief and narrow life. "Now there's a problem," she said. "But not a new one. Nossir, that's been a big problem from the beginning. Jimmy Duane never did make friends with money."

Miller reached into his pocket and counted out the bills he found. Forty-three dollars. He hadn't thought this out. He had been planning it in an oblique sense, but he hadn't really thought it out properly.

"This is all I have today," he said, "and the banks are closed, but I could come back Monday. Or, wait—I could get more at an ATM. Yeah. I could bring it back right away. In the next half hour or so."

She was silent.

"Or I could mail you a check?" His hand reached out into the air, but the girl did not move.

"What for?" she asked.

He pushed the money back into his pockets. "I'm not making sense, am I? Look, when I jumped into the lake after your husband, I became involved in your life. I didn't mean to. It just happened. I can't . . ." His throat ached and his hands shook a little. Maybe he was getting sick. "I can't explain it. I mean I can't just *leave* you like this."

She did smile then, smiled the way a grown-up smiles at a child who has said something naive. "You don't even know me."

He ran his hand through his hair. "Let me try this again. What I mean is that it was traumatic—upsetting—for me, too. And for my wife. I . . . I've had a difficult time. We both have. Not that my experience can compare to yours in any way. Your loss, I mean. God, no. I didn't mean that. It's just that . . ." He stopped, desperate, and looked at her thin, unrelenting face. "Just please let me help." Now he was laughing. He felt close to hysteria. "You know what?" he said. "You're making this awfully hard for me."

"I don't need your money, Mr. Miller Sharp. I got some insurance money from Jimmy Duane's company—Bakeless. Three thousand dollars."

"That's all?"

"It's the most money I've ever seen."

"But three thousand dollars? That won't last you more than a couple of months. The funeral alone . . . And you have that baby to take care of."

As if she didn't know that.

She laughed again. "I'll tell you what's the truth, Mr. Miller Sharp. I can't for the life of me figure out why this is such a problem for you."

From the shadowy depths of the house, the baby howled. Miller was startled by the sudden cry, but the girl did not move. Her eyes were still on Miller. She waited for another long minute and then she inclined her head backwards. "My baby's cryin'."

Miller shifted from one foot to the other. "I heard. Wait, though. Don't go yet. There must be something I can do."

"About what?"

"About . . . There must be something I can do to help."

She kept feeding him rope to hang himself, he thought, as if she were laughing at him, but her eyes glittered fiercely. "My baby's cryin'," she said again. Still, she did not move.

Miller nodded and turned to walk down the steps. He looked back again into the heat of her impenetrable stare, at her stiff, unyielding shoulders. He kept walking. When he looked down at his hand on the door handle of the Saab, he did not recognize it as his own hand. He was frightened and angry at the same time. Whether it was at himself or Adra Goodfriend, he didn't know. What he did know was that if he had it to do over again, he would not have jumped into the water after Jimmy Duane Goodfriend. He would have started up his motor and raced across the lake toward home. The hell with her, the hell with all of them.

He climbed into the car and turned the ignition key and pressed the accelerator so hard that the tires spit out rocks behind him. He sped down the driveway as fast as he dared, bouncing over the rutted surface like a roughrider. He never looked back but he knew that she was still standing there in the same position behind the screen door, watching him.

5

For the next few weeks he tried to forget about it. He was attentive to Katie and patient and friendly with Judd, even though the boy seemed more and more like a stranger who came home only to sleep and eat. Katie was still distant—not the old Katie—but occasionally a little of her true spirit would seep through the coolness, and then she would blush and look away from him. She started coming home on time again and there was an awkward truce between them. In a way, it was as if they were starting from scratch. Miller had been careful, studiously courting her, but considerate of her wariness. In bed he patted her shoulder when the lights went out, but he knew that neither of them was ready yet for anything more.

Miller didn't tell her about his dreams. Almost every night he slipped into a terrifying nightmare in which he was swimming through a cloudy veil of water. When he moved his hands in the breaststroke, the water parted like a curtain and he saw the bloated face of the drowned boy, the pale, flaccid lips and the long dark tunnel of his throat. As soon as Miller opened his mouth to scream, his own teeth floated out into the current one by one, then drifted slowly downward and came together on the river floor in the perfect shape of a bite.

On Thursday Katie reminded him that she had ordered tickets for the benefit symphony on Friday night. It was an occasion that Miller always dreaded, not because of the music, which he genuinely enjoyed, but because the concerts were always preceded by noisy, tedious dinners at the country club with Katie's friends. He tried to be cheerful about it to please Katie, and for the first time in weeks she seemed more energetic as she dressed in a white chiffon dress and high-heeled sandals. Miller sat on the edge of the bed and watched as she pulled on her sheer, pale stockings. He loved the clothes women wore in the summer. It was romantic, the way the light insinuated itself through the filmy fabric of their skirts, outlining hips and smooth tanned legs. He liked the way the heat brought out the sheen of their skin, heightened the color of their cheeks, lending an exotic allure to their dusky faces.

Katie's white dress reminded him of the first time he had seen her, at a party the summer of his sophomore year in college. She'd worn a white dress that night, too. He remembered also a thick gold bracelet that slid up and down her narrow wrist when she moved. Her blonde hair was long then, well past her shoulders, and that evening she had tucked a white gardenia behind her ear. The occasion was a birthday party for one of his father's friends, and beforehand, Miller had made all sorts of excuses to stay away. "Fifteen minutes," his father had insisted, "and then you can leave. Just pay your respects to Bill and then you can go."

In the end Miller had stayed until after midnight, trailing Katie Monroe, the visiting niece of his father's friend, around the garden, making her laugh, flirting outrageously. He ambled along beside her over the thick summer grass of the yard, acutely conscious of the enormous difference in their heights, and, from his vantage point as he towered above her, he could see the pale freckles along the swell of her breast. He said ridiculous things to her, but she only laughed when he babbled, "My name is Miller, but I don't care what you call me, just as long as you promise to call me." It was something he had heard a friend say to a girl once, and afterward he was embarrassed that he had repeated it to a girl as classy as Katie.

Something worked, though. He walked her home to her uncle's house and when she said good night, he asked for a drink of water. Anything to delay his departure. She smiled and glanced up at him under half-lowered lids, and he followed her down the long hallway to the kitchen. She snapped on the bright overhead light and leaned against the counter, contemplating him boldly as he sipped his water. Miller was so self-conscious that he could barely swallow. At last he was able to get down the water in one noisy, concentrated gulp, and they both laughed. The whole time, he had watched her distorted image through the thick base of the glass. He wanted his hands there where her hips touched the counter, just below the waist. He wanted to feel the slight swell of her hips and the inward curve of her waist and then maybe to slide his hands up along her ribs, where he could judge the juncture where the rise of her breasts began. "I think I need to sit down," he said, flushing with his own heat, and he sank into the nearest chair, an oak ladderback by the kitchen table.

Katie laughed and took the glass from his hand. She hitched the skirt of her dress up over her sun-browned knees and sat down on his lap, facing him, her smooth legs straddling his. His impulse was to slide his hands under her skirt and along her thighs, but instead he was prudent and fastened them around her waist. "Jesus," he whispered as his fingers pressed gently against her ribs. She laughed again and leaned forward to kiss him. Their mouths at first met each other tentatively, and then she brushed her tongue lightly across his lips.

"Where did you learn that?" he asked, but he didn't wait for her answer. As long as she was doing it to him, he didn't care. And when he moved out of the ripe heat of her mouth, he moved his lips against her neck and touched his tongue to her glistening throat. It tasted salty.

He moaned, half in jest, half in earnest.

"Oh God," she said, moving against him. And then she whispered his name. "Miller, Miller, Miller." Three times. It was the first time he had ever felt at home with his own name. She had baptized him with her desire.

They left the house and drove to a deserted place he knew at the beach and they lay together on the cool silky sand, listening to the rough crash of the waves beyond the dunes, and he told her about his mother, how she had left, walked out on them when he was fifteen. When Katie cried he was moved to passion and he realized from her eager response that she had more experience than he, but their hunger for each other seemed inevitable. The next night and the next and the entire summer thereafter they spent making love in his convertible, parked along deserted roads or on beaches, even in Miller's childhood bed when his father was out. Every night was spent that way, but it was never enough for either of them. By the next summer they were engaged, and the year after that, the summer of his graduation, they were married.

It was the great American love story.

Now, in their bedroom, with twenty married years behind them, Miller felt his desire growing as Katie fastened the strap of her sandal. For the first time in a long time, he felt oddly happy. "Let's stay home," he said. "Or better yet, let's go to a hotel." He sat beside her on the bed and put his hand around her ankle, letting his fingers slide down the arch of her foot and across her instep. He felt her flesh rise, though she had not moved. But he could tell she was pleased, even though she tried not to smile. "Come on, Katie," he whispered, "let's stay home."

Maybe he imagined it. He thought he felt her pulse quicken, but she was still holding back. She pushed him away. "Gina and Phil will be here to pick us up any minute. They're probably halfway here right now."

"So we'll say we changed our minds. Or we won't answer the door. We'll tack a note on it: 'Overcome by passion.'" He reached over and cupped his hand over her breast.

"We paid a hundred dollars for these tickets," Katie said. "And you love Respighi."

"Who's Respighi?"

"You know," she said. "The composer. He wrote *The Pines of Rome*. You love it."

"I do?"

"Yes, Miller, you do."

"I love *you*," he said. He moved closer and ran his finger along the rounded curve of her suntanned shoulder. His lips came down on the indentation where her collarbone ended and he let his mouth linger there, measuring her reaction. When he looked up, he noticed that her eyes were glistening and he rushed on, now that he had the advantage. "Come on, sugar. Let's stay home." He pulled her toward him again and moved his lips along her throat. Her neck smelled good, and he began to feel aroused as her head fell back slightly to accept his kisses.

She was murmuring something but he couldn't make it out. What he wanted from her was something of the girl who had sat on his lap in the kitchen all those years ago, the girl who had desired him openly and without recriminations. No strings. He coaxed her shoulders back toward the pillows and then he understood what she had been saying. "No."

"No? Why? Why in the hell not?"

Katie ducked out from beneath his arms. Blood rose to her cheeks. "Who do you think you are anyway, Miller? You can't ignore me for weeks and then suddenly treat me like . . ." Her eyes filled up.

He sat up suddenly. "Like what? Say it. Like what?"

"Like a sexual object."

His laugh sounded like a bark. "A sexual object? Jesus Christ, Katie. How long have we been married? Twenty years? Do we have to play games now? I said I love you. What more can I say? Frankly, I just flat out don't know where to go from here." He got hold of her wrist. "Look at me, Katie? Do you realize what I've been going through? Do you?"

She shook the skirt of her dress and wiped at her eyes. There was a little smudge of mascara on her cheek. "We're late," she said. "Let's talk about this when we get home." Her heels clicked against the floor as she hurried out of the bedroom.

"Katie," he said.

She turned to look at him from the doorway and suddenly all the wind went out of him. "You need to fix that," he said. "Your makeup."

Whoever had written the synopsis in the symphony program had called *The Pines of Rome* a work full of brilliant color and rich, varied orchestral textures. In the concert hall, Miller shifted in his seat, thinking not of the music, but of the anticipated confrontation with Katie later at home. Because that's what it would be—a confrontation, since Katie had already decided, after all the years of tender affection between them, that Miller was treating her like a sexual object. At first he was only upset, but then he was angry. He had made the move to make up with her and she had turned him down. *Words were said, shots were fired, people were hurt.*

Somehow he managed to be civil to Gina and Phil, and with Gina in the car, conversation wasn't a problem. She always monopolized it. Phil kept laughing and shaking his bald head in agreement with everything she said. Once in the theater, Miller was able to manipulate the seating arrangement so that he was on the aisle, next to Katie, and he wouldn't have to indulge in small talk with anybody. When the music began, he found himself unable to concentrate, even though the symphony was usually soothing for him. He had grown up with good music. His father had listened to the Metropolitan Opera every Saturday on the radio and he had once told Miller that a Mozart symphony could temporarily raise your I.Q. by ten points. He leaned back in his seat and looked up at the cupola of the theater's ceiling with its Byzantine carvings and the shadowed figures encircling the auditorium. Finally he looked down at his program again and in the oblique reflection of light from the stage he read the composer's own description of the work: "Part I. The Pines of the Villa Borghese. Children at play in the pine grove of the villa; . . . twittering and shrieking like swallows at evening. . . ."

That day after the drowning, children were running in Adra Goodfriend's yard, shrieking, tumbling through the ragged grass, and jumping from the flatbed of a rusty truck, oblivious to sorrow and loss.

Gina leaned across Katie and put her damp hand on Miller's knee. "Isn't this wonderful, Miller?"

Katie watched him anxiously, like a mother nervous about her child's social manners. Miller made a circle with his thumb and index finger, nodded his head, and went back to his program. "Part II. The Pines Near a Catacomb. . . . From the depths rises a chant which re-echoes solemnly, like a hymn, and is then mysteriously silenced."

The depths. Water weighs eight pounds per gallon. It takes eighty-two seconds to drown, maybe a little longer. Then ventricular fibrillation sets in and except for the brain, the body shuts down. After the first two minutes, Jimmy Duane was unconscious, though he could have been saved at that point. He could have been saved if he had been pulled up in time.

"Part III. The Pines of the Janiculum. There is a thrill in the air," Respighi wrote. "The full moon reveals the profile of the pines of Gianicolo's Hill. A nightingale sings."

A nightingale sings. Miller glanced sideways at Katie's profile. Her lashes were wet.

Read on. Don't think about Katie and how you have hurt her.

"Part IV. The Pines of the Appian Way. Misty dawn on the Appian Way. . . . To the poet's fantasy appears a vision of past glories; trumpets blare, and the army of the Consul advances brilliantly in the grandeur of a newly risen sun toward the Sacred Way, mounting in triumph the Capitoline Hill."

Above all, don't think about Adra Goodfriend. Try to stop wondering how much she knows. Don't think about the bruises or the rusty roof or whether the baby is hungry. Don't speculate about whether her child is crying, whether she is hungry, or if the insurance money has run out. Don't wonder whether her gaunt face might be glowing in the blue light of a television set, or whether she might be sitting alone in the dark, mourning her dead husband. Don't think about what you have already lost or what you will lose in the future or what you might already have let slip away without ever realizing its value.

He stayed in his seat during the intermission while Katie, Gina, and Phil went to the lobby for wine. As they filed back into their seats, Katie kept her distance as she stepped around him, but Gina brushed against him as he stood to let her pass. He felt the swell of her breasts and the slope of her soft belly as she inched by him.

Miller never even noticed when the concert ended. But people were standing to applaud. Katie, standing next to him, looked down, frowned, and nudged his shoulder. Miller heard laughter and the rustle of programs and the whisper of silk dresses and smelled the pungent odor of perfume and musk. When he stood up, his legs felt weak, as if he were recuperating from a long illness. He straightened his back and shoulders and forced a smile and began to clap with a feigned enthusiasm.

He had not heard a single note.

"Yes, it was wonderful," Katie was murmuring to Gina. Miller was trying to think up an excuse to skip drinks, which, logically, since the Carsons had picked them up, would have to be at their house. He found them a particularly tiring couple. At dinner the conversation had centered partly on Gina's shar-pei puppies and how much her dog was worth as a stud, and partly on the success of her real estate business. Phil, a gynecologist, was Gina's second husband. The first, an orthopedic surgeon, had also been named Phil. Miller had joked about Gina's predilection for physicians named Phil and had dubbed the gynecologist Re-Phil. At first Katie had laughed at the joke, but now that she had grown closer to Gina, she no longer thought it funny.

Gina was what people called a man-eater, red-haired and voluptuous, and physical—a toucher—and Miller shied away from touchers, even in the best of times. She wore her hair longer than she should have for her age, Miller thought, with part of it pinned up so that tendrils fell against her cheeks and forehead and the rest was swept back into great waves that made her round face seem inordinately smaller.

In the crowded aisle of the theater, Gina swept past Katie and grabbed Miller's elbow in a proprietary manner. He felt the weight of her ample, freckled breast on his forearm as she leaned against him. When he looked down at her, his eyes gravitated to the deep chasm outlined by the neckline of her green silky dress. "Katie's been so *depressed*," she whispered, her voice conspiratorial, as if the information were news to Miller. "I'm worried, aren't you?"

He put his hand to his ear to indicate he couldn't hear above the noise of the crowd, but Gina would not be deterred. "Maybe she just needs a little TLC," she suggested in a louder tone, glancing back at Katie. Miller hated that acronym. He had hated it since the first time he heard it—in high school, probably. Gina's warm fingers pressed into his wrist and he could have sworn that she leaned her head momentarily against his shoulder. Miller felt smothered in the fragrance of her heavy perfume. There was no graceful way he could pull away from her clutches. Now he began to wonder if Katie had confided in Gina and whether she had mentioned the marital problems or the story of the drowning. In the lobby he finally disengaged himself by saying he needed to go to the men's room. On the way down the stairs, sliding his hand along the brass banister, he nodded to people he knew and fought off an unaccountable urge to weep. Maybe it was a good thing Katie had turned down the hotel room. He wouldn't have been very good company. Whatever excitement he had felt earlier in the bedroom had now dissipated. All he wanted was to go home, have a drink, and go to sleep.

On the drive back, Gina insisted on sitting in the back with Miller. She leaned against him from shoulder to knee, and the scent of her thick perfume overwhelmed him. Miller smelled the odor of gardenias, and lavender, and roses, probably. Re-Phil was rattling on about the deplorable value of the dollar overseas and the rampant crime in Europe and how crowded the slopes at Aspen had been the previous winter. It was what Miller later described to Katie as "doctor talk."

"Why don't you guys come along with us this year?" Re-Phil said. "We go the week before Christmas and stay through New Year's."

"Christmas?" said Miller. "No. There's Judd."

"Well, bring him, too," Re-Phil said, waving his right arm in a huge, encompassing gesture.

"Yes," said Gina. She wound her fingers in Miller's and he felt the hard edge of her diamond solitaire against his hand. "Oh, Miller, it would be such fun." She leaned forward and patted Katie's shoulder with her free hand. "Come on, Katie, talk to this old grouch."

"We saw some movie stars there last year," Re-Phil said. "Who else, honey? Oh, the Kennedys. God, that Ethel has aged."

"I'm not into celebrity-watching," Miller said.

Katie turned and frowned at him.

"We always have a family Christmas at home," Miller said. He pulled his hand away from Gina's on the pretense of straightening his tie.

"Summer, then," said Re-Phil. "I have a sailboat down in Mexico. You guys could take a cruise with us."

"I get seasick," said Miller, though that was a lie.

"Let us think about it," Katie said quickly. "Imagine, Miller—sailing off the Baja peninsula. It sounds so romantic."

Miller took a deep breath. He felt as if he might burst out of his clothes, his very skin, and run screaming into the night. He almost thanked God aloud when Re-Phil pulled up in front of their house. "We'd ask you in," said Miller, "but I've had this horrible headache all evening." He opened the door and jumped out, not even waiting to walk Katie up the sidewalk.

He went directly to the kitchen and poured himself a drink. He heard Katie slam the front door and stomp up the stairs. When he went up, Katie was unzipping her white dress. "Did you have to be so rude, Miller? When we were at the symphony, I had already invited them to come home and have a drink with us, and then you start complaining about a headache. You don't really think they believed you, do you?"

Miller ripped off his tie and threw it across the room. "I really don't give a damn whether they believed me. Those people are frauds—shallow, nouveau riche frauds who are too stupid even to add up all the money they make."

Katie pulled her dress over her head and sat down on the edge of the bed. It was obvious to Miller that she was making a try at patience. "Phil's actually a very nice man, if you'd only make an effort to get to know him. And Gina's harmless. She's very funny, really, and nice when you get past the hair and the clothes. When did you start becoming so impatient with all our friends?"

"*Your* friends," Miller said. "Gina and Phil are *your* friends. Jesus—that perfume of hers. I could barely breathe in the car. And those nails. How does a person function in real life with nails that long?"

"Let's drop it, Miller. In fact, let's try to forget the whole evening." Katie bent forward to remove her stockings. She was wearing the white lace garter belt he had given her for Christmas, which, until this evening, had remained wrapped in tissue paper in her lingerie drawer. It was an overt invitation, he knew that. Hours earlier he would have been thrilled, but now all he felt was a cold and solid dread. When Katie unhooked her brassiere and let her breasts fall free, his heart began to pound, not with excitement, but apprehension. And when she looked up at him and smiled, some basic reflex made him step back. Seeing his reaction, she quickly moved her hands to cover herself and rushed into the bathroom.

He knew she was crying but at that moment he wasn't strong enough to deal with her anguish. It is a kind of attrition, he thought, maybe a necessary one, this falling off of love, like a falling off of light. It leaves you in darkness through no fault of your own except that a piece of your heart has finally worn out. He grabbed his pillow from the bed and went downstairs. He tossed the pillow onto the sofa and then went into the kitchen and opened the cabinet. He had replaced the bottle of whiskey several times in the past few weeks. It was the only way he could get to sleep at night. He considered it a temporary aberration—medicinal. It was something he could give up easily enough when the time came. But now he needed it. It was that simple. *I'll just finish off this one bottle*, he told himself, *and that will be the end of it.*

He poured himself half a glass, hesitated, then filled it almost to the top and carried it out to the back porch. The square of light on the grass suddenly disappeared and he realized that Katie had turned off the bedroom light upstairs. He walked out into the yard and put his hand where the square had been, surprised that it was not warm. In fact the place was cool and a little damp, but he sat down anyway and sipped his whiskey. This darkness—the broad deep canopy of night—made him feel agoraphobic. That endless space up there was too uncharted—limitless, and that's what frightened him. He was seized by the sudden realization that his father might meet up with Jimmy Duane Goodfriend in death and learn what Miller had done. Probably he already knew. Of course he did. The clue was in Miller's dreams. And maybe that was a clue, too, that death was not the place of peace the preachers promise, but a place of mourning and unrest. That's the way death comes, he thought, as fierce and determined as a screaming warrior. Maybe that's why men die with their eyes open.

In the quiet, Miller had the sensation that the earth was rumbling beneath him, gathering energy and momentum. He looked around and saw that nothing had really moved, yet he was suddenly aware of things going on without him. And far off in the distance—he was sure of it—he heard a door close, and with great finality.

6

Hammer, sixteen-penny nails, circular saw. What else? Screws, electric drill, screwdriver, level, extension cord. Crowbar—that, too. Miller stood in the shade of his garage. It was quiet there, and cool on a morning already clenched in the enervating fist of summer heat. He rummaged through his toolbox, making a mental inventory of its contents. He would have to stop by the lumberyard to pick up a couple of two-by-tens for the stringers and some two-by-twelves for the risers and treads.

Adra Goodfriend didn't know he was coming, not yet. He himself hadn't known until a few minutes before, when he had found himself picking up things he would need to repair her front steps.

His heart bumped wildly against his chest as he snapped the toolbox shut and carried it out to the trunk of his car. When he went back for the saw and cord, he hesitated. As usual, Judd had gone to the club swimming pool, and Katie was only God knew where. Miller had slept on the sofa after the concert the night before, and earlier that morning Katie had swept through the living room without speaking and then driven off in her car.

Maybe he could do what he had to do for Adra Goodfriend without Katie's even knowing about it. If Katie was angry enough to stay away for a few hours, maybe Miller could replace the steps and get back home before she did. Six steps, if he remembered correctly. That shouldn't take long. He thought back to the first time he had walked up those steps, the *only* time. The whole place was falling apart, not just the steps. Maybe there were other things he could do to help the girl, too.

He picked up the cord and the circular saw and put them into the trunk along with the toolbox. Then he closed the garage door and got into his car. It was amazing how fast his heart was skipping, yet the sensation was not unpleasant because it was the first time in weeks he had really felt alive.

He pulled out into the street and turned on the radio. In a few minutes he was humming along with the music and slapping the palm of his hand against the steering wheel. By the time he had picked up the lumber and was driving along the interstate with the boards sticking out the passenger seat window, he was singing out loud. A pretty girl in a green convertible passed him and gave him a thumbs-up sign. Her long, gold-threaded hair whipped across her eyes when she turned her head to look at him, and she laughed and pushed it away from her face. Miller tried to imagine how the girl's hair might feel against his fingertips. Silky. The way Katie's hair had felt when he first met her. He had a sudden reverie of her leaning above him, her gold hair spilling into shiny pools on his chest. He remembered sand dunes and the crash of waves on the beach. He sped up and kept pace with the girl in the green car for a while, and when she turned off a few exits later, she blew him a kiss. A beautiful girl in a convertible, and she had blown him a kiss. Summer. He felt happy again, and younger. Maybe his life was taking a turn for the better.

By the time he turned off at the exit for Blue Creek, his mood had evened out somewhat, but his hands shook a little. What if Adra turned him away? What if she called him a murderer? What if she knew, and had been saving up her anger for one huge confrontation? For revenge, maybe, or blackmail? He drove slowly down her driveway, feeling hesitant now. When the house came into his view it seemed to be staring at him blankly, with the uncurtained windows and the gaping mouth of the open front door.

Adra was in the yard beside the house, hanging sheets on a rusty wire clothesline. Behind her, under the shade of a locust tree, the baby lay sleeping on a blanket. Adra turned her head when Miller pulled in, and he watched her face, but as before, there was no hint of emotion, just a level stare. She stood with her hands poised on the clothesline as Miller pulled into the turnaround space by the barn.

He turned off the motor and sat still for a minute, watching Adra's reflection in the driver-side mirror. *Objects in the mirror are closer than they appear.* Adra dropped her clothespins into a willow basket and stood with her hands on her hips. She was barefooted and wore a long, faded sundress. Beneath the flimsy cotton of the dress, Miller saw the shape of her small, round breasts, even the sharp line of her hipbone. Her dark hair was pulled back from her face and secured with some sort of band. A flush of heat colored her cheekbones.

Miller climbed out of the car, bowing slightly. Adra pushed her hands into the pockets of her sundress and walked around the car to the passenger side. She ran her hand slowly along the smooth length of one of the boards sticking from the window and leaned forward to smell the fresh clean wood. It was a move that seemed unconscious but somehow graceful, even lovely. Miller remembered the girl in the convertible, the long silky hair. He wondered how Adra Goodfriend's hair would look freshly washed and brushed. In the sun there were glints of red and blue in it.

"So," she said. "Where are you going with all this new wood, Miller Sharp?" She seemed to gain some perverse pleasure from saying his name, as if it were a secret joke. But she wasn't smiling.

Miller shrugged. "If it's not too presumptuous, I thought I might repair your front steps for you."

Her laugh was abrupt and unnerving, like a bark. "You're making play of me."

"No," he said. "No. When I was here the last time, I noticed the steps were . . ." He struggled to think of an appropriate adjective that wouldn't hurt her feelings. "A little shaky. So I thought"—*how could he say this?*—"with your husband gone, you might need someone to help you with things like that."

She crossed her arms over her chest and cocked her head at him. "Jimmy Duane wadn't never very good at fixin' things. Leastwise, if he was, he wasn't about to let me know he was. He didn't much like work."

Miller opened the passenger door, slid out the boards, and dropped them onto the grass. The hollow repercussion of the wood woke the baby, and Adra walked across the grass and picked her up. When she came back, Miller looked into the baby's face and saw in it her father's expression. The thin blonde hair was like her father's, too, and the pale, round eyes. Her screaming seemed unbearably loud and her thin little arms moved in a stiff, mechanical rhythm. "How old?" Miller asked, trying to smile.

Adra patted the baby's back and lifted her over her shoulder. "Nine months. I call her Sister."

Miller nodded. He wanted the child to look more like her mother

than Jimmy Duane. "Do you have a sawhorse, anything I could use to cut these boards on?"

The baby's wails reached a new crescendo. "I've not said you could do this yet, have I?" said Adra.

Miller's heart began to thump erratically again. Why did the girl have to be so damned intrepid? "Am I fired, then? Before I even begin?"

A corner of her mouth pulled up. "How can I fire you if I ain't hired you? Anyway, you didn't say how much you charge."

Miller grabbed his advantage. He opened the trunk and started taking out his tools. "I come cheap," he said. "A beer, a glass of tea. Ice water." He smiled at her.

She raised an eyebrow and took a few steps backwards. Her slight retreat seemed to open a space into which Miller could move freely. She seemed more accessible now, less suspicious. When Miller carried the toolbox and the saw over to the bottom of the steps, Adra nodded toward the back of the house. "Sawhorses are around back."

Miller positioned the crowbar under the board of the first step. "Call me Miller," he said. "Please."

She looked at him without comment and then went up the back stairs of the porch with the baby, and in a few minutes the crying stopped. When she came back out the baby was sucking on a bottle, and Adra laid her down on the blanket again and returned to hanging up her wash. She moved like a woman who knew she was being watched, but didn't care, maybe even liked it. When she leaned over and picked up a wet sheet from her basket, Miller remembered that his mother had owned a willow basket like that. He had loved the sunny smell of the sheets when she took them down from the line, the fabric so worn and soft you could almost see through it.

The screech of the first step as the nails pulled away from the wood made the baby cry again. Her bottle went rolling across the blanket.
Adra retrieved it, fitted it into the child's hands, and went back to work. Every move she made seemed businesslike. She matched up the opposite corners of the wet sheet she took from the basket, snapped the length of it into the air, and folded it once. Then she held the open ends together and pinned them to the clothesline. "Just go on about your work," she said to Miller. "Don't fret about the young'n."

Miller pushed the crowbar into the space between the second step and the riser and put his weight behind it. The rotted wood splintered into shards. Whenever he looked around at Adra Goodfriend, she seemed occupied with hanging her wash. Carrying the boards from the car, he noticed the old wringer washer on the porch near the back of the house. What a job that had been for his mother, pushing the family clothes and linens through those thick rubber rolls. Once, she had caught her fingers, and when she got them out again, she had sat down in the laundry room and cried for a good half hour. Even at his young age, Miller suspected it was something more than physical pain that had made her grieve like that.

"I saw your old wringer washer back there," he called to Adra. "My mother used to have one of those."

When no comment came in reply, Miller resigned himself to the fact that Adra Goodfriend was not much for conversation and he concentrated on the steps. The rotted wood crumbled beneath his crowbar and pulled away easily from the foundation. He laid the broken boards and nails in a pile near the porch, to be carried away when he was finished. When he looked up again, the clothes basket was empty, and Adra was carrying her baby through the grass near the edge of the woods. Her shoulders were slightly curved with the weight of the child and her head was lowered as she murmured something into the baby's ear.

Between them the hanging sheets gleamed white in the hot sunlight. There was no breeze, not even a breath of air, and everything seemed portentous in that weighty atmosphere. The wringer had started him thinking about his mother, and there came into Miller's mind a memory of the last time he had seen her. He recalled that his parents had argued about her spending so much time at rehearsals for a little theater production she was acting in, and his mother had asked his father how she could be missed when he spent most of *his* time fishing and hunting, anyway. Then at the party after the opening night performance, the man who had directed the play—a shoe salesman at the local department store—shook Miller's hand and told him that his mother had real potential as an actress—maybe she would even end up in the movies—and although Miller saw from his mother's expression that she wanted him to be happy about that prediction, he had felt a vague premonition of danger.

After that play there was another and then another, and even when the season was over, his mother was often gone from home and his father was not as talkative as usual. It was an accident that Miller had even been home the day she left. He had felt sick at school and when the school nurse sent him home in the middle of the day, there was a big black Pontiac parked in the driveway of the house. He walked inside, almost tripping over the suitcases in the dim hallway, and when he peered around the corner into the living room, there was his mother, wearing a new yellow dress and sitting on the old brocade sofa with the director, a man at least fifteen years younger. There was a red smear, like lipstick, on the man's cheek. When Miller's mother tried to kiss him good-bye, he pushed her away and locked himself in the bathroom. He lay on the cold tile floor until he heard them drive away, and then he vomited. He stayed on the floor all afternoon, gliding in and out of sleep. When his father came home that evening and realized what had happened, he looked as if someone had slapped him across the face. He grabbed Miller's shoulder and pushed him back against the stairs. "Why in the hell didn't you call me?" he yelled. Then just as abruptly, he dropped to his knees and pulled his son into his arms. "No, no, forgive me, son, forgive me. It's not your fault. I saw it coming. Nothing could have stopped her." He laid his hand on Miller's head as if delivering a benediction. "It's not your fault, son, I'm the one to blame." He held Miller tightly for so long that the boy's neck began to ache and his shoulders were forced into an unnatural position, but he did not move, because he felt that if he did, the entire house might come down around his shoulders.

For years after that Miller flipped through movie magazines at the newsstands to look for his mother's picture, but he never found a trace of her. Lauralee Sharp, a real live person and one-time mother, had disappeared from the face of the earth. His earth, anyway. Then, two years after he was married, a card with a Minnesota postmark came to him through his father's address. It began, "My darling boy." She was working in a restaurant, she still loved him, he should write. But he never did. What would he have said? Then, only months later, his mother's landlady wrote to say that Lauralee had died of cancer. Her wedding ring gleamed in a corner of the envelope. His father took the envelope and pushed it into his pocket, and neither of them had ever spoken of her again.

Miller sighed and leaned over to pick up one of the two-by-tens. When he turned around to reach for a nail, he noticed that Adra was watching him from the blanket on the other side of the yard. The baby was crawling through the grass, engrossed in pulling up dandelions and trying to stuff them into her mouth. Miller marked the length of the treads with his carpenter's pencil, then cut them to size with the circular saw. The work went fast, but he was sweating, and the crown of his head began to burn where his hair was thinning a little.

After a while Adra carried the child into the house and came out with a pitcher of lemonade. Miller followed her to the shade tree and sat down beside her. He sipped from his glass, a jelly jar with a threaded rim, and noticed the thin beaded line of perspiration along Adra's upper lip. She stared at him unself-consciously, just as she had been staring at him most of the morning. "This is good," he said. "Is the baby asleep?"

She nodded.

"It's good lemonade," he said again. They sat in silence for a while and then finally Miller said, "It's hot today."

"Been hot," she said. "And summer not half over."

"Makes you want to be at the beach," Miller said. "Do you like the ocean?"

"Never been there."

"Never? You ought to go, then. We go there every summer, rent the same house the first two weeks in August."

"August," she said. "That's coming up. Where is it, this house you go to?"

"South Carolina. Pawleys Island. We rent this place right on the beach—an old house, rambling, comfortable. Same one every year. You get up in the morning, look out the window, and there's the ocean, right in your front yard." His voice trailed off. Right now, it was hard to picture it.

"I can't swim," Adra said. "My grandmama drowned and Mama would never let us go in the water. Not ever. Not even wading."

Miller swallowed, then rattled on. "You should learn to swim," he said. "It's important. Your baby, too. You never know . . . Anyway, babies take to water naturally. But you don't have to swim. Not if you don't want to. At the beach you can do other things. Walk on the sand, collect shells, crab."

Adra looked off into the woods. "What's your wife's name?"

Miller didn't want to talk about Katie. This was a world where she didn't belong, a crude and simple place that he did not want to share with her.

"You've not forgot it, have you?" Adra said. A trace of a smile brushed across her mouth.

Now Miller was the one to look off into the woods. "Katie," he said. "Her name is Katie." He leaned back against the tree. "It's cooler here in the shade, isn't it?"

She ignored his question and leaned forward to pull a blade of grass. "Young'ns?"

"Pardon?"

"Do you have any young'ns?"

"Oh, yes, sure. Judd, my son. Just the one boy. He's seventeen." He frowned. "I worry about him."

"Why?"

"Because he's drifting."

"Driftin'?"

"He has no goals, he wastes time. He . . . You don't want to hear all this."

"Why don't I?"

"Maybe it's me. Maybe I don't want to talk about it." He stood up. "I need to finish up those steps. Thanks for the lemonade."

Adra reached out for his empty glass, and when their fingers touched on the frosted glass, Miller pulled his hand back quickly.

Flushing, he turned back to his work. He started on the risers, drilling holes for the nails. He would build Adra Goodfriend a set of steps that would outlive her rickety house. He imagined a time in the future when the lot would be overgrown and the house gone, crumbled into ruin, the little family moved away, but the steps—the steps would still be there—sturdy and level, rising into the empty space that had once been the porch. He was all at once struck with the idea that this could be the way he might spend his life in a more productive way than at the aircraft company—out in the open, in the country, in the sun. The wind and rain, too. Or snow—it didn't matter. He would be content because it was the kind of work that was honest and fulfilling and you could reap immediate satisfaction from the finished product. Instant gratification.

He struck the nail and a sudden spark created by the friction ignited and spun into the air and just as quickly disappeared into the sunlight. He took that explosive show of energy as a sign that he should follow up on his feelings. He should do it. Leave his job. Quit, walk away. Already he could imagine people shaking their heads—Katie, Jack, Judd—even his father, if he were still alive. But maybe it was exactly what he and Katie needed to revitalize their marriage—give up the house, the furniture, the trappings. He could work odd jobs in summer, do construction, landscaping. They could buy a boat with the money they got for the house, go south in the winters. It was perfect. Why hadn't he thought of it before? Judd would be off to college in the fall, but he could join them in the summers in exotic places—the Caribbean, Mexico, New Zealand.

He fitted the last step into place and drilled holes for the screws. The sun was lowering a little and the baby was crying again. Adra had gone into the house an hour before.

When he finished the steps, he stood back to admire his work. The greenish tint of the pine gleamed against the older, weathered gray boards of the porch. The next thing would be to paint the entire place—new steps, siding, shutters and all. He would have to come back another day and rehang the shutters, too, maybe patch a few places on the rusty tin roof. He was sure it must leak in a good hard rain.

The screen door creaked. Adra stepped outside and sat down on the top step. Her sitting there was a sort of christening, Miller thought. He smiled and swung the hammer in his hand, feeling its satisfying weight. For a moment everything seemed exactly right. "I could come back and make some other repairs for you," he said. "Next weekend? Maybe even tomorrow. I'd have to see about that, though. Tomorrow might not work."

Adra smoothed her skirt around her legs and rested her chin on her knees. Then she reached out and ran her hand across the wood of the step she was sitting on. "Katie," she murmured, her eyes lowered. "That's a pretty name. Is it short for something?"

"What?"

She looked directly into his eyes. "Is it a nickname?"

Miller started gathering up his tools. "Katherine," he said. "That's her given name." The hammer suddenly felt awkward in his hand. He tossed it into the toolbox. Now he was eager to be gone. "Where can I take all this old wood?" he asked.

She scrambled to her feet. "Wheelbarrow's in the barn. I'll show you."

Miller followed her along the gravel driveway, noticing the muscles slide in her calves as she picked her way through the gravel with her bare feet. Her hips were straight and narrow, her bare arms shapely. She was strong, too. Miller helped her pull open the wooden door of the barn. One of its hinges had broken and it took the two of them to drag it across the long grass and wildflowers in order to open a space big enough to get the wheelbarrow out. The windows of the barn were boarded, and it was so dark that Miller could barely see. They had to squeeze their way around boxes and bulky shapes covered with tarpaulins and cartons stacked by the dozen. "What's all this?" Miller asked.

Adra's eyes were lowered. "Jimmy Duane's stuff," she mumbled, and then she pointed out the wheelbarrow. Miller saw that its tire had gone flat, but he figured he could make do with it for the time being. He knelt in the hay to examine the wheel and when he looked up, a bar of light that had entered through the slats of the barn fell across Adra's face, and in her dark eye he saw a splinter of gold.

He looked away quickly. All at once he felt breathless. "Let's get this outside," he said. He stood up and struggled with the wheelbarrow, manipulating it through the moldy straw and out through the door. It bumped along erratically on its flat tire, continually steering itself off course. He parked it next to the steps and started tossing in the old wood and nails. Adra stood by, watching, but did not offer to help. When Miller had loaded the wheelbarrow, Adra directed him to a ravine in the woods behind the house where he could dump the wood. By the time he had gone back for the second load she had disappeared, but when he returned the wheelbarrow to the barn, she was there in the shadows. He could not see her face but her voice was tight. "Miller Sharp." She said his name slowly, giving it a weight it had never had before.

He stared toward the dark where she stood and waited. She moved forward a little and her shoulder was scribed in light, but her face was still obscured. "I 'preciate you," she said abruptly. Miller realized that she was unpracticed at being thankful, perhaps because in her life she had been given so little to be thankful for. He reached out his hand, meaning to touch her somehow, but she pulled back her shoulders, making herself smaller, and slipped around him. When he followed her outside he found her standing on the new steps, sliding her hand along the railing. "It's right pretty," she said, and Miller realized that it was the first time he had ever seen her smile.

"That's it, then," said Miller. "For today, anyway." He opened the car door and stood looking back at her. He started to speak, then thought better of it. His breath was erratic as he drove down the bumpy driveway and onto the country road, and only when he reached the main highway did his heart slow down again.

7

Dr. Sidney M. Buckman, M.D., psychiatry, was a big man, loosely jointed, with a cherubic face whose roundness was emphasized by his large, bald head. His lips were rosy, as if they'd been rubbed with lip gloss, and his cheeks glowed as well. He was so benign looking that at first Miller imagined he might actually be able to wade into the man's protective aura. But when he thought about the circumstances of his being there—his coming home late from Adra Goodfriend's house that Saturday evening the week before, and Katie's threats of separation if he didn't agree to therapy—he remembered that he had gone to Buckman's office more as unwilling victim than as supplicant.

Miller stared out the window, planning his escape. Had they been on the ground floor, he could have cleared the window sill in one energetic leap. This was a waste of money, because even with Buckman, he had left out the part of his story that made him a murderer. That alteration created another lie of omission. And now he was being called a hero.

"Believe me," he told the doctor, "I'm not a hero."

"But Miller, it was a heroic act," said Buckman, "and contrary to popular opinion, a heroic act doesn't always have a happy ending. Yes, the young man died, but your *act*, you see—your attempt to rescue him—was *heroic*. And often, Miller, heroes such as yourself"—here he leaned forward to empty his pipe into the ashtray on the coffee table between them, forgot his place, then started over—"heroes such as yourself often suffer from guilt simply because they survived and the victim died."

Miller flinched. *Heroes such as yourself*. What kind of grammatical construction was that? He crossed and recrossed his legs restlessly as the psychiatrist filled and tamped his pipe and began the long, tedious process of relighting it. *Jesus*, Miller moaned to himself as Dr. Buckman struck another match and held it to the bowl of the pipe, sucking in his bright, mottled cheeks and emitting small grunts of pleasure as he worked to pull the flame down into the tobacco.

"Do you mind?" Dr. Buckman had asked, indicating his pipe, when they had first sat down across from each other in the well-appointed office. That had been thirty-five minutes earlier. There were still fifteen interminable minutes remaining in the fifty-minute hour. Miller's nostrils were filled with the overwhelming aroma of Buckman's vanilla-scented tobacco, and he was paying for therapy that would be completely ineffective because he wasn't giving the psychiatrist all the facts. He had never been so uncomfortable in his life, and it was costing him one hundred and sixty-five dollars an hour. For half of the thirty-five minutes they had sat in silence so thick Miller could have sworn he heard the second hand ticking on his battery-powered watch. Dr. Buckman had waited him out patiently, breaking the vacuum occasionally to say, "This is your time, Miller, your time to use as you deem most productive. The clock is ticking, but it's your clock." *Damned expensive clock*, Miller thought. He was so tense he felt close to bursting into maniacal laughter. Dr. Buckman kept asking the same question but applying it to different situations: "Now what is about that incident that bothers you most?"

Miller kept thinking of a joke that Jack had told him the week before. Buckman, poor sucker, had no way of knowing that, of course, no connection. *Jack leans across the lunch table, grinning. It is obvious he wants to cheer Miller up. Listen, Miller, he says. There's this woman who goes on an African safari, and this group, this column of tourists, is walking through the jungle, and the woman happens to be the last in line, see? So this big white gorilla reaches out from the undergrowth, grabs the woman, and carries her back to his cave. He keeps her imprisoned for a year, and every day he—you know—he has his way with her. So one day the woman manages to escape and get back to civilization. She's going nuts, though—she can't get over it—and finally she consults a psychiatrist. "It's been a almost a year now," she says, "since I escaped from the gorilla." The psychiatrist nods, leans forward in his chair, and says, "Tell me, what is it that bothers you most?" The woman starts boo-hooing, wrings her hands and says, "He never calls, he never writes."*

Miller covered his mouth and feigned a cough to cover the hysterical giggle that bubbled up in his throat. Dr. Buckman was making some sort of observation, his voice deep and resonant, and it seemed to Miller that at the end of every word there was just the slightest hint of an echo.

"Guilt was a classic response among the Jews who survived the concentration camps," the psychiatrist was saying. "Which is undoubtedly why Jews themselves use black humor when they talk about the Holocaust. You know, how many Jews can you put in a Volkswagen?" He smiled at Miller expectantly. "No offense, Miller. I myself am Jewish, you know." He cleared his throat. "That example was meant only to be an illustration."

Miller felt lost for a moment. He knew he was supposed to say something, but he couldn't think what. "Excuse me?" he said.

Dr. Buckman held up a finger while he drew deeply on his pipe. The bittersweet odor hung over the room like a cloud. "Guilt," said Dr. Buckman at last, once he had finally got the pipe going again. "The survivors of the camps felt guilty because they lived and their families and friends died." He glanced at his watch, nodded, and then repeated, "Guilt."

There it was again—a definite echo. The "t" at the end of the word *guilt* reverberated for a second in the air, then faded away. Miller slid lower into his seat, a buttery soft brown leather wing chair. Then he deliberately closed down. He had neither the energy nor the inclination to converse with Dr. Buckman, much less to confess his deepest fears or reveal the true source of his anxiety. If he had had his choice of doctors, he would have picked one who was leaner both physically and philosophically, one who owned a slight tinge of sarcasm and a swift sense of humor. And no pipe. Definitely no pipe.

"We can, after all," Dr. Buckman continued, "through our will power, determine our own destinies. And life—with its seemingly simple, everyday events—life forces us to make decisions about our own destinies and sometimes"—he smiled here, he actually smiled—"*sometimes*—even to assume responsibility for *other* people's lives."

As if that were some sort of profound revelation. Miller glanced at his watch and saw that only four minutes had passed since he had last checked.

"You see, Miller," Dr. Buckman said, "the problem is that there is always the accidental element." He paused, smiled his beatific smile. "In your case, for example, this was the drowning of Mr. . . ." He hesitated, leaning toward Miller.

"He wasn't a *mister*," Miller said. "He was a kid."

Buckman had a shrill, nervous laugh. "All right, Miller. He was a kid, but he had a name, didn't he?" Now Miller was making progress. There was a hint of irritation in Buckman's voice.

Miller stared up at the ceiling fan, the blades of which were obscured in a blurred circle of cane and mahogany. "Jimmy Duane Goodfriend," he said slowly, enunciating every syllable slowly to stretch out the time. He looked down at his feet. Beneath his leather chair lay a thick Oriental rug woven in shades of red, black, and navy, with occasional touches of yellow and pale blue. There was another equally sumptuous carpet under the Regency writing table that served as Buckman's desk, and other rich appointments were scattered throughout the room. A drawing on the wall looked like an original Picasso, and on a corner console table lit by a marble-based lamp stood a group of ivory figures. Miller wondered how many bloody-masked elephants had died for that little collection. It made him dislike Buckman that much more.

Buckman was droning on, apparently driven by his own insights. "But you see, Miller," he was saying, "the real hero *assumes* responsibility—that is his cross to bear, so to speak—he *assumes* responsibility . . ."

He keeps leaning on that word "assumes," thought Miller. He keeps *leaning.*

"Unfortunately, though, he often assumes responsibility even for accidents." Having said that, Buckman sat back and waited for a response from Miller. The only noise now was the soft sucking sound he made as he nursed his pipe. Finally he spoke. "Tell me, Miller, what is it that bothers you most about this incident?"

It was a mistake, that question. Miller saw the white gorilla against the brilliant green background of the jungle, and the kidnaped woman cowering in a corner of his lair. *He never calls, he never writes.* A sharp, unbidden sound exploded from Miller's throat.

Buckman jumped. His hand held the lighted match in midair. When the flame reached his fingers, he dropped the match on the rug and stamped it out with his foot.

A series of giggles erupted from Miller as if pulled from his throat by a tentative string. The laughter quickly intensified, until Miller's chest was heaving. Buckman pushed his chair back a few inches, then collected himself and handed Miller the box of tissues that had sat on the coffee table. Even as Miller was gasping for breath, he was reviling Buckman. So the man was, after all, he thought, a coward. Miller took the advantage that his discovery afforded him and leaned toward the doctor. "Stop it," he said. The pitch of his voice was a visible sign of his impending disintegration. His breath snagged every few seconds and then erupted in a rough shudder. "Stop fucking patronizing me."

Dr. Buckman looked toward the door, as if confirming the direction of the exit for an imminent escape. "There is something I want you to understand," said Miller, still unable to stop the giggling. He was shaking now. He held on to the arms of his chair for support. "I am *not a hero*. I am not—I repeat—*not*—a fucking *hero*."

Buckman's eyes bulged. "Now Miller," he said, "let's calm down here . . ."

"You talk too much," Miller managed. He was gasping for breath. "Christ, I thought you people weren't supposed to talk so much, let alone pontificate! You're supposed to listen, for Christ's sake. And that pipe—that ridiculous fucking pipe! You want to hear a diagnosis, doctor? Let me give *you* a diagnosis. I think you suffer from some kind of oral compulsive disorder. And if that upsets you, doctor, why don't you tell me what bothers you most about it."

Miller's breath failed him then and he had to shut up, because otherwise he would have collapsed right there in Buckman's office. And then whatever it was that was squeezing the life out of him dipped down into his belly, turned inside out and forced its way up through his chest and throat. It pushed out in a bellow, a fierce rough wail that surprised and frightened both Miller and Buckman. Miller heard his own howl as if from a distance, as if it were disconnected from whatever was going on in his head. He jumped out of his chair, threw open the door of Buckman's office, and stumbled down the corridor, banging against walls and doorways.

When he was halfway down the corridor, he heard Buckman's door slam and then the click of the deadbolt being pushed into place.

8

Katie was waiting at the window. She had never been a window watcher, but then things were changing so quickly, Miller thought. His mother had been a window watcher, or maybe what he had noticed back then was only the curtain moving when he and his father came in from fishing or hunting. Late, they were always late, sometimes hours, sometimes days. Lauralee would confront them with tears in her eyes and what his father called her stock complaints: "I thought you'd (1) been shot, (2) drowned, (3) had an accident with the car." Fill in the blanks, his father always joked, trying to make her laugh. She owned a fear appropriate to every possible scenario. The truth was that the time always got away from them when they were out in the woods or on the stream. Hollis especially became completely involved in nature. He never thought of anything else, not time, not food or sleep, not other women, not even his wife, whom he dearly loved.

And she never learned, either. And then one day she acted on her anger and disappointment, but leaving had seemed to Miller far too exacting to suit such innocent and spontaneous offenses.

Miller opened the front door and Katie stepped into the middle of
the living room. Her movement seemed deliberate, almost practiced,
as if the room were a stage on which she would repeat the lines she
100 had rehearsed in her head while she waited for him to come home.
Her mouth was a tight, narrow line. Miller had never before noticed
how exceptionally thin her lips were.

"Dr. Buckman called," Katie said.

Miller brushed past her and headed for the kitchen. "That son of a bitch," he said. He couldn't help it, he started laughing again. As he opened the cabinet and took out a glass, he was rehearsing the way he would tell the story to Jack. Then he reached behind the newspaper recycling bin where he had been hiding his bottle of whiskey.

He put the glass on the counter and just as he uncapped the bottle Katie moved to put her hand over the rim. "No. Not now, Miller. Put that away and listen to me." Peripherally, Miller noticed that she was watching his face but he would not meet her eyes. He stood poised, waiting for her to move her hand. "He said you were hysterical," Katie went on. "That was the word he used. *Hysterical.*"

Miller stared at Katie's hand on the rim of the glass. He saw the freckles on the back of her hand and the soft petal-shaped pink of her nails. "He wants to talk to you some more. He said something about putting you on antidepressants. You can't be drinking when you take those, though."

"Katie, have you ever considered what *I* want?" Miller said.

"No, tell me. Why don't you tell me?"

"The first thing I want is for you to move your hand."

"Dr. Buckman says you shouldn't be drinking under any circumstances. It just makes things worse. It compounds all your problems."

"Buckman is a self-absorbed son of a bitch idiot who loves the sound of his own voice. He'd already made his analysis just from talking to you when you made the appointment. He wasn't the least bit concerned about how I felt or what I wanted. He just kept talking nonsense, calling me a hero, trying to convince me and himself—mostly himself—that it was all that simple. And he kept sucking, sucking on that goddamned pipe. Who gave you his name, anyway?"

She hesitated. "Jim."

"Jim Skinner? You told Jim Skinner about our problems?"

"He won't tell anyone, Miller. We were playing a round of golf together, and he mentioned that I didn't seem focused, because I was off my game. And then, it just sort of all came out. I had to talk to somebody, Miller. God knows *you* won't talk to me."

"Oh, great, so now it'll be all over the club. I can see them laughing at me in the locker room, taking bets on how long our marriage will last. And you. You're having drinks with Skinner, playing golf . . ."

"It's harmless. I need a friend."

"Oh yeah, sure."

"Miller . . ."

"Enough." He held up his hand. "Are you going to let me pour this drink or not?"

Katie stepped back, folded her arms around herself, and began to cry. Miller felt nothing—not pity, not anger, just a void, an empty space that was like an excision at the core of his soul. When he tilted the bottle his hand shook so fiercely that he spilled half the whiskey on the counter. A terror filled his heart. Now he could not even count on his body to obey his signals. He gripped the glass with both hands and drank.

Katie moaned. "You're killing yourself, Miller. You're killing me." Tears ran unchecked down her cheeks. "Talk. You said you wanted to talk. Tell me what you want."

He slammed the glass down on the counter, gathering strength from his own bravura. "Okay, you want to know what I want?" He grabbed her wrist. "Listen to me, Katie. No, listen, I'm serious, I'm not crazy. I'm not fucking crazy. In fact, I'm saner than I've ever been. All this—this stuff we have, this house, my job, your job, all the . . . *trappings*. They mean nothing. I don't want them anymore. My God, people are dying out there, Katie, people are *dying,* of—of AIDS and ebola and starvation and war. Women are being raped, children shot, and we're worrying about how green the lawn is or where we can afford to send Judd to college. I want to sell this house, chuck my job, leave this town, start over. Buy a farm someplace maybe, or a bait shop at the beach. Judd will be going to college. It will be just you and me, the two of us starting over. I want to leave everything else behind—vacuous people, the job, stress, deadlines, the country club. Jesus, most of all, the country club."

Katie tried to pull her hand from his grasp. Miller saw the look of horror on her face and he quickly released her. He poured himself another drink, this time without spilling a drop. "You asked, so I'm telling you. This is really what I want. Really. I've been thinking about this for weeks. We could get—what?—three hundred and fifty thousand for this place, maybe four? We have some stocks, we have that property Dad left us. His house, too. We could just walk out of here, start a new life."

"What about Judd's college? How would we pay for that?"

"He can go to a state university. I did. He can work for a change, put himself through school."

"What about *my* job?"

"Katie, you're wasting your talents there. A business school? No. I see you on a farm. Out in the open air. You could do what you've always wanted to do."

"Oh, and you *know* what I've always wanted to do?" She picked
up a paper napkin from the counter and blew her nose. "What is it, Miller? What in the *hell* is it I've always wanted to do?" Her eyes were red and a single streak of mascara threaded its way down her cheek.

"Well, you could paint, write, anything."

"I can't paint, Miller. I don't write. I love my job. I love this house. I love this town."

Miller laughed. "You don't get it, do you Katie? Change. That's what it's all about—change. Do something brand new, charge up the old spark plugs." He spread his arms and smiled. A keen excitement flooded his chest. "Think about it. We could raise fruit trees, maybe a few head of cattle. Horses. Chickens. We could live on the land, harvest what we need with our own hands."

Katie leaned back against the wall and slid slowly to the floor. She covered her face with her hands. Her shoulders were shaking. "Miller, I don't even know who you are anymore."

He squatted down in front of her and pulled her hands away from her face. "No, no, Katie. Listen. It's just that you didn't know this *side* of me. I never *told* you. How *could* you know? And maybe I never realized it *myself*. I just knew something was terribly wrong. But now I *do* know, see? Now I *know*."

"A farm?" she said, weeping. "A *farm*? Please, Miller. That's not what *I* want. What about me? Ask me what I want. I want our life back the way it was."

"See, though? I hated that. I *hated* it. Let's try to compromise. A bait and tackle shop, then. A place at the beach. We could live in the back of the place and, hell, if we felt like it, we could close up early and just go fishing or walking on the beach. You *love* the beach, Katie."

You love Respighi, Katie had said.

Miller kissed the damp palms of her hands. "Think about it, honey," he said. "Give it a chance. We could live moment to moment." Katie's eyes were swollen. Her nose dripped. Miller rocked back on his haunches and then leaned against the wall beside her. He held his drink between his knees. Katie reached for his hand and held it in both of hers, staring at it. She kept crying, choking on her own words. "Maybe this is only a bad dream," she said. "Remember how I used to have those awful dreams, Miller, when I was pregnant with Judd, after I'd already had those three miscarriages—nightmares about deformed babies, or dead babies, or losing a baby? And you'd hold me and stroke me until I felt safe and peaceful again? That's what I want now. I want you to wake me from this nightmare. Hold me, Miller."

Miller banged his head slowly against the wall. He could not look at Katie. Her hand holding his felt awkward and unfamiliar. "I can't," he whispered. "I don't know why, but I just can't."

He was not sure later whether that was the point from which he could not turn back or whether it had been the session with Buckman. The next day he drove to the plant at the usual time, walked straight into his manager's office and quit his job. From the manager's office he went to the mailroom in search of a cardboard box, returned to his desk, and started emptying the drawers. Jack came rushing into his office. "Miller," he said in a coarse whisper, "what in the hell do you think you're doing?" Miller turned his top desk drawer upside down and dumped the contents into the cardboard box. People stood in the doorway, staring. Jack closed the door and put his hands on the glass surface of the desk. "Jesus Christ, man," he said, "slow down and think about this for a minute. You're throwing away your future here."

Miller picked up a gold-framed photograph of Katie and Judd and tossed it into the box. "I *have* thought about it." He yanked open his file drawer, then slammed it shut again. Nothing there he would ever need again.

"Miller, please, let's go somewhere and have a cup of coffee and talk about it."

"There's nothing to talk about. I'm starting a new life. I know exactly what I'm doing." He bent over and started clearing out the lower drawers. So much junk. Rubber bands, dried-up pens, unanswered faxes, an old birthday card.

Jack ran his hands through his hair and looked around desperately. "For God's sake, Miller, what's going on with you?" He leaned closer and lowered his voice. "Is it that girl? It is, isn't it? It's that girl. Oh, man, for Chrissake, it's her."

"No. Not the girl, not Katie." He looked pointedly at Jack. "Not my father's death, either." He stood up straight and looked around at his work area. "But all of the above, I guess. All of the above."

Jack grabbed his arm. "Look, Miller, just go see the shrink a few more times. Or, Jesus, if you didn't like him, try another one. Get a mood elevator, something."

"Chemicals? An artificial painkiller? No thanks."

Jack lowered his voice. "No thanks? No painkiller? Well, then, what in the sweet name of Christ do you call that stuff in the bottle you've been dosing on? Get a grip, Miller. You can smell it on you first thing every morning. Everybody's talking. It's coming out of your fucking *pores*, for Chrissake."

Miller pushed at Jack's shoulder. "Get out of my way."

Jack followed him out of the office and down the corridor, trailing him so closely he stepped on his heel. "Miller. I'm sorry, man. Come back here. Hell, you know I love you, buddy."

Miller kept walking, and Jack grabbed his elbow. "Come on. It's not too late to change your mind." At the elevator, Miller shifted his box to the other arm and pushed the down button. When the doors opened before him, he tossed the cardboard box into the trash can by the water fountain and stepped into the elevator. The last thing he saw before the doors closed was Jack's anguished face. Walking through the parking lot, Miller felt elated yet strangely displaced, as if he were suspended in an atmosphere where none of the usual rules of physics applied.

From the plant he drove directly to Adra Goodfriend's house. When he pulled into the driveway, Adra walked out onto the porch. She wore sandals and a long, flowered dress with a scooped neck that showed the thin bones of her shoulders. She looked at him expectantly, waiting, probably, he thought, for him to explain what he was doing there on a workday morning. He walked as far as the bottom step of the porch, the step he had built, and looked up at her. "Pretty dress," he said. "It makes you look . . . It's pretty."

She glanced down at herself and folded her arms across her breasts. "I had to go into town for groceries. This is my Sunday-go-to-meetin' dress."

"Pretty," Miller said again. He hesitated, then looked up into the sky—for what, he did not know. Then he looked back at the girl. "I can help you out here more now," he said. "I quit my job."

Her voice was thick and stringy, yet faintly melodious. "When was this?"

He laughed and looked at his watch. "This was—oh, half an hour ago."

Adra sat down on the top step. Through the open straps of her sandals he saw her toes, long and flat and brushed with the silky dry dust of summer. If Miller had dared reach for her ankle, he could have closed one hand around it, her bones were so fine. Her hair was newly washed, and the lights in it were blue.

"Half an hour ago," Adra repeated. She laughed. "You do surprise a body."

Her laughter heartened him. He sat down on the bottom step and looked up at her. He could see the curve of her thigh just inside the shadow of her skirt, the parabola of knee and calf. She was a mystery to him, a puzzle layered and intricate and elegant.

"I could come Saturday," he said. "Hell, I'd start on the roof today, but I didn't bring my tools."

"Saturday? I thought you and Katie were going to the ocean."

"You remembered that?" He shook his head. "Well, we're not going. My wife wants me to call the rental company and cancel." He looked away, out into the long yard that disappeared into the trees beyond the clearing—mostly locusts and pines. "I haven't done it yet, though. I can't seem to get things done these days."

"What about Katie?" Adra said. "Is she worried about the money now? I mean you with no job?"

Her question jerked Miller into another realm. "Katie doesn't know I've quit, not yet. I talked to her about it last night but things sort of . . . deteriorated."

"You've not told her?"

He shrugged. Adra frowned and pushed her hands through her hair, lifting it off her neck. A blue vein ran up the length of her pale arm. Miller wanted to follow it to where it disappeared into the sleeve of her flowered dress. He shouldn't think about such things, but he could not stop looking. "*You* could go," he said suddenly. "Of course. Why didn't I think of that before? You and the baby could go."

Adra let her hair fall back against her neck. "Go where?"

"To the beach. You could use the beach house, you and the baby."

She shook her head and laughed.

"Really. I mean it. I'd lose the money anyway, if you didn't. I've paid for half of it already. You'd be doing me a favor."

"No." She twisted her hair and pursed her lips. "You're playing with me."

"No, no, I'm serious, Adra." He loved being able to say her name, to have an excuse to say it. "See, you have to pay a week in advance when you book the house, so I paid the deposit way back in January, and if you want to go, I'll spring for the other half if you decide to stay two weeks. It's the least I can do."

"Why the least? What do you mean?" He shrugged. "No, "she said, suddenly fierce.

Miller stroked his jaw and felt the rough beginnings of a beard. He had forgotten to shave that morning. It didn't matter anymore. Why should he shave? His power now was almost unlimited. To quit his job. To change his appearance. To grow a beard. To alter the direction of his life. He looked down at his hands and whispered, "Adra, I want you to be happy."

"What?"

He looked up and raised his voice. "I want you to be happy. To have a happy life. That's very important to me."

She turned her head away and laughed again. "I swear you are a pluperfect puzzle."

Miller's emotions rode on her laughter. "Will you go, then? It would mean a lot to me."

Her face went sullen again. "I've never drove that far in my life. Besides, my old truck wouldn't make it even if I could."

"I'll take you. I'll drive you to the ocean and then come back for you when the two weeks are up. I'm free now. My time is my own. Anyway, you don't really need a car there, not if we stock up on groceries when we get there. You could walk to the store for milk." He rubbed his chin again and grinned at her. "Will you do it?"

She hesitated. She bent her head so that her chin rested on her knees. "You'd really drive us there? Me and Sister?"

"I'd drive you there."

"And bring us home again?"

"I promise."

"Lord have mercy." She pulled her skirt around her ankles and thought for a while. "What about Katie?"

"What about her?"

"Wouldn't she care? Wouldn't she be mad? Hell's fire, *I* would. Jimmy Duane would go out most weekends and I heard tell he was dancing with other girls. Sometimes he didn't even come home until morning." Her voice trailed off. "I hated him for that."

Miller rubbed the stubble on his chin. The short rough whiskers felt good against the tips of his fingers. There was nothing that seemed more important in the world than for him to do this thing for Adra. "I'll work it out with Katie," he said. "I'll work it out."

9

Miller squinted at the highway before him. Usually when he came home from work at five, the sun was in the west, behind him, but now, this early in the morning, things looked different. It was like exploring an entirely new world. He turned on the radio and tapped his fingers against the steering wheel. Ahead, a neon sign in the shape of a pig advertised a barbeque restaurant. He pulled into the parking lot and glanced at his watch. Ten-thirty A.M. Despite the "closed" sign in the window, he tried the door, only to be waved away by a man who was mopping the floor.

Miller shuffled back to the car. Across the roadside strip of scorched grass, the highway sent up heat in iridescent waves. His shirt stuck to his back and chest. Hot already. Too hot. He glanced up at the sun and loosened his tie. At this time of the morning he would have been in his climate-controlled office, drinking hot coffee, probably leaning over a set of designs or safety specifications. Well, that was finished, and good riddance. He climbed back into the car and, leaving the door ajar, leaned against the headrest. When he closed his eyes he saw a red field across which a ragged black spider danced. "Middle age," his ophthalmologist had said cheerfully. "Some people get cataracts, some get floaters." He had said this as if Miller were somehow a lucky man.

Miller blinked a few times to try to dislodge the floater and then dozed for a while. When he woke up, the light had changed again, the shadows were shorter. He pulled off his tie, hung it over the rearview mirror, and opened the top two buttons of his shirt. The "closed" sign still hung in the window of the restaurant. Reluctantly, he started the engine, shut the car door, and pulled out onto the highway.What did people do, anyway, at eleven o'clock on a weekday morning? Thinking about it, Miller felt a little breathless. He liked the powerful rocketing sound of cars rushing by in the other lane, the tindery smell of the highway. He could have turned on the air conditioner, but it was good to be so close to the road and the weather. It was real. And for too long, he had distanced himself from reality, the way people lived. His own life had been meaningless—all that empty convention, the unfulfilling cultural events, the effete atmosphere of the country club, the petty politics at the office. Why hadn't he noticed all those things before—things that left you longing for something solid, things that left you sad and empty? He needed something else. Something.

And what about Katie? How was he going to tell her? *What* was he going to tell her? That he had quit his job of twenty years seemed almost incidental to the fact that he had just made plans with Adra Goodfriend to drive her and her baby to the beach on Saturday morning.

The driver behind him honked his horn, and Miller glanced into the rearview mirror and then at his speedometer. Thirty. He motioned the driver to pull around him. Even on this familiar highway, he kept seeing things as if for the first time. On the left was a new hardware store and a garden shop that had moved into a former restaurant site. He had passed it every day, maybe for years, and never noticed it. Ahead was the new shopping mall, a place he ordinarily avoided, but when he came to the entrance, he impulsively turned in.

He walked in through the main entrance, bracing himself against the cool, green air, amazed at the indoor presence of full-sized trees with their broad leafy canopies and the soaring heights of the glass ceilings. Noise bounced through the broad corridors, sailed off into space, hovered, and then fell. Everything echoed, giving the place a sense of unreality. In his office there had always been a soft undercurrent of sound—muted voices and the subtle click of computer keys, occasionally the whine of the printer and the purposeful crank of fax machines. There in the mall, footsteps multiplied and voices rose and fell in a cacophonic babble.

School kids on summer vacation strode along in packs of three or four—the boys long and lanky, wearing oversized pants and expensive tennis shoes. They were ogling the girls, who seemed only half-dressed in shorts and cropped shirts that bared their flat, creamy midriffs. Their hair was studiously casual and shiny and their mouths and eyes were made up like movie stars. Older couples walked briskly in whispering nylon jogging outfits and tennis shoes, and young mothers pushed their babies in strollers. All the older people seemed to know exactly where they were going, while the kids ambled along in a listless but glorious limbo. Miller, too, wandered, recognizing that as a middle-aged, unemployed man, he no longer fit into any category in a place like this. It was like being 4-F in a country at war. Only the weak and the wounded were left behind with the women, children, and old people.

Then he noticed something in the window of a lingerie shop—an elegant black satin nightgown. He stood in the doorway, looking, and was finally enticed inside by the satins, silks, tulles, and lace. Katie wore mostly white cotton under her clothes, but Miller was drawn to the vivid purples, golds, emeralds, and inky blacks. Everything gleamed, glistened, or glittered. Some of the pieces were slippery, others were stiffly wired and boned so firmly that they seemed to have form and character of their own. Miller, caught up in the subtle excitement of the place, pulled out his wallet and bought Katie a peacock green satin bodysuit overlaid with black lace and bolstered with an underwire brassiere. Then he chose a pair of amber satin pajamas and a silk, leopard-print robe. While he looked through his wallet for his credit card, he leaned toward the salesgirl and whispered, "Just what *is* Victoria's secret, anyway?"

The girl didn't get it. "I really don't know, sir," she said. "Will this be cash or charge?" Just as she was totaling his purchases, Miller impulsively added a purple push-up brassiere with matching bikini and garter belt. The bill was over three hundred dollars, but he walked out in a buoyant mood, swinging the shopping bag and feeling reckless and lighthearted.

Riding on that initial excitement, he bought CDs for Judd, a new jigsaw for himself, and a book for Adra about southeastern beaches. In the noisy food court, he ordered a couple of pizza slices and a hot dog and sat down at one of the small tables overlooking the concourse below.

When he finished eating, he glanced at his watch. One o'clock. The day was dragging. He strolled along the corridors of the mall and was delighted to see a movie theater at the end of the concourse. It didn't matter what was showing, but the girl at the window was reluctant to sell him a ticket. Her fingernails were painted alternately black and green and dusted with gold. "You don't want to go in now," she told him. "The feature started seventeen minutes ago."

Miller slid a ten-dollar bill through the slot. "You won't understand this," he said, "but I've already missed forty-three years."

The girl eyed him with a jaded expression, sighed, and pushed his change forward with her multicolored nails. Miller hooked his shopping bags over his elbow as he juggled a large box of buttered popcorn and a giant-sized soft drink. In the near-empty theater he settled into his seat and watched a film about a woman so consumed by the death of her lover that she imagined—or perhaps it had really happened—that was the beauty of it, that you weren't really sure—that her dead lover had come back with several dead friends in tow, and the whole bunch took over her apartment. They busied themselves watching videos of old movies, rearranging her furniture, and turning up the heat against their incessant chills. *Be careful what you ask for. You might get it.* That was the theme, because eventually the girl found her dead lover's demands too irritating and bothersome to put up with.

When Miller came out of the movie and stepped into the parking lot, the afternoon light blinded him. He looked at his watch. Three-thirty. He couldn't go home yet. He decided to go by his father's place. In the six months since Hollis had died, Miller had been unable—maybe unwilling—to put the house up for sale. Inside, everything was just as his father had left it. Katie had gone by one day after the funeral and emptied the refrigerator, but other than that, Miller paid the taxes and the utilities and the phone connection and kept the yard mowed. The perennials had pushed up as usual. It was surprising how luxurious they looked, even in the overwhelming heat and without regular care and watering. Miller usually turned on the sprinkler when he went over, but he hadn't gone to the house for a month—not since the incident with Jimmy Duane. He expected to see knee-high grass and drooping flowers.

He pulled into the driveway and was surprised to see a woman with a thin halo of white hair kneeling by the rose bed. At the sound of his tires on the pea gravel drive, she looked up, squinting against the sunlight. Miller got out of the car. "Mrs. Donaldson. Hello." It was their old neighbor. She'd lived there long before Miller was even born, and she'd been good to Hollis and Miller after Lauralee went away. She was always bringing over casseroles, vegetables she'd put up, and later, keeping his father company after Miller left home. Whenever Miller came by the house, he made it a point to stop in and say hello to her.

Mrs. Donaldson wiped a hand across her forehead, leaving a damp smudge of dirt from her garden gloves across her velvety brow. "Is that you, Miller?" She laughed and started to get to her feet, but the effort seemed too much, and she sank down again, as if she had slowly settled into her old bones. "You haven't been by lately. I've missed our little visits."

Miller hesitated, waiting for her to explain why she was weeding his father's garden. Maybe she was confused about whose yard was whose. Maybe her mind was failing. Mrs. Donaldson sat back and contemplated the wilted dandelion in her gloved fingers. "You don't mind, do you?"

"Mind? The flower beds, you mean? No, of course I don't *mind*, but . . ." He smiled. "Oh, now I understand. You're the reason the flowers look so lush. You've been tending them."

Mrs. Donaldson tossed the dandelion into a pile of weeds and tamped the soil with her pointed spade. "It's for your father. For his memory."

"Ah." Miller nodded. He waved his hand to take in the flower bed, the yard. "You should have a hat, working out here in this hot sun."

He squatted down beside her and his knees popped a little. The sore knee gave him a momentary pinch of pain, too. When he looked into Mrs. Donaldson's flushed face, he saw the sharp blue eyes he remembered from his boyhood, the eyes of the pretty neighbor who had fed him cookies and lemonade, the friend who had ironed his shirts after his mother left home and who had tied his bow tie the night of his senior prom.

She smiled and gazed off into the distance for a minute. "Remember these roses, Miller? Hollis loved them. I remember the day he planted them. You were gone—just married, you and Katie. How is she, that sweet girl?" But she went on before Miller could answer. "Hollis was lonely. He wanted something to do, so he dug this rose bed. And look at these bushes now. I wish he was here to see them. Some of them are six feet tall."

"You're very good to do this," Miller said. He struggled to recall her first name. It was, he remembered, something sweet and old-fashioned. Elsie? Effie? No, there it was. *Evelyn.*

"It's for him," Mrs. Donaldson said again. There was a silken beauty to her soft, folded skin. She reached up and bent one of the lower branches that hung close to her face. "This one's named Paris d'Yves St. Laurent." She pronounced it in the French way.

"Ah." Miller said again. He looked up at the salmon-pink blooms and pulled one close to his face to smell it. The fragrance was spicy. "I should go check the house," he said. He got to his feet and walked along the herringbone-patterned brick pathway that led to the back porch. The flower bed by the steps was thriving, too—with bright pink larkspur and liriope whose lavender spiky blooms were just beginning to form. For a minute, he turned back to Mrs. Donaldson, who watched him almost breathlessly. "It's lovely," he said. "Thank you. For my father, for myself. Thank you." For some reason he felt close to tears.

There was the blush again, the bashful smile. Mrs. Donaldson pushed her spade into the loamy soil and immediately became absorbed in her work, as if there had never been an interruption. Miller called her name and nodded toward the house. "I'm just going inside to check things." For some reason, he felt that he needed her approval, as if he, not she, were an intruder here. He started up the porch steps, then turned back. "Would you like a key?"

"A key?"

"Yes. So you could come in occasionally. For old time's sake. You know."

She raised her hand to shade her eyes and stared at him across the dry expanse of grass. "I have one, dear. Hollis gave me one years ago." She nodded again and went back to her weeding. Miller stood with his hand on the doorknob. Why would his father have given Evelyn a key? He opened the door and stepped into the bright, echoing kitchen. His memories of this room had more to do with his father than his mother. He and Hollis had cooked here together, or Hollis had cooked and Miller had sat at the round oak table doing his homework. Miller could even call up the odors that over those years had accompanied his comprehension of facts and figures. *Who was Abelard? What did he write? Give an account of his romantic life.* Chicken and dumplings, the smell of sage and the fragrant transparent aroma of onions wafting through the house.

Show how changing the position of a comma may alter the meaning of a sentence. Baked apples, scented with cinnamon and nutmeg.

Explain the conditions that brought Norway under the rule of Queen Margaret. What other countries did she rule? Fried fish, hominy grits, the delicate buttery fragrance of steamed cabbage from the summer garden. His father had become quite the chef.

Miller laid his hand on the counter, as if he could feel the pulse of the house. He wandered down the hallway, his heart and feet growing heavier with every step. He picked up his bronzed baby shoes from his father's desk and sniffed at the green sour smell of the metal. His hands carried away the metallic tinge of his childhood and he remembered buying his girlfriends dime store rings that had turned their fingers green. Still, those gifts had been valued beyond all reckoning. With his foot on the bottom tread of the steps, he had a sudden realization and looked back into the living room. Everything was polished and dusted—the tabletops and trinkets, photos on the mantelpiece, the piano. And the slight indentations on the carpet showed it had recently been vacuumed.

Evelyn Donaldson.

As he trudged up the stairs, his stiff knee rebelled against the weight of his own body. He looked into his parents' bedroom, a room never used after his mother left. The lace curtains were freshly washed and the room smelled of potpourri. Sunlight slanted in long beams through the windows. In his old bedroom, the shelves were still lined with basketball trophies, the baseball signed by Joe DiMaggio that his father had given him on his sixteenth birthday, and in the closet, his old high school letter jacket. Judd wasn't interested in inheriting these treasures, not yet, but maybe some day. He swallowed the lump in his throat and started back downstairs. The grandfather clock in the living room stood silent, unwound for months. Miller sank down on the worn, rose-patterned carpet and rested his head on his knees. He smelled the odors of his own body, his woodsy shampoo, the detergent on his clothes, his own bitter sweat. He felt desperately lonely, for his father, for Katie and Judd, maybe even for his old self. "Help me, Dad," he whispered. "Help me get straight."

When he finally pushed himself to his feet and went outside, he saw that Mrs. Donaldson was still working in the rose bed. "Don't you think you should get out of the sun for a while?" Miller asked.

She laughed. "It feels good on my bones. I don't warm as easily these days." Her nose glistened with perspiration and she smelled of lavender powder. "Why don't you take some of these roses for your wife?" she said. Before he could refuse, she leaned forward and snipped a dozen stalks with her garden shears. "Remember to tell her the name of them," she said. "Those things are important to women."

Miller held the bouquet in his fist. "Yves St. Laurent," he said. "I remember."

Mrs. Donaldson stared at him. "You look like him, you know. Especially since you've gotten older." She laughed a pealing, girlish laugh. "I meant your father, not Mr. Laurent."

"I knew that," Miller said. He felt awkward and was glad to have the roses in his hands, to have something to hold onto. "I'll be back soon then," he said, and she went on working, bent to her task, smiling at some small thing that memory had pulled up.

At the end of the driveway Miller turned around again. "Why don't I go inside and get you one of my dad's hats?" he said. "This sun . . ."

She smiled at him as if he were a boy again. "Get those roses on home to your wife before they wilt," she ordered. "And don't you worry so much. I may look old, but inside I feel as young as you do."

Pity you then, Miller thought as he climbed heavily into the car. *Pity you.*

10

Judd's car was in the driveway when Miller got home. Lucky kid, Miller thought, to have so much free time. During the summers of his own adolescence, time had stretched endlessly. A single afternoon often embodied the weight and substance of years. He could still call up the old sounds and smells of those summers—the scorched tarmac of the swimming pool parking lot, the sharp, antiseptic chlorine of the pool, the coconut fragrance of suntan lotion. And girls. Girls with taut, oiled skin so slick and smooth that drops of water stood like glistening beads on their tanned and gleaming legs. Miller had loved their burnished cheeks and shoulders, clean hair bouncy and smelling of fragrant shampoos, toenails polished on dusky, sandaled feet. He had loved their crisply ironed cotton shorts, their bare-shouldered sundresses and halter tops that exposed necks and backs and parts of the body forbidden under other seasonal circumstances. Everyone fell in love in the summer. The atmosphere was perfect for it—tender air, open convertibles, silky lakes.

He parked his car beside Judd's, gathered up the roses from Mrs. Donaldson and retrieved his packages from the trunk. Maybe Judd wouldn't notice that he was coming home a little early. If he did, Miller would think up some excuse.

This was strange. The front door was locked. Miller put down his bags and dug into his pocket for his keys. He opened the hall door and stood listening. Something was different about the house, something had changed the feel of it. He started to call Judd's name and then he heard a noise, a soft, high-pitched wail, and then a long, low moan. His skin prickled. He laid the packages and the roses carefully down on the floor and walked to the bottom of the stairs. It was quiet for a moment, and then the noise started up again. It was coming from upstairs.

He started up the steps on tiptoe. At the landing he noticed other sounds—a sudden thump and then a groan. Judd. Someone was hurting Judd. The sound wasn't coming from the direction of Judd's room, though. It was coming from his own bedroom. Maybe someone was attacking Katie. Maybe Katie had come home early and an intruder had been in the house. Miller abandoned his caution and ran up the stairs three at a time, hurling himself at the bedroom door.

The girl screamed and ran into the bathroom, dragging the sheet with her. Judd was still in the middle of Miller's bed—crouched naked, like an animal, his eyes wide with terror. When he saw Miller, he collapsed, beating his fists against the mattress.

Miller lunged at Judd and pushed his shoulder, knocking the boy off balance. "You're having sex in *my* bed? Your *mother's* bed? What in the hell is going on here?" He shook him roughly. "Answer me, Judd, answer me. What the hell do you think you're doing?"

Judd peeled Miller's hand from his arm, rolled over and reached for his jeans. "What does it look like I was doing?" he said.

Miller pushed at Judd's shoulder again with the heel of his hand. "You don't do that, Judd. You don't speak to your father that way."

Judd stood up and pulled on his jeans. He closed the zipper with great deliberation. His face was flushed with anger. "You pushed me," he said. He looked Miller in the face and his hand came forward, palm out. "Don't you ever do that again." His teeth were clenched, and he came around the bed with his fist doubled.

Miller jumped back. "Hold it right there, boy."

Judd took another step forward. "You hit me, didn't you?"

"I'm your father," Miller said. "You're . . ." He waved his arms helplessly. "You're a *kid* and you're having sex with a girl in my bed, and I'm not supposed to be upset?"

He could hear the girl crying in the bathroom. From the corner of his eye he saw her clothes tossed over the back of Katie's dressing table bench and Judd's underwear and tee shirt thrown on the carpet.

"You have no right to push me," Judd said. A vein throbbed in the boy's temple. He was still poised to attack.

"There are certain . . . rules of etiquette . . ."

Judd laughed. It was a cruel, angry laugh that pierced Miller's heart. "Rules of etiquette? Who are you?" he asked. "Miss fucking Manners?" He walked over to the door and slammed his fist against it. "Fuck you," he said, "after the way you've been treating Mom."

Miller swung at the boy's arm, feeling a ragged pain in the shoulder he had used to break through the door, but Judd ducked and came back at Miller with a jab to his ribs. "Fuck you," he screamed again. Tears ran down his cheeks.

"I'm your father," Miller cried. He gasped for air. "I'm your father."

"Go to hell," Judd snarled and wheeled out of the room. He pounded down the steps, but by the time Miller got himself together, Judd was roaring down the street in his car.

Miller felt dizzy. He needed to lie down, but he had to avoid the bed. He took long, deep breaths through his mouth and ran his hand over his ribs where Judd had hit him. His son, his child, punching him and calling him names. God, it was all falling apart. Everything.

He had almost forgotten about the girl. The sound from the bathroom was rhythmic and pitiful—a wheezy hiccough of a sob and a rough inhalation of air and then a repetition of the whole pattern. Miller shuffled across the room and knocked on the bathroom door. "It's okay," he said. "It's Mr. Sharp, Judd's father. Please, stop crying. It's okay."

Silence.

"It's okay," he repeated. "I didn't mean to frighten you. Judd's gone."

That information started a fresh round of crying.

"Please, uh . . . what's your name?"

Through the broken sobs he made out her name. "Cindy."

"Cindy. Okay, Cindy. Your clothes are out here where you left them. In a minute I'll be out of this room and you can open the door and get your clothes. I'll be downstairs. All right? When you hear the bedroom door close, I'll be out." He thought a minute. "I might not be able to close the bedroom door, but I'm going down, okay?"

Silence again.

"Cindy?"

Nothing.

"Don't worry. Nobody's going to hurt you. It's fine," he said. "Everything's fine." He made as much noise as possible crossing the bedroom floor and then he closed the door as well as he could with the top hinge broken. No need to frighten the girl further. He hurried down the stairs and went into the kitchen and poured himself a drink. Leaning against the counter as he downed his whiskey, he heard water running through the pipes and then the toilet flushing. In a few minutes the girl appeared at the bottom of the stairs. She was a little thing, with big, dark eyes and sun-lightened hair cut short as a boy's. Her eyes were red from crying. She stood with her hand on the banister, looking like a condemned prisoner.

"Judd's gone," Miller said, shrugging. The girl's chin quivered. "I'm sorry he took off like that," said Miller. "He was pretty upset. We were all upset. I'm sorry if I frightened you."

She said nothing, just stood there looking down at her feet.

"Do you live far from here?" Miller asked.

She nodded. "Yessir."

"I'll drive you home."

The girl sank down on the bottom step and began to weep again.

"It's okay, Cindy. Stop crying. These things happen. Believe me." He laughed. "This is the way life works." He started to pat her shoulder and then thought better of it. Best not to touch her.

The girl looked around and snuffled. "Where did Judd go? I can't believe he left me like that."

"It was my fault," Miller said. "I was so shocked, I guess I wasn't thinking rationally." He plunged his hands into his pockets. "You kids," he mumbled, looking away from her, "you're too young to be doing things like that."

Cindy's chest heaved with sobs. "Mr. Sharp, I'm really a nice girl, really I am. It's just . . . I love Judd, that's all. We never came here before. This was the first time."

Miller wondered how he would feel if she were his daughter. "I know you're a nice girl, Cindy. I'm sorry. Things are different now, you know. Sex, I mean. It isn't that we didn't do things like that when I was your age. We did. I mean, it just wasn't so soon. Not so young."

He looked at her, her tiny wrists and ankles, the flat chest, the soft smooth nape of her neck. She was a baby.

She must have read his thoughts. "I'm seventeen," she said. "The same as Judd." Miller reached into his pocket and handed her his handkerchief. Cindy blew her nose and ran her hands through her hair. "I thought he loved me. He said he did. But then he just went off like that and left me? Oh God. Why did he leave like that?"

"It was my fault," said Miller. "He was mad at me." And, he wanted to say, what can you expect? He's only a kid. But the girl was only a kid, too, and she was suffering.

Cindy blew her nose again. "Did you hurt him?" she asked. "Is he hurt?"

Miller laughed. "I'm the one who's hurt. Judd landed a good right punch to my ribs, but it's mostly his feelings that were hurt." He hesitated. "Do you want an aspirin or something?" Miller asked. "A Coke?"

She shook her head. "I just want to go home. Please, Mr. Sharp."

"Come on. Let's go," Miller said. "It's okay, I'm sure you'll hear from Judd soon. I embarrassed him, hurt his pride. I wish this hadn't happened."

The girl trembled and sniffled occasionally as he led her to the car. As Miller drove, he thought it important to make conversation, to lessen the impact of the whole situation. "So you'll be a senior this year, too?"

"No. Next year," she said. "Judd's a year ahead."

"Did you two meet at school or at the club this summer?"

"The club. But I'd seen him at school, too. I mean, I knew who he was." She sighed and rested her head against the window. The air conditioning pushed out a cold, stale rush of air with a sharp, metallic odor.

When Miller pulled up at the girl's house he recognized the name on the mailbox as a judge who was prominent in community affairs. At least Judd was keeping good company, he thought. He reached across the girl to open the door. "Cindy," he said. "I'm sorry about what happened, my scaring you like that, I mean. I know that you're a nice girl. A *very* nice girl. I was surprised, that's all. What I did was a gut reaction. But my God, Cindy, I hope you realize that you're both too young for this. Way, way too young. I'm sure your parents would tell you the same thing."

Her eyes widened. "You won't tell them, will you?"

"Of course not. But if you were my daughter, I would want you to wait a while for experiences like this." He had almost said *save yourself for your future husband*, the way parents did in his day, but he bit his tongue. He remembered something Jack had said at lunch the day before. "It used to be," Jack mused, "that you'd go into a drugstore, ask for a pack of cigarettes, then whisper, 'And a package of condoms.' Now, it's the other way around. You go in, ask openly for condoms, then whisper, 'And a pack of cigarettes.'" Indeed, Miller thought, times have definitely changed. Miller pushed the car door open. "Go," he said. "Go. No more crying."

She gave him one last anguished look and then she ran up the driveway and disappeared through the front door of the house.

On the way home, Miller felt more sad than angry. Maybe it was just the realization that Judd was a man now, at least physically. He had been shocked at seeing his son naked on the bed and realized that he had not seen him totally undressed for the past couple of years. He felt the weight of a loss, not only for his son's childhood, but for his own innocence as well.

When he touched his bruised rib, pain shot through it. It was getting late. Katie would be home. Miller didn't know if he had the strength to tell her about the job or the promise he had made to Adra Goodfriend, and he certainly wasn't going to tell her about Judd, not on top of everything else. Maybe tomorrow. Maybe never.

But there was her car, parked in the garage. And she was sitting on the bottom step of the stairs, going through the packages Miller had dropped there earlier. The satin pajamas lay in a shiny heap at her feet. The wilted roses lay scattered across the floor. "Miller," she said, her voice trembling, "for God's sake, what is this? What in the world is going on here?"

Miller felt his heart skip a beat. "What do you mean, what's going on? I went shopping, that's all. I got those things for you, Katie." He sat down beside her on the step. "And I stopped by Dad's place. That's where the flowers came from. Mrs. Donaldson. Remember her? Evelyn?"

Katie reached into the bag and pulled out the silky robe. "God, Miller. You know I would never wear anything like this. A leopard print?"

"But couldn't you try? I thought these things were so beautiful. If *I* could imagine you wearing them, why can't *you* imagine yourself wearing them?"

She tossed the pajamas back into the bag. "And what happened at work? Jack called a minute ago and said it was urgent that you call him. Did you leave early?"

Miller nodded. "I was having a bad day."

"Please, Miller, spare me. What about the bedroom? What happened there? The door's broken, the sheet's in the bathroom, the bedclothes are torn apart. Did somebody break in?"

His mind raced. "I was taking a nap. I left work early and I was taking a nap and I got cold. I got cold and I wrapped the sheet around me and I guess I left it in the bathroom."

"How could you have taken a nap if you're just coming home?"

"Well, I came home, took a nap, and then went over to Dad's house."

"Just now?"

"Yeah."

"And you said the roses came from Mrs. Donaldson."

"Yes, Evelyn Donaldson. I went out there twice. She needed something fixed. Her hose connection. I came home, got a tool, and then went back."

"What about the door?" Katie asked.

"The door?"

"The *bedroom* door."

"Hell, it jammed. I tried to force it and the hinge broke."

"It was fine this morning."

Miller shrugged, but Katie rushed on. "And what happened at work? Jack wouldn't tell me anything."

Good old Jack. "Katie, you know how unhappy I've been for a long time at work. It was another one of those days, nobody listening to me. If you complain, they think you're a troublemaker."

Katie held up her hand. "Please, Miller. We've been through this a hundred times. You're forty-three. You have at least twenty years until retirement. If you don't like conditions at work, change them. Speak up."

"It's not that easy." He studied her face, weighed the resistance in her eyes. "Oh hell, what's the use? You don't understand."

"It's a moot point," Katie said. "We can't afford for you to quit your job."

Miller heard it again. A door slamming. "Oh I really love this Katie, I really do. You and Dr. Buckman, making plans for me, deciding how I should live my life." He pushed himself up and started picking up the packages and the flowers. The heavy heads of the roses swayed and drooped.

Katie sat silent, watching him. When he started up the stairs, she spoke to his back. "I've been thinking. Maybe, since your vacation starts day after tomorrow and you've already paid for the deposit at the beach, why don't you go by yourself? It might be good for us to spend some time apart."

Miller stopped. The shopping bag swung in his left hand. He heard the low hum of the air conditioner, a dog barking outside. He could hear breathing, too, but he didn't know whether it was Katie's or his own. It took a minute for him to will his feet to move and then he started up the steps again.

"Miller?"

He kept going. "I'll think about it," he said. "Let me think about it."

He went into the bedroom and tried to close the sagging door. Finally he gave up and put the shopping bag and flowers down at the foot of the bed and began to strip all the bedclothes off the mattress. Then he carried them into the bathroom and stuffed them into the laundry hamper and lay down on the bare mattress. He stared up at the ceiling, studying the texture of the plaster. There was a vast geography there, ridges that carried him away like tributaries to greater rivers, to the feet of mountain ranges, the shores of strange seacoasts. All these years sleeping in this bed and he had never noticed that aerial landscape right above his head. He had ignored so many things. He was sad more than sorry for having taken so many wrong paths. He was frightened, too. It seemed as if his very life were in danger. And it would get worse. It would get worse when Katie found out about his quitting his job. And because Katie had just given him carte blanche to go to the beach without her, he felt duplicitous and afraid that her suggestion and his silence might lead to a greater chasm between them.

He rolled over and pulled the pillow to his chest. It had a smell of something fresh and sweet—kiwi, maybe, something a pretty young girl would use to shampoo her hair. He hoped Katie wouldn't notice it. He would make sure to keep that pillow on his side of the bed so he wouldn't have to explain the episode with Judd. He flexed his arm and was jolted by the pain in his shoulder. Then he ran his hand tentatively over his ribs and found the tender spot Judd's punch had left. When he pressed it, he felt an exquisite little pain. He pressed again, somehow savoring the sensation. Maybe he could ride on that pain instead of being cowed by it, see how much he could take.

The next thing he knew, Katie was standing over him, shaking his shoulder. "Miller. Miller. What's wrong? You were crying, sort of. Moaning. Were you having a bad dream?"

Miller sat up and rubbed his eyes. He had seen Jimmy Duane again, under the water. This time he was swimming after Miller, reaching out to catch him and pull him down once and for all. "Yeah," Miller said. He shivered. "It's so damned cold in here. Can you turn that air down?"

"Why is everybody in such a bad mood?" Katie asked. "I was holding dinner for Judd and he just came in and almost snapped my head off. All I did was ask him where he'd been. Why don't you go find out what's wrong, and then both of you come down to dinner." She started out of the room and then turned back. "And Miller, he wasn't wearing a shirt. He shouldn't be out in public like that. Talk to him, okay? Suddenly everybody around here is going crazy."

Miller sat on the side of the bed, shivering. That was one of the things he liked about the beach house. No air conditioning and no telephone, open windows. Peace. Quiet. You could lie in bed at night and hear the waves crashing on the shore. Here in this over-insulated house, they were missing all the outside sounds of summer—cicadas, thunder, tree frogs, rain.

He shuffled into the bathroom and washed his face. Then he pulled on a long-sleeved shirt and walked down the hall to Judd's room. He knocked on the door.

No answer. Miller tried the knob, but the door was locked. "Judd, I know you're in there. Otherwise, why would the door be locked?"

Silence.

Miller knocked harder. "Let me in, Judd. Your mother has supper waiting, and you and I need to talk." He waited, and then spoke in a firmer voice. *"Now."*

No response. "Okay, Judd," he warned, "let's put it this way. I can have this conversation with you, or the two of us can have it with your mother."

There followed a suspenseful silence and then the knob turned. Judd shut the door behind Miller and then flung himself down on the bed. He hugged his pillow and stared at the wall.

"Judd," said Miller, "we need to talk about what happened today. Your mother—" Judd sat up abruptly and Miller held up his hand. "Don't worry. I haven't said anything, and I don't intend to, but unless we straighten this out between us, she's going to press me for details. Let's get our stories straight here." He sat down on the edge of the bed and looked at his son.

Judd grunted. Miller tried humor. "You really busted me one there, Tyson. I think you may even have cracked a rib for me. To say nothing of my smashing my shoulder when I crashed through that door."

"You shouldn't have pushed me like that," Judd said, facing the wall again. "You treated me like some kind of criminal in front of Cindy."

"She was in the bathroom."

"She could *hear.*"

The pink sheen of Judd's cheeks was purpled with the pale shadow

of a beard. Miller cleared his throat. "Right. I shouldn't have pushed you, and you shouldn't have hit me and we shouldn't have cursed each other. We both acted like a couple of thugs. But Jesus Christ, Judd, how do you think I felt? I mean," he lowered his voice, "it would have been shocking enough to find you—my son—having sex—okay, making love—whatever, to a girl in *your* bed. But in *my* bed?" He watched Judd for signs of acquiescence. "And by the way, why our bed instead of yours?"

Judd shrugged, rolled over, and stared up at the ceiling. "Yours is bigger and nicer. Besides"—he couldn't help smiling here—"my room was a mess."

Miller tried not to laugh. "Listen, Judd. I don't like what happened this afternoon anymore than you do. I embarrassed you, and you embarrassed me. To say nothing of poor Cindy. The thing is, your behavior was unacceptable, your judgment was faulty, and the timing was absolutely lousy."

"So what were you doing home so early?" Judd wanted to know. "If you hadn't come home early, you never would have known." He was looking Miller in the eye now. Maybe they were making some progress.

"Oh, and that would have excused your irresponsibility? For one thing, that girl—and she *is* a nice girl—we had a talk after you bailed out on her—that girl is under age, and even if you are, too, that doesn't keep you out of trouble if you get her pregnant."

"She won't get pregnant."

"Oh Jesus. You are so damned naive. And what about diseases?"

"I don't have any."

"Well, what if she does?"

"You just said, she's a nice girl. She was a virgin, Dad."

"Oh, that's terrific. She was a *virgin*. There are plenty of nice girls and nice guys, Judd, who get sexual diseases by accident or misin- formation or disinformation. Did you—did you use something?"

"*Yes*, Dad, I *used* something. Will you please stop asking me all these personal questions?"

Miller nodded. "I will in a minute. This is a talk we should have had a while back, anyway. I just didn't realize you were a little ahead of me. There's just one more thing. What was that crack about how I was treating your mother?"

"Well, I *live* here, don't I, Dad?" Judd said. "I can hear you fighting. You've been sleeping on the couch downstairs and she's been crying every night." He sat forward again suddenly and Miller brought his hands up to protect himself. But Judd was only trying to emphasize his point. "No, you *couldn't* know that," he said, "or maybe you don't care, because you've been drinking every night."

The remark was like a blow to his belly. In fact, he would have preferred a blow to Judd's comment. Miller put his head in his hands and tried to gather his thoughts. "You're right, Judd, you're right. It's just . . . Well, listen, son. There's something I have to explain to you. I told you about this drowning incident. It's sort of turned my life upside down. A man—a kid, really—only a few years older than you—he lost his life. I couldn't save him. I *didn't* save him." He stopped. "I *should* have saved him. I can't explain this very well, but it's thrown me off balance." He reached out his hand. "Son," he said, "help me with this. Give me some slack here. I love you, I really do. I need you to be patient with me until I get through this thing."

Judd's face crumpled, and Miller lay down beside him and put his arms around him. It was the first time in a long time they had embraced. Miller felt the thick, tight muscles across the boy's back, the broad hard stretch of his shoulders. "I'm working on it, Judd," Miller whispered. "It'll be all right. You'll see. We'll be back to normal before you know it."

Judd wiped his eyes. "Are you going to get a divorce from Mom?" he asked.

Miller's mouth fell open. "Where did you get that idea? Listen, Judd, all marriages go through rough spots, all of them. In this case I take complete responsibility. It's this outside circumstance that's caused the tension. The drowning." He held Judd tighter, smelling the musky male smell of him, the chlorine in his hair from the pool, the yeasty smell of sweat. He held him with pleasure but a touch of regret for what he himself had lost—that youthful expectation, an unwritten future ripe with possibilities, the lithe, hard body and the ever-present sexuality.

"I don't want you to leave," Judd said. "Promise me you won't leave Mom."

At that instant it did not seem within Miller's power to make such a momentous promise. He sidestepped it, hugging Judd again and kissing his forehead. "Judd, Judd, everything's going to be all right." Judd shrugged, trying to ease out of Miller's embrace, but Miller was holding on tight, clinging to the moment.

"Dad," Judd whispered. "I'm sorry. I really am. You're right. That was a really dumb move on my part." He sat up. "How did Cindy get home? Is she pissed at me?"

"If I were you," Miller said, swinging his legs over the side of the bed, "I'd send her flowers. And please remember, you have college ahead of you. Don't end up with a pregnant teenaged wife and no education. Cindy's sweet and beautiful, Judd, but slow down, okay?"

Judd nodded. "Okay. And thanks, Dad. For not telling Mom, I mean."

Miller hugged him again.

"You can let me go now, Dad," Judd said, laughing.

"Fine, fine." Miller loosened his grip and the boy stood up. "You know what?" Miller said. "Your room really *is* a mess."

11

Adra was waiting on the porch at six thirty-five A.M. When Miller pulled into the driveway, her face brightened. It was the first time he had ever seen her so unguarded. Despite his apprehension, despite his guilt about not telling Katie the truth, he knew he was doing the right thing. Here was a girl who had never been to the seashore, had probably never even been on a real trip, and he was giving her a chance—a magical chance—to do something she'd never done before. He was nervous, though. Lots of his friends went to the same beach in the summer, and it was possible he'd run into somebody at the rental office. Well, he wouldn't be there long. He'd drop Adra and Sister off at the house, make sure they had groceries, and then he'd find another place to stay, maybe a hotel at Myrtle Beach or a cheap place north of the island. He'd have to watch his money more closely now that he had quit his job. He'd taken seven hundred dollars out of the joint checking account for the trip, and he could pay for the balance of the rental with a check. A few days before, he'd finally worked up the nerve to tell Katie he'd take her up on her suggestion—he'd go to the beach alone and think about his "situation," as Katie referred to it. But he would not go back to Dr. Buckman, he was adamant about that. Now, though, Katie was talking about marriage counselors. Whatever they did, she said, they needed outside help.

But at least for those two weeks, Miller wished only to push all that business to the back of his mind, get some fishing done, see that Adra had a good time.

Adra was wearing the same dress she had worn the day Miller came to repair her steps—her "Sunday-go-to-meetin'" dress. Her hair was tied back, and stray damp tendrils fell around her ears and forehead. With the rising sun behind her and the light obscuring her features, she looked like a girl in an old sepia photograph. Around the house a vague mist had pushed itself up from the long grass and the trees were silvery with dew.

"You're late," she said when Miller stepped out of the car. Still, she was smiling.

He looked at his watch and laughed. "Five minutes." He stood at the bottom of the steps, enjoying the sheer pleasure of looking at her. The smile, the flushed cheeks. There was a light in her eyes he had never seen before.

Adra blushed, folding her arms across her chest. "What?" she said.

"You." Miller allowed himself another minute of looking at her, then reached for her suitcase, a scarred old leather satchel with crumpled corners. "Is this it? This is all you're taking?"

She looked puzzled. "Did I forget something?"

"No, it's okay. If you need anything else, we'll buy it there."

"Really. Tell me. I don't have much money, but . . ."

Miller held up his hand. "It's fine, I'm sure. You don't need money. All you really need is a bathing suit and some shorts. Tee shirts. You do have a bathing suit?"

She nodded. "I got one yesterday."

"And diapers? Milk for the baby?"

She nodded.

"Fine, then," Miller said again. "Everything's fine." She smiled at him, looking a little uncertain, he thought, then opened the screen door and disappeared into the house. Miller was amazed that Adra would carry so little with her, especially with the baby. Every time Miller and Katie and Judd headed to the beach, they took Katie's SUV, and it was always loaded with beach chairs, fishing gear, bait buckets, straw hats, beach mats, food, books—dozens of books, tapes and records, magazines they hadn't had time to read at home, Judd's floats and inner tubes, suitcases and shopping bags full of more clothes than they would ever need. They spent their evenings sitting on the porch in the dark, drinking and talking and watching the moon and the milky constellations. Sometimes they listened to music and other times they just listened to the waves. Once, Miller had taken his father's scratchy old Caruso records, which they had played on the dusty Victrola in the downstairs living room.

Katie, a consummate cook, always prepared sumptuous suppers at the beach—lobster, skewered shrimp, mussels, clams, flounder with amandine sauce. They ate on the deck in the rich pink light of the sunset that seemed to illuminate their sun-darkened skin from within, and they licked their fingers greedily and drank white wine and rejoiced in being there and in being alive. Some nights after Judd had gone off to Myrtle Beach with friends he knew from previous years, Miller and Katie would lie down between the dunes and make love, just as they had done in the early days. The sand was still warm, and the sea oats hid them from view. But above them was the whole wide, open sky, and at moments Miller had the feeling that they could spiral upwards in each other's arms and become part of the luminous universe. Those times were the most intense in their personal history together, times when they were both wholly absorbed with their love for each other, when every look and touch was sensual and explosive. Love did wonders for the self-esteem, Miller thought. As if you could see yourself as the lover saw you, beautiful and without blemish, charming, clever, intelligent. In a word—flawless. So love essentially also became an exercise in egoism, sensing how your own perfection was reflected in the eyes of the woman who loved you. Together, you rode in the core of a concentric circle that revolved around you both, invisible, impenetrable, and immune from hurt and criticism.

When Miller opened the trunk of the car to stow Adra's bags, he shoved aside his own leather suitcase, his fishing gear, and the package with Adra's book in it. It was then that he noticed the bag with the lingerie he had bought for Katie. He moved it back into a corner of the trunk. He had meant to return it the day before, but on the pretense of going to work, he'd left the house at the usual time and driven to the mountains. He'd spent the day in shirtsleeves and tie, just sitting on a rock overlooking a rushing stream. He pushed the bag into a corner of the trunk and slammed the lid.

When everything was packed, he stepped up onto the porch and knocked on the screen door. "Back here," Adra called. It was the first time Miller had ever set foot in the house. The wooden floor was bare but clean, and the walls were plastered and freshly whitewashed. He walked down the narrow corridor and found Adra in the baby's room. There, the floor was covered with a cracked but clean linoleum patterned in black-and-white checks, and there was no furniture other than the crib and an old-fashioned chest of drawers pushed up against the outside wall. Miller leaned over the crib. He had loved that time in his life when Judd was an infant, smelling the warm, moist odors of a child's room—powder, baby oil, soap, the sharp smell of wet diapers. But again, looking at the baby, he saw the face of Jimmy Duane, and though the child was smiling, Miller felt a frightening chill of recognition.

"Is something wrong?" Adra asked.

Miller shook his head. "We need to get on the road."

Adra picked up the baby, who stretched luxuriously, made a few sounds, then reached for the bottle Adra had heated for her. Miller followed Adra back through the hallway, past what he supposed was the living room with its faded rag rug, a green vinyl sofa, and an oil stove. A battered television set was pocked with cigarette burns. The kitchen was small and dark, with a Formica table and three orange plastic chairs with cracked seats.

He was glad to get out into the sunshine again. He still felt cold, and there was an odor in his nostrils he couldn't identify. Adra tucked the baby into the car seat Miller had bought the night before and ran back to lock up the house. Miller opened the passenger door for her and stood waiting. When she came off the porch she looked at him and hesitated. "My mother said something," she murmured.

"What? What did she say?" Miller asked.

"She asked me what did you want from me."

Miller stood still, his hand on the door handle. "What?"

"My mother said what did you want from me."

He closed the door and took her hands in his. "What I told you," he said. "I want you to be happy. I want you to have a good time."

Her hands felt cold and unbearably fragile. "That's what I told her. That's what I said."

"Good." He opened the door again and she climbed into the car and glanced back at the baby. As Miller walked around to the driver's side he saw her sliding her hand over the smooth black leather of the seat.

"That was nice of you," Adra said, "buying that car seat. I haven't had the money to get one."

"You can keep this one when you get home again. God knows I don't need it." Sitting there with his hand on the ignition, Miller suddenly had a feeling of impending doom.

Adra must have sensed it, too, he thought, because her mouth wobbled a little. "Do you want to know what else I told my mother?"

"Only if it's good."

"I told her you were the first real gentleman I'd ever met."

Miller laughed. "Well," he said, "you are young yet." She laughed, too, and Miller felt better. "So," he said, "we're off," and he turned the key. He was eager to get on the interstate, to get out of town, to put his present life behind him.

Once they were on the highway, a silence fell between them. The first years that he and Katie had driven to the beach, they had worked crossword puzzles, she filling in the squares and Miller supplying most of the answers. Sometimes they played word and memory games, sometimes they sang. The first summer they met, they had driven together to a house party at Myrtle Beach, and on the way there, Miller stopped every few miles to pull over on the side of the highway and kiss her.

Close to Asheville, the tension was broken when the baby began to scream. Adra looked at Miller, anxious. "Can you stop so I can hold her?"

"Tell you what," said Miller. "Let's stop at a restaurant. There's a good one at this exit." He turned on the signal and eased into the exit lane, but when he pulled up at the restaurant Adra made no move to get out of the car. Miller walked around to the passenger side and knocked on her window. She rolled it down slowly. "Are you coming in?" he asked.

"I'll wait here," she said.

"Why?"

Tears welled up in her eyes. "You don't understand," she said. "I

can't afford it."

Miller put his hand on her shoulder. He was startled by the sharpness of her bones. "Adra, I should have told you that I'm paying. I'm sorry you didn't know that. I meant all along to buy you breakfast." He reached inside the window and released the lock on the door. She climbed out hesitantly, and Miller tilted the seat and retrieved the anguished baby from the back seat. Standing in the sun with the child in his arms, he felt years peel away. It was déjà vu, waiting for Katie to get whatever she needed from the back seat of their old Volkswagen van while he held Judd in his arms.

The restaurant was crowded with tourists—families on their way to the beach or to the mountains, college kids out of school. Miller looked around but saw no familiar faces. The waitress brought a high chair and Miller sat with the baby while Adra went to the breakfast bar. When she came back with her food, she slid into the booth and showed Miller her plate. "Did I get too much? Will they make you pay more?"

"It's a buffet, Adra. That means it's all one price, for as many refills as you want." He laughed and suddenly he understood her mysterious allure. She was part woman, part child, the daughter he had never had, the mother he had lost long years before.

She blushed under his scrutiny and looked down at her plate. "You think I'm backward, don't you? You think I'm backward 'cause I've never been anywhere and I don't talk as good as I should."

Miller patted her hand. "Adra, I like you as you are. Exactly as you are. You're a very special woman. If I didn't like you, we wouldn't be here."

"Do you feel sorry for me then?"

"Sorry? You're the toughest female I've ever met. In fact, sometimes you scare the hell out of me."

When she laughed, it was as if her old protective mask had fallen away at last. They looked at each other as if something important had occurred between them. "You go now," she said. "Get yourself something to eat." And when he stood up, she said his name, just to be saying it. "Miller."

Walking across the room, he looked back, and she waved and smiled at him, her head tilted. She could be Judd's wife, give or take a few years on both sides. The baby could be his granddaughter. He filled his plate with eggs and sausage, bacon and grits, and as an afterthought added melon slices and strawberries. He was hungry, really hungry for the first time in weeks.

It was better after that. Before they left the restaurant, Miller bought some magazines and Adra flipped through the pages while he drove. "Oh Lord Jesus," she said. "Look at this. A shark. Will there be sharks in the water where we're going?"

"No," Miller promised. "No danger." He didn't want to tell her that the sharks swam beyond the sand bar and were often hooked by fishermen on the pier. "And besides, that's a whale shark you're looking at. They don't bite people. They just feed on plankton."

"What's that?" Adra asked.

"It's little stuff—microscopic plant life and minuscule animal life that swirls around in the ocean. It's so small it's hardly noticeable to us."

He sensed that she was watching his profile and he glanced sideways at her as he drove. "You know everything, don't you?" she said.

He frowned. "I wish."

"No, you do, you really do. You know what this plankton stuff is, you know about sharks, you know how to fix things. You jumped in and you pulled Jimmy Duane up out of that lake and you did that thing . . ."

"CPR?"

"Yes, that. I mean, even if it was . . . too late, you knew how to do that." She was quiet for a minute. Miller was aware of the sounds of the road—cars streaming by, a truck gearing up to pass, the tires spinning them on their way to the next phase of their lives.

"Remember when I tried to hit you?" Adra's voice rose a decibel, and Miller's fingers tightened on the steering wheel. "I'm sorry I did that. I was just so crazy. We all were. We were so scared, and you were the only one who knew what to do. I just went crazy, that's all."

Miller's felt his breakfast pushing up in his throat.

Adra looked at him for a minute and then she started flipping through the magazines again.

Suddenly the baby began to scream and a fetid odor filled the car. Miller held his breath and rolled down the window.

"Maybe we should stop at a gas station or something," Adra said. "I need to change her and wash her diaper out."

Miller pulled off at the first exit and found a convenience market. Inside he bought two boxes of disposable diapers and instructed Adra to throw the dirty cloth diaper into the trash can. "Throw it away?" she said. "But I can wash it out."

"Adra. I insist."

"I can't let you keep buying me things," she said.

Miller was getting tired. He couldn't remember the trip seeming this long ever before. It was hot on the asphalt parking area. The smell of gasoline and the soiled diaper and the hot, rubbery tarmac nauseated him. He glanced at his watch. Three more hours at least to the coast. He was beginning to think he had made a terrible mistake. He saw a telephone enclosure near the edge of the asphalt. Maybe he should call Katie and confess everything to her—everything, starting with what had really happened at the lake. Then the job, then this trip. He could still turn around and take Adra and the baby home.

From the look on Adra's face, Miller realized that she had sensed the change in his mood. "Want a cold drink?" he asked. He forced a smile.

She nodded and watched him as he walked in to pay for the gas.

Inside, Miller went to the rest room and washed his hands. He examined his face in the mottled mirror above the sink. At first he didn't recognize himself with the new growth of beard. The fact that Katie hated it had made him that much more determined to keep it. Adra, on the other hand, had said nothing. She accepted him as he was, without question.

He turned off the water. When he saw that the paper towel dispenser was empty, he banged it with his fist. He left the bathroom cursing and drying his hands against his jeans, and went directly to the telephone. He inserted some coins and dialed zero for collect but when the operator answered, he hung up. He bought canned drinks for himself and Adra, and after that, the silence in the car was so thick that he could actually hear Adra swallowing. But with the first view of the ocean at Georgetown, he felt better. He opened the window and let the salt air rush in. "We're close now," he said. "We'll be there soon." He smiled at Adra. "Smell that? Smell the salt air?"

"The ocean?" Adra asked. "Already? I thought it would be dark when we got there."

"Roll down your window," Miller said. "When we come to this bridge up ahead, you'll see the marshes and inlets. Watch for herons. Big white birds with long legs."

Adra lowered her window. She turned and looked over her shoulder at the road behind them. "How far to back home now?" she asked.

"Four hundred miles or so," Miller said. "Adra, don't worry. I'm sorry I hurt your feelings. I know I've been moody lately."

Adra bit her lip, but when she looked out the window she gasped. "Oh look. I see it. The ocean. That's it, isn't it?"

"That's an inland marsh," said Miller. "Look out as far as you can see to your right. The ocean's out there."

"Oh thank you, Jesus," Adra whispered. "The ocean. My mother and daddy have never even seen the ocean. Jimmy Duane neither." She glanced at Miller and then back at the water.

Along the narrow highway, the pines exuded a bittersweet fragrance that was sharpened by the heat of the afternoon sun. Beneath the trees the fallen pine needles had woven a rich brown carpet. Soon the roadside forest thinned and buildings came into view—peeling shacks and occasional small stores, then the intersection for the turnoff.

Miller pulled up at the rental office and looked around at his little family. *So now what? Where do I stay tonight? Why have I taken this terrible gamble, and for what?* He went inside to pay the balance of the rent and was relieved that the woman who would recognize him from past years was occupied with another family. He kept his face turned away from her as he signed his check. Outside he gathered Adra and Sister from the car and they all headed for the supermarket at the end of the parking lot. "Anything you want," he kept telling Adra, as she examined prices and ran her hand along the shelves. He was beginning to feel better, as if they were halfway home. Every time he tossed something into the basket, Adra would try to put it back, saying it was too expensive. Then Miller, feeling generous and expansive, would laugh and deposit it in the basket again. It soon became a game that set them laughing. At one point he slid his arm around her waist and she leaned into him slightly. "No beef," said Miller. Katie usually made such decisions, and he was enjoying the role of overseer. "Not at the beach. Fresh seafood every night, okay? If we can't catch it, we'll buy it." He bought beer and soft drinks, orange juice and lemonade. Pushing the cart down the aisle with the baby in it, Miller felt young and serious, endowed with a new chance at life.

He especially loved the aisle with the fishing supplies—the supple rods, shiny silver bait buckets and white plastic minnow traps with yellow doors, shelves of bright fishing line and string and lead weights, leaders and sinkers. Nets of various shapes and sizes hung along the wall. When they had loaded the groceries in the car and started across the bridge to the island, Miller kept watching Adra's face. Her joy was more precious to him than his own excitement. A few fishermen and crabbers lined the narrow sidewalk along the two lanes, and they nodded lazily as Miller drove past, as if they had nothing to do but wait for strikes and greet new visitors to the island. On both sides of the bridge lay the marshes and the inlets that drank up the ocean at high tide, then spit it out again twelve hours later.

Once on the island, Miller turned right, past the old church, and started looking for the house. It was oceanfront, center-island, with a long deck that led down to the beach. The ocean side was banked with dunes grown wild with sea oats and trumpet vines. Miller turned into the driveway and parked between two twisted myrtles. He looked triumphantly at Adra, but she looked more stunned than happy. Miller went around to the back and lifted the baby out and then waited for Adra to emerge from her side of the car. She walked behind him slowly, taking it all in. A humid dampness permeated the shaded driveway, but when they climbed the long steps to the porch the ocean breeze hit them and the sky lifted the whole world into view—ocean, beach, horizon, a regimented flock of pelicans. Adra sucked in her breath. Miller handed over the baby while he went around throwing open windows and doors. Then he went down for the groceries and luggage. He carried Adra's suitcase up to the front bedroom and left his own in the trunk of the car. Later, there would be time to decide where he would stay that night.

While he put away the groceries, Adra was upstairs, running from room to room. When he was finished, he walked out onto the shaded back porch. He took off his shoes and leaned into the sun, breathing in the salt air and listening to the sound of the breakers.

"This house is too big for me," Adra said, breathless, when she came outside. "Lord, Miller, there's four or five bedrooms. I'd be afraid at night. I don't think I can stay here by myself. Maybe we should go back."

Miller laughed and held out his arm as if to pull her close to him, and then he quickly pushed his hand into his pocket. "Come on, let's go down and take a look at the beach."

"Should we put on our bathing suits?"

"Not yet. We'll just look right now."

When they stepped onto the deck, the wind lifted Adra's hair and she laughed. "Take off your shoes," Miller said. Obediently, Adra sat down on the top step, the baby in her lap, and Miller reached for her ankle, the way he had longed to do weeks before on her front porch. He slipped off her sandals, letting his fingers brush across the arch of her foot. Her long narrow toes glistened with silvery flecks of sand. Miller dared not look at her face, but at his touch she drew her foot back slightly.

When they stepped off the deck and onto the hot, silky beach, Adra stared openmouthed at the water. "How deep is it?" she asked.

"It gets deep gradually," Miller said. "You start in ankle-deep. You can stop whenever you want." Adra stepped into the shallows. Her progress was tentative but somehow graceful, as if she were a dancer learning a new choreography. Her pace was measured not by fascination, but by hesitation. "It looks so deep," she said, gazing out over the horizon. "There are ships out there." She shifted the baby on her shoulder.

Miller put a hand on her elbow as foamy water swirled around their ankles. "Don't be afraid. It's shallow where we're standing. Come on, step out a little farther. Come on." When he said that, he thought of the dream about his father. *Come on, son. It's not so bad once you're in.* He put his arm around Adra and pulled her forward a little.

She leaned toward the shore, pulling back against his touch. "Don't let go," she kept saying, "don't let go."

Miller had not thought about what the water might mean to her, what symbols or fears it might represent. Maybe she was thinking of Jimmy Duane. To Miller, the ocean, with its constant change and movement, was more alive and electric than the dark silent depths of the lake. But he had seen drownings in the ocean, too, seen a lost child pulled up once with a crab on his ear, seen a dead fisherman brought in on a boat, his bloated belly white as the underside of a flounder.

He tightened his hold on her waist. "I won't let go," he promised. Water licked at their ankles, soft and caressing. "I won't let go."

He wasn't certain, but he thought he saw tears in her eyes. "Look, I can stay if you want me to," he told her. "I can stay here in the house with you and take care of you. There are plenty of bedrooms." She pulled back and shaded her eyes as she stared at him. "It's all right," Miller said. "Katie thinks I'm staying alone here these two weeks." He cleared his throat, looked away. "I guess you could call it a separation of sorts."

"Because of the job?" But then it seemed to occur to her suddenly that there might be other reasons. "Does she know about you bringing me here?"

"No, no. I didn't lie, really, but I didn't exactly tell her, either. She wouldn't give me a chance. I was going to, but she just wanted me away for a while. She said she thought we ought to be apart to think about our problems."

Adra bit down on her bottom lip.

"So I can stay here with you," Miller rushed on. "I'll sleep in the back bedroom, or downstairs on one of the sofas, whatever would make you more comfortable."

Adra looked back toward the house. "Katie don't know? She don't know about any of it?"

He shook his head. "It's okay, Adra. Don't worry. Just try to relax and have a good time. That's what I'm going to do."

Adra backed out of the water and looked down the beach. Finally she turned and faced Miller. "You can take me on back home if you have a mind to. I won't be mad."

"I don't want to take you back, Adra. That's the last thing I want." He put his fingertips to his lips and then made the motion of a cross over his heart. Adra smiled and dipped her head and then the angle of the sun moved into his line of vision and he blinked. He turned back to the sea and looked out at the gently breaking whitecaps. A gull screamed and swooped down toward the glittering surface. For a second Miller thought he saw something pale rise up in the space between two incoming waves—rise, then disappear. Nothing, it was nothing. It was only the light. It was only the wind.

12

That night, with the baby finally asleep in the upstairs bedroom, Miller and Adra sat on the rooftop deck and looked out over the ocean. The water was black, fringed with luminous white caps, and the summer sky was riddled with stars. Adra's presence beside him created an electric current that both disturbed and comforted Miller. All he understood was that he was excited about life again. Sitting there in the dark, with the space between them charged with expectation, he talked about everything except what was in his heart. He told her the names of the constellations and the stories behind them. Aquarius the Water Bearer, Leo the Lion, Pisces the Fish, Aries the Ram. With his hands, he scribed the outline of Sagittarius the Archer, and he was transported to his childhood backyard that summer after his mother had left. It disturbed him that after all those years, he heard in his memory a catch in his father's voice that he had never noticed before.

"What's that one?" asked Adra, pointing. "That bright star over there."

Miller squinted. "I think that one's a star of the first magnitude. That's what they call the brightest ones."

"And what are the dimmest ones?"

"The sixth magnitude. Those are the faintest stars that can still be seen with the naked eye." He smiled. "My father taught me that when I was a kid."

"He sounds nice, your father," she said. "My daddy never had time for us kids. Plus, we were scared of him. He was a drunk, a mean one."

Miller wanted to hold her, protect her. The night cradled them there, halfway between sky and sea. "Look over there," he said. "There's a star of the first magnitude."

"Where?" She turned her head. He saw the flash of her teeth and the whites of her eyes. Miller put his hand on her shoulder and moved it slightly, so that her vision was aligned with the direction in which his arm pointed. "See? No, this way." He moved his hand to her chin and tilted it a little. "That one. That's a blue star. A blue star has more energy than a red star, so it's hotter." He kept talking, but if he had been asked to repeat what he was saying, he wasn't sure he would remember, because in touching her he lost all sense of the wider universe. It was just the two of them, burning as intensely as a light of the first magnitude.

"That seems backwards," Adra said. She giggled a little. They had been drinking wine since dinner. White wine with seafood, he told her, and wine to celebrate his decision to stay in the house with her. She would take the front bedroom, he would take the back. It would all be circumspect. "I mean," Adra went on, "red stands for hot. Blue stands for cool. How can the blue star be hotter?" When she turned to him for an answer, he could not help touching her face. She grasped his hand with both of hers and guided it down the column of her neck and across her throat and held it just above the rise of her breasts. "I like your hand on me," she whispered. "I like you touching me. It burns, sort of."

Miller felt blood beating, but he was not sure whether it was his own pulse or hers. For a minute neither of them moved. Miller heard, or imagined that he heard, her halting breath over the pounding of the breakers. Then, still guiding his hand, she slid it beneath her dress, so that he felt her bare skin and the hardened point of her nipple under his palm.

He sat perfectly still. Breakers crashed against the shore below, and a soft riff of wind moved across his cheeks, yet all his senses were focused on his hand and the heat beneath it. When Adra shifted in his chair, he moved closer, feeling her heart beat beneath his hand. His voice was low, cracked with emotion. His lips moved against her shoulder. He whispered. "Remember that day in your barn, the day I fixed your steps?" He stumbled on. "You were so distant, so hard. I thought you hated me. I wanted to find out what you were thinking—Jesus I just wanted you to blurt it out, so I would know one way or the other how you felt about me. You were so damned . . . you were a puzzle. But whatever you were feeling, I wanted you. This sounds crazy, but that day in the barn I saw gold in your eye where the light fell across it, like you were some kind of gift or prize. I wanted to touch you, and I almost did, but I was afraid to, and when I reached out to do it, you moved around me somehow."

Her heartbeat quickened, he was sure of it. "Look at me," Miller said. "I think I've always wanted you. From the first moment I saw you—that day on the dock. I think I would have been willing to drown myself, if I could have taken you down with me, held you in my arms."

She made a low sound that came from deep inside her. He pulled her closer, so that her chair tilted against his own. She allowed herself to be held but she kept silent and was absolutely still, as if poised on the edge of a precipice. But then a little shudder rippled through her frame. Miller moved his hands briskly against her skin to warm her and a soft, almost inaudible, cry came from her throat, but she did not move even when his hands followed the sloping curve of her shoulder and slid smoothly under the narrow strap of her dress. But then her chair, which was canted toward him, tilted and she lost her balance. Laughing, she clutched at his shirt and Miller smelled the salt in her hair and felt the heat of her skin. Together, they tumbled to the deck and he lay next to her, holding her close against the length of his body.

Once the strap on her left shoulder lay across his knuckles, he lifted it, then pulled it slowly over her shoulder and the dress fell away on one side. Her breast was pale in the moonlight, so small that his opened hand covered it completely. Then he lowered the other strap and slid the dress down to her waist. Her mouth was partly open and there was a glint of moonlight on her lower lip. Her shoulders were thin, the blades sharp and defined in the hazy shadows, yet her skin was unbearably soft under his touch. In his warm hands she was a medium to be molded, shaped into whatever his creative heart might desire. He needed someone to love him without reservation, he wanted unquestioning allegiance, he wanted complete surrender. He felt a sharp, slicing hunger for her and a terrible fear that if he did not cling to her, he might spin off into the universe, he might become one of the hot blue stars that burn for billions of years in the galaxy and then disappear.

When Adra slid out of his embrace and stood up, he was afraid he had gone too far. But she reached for his hands and helped him up and her dress fell to her ankles and she stepped out of her undergarments at the same time he stood to shed his own clothes. Then Miller sat down again on the chair and lifted her, facing him, onto his lap, and they made love under the brilliant, star-studded sky.

At the end, Miller was frightened because Adra clung to him and cried so brokenly. "What?" he whispered. "What? Did I hurt you?"

"No, no," she said. "It was just . . ." She fitted her face into the curve of his neck and shoulder and kissed his neck. "Jimmy Duane never did love me like that. Never. He was rough. He hurt me. But with you, it was sweet. It was so sweet."

"Adra."

"I don't mean to cry. Don't be mad at me."

He held his arms tight around her. "How could I be mad? I could never get mad at you."

"Jimmy Duane always got mad when I cried."

"But why?"

She ran her hands across his shoulders. "I don't know. It upset him. He didn't like crying. But he liked hitting all right."

Miller pulled back slightly so he could look at her face. "He hurt you, didn't he? I remember that day at the lake, you had bruises on your wrist. Did he do that?"

Her face crumpled again. "It was my fault. He did it because I cried. Sometimes he would hit me because he was drinking. It was the whiskey. He didn't know no better when he was drinking." She shook her head. "But that day the baby had woke up crying, and Jimmy Duane was mad because he couldn't sleep, and he grabbed her and shook her and I kept hitting him to make him stop. He pushed me against the wall and twisted my wrist, but it got his attention away from Sister. That was all I cared about. You reckon she coulda got—what do they call that—shook baby syndrome?"

Miller held her and smoothed her hair with his hands. "Oh my poor sweet Adra."

She wound her arms around his neck. "I'm happy now, though,

see? Tonight I cried because you made me so happy. I can't explain. It just come out of me, I couldn't stop it."

"I'm happy, too, Adra. For the first time in a long time."

"You're not sorry?"

"Sorry? How could I be?"

"Because," she said. "Because. Everything. Katie, mostly. You couldn't just flat stop loving her all of a sudden, could you?"

Miller laid his finger against her lips. "Please, no more talk about Katie or Jimmy Duane. It's just the two of us now. Miller and Adra." With the unexpected mention of Katie, his spirits sank. "Are you getting cold out here?" he asked. "Let me get your robe for you."

She pulled at his neck. "I'm not cold," she said. "Stay here. Just hold me."

"No. I could feel goose bumps on your arms. I want to get something to cover you up."

"I don't have a robe. At home I just wear one of Jimmy Duane's old shirts."

Miller stood up and pulled on his jeans. "I'll be right back." He ran down the stairs and out into the dark driveway and all at once he felt dizzy and short of breath. Everything seemed magnified—the pounding waves on the beach and the shrill lament of tree frogs in the live oaks that crowned the sandy driveway. The chaotic rhythm of his heart. After what he had just done—and there was no way he would have changed that—there was no turning back. How could his life have altered so dramatically in twenty-four hours? Here he was, making new ties while he cut old ones. He was shaking a little, afraid of something he could not name, some unseen enemy that he all at once realized might well be himself.

He lifted the trunk latch and stood blinking against the sudden light, then gathered up his own suitcase and the packages he had bought for Katie and went back inside.

Adra was sitting on the edge of the bed with a sheet pulled around her. She looked at Miller expectantly when he came up the stairs, as if she were waiting to be told what to do next or how to feel. Miller feigned cheerfulness. He rummaged through the bags and found the one with the amber silk pajamas and the animal print robe. When he held them out to Adra, she smoothed her hand along the length of the sleeve. "Oh my God," she whispered, "I've never seen anything so pretty."

Katie had said, You know I would never wear anything like this.

"Try them on."

"What?"

"Try them on. They're yours. They're a present."

"For me? You bought these for me?"

Miller nodded. It wasn't a lie exactly, that nod. Not exactly. "Try them on," he said. He wanted to see her in something silky. He wanted to buy beautiful clothes for her. He wanted to give her everything she had always been denied.

As the smooth silk flowed through Adra's narrow hands, Miller saw it as a dark golden river. Perhaps she was the conduit, he thought, through which he might save his own life. He stood above her and combed his fingers through her hair, pulling it back from her face and exposing her long pale neck. A yellow light from the bedroom lamp cast a soft golden tint to the skin of her throat. "Try them on," he said. "I'm going out on the beach for a while."

She looked up quickly. "You're going out?"

This must have been a familiar scenario for her with Jimmy Duane, Miller realized. "Only out on the beach," he said. "I just need to think." He leaned over and kissed her mouth. "I won't be long."

She nodded, holding the lingerie to her chest.

At the top of the stairs Miller looked back. She was still watching him. The silk swam in her hands. He blew her a kiss, but she only nodded.

On the downstairs landing, Miller stopped and turned on the light in the small bathroom that the owners had built into the corner of the house. When the bulb came on, a huge swamp roach scuttled across the floor and disappeared under the blue baseboard. Miller shuddered. He flushed the toilet, then turned to wash his hands. When he looked at his face in the mirror, the beard seemed right for the first time because he did not recognize himself as Miller Sharp. He was someone else, a stranger on the verge of a new life.

When are you going to shave that thing off? Katie had asked him.

He liked it, though. It gave him some mystery. He moved closer to the mirror. There was not so much of his father in the reflection now, but somebody his father might like to know, perhaps. As he dried his hands he turned his face to different perspectives, trying to absorb what it was he was evolving into. The fact that he was a new man tempered his guilt, made it less acute, and that gave him hope because he knew that his life would have to change in order for it to be saved.

The roach emerged from the baseboard again and scurried across Miller's bare foot. A basic reflex made him kick outward, and the creature flew off his foot and slammed against the wall. Miller turned out the light and hurried outside.

The moonlight illuminated the path to the ocean and spilled across the surface of the waves. The white dunes were branched with sand burr grass and purple flowering railroad vines, and close to the house, saw palmettos and sea grapes, stunted by the ocean wind, grew through thick clusters of yaupon, bayberry, and wax myrtles. Sea oats and the dry reeds of shorerush made dark shadows against the pale sand.

At this hour the sand was cool, and Miller stepped off the deck and headed toward the thick white fringe of the breakers. He could see a slight chop farther out, glowing in the dark ocean, and he walked to the shoreline and stepped into the water. The surf was still warm from the day's heat. He backtracked a few feet and sat down on the damp sand, thinking of another time he had stepped into the surf, but that day was cold and heavy. After Hollis's death, Miller had driven to Cape Hatteras, where they had often surf-fished together, to scatter Hollis's ashes. It was January, and the sky was spitting snow that day. The freezing surf had slapped mercilessly against Miller's legs and a northerly wind whipped the breakers into brown-tinged froth that rolled along the beach like dark balls of cotton. Miller had stood knee-deep in the icy water while he opened the top of the urn. Then he swept his arm in a wide arc and let the ashes blow into the sea. Some, wet by the ocean spray, swept back against his jacket and stuck there. He brushed them off with stiff, chapped fingers. It was a wild place. Yet it seemed a fitting burial site for his father's boundless energy.

For a long time after the urn was empty he had stood in the water and squinted against the unforgiving wind. The surf and sky were tinted a steely gray, blending at the horizon line. Finally, when his legs were almost too numb to stand, Miller went back to his motel room, took a hot shower, and then lay across the bed, exhausted. It was over. That whole part of his life was over. He slept the rest of the day and through most of the night, and when he woke in the early hours the following morning, he signed out of the motel and started for home, driving straight through to Knoxville—a fourteen-hour drive. At one point he looked down at his windbreaker and discovered a gritty gray spot. His father was still with him. He dampened his finger, lifted the ash, and touched it to his tongue. It was a communion service of sorts.

Now, on this warm August night, he looked down at the surf and wondered whether his father's ashes had become part of the very water that now lapped languidly at the beach. They might have traveled far in those intervening months. Phosphorescence blinked in the shallows, and broken shells washed up, tumbled, and disappeared again. Even when the tide licked at his feet, he couldn't move. The incident with the roach had frightened him. After the lovemaking with Adra, after the magnificent stars, the lowly cockroach had shaken his soul, reminded him of ugly, nameless, formless things.

The night obscured the division of sea and sky. It was all one piece, all one dark puzzle of air and water and burning stars. In the morning, it would be clear where things began and ended, but now he feared the mystery as strongly as Adra feared drowning. So many things threatened. Lightning, wind, hurricanes, childbirth, inalterable sorrow. And death. Don't forget death, he told himself. He tried to pray, but he was no good at praying. How could he ask God for favors when lately he had broken every rule?

He looked back at the house, where the yellow light in the window of the living room burned, and he believed it was the only beacon that could save him. He shuffled toward the house, rinsed his sandy feet under the faucet on the deck, and went in. Adra was in the living room, sitting under the floor lamp. She was wearing the gold silk pajamas. Before her, spread out on the bare wooden floor, was a pile of old *National Geographic*s that had sat on the shelf in that room for all the years Miller could remember coming there. Their coated covers gleamed under the lamplight. Adra looked up at Miller with uncertainty. "It says here," she told him, "that a hummingbird's nest is no bigger than a doll's teacup."

That was all it took to transport him from chaos to order. Miller laughed and sat down on the floor behind her, circling her waist with his arms as she read, his chin resting on her gold silken shoulder. It grounded him, this girl in this house, the sleeping baby in the room above, the rich overripe smell of the marsh drifting in through the window, the unrestrained sea where his father's ashes alternately danced and drifted forever. He closed his eyes and held his breath for a minute until he could adjust his rhythm to Adra's, and then he floated, letting her breathe for him, letting her heart pump for both of them.

13

The sound of the surf woke him just before dawn. It took a minute for him to get his bearings, to remember that he was at the beach and that the woman beside him was not his wife. In the pale shadows he saw the disorder of the room—the gold silk pajamas thrown across the foot of the bed, his own clothes strewn on the floor, the half-open suitcase and the peeling satchel with clothing spilling out. There were two glasses on the dresser top and a pile of diapers on the rush-bottom chair by the door. Two of the dresser drawers were pulled out and the sleeve of a white shirt hung limply from one. As a child Miller had refused to sleep in a room in which a drawer or a closet was open. It had something to do with an unnameable fear of lurking monsters or demons—whatever one could call the unknown—waiting to be set free by the dark.

He lay staring at the ceiling, which he knew to be pale green, but in the half light, it looked gray. The walls were whitewashed and the floor was worn to a soft gray-green patina. He had always liked this room because it reminded him of the colors of the sea. But this morning he felt a vague foreboding and a physical discomfort that would not let him drift back into sleep. He noticed a slight twinge in his chest, as if something had snapped there and caught, and then he felt a bump in his breathing, as if it were too slow, or too fast, but wrong—somehow broken. He turned over slowly, so as not to wake Adra, and tried lying on his right side in order to give his heart more room. It could be something as simple as a muscle cramp, he assured himself, but the constrictions gathered force. This is what had happened to his father. Maybe he had lain awake all night, or maybe he had just sat in his chair where Miller found him, wondering until it was too late whether the pain was serious enough to do something about.

Fear balled up inside him like a fist. He rolled back to the left, and Adra stirred and made a soft sound in her throat. He was filled with dread. He wasn't ready for her to wake, and he certainly didn't want to confess his apprehensions. He turned on his back again and eased away from her. Adra raised up on her elbow and looked down into his face. Her dark hair fell across her eyes. She was expecting something from him, he thought, and maybe if he did not meet her eyes, she would lie back down again. But she didn't. Miller looked up at the ceiling, at the parallel lines of the boards. "My father died," he said.

He had not meant to say such a thing. He did not understand where the disclosure had come from. But Adra seemed neither surprised nor disturbed. She lay back down and pulled the sheet up across her breast. "He taught you about the stars," she said.

Miller laughed. He could not have said why he laughed, except that her response had pleased him, had been exactly right. He turned toward her and laid his hand on her hair, remembering that when he and Katie were first married, Katie's hair had done this—spilled brightly over the pillow. "It's all mixed up," Miller said quietly. "The way I feel about you, the way I miss my father. Katie and Judd. It's hard."

She was silent, waiting, but she watched him with her penetrating stare.

"I went over to my father's house, and usually when I pulled up in the driveway, he'd hurry out. He'd say, *Son*. That's all. *Son*. Like it was some kind of great revelation. But this time it was quiet, dead quiet, and when I stepped onto the porch the door was partly open. It was December, just a few days after Christmas, so that wasn't normal—the door being open like that. And then I went in and he was in his chair, the one he sat in when he watched television, and he was wearing his coat, so he must have been outside sometime that morning. And I figured the pain must have started out there and when he came in it must have been so bad that he couldn't even close the door. Or maybe he hoped to call for help, I don't know. Anyway, the way he was seated in the chair—sort of sprawled across it—looked as if he had just made it there, fallen into it, sort of. And his eyes were open. I think that was the worst part. His eyes were open but there was no life in them, they were flat and dark like the ocean before a storm, before the wind comes up."

He moved his hand to Adra's cheek and she covered it with her own hand and held it there.

"When I woke up a while ago," Miller said, "I had pain. And I thought it was the same kind of pain that killed my father."

Adra rolled on her side and put her fingers on his throat. "Let me feel your pulse."

"No, no," Miller said. "I'm okay now, I swear. It's tension, I guess. Anxiety." He pulled her toward him and kissed her face. "Worried about me? Don't be. I'm sticking around to take care of you and

Sister." He lifted her onto himself and held her close with his arms. Her body was so slight, she had the weight of a child. He could feel the wetness of her mouth against his neck. He forgot about the pain then, but just as his excitement began to grow, the baby cried. Adra laughed and rolled off him. "Oh Lordy," she said. "That child has a bad sense of timing."

"Wait, maybe she'll go back to sleep." His hands held her firmly at the waist. "Don't go. Don't get up. Please, Adra. Stay with me."

"I got to get her," she said. "She's hungry. And she's in a strange place. She'll be scared if I don't come." She slid away from him and swung her legs off the side of the bed. Her nakedness blurred against the blooming light from the window. Her body was pale, luminous. She reached for the pajama shirt and slipped her arms into it. Then she pulled on the silky pants. "They feel so good," she said. Her voice in the morning was even deeper, more layered, than usual.

"Come back here," Miller said. "Come back to me." But the baby cried again and Adra looked at him.

"You ain't mad?" she said.

He *was* angry. Angry at the baby for crying. Angry at Adra for leaving him. Angry at himself for being angry. But he shook his head. "It's fine," he said. "Fine." When Judd was a baby they used to take him into bed with them in the mornings, but Miller found it difficult to look very long at Sister. Those pale eyes, hair like her father's.

"I'll just go downstairs and warm her bottle," Adra said. She was watching Miller's face. "Maybe she'll go back to sleep. Sometimes she does." She hesitated. "Ever once in a while she will."

Miller sat up. "Never mind. I'm wide awake now. I think I'll go see if I can catch some fish for our breakfast. You feed the baby and then cook up some grits and eggs and I'll bring the main course." He laughed. "Stop looking at me like that, Adra. I *said*, it's okay."

She nodded and left the room. The baby's screams were even more intense now, and all he wanted was to have them stopped. While he was dressing, he noticed the pinching in his chest again, but it had disappeared by the time he walked downstairs. He followed the path to the ocean just as the sun edged over the horizon. For a few minutes he stood in the shallows, getting used to the chill of the water. Then he filled his plastic bucket with sea water and tied a shrimp on the line and a two-ounce sinker for weight against the current. He waded out to his waist, shivering a little in the cool morning breeze. He cast his line out beyond the breakers, and the spool sang as the reel released. The first fish hit the bait hard—a blue—and he pulled it in slowly, occasionally letting the line play out to relax the tension.

In a little while, he had six fair-sized fish in the bucket. He reeled in his line and waded in to the beach. An old man he had noticed the day before was walking along the shore with his dog. He stopped and glanced into Miller's bucket. "Have any luck, neighbor?"

Miller showed him the fish. "You're up at the Smith cottage, aren't you?" the man asked. Miller nodded. "Nice family you got there," the man said.

Miller smiled. "Thanks."

"First grandchild?"

Miller felt his cheeks flush. "Pardon?"

"The baby. Is it your daughter's first?"

Miller busied himself gathering up his bucket and bait. The man stood there while his dog danced around Miller, sniffing the shrimp in his hand and nosing the bucket. Miller didn't know what possessed him to lie. "She's my wife," he said. And then he repeated it, more for himself than anything else, to make sure that was what he had really said in the first place. "She's my wife."

The old man bowed, lowering his narrow, freckled shoulders and backing away in an embarrassed little two-step. "Sorry, friend," he said. "I thought . . . Well, she's so young." The two men stood contemplating each other while the dog poked his nose into the bucket of fish. "Wellsir," the man said, "I would say then that you are a very lucky man."

Miller nodded and touched the back of his hand to his forehead in a vague salute. The old man started up the beach again. After a few feet he looked back at Miller and held up a hand in apology. Then he made a thumbs-up sign and went on down the beach, shaking his head.

When he started up the path to the house, Miller felt his face burning. Up until this point in his life, he had rarely lied. Now it seemed to be the only thing he had a talent for anymore.

He propped his fishing rod against the corner of the porch and carried the bucket into the kitchen through the back door. The pans and skillets sat empty on the stove, waiting for breakfast. He caught a glimpse of Adra's gold silk pajamas in the living room and then she came through the doorway into the kitchen, carrying the baby. Miller smiled and held up the bucket of fish. But Adra put her hand to her lips and nodded toward the living room.

Miller felt a little bubble of apprehension expand in his chest. He stepped into the living room and looked around. Katie was sitting on the sofa. She sat stiffly, her hands clenched together on her knees. Her body was shaking.

A chill rippled across Miller's skin and his tongue felt thick and swollen. He stood before his wife barefooted, his wet bathing suit dripping. He was still holding the bucket of fish.

She spoke first. No tears. Just a cold, imploding anger. "You could have saved me the trouble of an all-night drive if you had let me know you weren't going to be alone here. Just tell me one thing. How long have you been planning this?"

Miller put down the bucket and shook his head. He was trying to stay calm."Katie, I swear to you. It's not the way it looks."

"Well, Miller, let me tell you what I think. I think you've been planning all along to bring your grieving widow slut to the beach. I think it looks like you bought those silk pajamas for her and I came across them by accident." Her voice rose in intensity. "I also think—I *know*—that you're pretty well into lying and cheating these days." Katie's face was getting redder and redder.

Miller held up his hand and moved toward her. "You've got it all wrong, Katie, I swear."

"Don't touch me," she warned. Her voice rose to a dangerous level, threatening. "I came here hoping to make up with you, and you're sleeping with an ignorant redneck tramp. She can't even speak proper English. The poor young widow. What a joke. She looks like she's thirteen years old."

Miller sat down in the rocking chair facing the sofa and at last released the bucket. Moisture from his wet bathing trunks dripped through the wooden slats onto the floor. Without his shirt, he felt strangely naked. "Listen, Katie. Let's try to talk about this in a civil way, okay? I mean, all this stuff, everything that's happened, has been a kind of synchronicity. I mean, it just happened. Let me explain. I was only going to leave her—Adra—here at the house. Alone, I mean, I was going to let her use it because first you said you weren't coming, and then you told me to come alone, but when I drove her here she was afraid to stay alone."

"Oh," said Katie. "So now you're going to blame it on me. I *told* you to come here."

"Damn it," said Miller, "that's not what I meant."

Her mouth twisted. "And Jack called." Now she was beginning to weep. "Jack said you had quit your *job*, for God's sake. Miller, what are we supposed to do for money?" She leaned forward and hugged her knees, rocking back and forth. "Or," she said abruptly, "is there even a 'we' anymore? A me and you? Or just you and her?" She laughed. "Migod, I just realized that you must have had her in our bed, too. I smelled coconut on the pillow, but until now, I never put it all together. First you screwed her in our bed and now you're screwing her in the beach house that has meant so much to our family all these years. You're desecrating our entire marriage. You and that little whore."

"Katie, Adra is not a whore. Please don't call her that."

"What would you call her, Miller? Good God, her husband's not even cold in his grave."

Miller looked back toward the kitchen, but Adra was out of sight. If she had taken the baby outside he had not heard the screen door close. He had a sudden illogical fear that if they had gone outside, the baby would get sunburned without her hat.

Katie had noticed his backward glance. "What in the hell are you looking at, Miller? Are you worried about *her* feelings? What about *mine*? In fact, hasn't that been the issue these past few weeks? That you no longer care about *my* feelings?" She stood up and paced around the room. Miller flinched whenever she moved close to his chair. "I left home in the middle of the night to come here," Katie said. "The middle of the night! Oh, God, Miller I was so worried. I was worried about *you*. Can you imagine that? Isn't that absurd? I thought you had gone crazy, that you were here lonely and depressed and scared—yes, scared—and that maybe I was being unfair to you, Miller. *Unfair*." She laughed that strange theatrical laugh that Miller had never before heard from her. " And then I walk in at eight A.M. and find this." Then, without warning, she lunged at him, flailing at him with her fists, throwing her weight behind the punches so hard that she fell to her knees. "No," she screamed when he tried to help her up, "don't touch me, don't you ever touch me again." She gave him a final, abortive shove and ran out of the room and down the steps to the driveway.

Stunned, Miller sat for a minute on the floor and then he heard Katie slam the car door and start the engine. Somehow Miller managed to pick himself up and run after her. But when she saw him coming down the steps she threw the gear into forward, gunned the motor, and headed straight for him. The car came hurtling across the small sand dune at the foot of the wooden stairway. Miller stood frozen, unbelieving. He held onto the railing and braced himself for the jolt, but the dune slowed the momentum of the car so that only the first five or six steps were smashed. Yet the impact was strong enough to shake the entire structure of the porch. The steps beneath him swayed, and Miller put one hand against the side of the house and held onto the rail with the other. It was like being in an earthquake. There was a sickening screech of wood being ripped away from nails as Katie backed the car away from the wreckage, pulling the bottom step askew with her fender. Miller held on for the next attack, but Katie spun her wheels in the sand and then careened out of the driveway. He heard the scream of her tires as she swerved onto the bridge and then a long silence.

Miller dropped down on the steps and the whole stairway pulled a good six inches away from the house. Overhead, the sun was burning hotter, but Miller shivered and hugged his arms around himself. After a while he was able to hear the other, usual sounds of the beach—waves falling against the sand, seagulls screeching, the whine of a motorboat. He held his head in his hands and sat waiting for someone or something to save him from himself. He was so still that a chameleon raced across his foot.

He heard footsteps in the house above and Adra came to the porch door and opened the screen. "I made coffee," she said. When Miller didn't answer, she closed the door and went back inside the house. Miller sat there, his head in his hands, trying to make sense of things. He could hear Adra talking to Sister, the dull clatter of plates being laid out. The baby fussed a little and then settled down. Then Miller heard the radio come on in the house next door. It was a Myrtle Beach station. The weather reporter announced the expected temperatures and the wind and tides predicted for that day. When Miller stood up, the stairway shook dangerously, but it held as he started up toward the back porch and whatever remaining surprises the rest of the day would bring.

Dazed, he walked into the kitchen and sat down at the table. Adra had already poured him a cup of coffee, and when he picked it up, it felt cold. Adra stood at the stove with her back toward Miller. She pushed a spatula under the fish frying in the pan. "You cleaned the fish?" Miller said.

"Jimmy Duane taught me how. He was a good one for fishing but not for cleaning." She kept her head down and her voice low, as if any sudden sound or movement would disrupt the balance in the room.

Miller pushed the coffee cup away and looked out the window. The sun was suspended over the horizon like a bright silver ball. He was surprised that it had climbed only halfway in the sky. It was not even nine A.M. yet, and so much had already happened that morning. In retrospect, the pain he had awakened with earlier now seemed prescient. He could not believe that Adra seemed to be ignoring the incident with Katie. At the very least, she could turn around and face him. He waited while she stirred the grits and turned the flame down under the fish. Finally it was too much for him. "What in the hell is wrong with you, Adra?"

Adra flinched, hunching her shoulders as if to protect herself.

"I cannot believe," Miller said, "that after what happened here this morning—Katie insulting you, then running her car into the goddamned *house—the goddamned fucking house*—that you can pretend that everything is all right, everything is fine. I mean you're serving me *coffee,* like there's nothing *wrong*. There *is* something wrong, Adra. *Everything* is wrong."

Her voice was guarded. "I'm not pretending nothing."

"*Anything,*" said Miller. "You're not pretending *anything.*"

Adra's head dropped back. She appeared to be looking toward the ceiling. "That's what I said."

"Jesus Christ, I can't believe this. Are you missing some part of your emotional makeup? Did Jimmy Duane beat that out of you too?" Miller slammed his fist down on the table.

The baby howled and Adra gripped the edge of the counter with both hands. Miller noticed the flat splayed ends of her fingers, the rough, bitten nails. "She was pretty," Adra blurted out. "Katie was real pretty."

"Adra, for God's sake. What does that have to do with anything?"

"She called me a whore. Before you came up from the beach, she called me a whore and asked me if you had been coming around to see me before."

"Before what?"

"Before Jimmy Duane died."

"Oh, Jesus," Miller moaned. "What did you say to her?"

"Nothing, I didn't say nothing." She started tending to things on the stove. Her back seemed vulnerable.

"Turn around, goddamit," Miller said. "Do you know *anything at all* about double negatives?"

Adra turned around slowly. Her eyes were filled with tears.

Miller pushed his chair back and as he started toward her, she shrank against the refrigerator, her hand against her cheek as if expecting a blow. "No," Miller said. "No."

Adra slid to the floor, her arms crossed above her head. "Don't," she cried. "Please. Don't hit me. I'm sorry, I'm sorry. I'll do better, I swear I will. I'll do whatever you tell me."

"No, Adra, no, oh God no, I wasn't going to hurt you." Miller grabbed her elbows and pulled her up against him and buried his face in her hair. "I would never hurt you," he whispered. "I would never, ever, hit you." He sank into a chair and pulled her down on his lap. "Oh, baby, I'm so, so sorry. I'm only angry at myself. Can't you understand that? I've made such a mess of everything. I've made everybody crazy and miserable." He stroked her hair and felt her trembling against his chest. "Okay, I guess I *was* a little angry at you because I see how you avoid things, how you deny them, to keep from being hurt. But I understand that now, see? I've been doing it, too. I've been denying so many things I can't even sort out what's true and what's a lie any more." He lifted her hand to his mouth and kissed her palm, then each of her fingers.

"What did I do wrong?" she asked. "Tell me and I'll fix it. I'll change."

He had to laugh then. *How could she not know?* "Don't you understand what happened here a while ago? Didn't you hear the crash? That terrible noise? Katie tried to run me down with her car. She wrecked the steps, for Christ's sake. You *must* have seen that when you came out on the porch."

Adra lay motionless against him. She seemed not to breathe.

"Well, didn't you?" Miller asked.

She burrowed closer, as if she could escape his anger by hiding inside the shadows of his very body.

"Any other woman would have screamed, or—I don't know—cried, or something, run down to examine the damage. You ignored it."

She said nothing.

"Why?" he insisted.

Her voice was almost inaudible. "It's none of my business, I figured."

He cupped her chin and tilted her head so that she had to look at him. "Oh yes, Adra, it is your business. It is *our* business, yours and mine now." Her eyes were wet, staring into his, but her dark pupils seemed closed to light and comprehension. Miller leaned forward and kissed her eyelids and then her mouth. He moved his hands gently against her ribs. When he looked over Adra's shoulder he noticed smoke from the stove. "Oh my God," he cried, "the fish are burning."

Adra jumped up and both of them rushed to turn off the burners. Adra was laughing and crying at the same time. "It's okay," Miller said. "We can scrape them off. It's okay. And honey, please, for God's sake, pick up that baby and make her stop crying."

Miller took over as cook while Adra calmed Sister, and after breakfast he sent Adra upstairs to get her bathing suit. While he ran water in the sink for the dishes, he thought about what he must do later—drive into Georgetown for lumber to repair the steps, find a pay telephone to call home later in the evening to make sure Katie had gotten there safely. What else? Fix his life. Somehow fix his life.

When Adra came down with the baby, she stood watching him for a minute. "Miller," she said softly, "what did you mean by that?"

"By what, Adra?"

She shifted the baby in her arms. "What's a double negative?"

He put his arms around her, enclosing her and the child in one embrace. "Nothing you need to worry about, sweetheart," he said, kissing her forehead, "absolutely nothing."

On the beach Miller carried Sister on his shoulders and held onto Adra's hand. When they passed the beach umbrella of the couple next door, the old man looked up and waved. "Did you hear that commotion this morning?" he asked.

Miller felt invulnerable behind his dark sunglasses. "This morning? What time?"

"Just after I saw you on the beach. A crash of some kind."

Miller shrugged and tightened his hold on Adra's hand. "I missed that," Miller said, and kept walking. Out of the corner of his eye he saw that Adra was biting her lip to keep from giggling.

By the time they were halfway down to the north end of the island, the wind was gusting and the sky was darkening to the south. "Better turn back," Miller said. The horizon looked leaden now. A dark line defined the separation of sea and sky. Just as they were turning around a flash of lightning stabbed the water far out at sea.

Adra pulled at his hand. "We have to go back," she said. "My cousin died of lightning."

"Your cousin *died* of it?" Miller said. He could not quite believe it. "How?" He ran close behind Adra, juggling the baby, who was beginning to cry again.

Adra's voice bounced with every footfall. She was short of breath. "She was standing by the window, washing Sunday dishes, and lightning came in the window and hit the water in the dish pan."

"I didn't know that was possible," Miller said.

"She died, I tell you," Adra said, her eyes wide. "I ain't lying."

"I know you're not lying," Miller said. "Wait, slow down. The storm is still pretty far out to sea."

But she ran on. "Hurry," she said. "Hurry."

Miller struggled after her. By the time the first raindrops hit, the baby was hysterical. Now Miller, too, began to feel vulnerable to the lightning. He remembered his father telling him that when a man is struck by lightning in some parts of Africa, his body is left to rot where it falls, on the assumption that his death is retribution for some misdeed he has committed. He ran faster, cradling the baby against his chest.

The rain gathered itself into a slashing sheet, and with each crash of thunder, Adra shrieked. By the time they finally came to the path to their house, Miller's heart was pounding. *Maybe God is out to get me.* His footsteps squeaked against the wet sand as he ran toward the porch. Once inside the door, Adra backed up against the kitchen wall and started to cry.

Miller hurried into the bathroom for towels. He wrapped one around the baby and handed her to Adra and then he draped one over Adra's shoulders and began to dry her hair. She was sobbing. "Hush," Miller whispered. "Hush, hush. You're safe now." Just above the roof, thunder crashed and a bolt of lightning lit up the whole room. Adra screamed in terror. "Sit down," Miller ordered. He grabbed her arms and eased her onto the corner sofa, away from the window, then sat down next to her and held her in the tight circle of his arms. "Shhh, shhh," he said, "you're okay now. You're safe with me." Adra let her head fall against his shoulder but her eyes remained wide open. The baby continued to cry softly.

Finally the lightning moved up the beach and the thunder rumbled toward the north, making a worrisome sound like some fractious old man having the last word in an argument. By that time, the baby was asleep. "Come on and change into something dry," Miller said, and Adra, carrying the baby, followed him up the stairs. She dressed Sister in dry clothes and tucked her into the crib. In the bedroom, she turned away from Miller to undress but he put his hands on her hips and peeled down her wet bathing suit and when she turned to face him he pulled her close to warm her with his own body. Her cold skin felt like marble, polished and cold, but then his hands, his fingertips, warmed her and when he moved across her on the bed she looked into his face and what she said frightened him because it complicated things even more.

"I love you," she said. "I love you."

14

That night, Miller called home from a pay phone outside the supermarket. Somebody picked up the telephone, but there was silence on the other end of the line. And then as soon as Miller said, "Katie? Judd?" the receiver was slammed down.

It had to be Katie, Miller thought, because Judd wouldn't have done such a thing. Unless, of course, Katie had come back and told Judd what had happened that morning at the beach. But whoever had answered, at least Miller was certain now that Katie had made it home safely. He felt relieved, but sorry that he had wounded her so badly. He hung up the phone and leaned against the warm brick wall of the supermarket. Cars whizzed by, their lights scouring the tree-lined road. The rain-washed leaves on the live oaks rippled in the disturbance of air. Miller was enveloped in a jumble of sound—car radios, distant conversation, the nasal hum of tree frogs from the patch of woods behind the market. Suddenly out of all that noise he heard a familiar voice—someone calling his name. It sounded like his father's voice. Blood pounded in his ears, and he leaned forward, peering around the side of the building, but there was no one there. He looked behind him, but the lot was empty of people. He backed up to the wall again and listened.

Maybe he was going crazy or maybe that voice was only a warning, a sign for him to slow down. If Katie wouldn't speak to him, he had no idea whether he could go home again, or whether he even wanted to. He could drive back to Knoxville that very night—he could start that minute—and talk to her, make her face him and discuss their problems. That's what a man would do who was desperate to keep his marriage together. But he stayed flattened against the wall and grasped the jutting edges of the bricks with his fingers.

When his heart was quieter, he left the wall and opened the door of his car. He sat down in the driver's seat and reviewed the events of the day. Earlier that afternoon, when Adra had declared her love for him, he had mumbled something against her throat and avoided her penetrating stare. He could not deny his insatiable hunger for her. She had a raw unfinished quality that compelled him. He nursed a fantasy that he could reshape her life, her very being, but love? He had always believed that love was a state of immersion, one in which you sacrificed yourself completely for the other person—the loved one—and lately he seemed to be too busy doing things to save himself to think about other people, even the ones he himself had placed in jeopardy.

He turned the key in the ignition, rolled down the window, and pulled out onto the roadway. Driving back across the bridge over the inlet he felt the cool breeze hit his cheek and he experienced a sudden and inexplicable euphoria. And then he realized with horror that it might actually stem from relief, relief that Katie at last knew the truth, or most of the truth, and now that Katie knew about Adra and about his quitting the job, at least he did not have to worry anymore about covering up those particular areas of his life. He laughed out loud. It seemed ironic and deceitful, but he actually felt better somehow. Freer. He could not think beyond that feeling and he could not plan beyond the remaining week and a half until he would have to go back to Knoxville and decide which pieces of his life to pick up and which to walk away from.

He pulled into the driveway of the beach house and parked the car, skirting the pile of lumber he had bought that afternoon to repair the steps. To avoid the splintered stairway, he walked around the side of the house to the kitchen entrance. Adra sat cross-legged in the dim light of the living room, her *Geographics* spread around her like a fan, as if she had arranged them in a deliberate pattern. She was wearing one of Miller's blue denim shirts, and her usually pale cheeks glowed. After the storm the sun had come out again, and they had sat on the rooftop porch most of the afternoon because Adra was hesitant to venture far from the house. Seeing her now, Miller felt a quick flush of warmth.

"Look here, Miller," she said, holding up a tattered magazine when he walked in. "This story's about the Smoky Mountains." Miller glanced at the cover. July 1979. "Don't laugh," Adra said, "but close as I live to the Smokies, I've never even been there."

Miller knelt down beside her on the floor, closed his hand around her arm and slid it down toward her small wrist. "I'll take you there, Adra. When we get back. I'll take you there, and we'll have a picnic. We'll get a carrier for Sister, and I'll take her on my back."

She gazed into his face, squinting as if to read his thoughts, then turned back to the photographs. "It's best in the fall," Miller went on, "when the leaves change color. October. I want you to see it then. I want to show you everything. I want you to share all the things I love with me." He thought, *I want your past, your present, and your future. I want to write your life over, leaving Jimmy Duane out of the whole scenario. The baby, too.*

"Oh well," Adra said finally, "it's best not to plan for the future sometimes, ain't it?" She caught herself. "Idn't it?"

Miller lifted her dark hair and kissed the place where it gathered thickly in a point at the base of her neck. Then he slid his arm around her waist and pressed her ribs with his fingertips, as if he might memorize her very structure. He closed his eyes and pulled her into the space between his knees and bent over her, feeling the sharply defined topography of her body.

She did not speak. She seemed not even to breathe. She was waiting for him to make a move as she always waited.

Miller, his eyes still shut, closed his hands around the crown of her head and slid them down, across her cheeks, her shoulders, along the curve of her waist and the slight slope of her hips. "This is mine," he thought. "She loves me. I should be happy." He felt gratitude and, at the same time, something like pity. Adra's deprivations seemed enormous. How could it be, he wondered, that she had not seen, only thirty miles from her home, the magnificent rolling mountains of the Smokies or the sudden verdant valleys, the swift creeks and the thick rhododendron? What else had her life deprived her of? She knew the lake, of course. Miller remembered how Jimmy Duane had leaned toward her, never letting go of the rope that kept him from touching her. And then he had taken that last look, as if his fate were already sealed, as if the loop in his hand were a Gordian knot fate had tied for him. And Adra, that bracelet of bruises. Her refusal to step toward Jimmy Duane must have been retribution for his wounding her, threatening the baby.

In the dark space behind his closed eyelids, Miller suddenly saw Jimmy Duane's face, the desperate twist of his mouth, the raw red lips. Something rose in his throat. Water. He was drowning. His eyes flew open and he jumped abruptly to his feet.

Even before Adra opened her eyes, she threw her hands up to protect herself.

"No," Miller yelled. "No! Don't you for Christ's sake get it, Adra? I am *not* Jimmy Duane. I am not a fucking redneck *wife* beater. I am not for God's sake going to *hit* you."

Yet he wanted to. Because wasn't it her fault that he was in this predicament? Wasn't she the one who had tempted him? Yes, he wanted to hit her just because she expected him to. He wanted to hit her because of her lack of faith in him, her lingering doubt. He wanted to hit her for making him desire her, for chasing Katie away, for alienating Judd, and for precipitating his decision about his job. He wanted to hit her for being poor and ignorant, for bearing that child who looked so much like Jimmy Duane Goodfriend. He wanted to hit her because he needed to hit someone or something and at that moment she was the most likely and accessible victim.

Fear boiled up in him, fear of all his possible dark capabilities and his innate and untapped weaknesses. Because no amount of education or logic could dispel the basic animal instincts he felt emerging in his soul. He bounded up the steps to the bedroom and rooted in the closet for his duffel bag. He had hidden the bottle of whiskey in the zippered side pocket. Just in case, he had told himself when he packed. Just in case. And this was it.

When he rushed through the living room again on his way to the beach, he saw Adra from the corner of his eye, still crumpled on the floor against the sofa. The reflection of the lamplight bounced off the coated covers of her magazines. Information. So much information. And what did it teach us in the end? he wondered. In the end, after everything else is stripped away, reduced to its smallest factor, we are left with our fears and our emotions and no tools to deal with them except for our basic instincts, the same ones the cavemen had, the same ones Jimmy Duane Goodfriend had resorted to out there in the lake that day.

Jesus. Jesus have mercy on my soul. All our souls. All of us. All.

Outside in the dark he hurtled down the sandy path to the beach. When he felt the first strong ocean breeze, he skidded to a stop and uncapped the bottle. He dropped to his knees and took a long draft of the whiskey.

Now he could understand why Jimmy Duane had clung to him so tenaciously. When you are going under, you will grab at anything, anything that might save you, anything that might keep you afloat a little longer. He himself had discarded all the things that had pulled him down—Katie, Judd, the job—and he was clinging now to Adra because she represented a fresh life, a new start. Adra and the whiskey. Both were warm and liquid. Both offered change, comfort, promise.

A mosquito planted its stinger in his neck and he swatted at it, then pushed his finger into the bottle, tilted it, and rubbed the alcohol against the bite. When he had drunk the last of the whiskey, he shed his clothes on the steps and walked naked down to the water. He plunged into the cold dark waves. Sharks? Fuck them. If they took him, they took him. Amen. So be it. He swam straight out toward the horizon until his arms ached and then he floated for a while. As his vision became accustomed to the dark, he noticed luminous forms in the water below him and beyond the sandbar, the lacy caps of waves. He watched the bobbing lights of the houses on the shore, focusing on the light of the bedroom where he had slept with Adra and, in past years, with Katie as well. *Ah God he was a terrible human being.* He recalled reading something about Jonathan Swift, as he deteriorated into dementia. His last words as he was dying were, "I am a fool." Maybe he was, too. A fool.

The rhythm of the water lulled him as he floated on the swells. He thought how comforting it might be to drift until you were too far out to return to shore and then in that last moment, before you could change your mind, to drink deeply of the salty sea, to fill your belly and throat with water and slowly sink, letting your lungs take the last of it. For all its mysterious beauty, he thought, the sea might draw us at last to our own annihilation. His father had told him how Virginia Woolf had one day filled her pockets with stones and walked into the river near her Sussex house. He could not imagine summoning up the discipline such an act would require. You would have to be thoroughly weary of life, thoroughly. Still, for him, there would be that pinch of doubt—whether death would in fact be a forgetting or a sleep in which you forever dreamed dreams that reflected the nightmares in the darkest corners of your life. And what about the things you would lose? A woman's half-lit eyes closing beneath you, the sweet green smell of mountains, the ruffled fins of a brown trout in a clear mountain stream. He wasn't ready. Not yet.

Something, something big, broke the surface of the water and brushed against Miller's shoulder. He reacted so violently that he went under for a second and came up sputtering, thrashing his arms and legs in a frenzied rush to get to shore. Instinctively, he knew it was the worst thing he could do if it was a shark that had nudged him, but in his panic he was incapable of reason. Everything he did after that was strictly reactive. He moaned and prayed as he kicked and pulled his way to shore, he made desperate promises. When his feet touched bottom, he ran the rest of the way in to the shore, fighting the weight of the water that pulled against his legs. He fell exhausted on the wet sand and lay there shaking and coughing up salt water.

When he woke a while later he was cold and his body was covered with insect bites. The tide was licking at his feet. He sat up and turned to look at the beach house. He saw that the bedroom light was extinguished now. The house was a dark shadow shouldered against the dunes. He collected his clothes and dragged himself up the path. He stepped into the outside shower and rinsed off, letting the cold water sting his wounded skin. Then he found a damp towel on the clothesline and dried himself the best he could. Finally he went inside, moving naked through the rooms. He hesitated outside the open door where Adra slept, then moved on. In the dark he groped his way into the empty bedroom that faced the marsh side of the road and fell heavily onto the bare mattress.

Adra emerged from the dimness and stood at the foot of the bed. Miller saw her as ghostly and ethereal in her nakedness, a pale portrait in the rough white frame of the doorway. He lay still as she approached the bed. For a long time she stood looking at him and then she held out her hand. Finally he reached up and took her fingers in his and followed her along the dim hallway. She pulled him down onto the bed and he folded her into his arms and the last thing he remembered hearing her say before he fell asleep was, "You should have hit me. That would have been easier."

15

So then there was the problem of going home. Years before, Miller had thought that when you grew up, you could invent yourself as the person you thought you should be or could be, maybe the person you ought to be, but it had not turned out that way. Other things had interfered—fear, desire, boredom, need, a helpless and hopeless sense of destiny.

Driving west along the interstate, he glanced over at Adra and then at the baby in the back seat. Both slept soundly. The car moved as if fueled by their slumber. As long as they sleep, Miller thought, everything will be all right. The baby won't cry. I won't have to talk to Adra. He did not want to encourage or disappoint her. He did not want to bond with a child that was not his own. He felt righteous somehow, martyred, as if his own suffering mollified the pain he had inflicted on Katie and Judd.

In the last two weeks he had stepped into a new role—protector, instructor. He had taught Adra to crab and surf-fish. He had read bedtime stories to the baby, sung lullabies, and cooked most of the meals.

When he was performing these family duties, he felt free of guilt, as if he were serving an easy penance. On the next-to-the-last day of the vacation, he had been standing in the surf holding the baby in his arms when she touched his face and babbled something that sounded like "Dada." The child's small hand on his cheek was soft and trusting. Miller looked into her face and saw across her brow the thin scar that Adra attributed to Jimmy Duane's anger. It seemed Jimmy Duane would have done anything to stop his family's crying. Yet Miller could not bring himself to love the child. She looked too much like her father.

As he drove, the landscape climbed from the flat sandy terrain of the coast to the low rolling foothills of the Smokies. Yes, they were going home, but Miller wasn't sure where home really was now. Adra lay with her head against the window, lips parted. An occasional soft little snore came from her throat. Her eyelids were paler than the rest of her face, which was bronzed now by the sun. Miller noticed the white line of her breast just beneath the neckline of her dress. Every day his hunger for her had grown, and every day she had become more dependent on him. He wanted to compensate for whatever he had taken away from her that day at the lake, but as they drove toward Knoxville, Miller began to feel a vague dissatisfaction, something that seemed to distance him from her. Adra seemed to sense it, too, because when she woke, she was irritable, almost anxious, as if something was happening beyond her control. Now, with the beach behind them, the gift delivered, Miller felt unable or unwilling to comfort her. They drove in silence.

If he left Katie and Judd, it must not be a separation based on assuaging his guilt about Adra, though there was still that factor to deal with. First he had to try to work things out with Katie, but not, absolutely not with the job. He could not make himself go back there, but the marriage—the family—was different. There was too much invested in it—blood, bones, hearts, history. And as much as he hated to admit it, the house, too.

They drove into Adra's yard just as the sun was setting. The grass was knee high and the little house looked even more forlorn than usual. When Adra stepped from the car, all the tension and the unspoken regrets of the trip surfaced, and she burst into tears. Miller clenched his jaw and silently lifted the baby from the back seat. He could not bear to go into that house with Adra. Without looking directly into her eyes, he handed her the baby and then carried the bags to the porch. She stared at him, waiting for him to say something. "You're mad at me," she cried at last. "And I don't know why. What did I do wrong?"

He shook his head. "Listen, Adra," he said, "I'm sorry. I can't explain how I feel now. It's just that I have to try to straighten things out at home somehow. Driving back, I kept thinking of everything I have to do. I know I was preoccupied, and I'm sorry."

He started to reach for her, but instead patted the baby's leg. He didn't know how to touch her now without promising too much. He was halfway down the steps when he turned around. "I'll call you, okay?" he said, and then he remembered that she had no telephone. "I mean I'll come by."

He saw that in the brief space during which he had turned his back, she had put on the wary expression she had worn a few weeks earlier, the same one Miller had seen through the screen door that first day. Under the thin layer of her sun-darkened skin, her face seemed drained of color. She stared at Miller for a second, then turned the key in the lock and went inside with the baby, leaving her suitcase on the porch and closing the door behind her, as if eager to put some sort of barrier between them.

Miller trudged down the steps and got into the car. He sat for a minute looking at the house. Adra and the baby were shut up somewhere inside it now. Fortified. He started the motor and drove slowly along the dirt road to the highway. There had been no rain while they were gone. The flowers in the field drooped or hung burnt and shriveled on their long bent stalks. Nothing had changed and he was disappointed. Somehow, he had expected things to be different.

While he drove toward home, he tried to plan what he would say to Katie. They could start over, perhaps, if Katie were willing to sell the house and go away with him. He would have to insist on that condition at least. And this was the first time, the only time in their long marriage, that Miller had strayed. Surely Katie would consider that. And Miller could try to wean himself away from Adra. He would find some way to help her but end their physical relationship.

By the time he turned into his neighborhood, his heart was hammering and his resolve had weakened. But if this wasn't what he wanted, where in the hell would he go? He could not face the memories he would have to confront by staying at his father's house, and he could not picture himself living with Adra, not in that little shack, and not with the memory of Jimmy Duane permeating the air like a vague and putrid stink. If he was going to be with Adra, he would have to move her, move the baby, and with the money situation the way it was now—no. And what about his rage that night at the beach? What about the unresolved anger he had directed toward her? If she called up that kind of darkness in him, he wouldn't be doing her any favors, either. Another thing. He wasn't ready to be a father again. He couldn't start over with another man's child. Especially not a child with Jimmy Duane's eyes.

Miller brightened a little when he saw Katie's car parked in the driveway. Elated, he started up the porch steps, his mind tripping over all the excuses he would give her to explain his behavior, but then he noticed two cardboard boxes under the window with his name scrawled across the sides. He lifted the flaps of the top one and looked inside. His clothes, his college annual, his fishing trophies. "Shit," he muttered. It was worse than he had imagined. He turned the knob of the door. Locked. He fished in his pocket for his keys. His hands were shaking. His key slid into the lock but refused to turn. As Miller shook the knob, he realized that the brass was shiny and new. He cursed and slammed his shoulder against the door. Finally he lifted the door knocker and let it fall, then started pounding with both fists. "Katie," he yelled, "let me in, damn it. I know you're in there."

He leaned against the door and listened. Silence. He wondered what Katie was doing inside, where she was standing, whether she was crying, whether she felt as frightened and lonely as he did. He pictured her flattened against the base of the staircase, holding her breath. He pounded again, then walked across the porch and tried the windows. Everything was tightly secured against him. He peered inside. The living room was slightly disordered—a sweater thrown across the sofa, newspapers piled on the floor, a dirty plate on the end table. That wasn't like Katie. He vaulted over the railing at the end of the porch and hurried around to the back door. That had a new lock, too. He didn't even bother to try it. He felt like a criminal, excluded from his old life, as if it were now official that those borders were closed to him. He looked through the French doors of the dining room but saw no one, only a slightly dusty loneliness, three or four books piled on the table, a bowl of bruised and spoiled fruit. The candle centerpiece sat in a pool of white wax. He wondered what sort of occasion had called for candlelight, and with whom. He kicked savagely at the door, nicking the paint, kicked again, and finally sprinted down the driveway and got into his car. Then he remembered the boxes. He cursed, got out, and thundered up onto the porch. "I know you're in there, Katie," he bellowed. "Open the door, damn it. Open the fucking door."

If the neighbors were watching or listening, fuck them. Finally, Miller picked up the boxes and carried them to the car. When he opened the trunk, he saw traces of sand from the beach on the carpeting and that was the thing, more than anything else, that made his throat swell up.

Once he had backed to the end of the driveway, he was uncertain whether to go left or right. Finally he headed for the interstate and pulled off at the first motel, about five miles from the house. He checked in and carried the boxes inside. The room had a sliding glass door that faced the swimming pool. He opened the curtains and looked out. About a dozen people were frolicking in the water. Children were screaming with excitement, and all the sounds echoed and reverberated against the walls of his room. He thought about calling the desk to have the room changed, but it seemed too much of an effort, and, instead, he closed the drapery and fell face down across the bed.

When he woke up it was dark and it took him a minute to get his bearings. The room smelled of years of stale cigarette smoke and everything was slightly shabby and worn. The bedspread was faded, the carpet worn thin beneath the sink. And it was unbearably hot. He had neglected to turn on the air conditioning unit. He got up, switched on a lamp, and set the unit control to *air high*. It was after nine, but he wasn't hungry. He washed his face, changed his shirt, and drove to a bar he remembered passing on his way to the motel.

He walked in and took a seat at the bar. On the tiny dance floor, two couples were moving slowly to the disk jockey's choice—an old love song that Miller vaguely remembered his mother singing, but he couldn't remember the name of it. He thought maybe it was Peggy Lee on the tape, or Julie London. Whoever she was, she was singing a song about loneliness.

Miller ordered a whiskey and spun slowly around on his stool to watch the dance floor. A woman at a table in the corner was staring at him. She looked like a nice woman, probably about his age. She was pretty. Big eyes. Shiny hair. Well dressed. Nice legs crossed at the knee. A little too classy for a place like this, but there was the reason—loneliness was stamped all over her face. She watched him while she twirled a paper coaster around and around in her fingers. Miller broke the eye contact and swivelled the seat toward the bar again. The last thing he needed in his life was another woman to complicate things. God help him. He finished off the first whiskey and almost immediately ordered another. The second drink he nursed along for a while, and by the time he finished it he felt worse. The last few swallows of the whiskey backed up in his throat. He glanced at his watch. He still had time to get his own bottle before the liquor stores closed. He would not make a practice of this, he promised himself. He could quit once his life got straightened out. He paid the bartender and nodded at the lonely woman on his way out. When he acknowledged her, she looked hopeful for a second and then when he continued to walk past her, the light went out in her eyes.

The cold air in the motel room slapped against him as soon as he opened the door. He turned the air setting down and opened the sliding glass door. Warm air poured into the room and a strong smell of chlorine stung his nostrils. The pool was empty now, with soft lights illuminating the water. Miller tucked his bottle under his arm and walked outside. He read the sign wired to the gate at the pool entrance: "No running, diving, or horseplay. No glass containers or alcohol. Swim at your own risk." He sank into one of the damp chairs by the diving board and watched the lights play off the water.

What now? he wondered. He could not stay in this place for long. He should go inside and try to figure out his financial position.

Roughly, anyway. But all the papers were at the house, and Katie wouldn't let him in. It was Saturday. On Monday he could call Jim Skinner and find out exactly what his financial situation was. He'd give him a little grief on his recent friendliness with Katie, too. Skinner was a womanizer and Miller didn't want Katie hurt. He had to laugh at that. *He didn't want Katie hurt.* He unscrewed the bottle cap and took a swallow of whiskey. As it slid down his throat, he felt the warmth of its color—amber—and he thought of Adra in the silky gold pajamas. He heard her deep, throaty laugh. He thought about her small, fragile body beneath him, the look on her face when they made love—transported, incredulous, ecstatic. For a second he entertained the idea of driving out to see her, but no, it was too late, too far, and he'd had too much to drink.

He made himself concentrate on the financial arrangements. The house figured in the assets, and if they couldn't work it out, if Katie wanted a split, he would have to give her the house, just for old time's sake. He knew that under Tennessee law, all a husband owed a wife was half the assets. He remembered hearing Jack talk about that when Nadia had threatened divorce. That was it—he could call Jack. He went back to his room and asked the operator for an outside line, but when Jack answered, Miller hung up. Because for Christ's sake what was he going to say? Where would he even begin? *Jack, I fucked up? I need some help*?

He closed the door and pulled the curtains shut and then went into the bathroom for a plastic cup. The digital clock on the bedside table said twelve thirty-five. He poured half a glass of whiskey, sat down on the floor beside one of the boxes Katie had left on the porch and started pulling things out—the high school and college annuals, fishing trophies, personal things Katie probably didn't want to look at. At the bottom of the first box he found the love letters he had written to her when he was away at school. She had saved them all those years. They were tied together with a faded blue satin ribbon. So she was really serious, then, throwing away the past, erasing his presence in her house and heart. He opened the first one, hating the cramped and guarded scrawl of his youth, but he could get no farther than the first line. He refolded the letter and slid it back into its envelope, pushed the envelope back beneath the blue ribbon and laid the packet aside. At the bottom of the box was an old album of his father's, one Miller had found in Hollis's dresser drawer when he died. Inside were photographs of his parents together, of Miller as a baby and schoolboy, of his mother in her stage costumes, another of Evelyn Donaldson with Miller as a teenager. There was a picture of his parents on their wedding day, their smiles innocent and naive. *How could they have known?* He had to look at photographs to remember his mother now—it had been so long—but his father's face was imprinted on his memory—two deep horizontal lines etched across the broad plane of his forehead, two vertical marks between his brows. From the corner of each eye, four or five lines radiating outward toward his temples. Long upper lip. Mouth full and friendly. Fleshy pockets beneath the crinkled eyes. Blue eyes like Miller's.

Miller turned the page to an early photograph taken when he was about nine years old. He and his parents were standing in front of a beach house where they used to go in the summers. Another tourist must have snapped the picture. Miller's father had his hand on Miller's shoulder, but his mother stood slightly apart with her arms crossed, a serious expression on her face. The little house was situated at the end of a barrier island wooded with palmettos and pine trees, and in the evenings deer came out of the woods. His mother used to sit on the deck—very still—and hold out carrots or lettuce for them. For those thirty or forty minutes every evening at sunset, she seemed happy. Once, when the deer were visiting, Hollis accidentally let the screen door slam and the deer fled, leaping over shrubs like startled ballet dancers. His mother cried and would not speak to either of them for the rest of the evening, not even Miller, who had been lying in the hammock watching her. The next morning Miller followed her out to the beach and walked about ten yards behind her, stepping carefully into each of her footprints, which he imagined were still warm. He wanted her to explain why she was so angry. At one point she turned her head and looked at him but said nothing. She just kept walking, until Miller gave up and sat down in the sand, watching her retreating figure disappear out of sight at the curve of the beach where the marsh emptied into the ocean.

Miller closed the album and laid it back in the box. Then he put the other things back—the trophies, the letters, clothing. He did not even open the second box. This fraction of his belongings—the part that contained the most memories—Katie had meant to be symbolic, he felt sure. She had packed up hundreds of memories intended to inspire guilt and punish him.

He poured another glass from the bottle and turned on the television set. Then he lay down on the bed. The comedian on the screen blurred and disappeared and a few hours later Miller woke to the cadence of an early morning exercise program on the television set and the sound of people splashing in the pool outside. His head was throbbing, and when he sat up he felt nauseated. He rummaged in his luggage, but the aspirin bottle in his shaving kit was empty. He couldn't imagine why he hadn't thrown the bottle away, but then Katie usually did things like that for him when they returned from trips. On the chance that cold water would help clear his head, he put on his bathing suit, which was still damp and musty from the beach, and stumbled out to the pool. People stared. He must have looked dangerous, with his ragged beard and the rumpled bathing suit, but he walked to the deep end of the pool and jumped in, feet first, and let himself sink to the bottom. Submerged, he opened his eyes and looked up through the layers of water, at the white legs and kicking feet of the swimmers above, and then he pulled himself along the floor of the pool, which was patterned in diamonds of light and the shadows of forms floating on the surface. By the drain, several coins and a room key wavered against the white tile. He picked up the key, then dropped it again. The longer he held his breath, the worse his head hurt. When he came up against the wall at the shallow end of the pool he pressed his temples. He let the water buoy him to the surface, and he floated, the sun in his eyes and the cool water cradling him.

Jimmy Duane is drown-ded, Jimmy Duane is drown-ded.

He swam to the side, pulled himself out of the pool, and hurried back to his room. Shivering in the cool air, he pulled some wrinkled clothes from his suitcase and dressed. Then he picked up the telephone and dialed Jim Skinner's office number, and when the answering machine kicked in, he remembered it was Sunday. He had told Adra he would come by, and she would be expecting him, but he hadn't said *when*, had he? And that was lucky because he couldn't go, not yet, and at that particular moment he had no idea how soon it might be.

There was nothing left to do then but turn on the television set. He didn't even know what he was watching, but it had the sound of human voices and it was comforting enough to put him to sleep for the rest of the afternoon. For now, that was enough to get him through another day.

16

As a divorced man, Jim Skinner, Miller's accountant, was often cast as the eligible bachelor at Katie's parties. Miller and Katie had seen a lot of Jim in the past few years, mostly at the club. He was always with a new woman, and lately, that woman was younger and younger.

On Monday afternoon Miller sat in the leather chair across from Jim's desk, waiting while Jim shuffled through the papers in his portfolio. Miller waited, tapping his fingers on the arm of his chair. The headache he'd wakened with the day before still hung on stubbornly. He was eager to get this over with. "So what are the damages, Jim?" he asked.

"Damages?" Jim looked up from the papers. "Hell, Miller, you and Katie are in great financial shape, my friend. Right now, despite the present economy, you have very respectable assets, good solid investments in mutual funds and municipal bonds, IRAs, a good retirement program for you at the plant and a decent enough one for Katie at the university. On top of that, your house is almost paid for and it's worth—what? maybe three or four hundred thousand in today's market? Four-fifty? Then there's your dad's property. And you and Katie still have almost twenty earning years ahead of you before retirement. No, Miller, you have no damages at all." He leaned back in his chair and smiled. "What's up? Somebody trying to sell you a foolproof investment opportunity?" He took off his horn-rimmed glasses and held them up to the light.

Miller leaned forward. "What are the prospects without the retirement program? I mean, what if I take out what I've invested so far? How would the future look without additional investment?"

"Forget it, Miller." Jim put the glasses on again and tapped the end of his pencil on the desk for emphasis. "Look, the way you two live—if you want to maintain your present standard of living—you don't even want to *think* about retirement until you're sixty-two. Uh uh, Miller. You and Katie stick out your jobs for another fifteen, twenty years, and you can set your own agenda—travel, play golf, tennis, maybe buy a little retirement condo and still have enough to leave Judd a nice nest egg. And hell, Miller, the way the economy is going, you're going to need at least two million in the nest by the time you're ready to hang the job up."

"You didn't answer my question, Jim. I said, what about the future *without* the retirement program? What are the alternatives?"

"Christ, Miller, you're not thinking of quitting."

"No, not thinking."

Jim laughed. "Thank God."

"Not thinking," Miller repeated. "It's a done deal."

Jim looked stunned. "Jesus Christ, man. You *quit*? What, are you *crazy*?"

Miller smiled. "Some people seem to think so."

"What does Katie say about this?"

"I thought she might have told you."

Jim's face reddened. "Why would Katie have told *me*?"

Miller shrugged. "You two are spending a lot of time together lately."

Jim fidgeted with the silver pen on his desk. "Sure, we play a few rounds of golf together from time to time, maybe have a drink afterward, but all she's said is that things aren't so good between you right now. Jesus, Miller, this explains everything. Look, you're in management. You can probably get the job back. It will take a while to do a job search to replace you. You know, with equal opportunity and all those federal guidelines. Why didn't you talk to me about this before you took such a drastic step?"

"It was my decision to make, Jim. You're my accountant, not my muse. And anyway, it's irrevocable. Not from the company's standpoint. From mine. I'm not going back."

"But why, Miller? What in the hell?"

"It's a long story, Jim. And I have a pounding headache. All I want to know is what assets I have right now, or what I *will* have if I have to give Katie half."

"You mean *divorce*? Jesus, Miller."

Miller looked out the window. His head hurt when he nodded. "Maybe. I guess it's sort of up to her at this point."

Jim pushed back his chair and walked around his desk. He put his hand on Miller's shoulder. "Miller, you folks need to get some guidance here—a marriage counselor, a psychiatrist—something. Jesus, I thought you had a great marriage. I mean, you two were always the model couple for everybody else, you know what I mean? Okay, so Katie did mention to me that you're having a little trouble, but hell, she didn't give me a clue that it was this serious."

Miller felt strangely detached. "Well, sometimes you get surprised in this life, Jim." He moved his shoulder just enough for Jim to get the message that he wanted him to take his hand away. "What I need from you right now is a ballpark estimate on what I have without the house and half of everything else we own."

Jim sighed and went back to the papers. "You do know that in this state everything is divided equally between the parties unless some other personal agreement is arrived at."

"Yeah, I know that. But I'm not going to pull the rug out from under Katie. I owe her this, Jim. I don't want to hurt her anymore."

Jim raised an eyebrow. "Let me work on it and get back to you, okay? But even if you did decide to get a lump sum from your company's retirement program, you have to reinvest that, Miller. If you don't, you have to pay capital gains, and at the standard of living you have now, and today's economy, how long do you think this money is going to last you, even if it's close to a million? Unless of course you have another job lined up." A smile flashed across his face, as if a joke had been played on him. "That's it, isn't it, Miller? You have something else lined up." He laughed. "You really had me going there for a minute, buddy."

Miller sighed. "Jim, no. I do not have something else lined up. What I'm toying with is the idea of moving to the beach, opening a bait shop."

Jim exhaled sharply, as if somebody had stuck a pin in him. "Miller, you're shitting me."

Miller ignored that. How many times could he tell the man? "I wouldn't need much to live on now. It's later, I guess, that I have to worry about. When I get old. If I should get sick. If I got married again."

Jim blinked, then regained his composure. "We're talking retirement homes, long-term care maybe, disability, Medicare, Miller. For you, maybe Medicaid, if you're not careful. Anyway, we definitely need to talk long-term disability insurance."

Miller stood up. Even that small effort sent the pain screaming to the top of his head. He grimaced.

"You must have tied one on this weekend," Jim said. "You look pretty awful." He came around the desk again and laid his arm across Miller's shoulders. "How's Judd taking this?"

Miller shrugged off the arm. "We haven't talked yet." He edged toward the door. "Well, thanks, Jim. This is all I needed for today. Things might change, depending on what Katie decides to do."

Jim moved as if to hug Miller's shoulder again, but Miller backed away. "And you can rest assured, Miller," Jim said, "that I'll help Katie through this. Financially, I mean, if you guys can't work things out. I hope to God you do. Divorce is hell. But when Wanda and I split up, I saw that she was fixed for life, and we still do business together, even though she's remarried." He grabbed Miller's hand and pumped it vigorously. "Count on me, Miller. Okay, buddy? Okay?"

Miller nodded and put his hand on the doorknob.

"You're crazy. You know that, don't you, Miller?" Jim said. "I mean, your wife is a beautiful woman. Vital, and if you don't mind my saying, very desirable."

Miller looked him in the eye. "The truth is, I do mind your saying that, Jim. Under the circumstances, it doesn't seem to be in particularly good taste."

"I didn't mean anything by it, guy," Jim said. "I just meant that, well, if it were me . . ."

"Yeah, well, it isn't you, Jim," Miller said. He pushed the door open and walked out. But Skinner didn't know when to quit. He leaned out into the hallway and called to Miller's retreating back, "Hey, where's that beard going, friend? I know a good barber who can shape it up for you."

Miller kept walking. He headed for the stairs instead of the elevator and ran all the way down all seven flights.

When he got back to the motel room he opened the second box from Katie and found his mail. There was a letter from his boss at the plant expressing concern for his leaving and another from the bookkeeper saying that Miller had neglected to fill out the requisite exit papers. She had enclosed the necessary forms, but they looked too complicated for Miller to bother with at the moment. There were a few other letters—one reminding him of his twenty-fifth high school reunion the following week, and another telling him his *Atlantic* subscription was due to be renewed. Beneath the mail, his clothing was thrown in haphazardly, all wrinkled and creased. Well, that was okay. He wouldn't be dressing up much for a while.

He put the letters from the office back into the box. Then he called the house—he could no longer think of it as *home*—and left a message for Katie saying that he needed to talk about money. He couldn't blame her for whatever grievances she harbored against him, he added, and he wanted to make it easy for her—she could have whatever she wanted. And even if they couldn't work it out, she'd need money in the meantime. He left his motel room telephone number and asked her to call and suggest a time they could meet. "I want to talk to Judd, too," he added, but the recording timer had already cut him off.

He needn't have worried about Katie having enough money, though. When he went to the bank later that afternoon, he discovered that she had withdrawn thirty thousand of the forty thousand they had in their joint savings account. She didn't call, either, not that day or the next. Miller drove by the house a couple of times, but when he knocked on the door, nobody would answer, even when Katie's or Judd's car was parked in the driveway. He thought about going by the club in order to talk to Judd, but the prospect of facing the people he knew there was too daunting, and it would probably be embarrassing for Judd.

On Thursday afternoon he was lying on the bed in the motel room when the telephone rang. His heart raced. Katie was the only one who had the number. His voice sounded hoarse when he said hello, and he realized that he had not spoken to another human being since ordering breakfast in the dining room that morning. It wasn't Katie, though. It was Gina Carson, Katie's real estate friend. Re-Phil's wife.

"How did you get this number?" Miller asked.

"From Katie. Don't be angry, Miller. I asked her if I could call you, and she said she wouldn't mind."

"Wouldn't mind what?"

"My calling you about real estate. Honestly, Miller, aren't you just sick of living in that nasty old motel? Aren't you in the market for an apartment?"

Miller sat up and propped a pillow behind his back. "Do you know something I don't know? I mean, did Katie tell you she wasn't letting me back in? Ever?"

Gina's laugh was low and provocative. "Of course not, silly. But with what's happened between you and Katie, I think she needs some time alone, and I have the afternoon free and a couple of real nice furnished places have come up as available on the computer. Either one would be great temporary digs for a bachelor type."

Miller laughed.

"Is that a yes?"

"A laugh is not a yes," he said.

"But could it be?"

Miller shook his head. The woman had incredible gall. "Let me get this straight. You're supposed to be Katie's friend, and you're setting me up in an apartment instead of hoping we'll get back together."

"Look at it this way, Miller. You'd be more comfortable in an apartment and I would make a nice commission and Katie wouldn't be so worried about you."

"If she's so damned worried, why won't she answer my calls?"

"Oh Miller, you know women. They have to be ready. She's hurt. Correct that. She's *devastated.* We've talked several times and I can tell you she absolutely is not ready to talk to you. And in the meantime, you're stuck there in a motel without any view or privacy or a kitchen or anything. Come on, Miller, *please* say yes. Pretty please. I'm so *bored* this afternoon. I need to get out of the office. It's a slow day. Let me at least take you around to these two places. You don't have to make a commitment, just look. It'll do you good to get out."

"No."

"What about Judd?"

"What does Judd have to do with it?"

"Well, during this period of—separation—you need a place to visit with Judd, don't you? I mean, you don't want him coming to a depressing old motel room to visit you, do you?"

Miller hesitated. He hadn't thought of that. "What are these places that you have in mind?"

"They're both furnished. The owner of one—that's Arthur dePier of the dePier Art Gallery—is in Europe for several months and he wants somebody to water the plants, feed the cats, make sure the place is secure. The other belongs to a university professor who's away on sabbatical. He's paying double rent and he needs the money."

Miller sighed. After all, what else did he have to do? "What time?"

"Thirty minutes," Gina said. Miller could already hear her bustling, jangling her car keys, rattling computer printouts, possibly applying fresh lipstick. "I'll pick you up in front of the lobby. I know where the motel is."

"One thing," Miller said.

"What, sugar?"

"Can you bring me something for a headache?"

Gina laughed. "See you in thirty minutes, pain reliever in hand."

As soon as Miller hung up he was reviling himself for accepting the proposition. He didn't even know for sure if Katie was really adamant about his not coming home. He dialed her work number to ask her in person, and as soon as she recognized his voice she hung up.

"The hell with it," he said, and went into the bathroom to wash his face. "The hell with her, the hell with everything."

Gina's generous body seemed to dominate her little red sports car. Her breasts spilled around the confines of the seat belt that crossed her chest like a beauty queen's banner. She wore an emerald green linen dress and dyed-to-match shoes, a fashion idiosyncrasy that Miller had always thought was reserved for weddings. Gina was something of an enigma. She seemed outdated, but somehow bigger than life. Her face was bronzed with some sort of artificial tanning simulator, and her green eyes sparkled beneath her thickly coated lashes. Her lids were brushed with an iridescent gold. In general, she exuded vibrant health, enthusiasm, and energy, to say nothing of an overwhelming sexuality. As soon as Miller was secured in the car, a captive passenger strapped in with his seat belt, Gina seemed to wind up even more. She peeled out of the parking lot and started weaving in and out of traffic. "I'm going to show you both places, Miller," she said, missing the pristine fender of a white Mercedes by mere inches. "But I think you'll like the professor's place better than Arthur's." She patted his knee. "I could be wrong, but I can usually read people's needs pretty accurately. Did you know I'm in the Million Dollar Club? Top seller in my firm." She went on without waiting for his reply. "Still, I want you to see Arthur's apartment because the view is so spectacular. It's up on Cherokee Bluff, overlooking the river. I mean, the view alone counteracts the negative aspects of the French Empire."

"French Empire?" Miller said.

"Yes. The furniture. Oh you know French Empire, Miller. All those busy motifs—swords and spears, stars, sphinxes. Little bees, rosettes carved into the furniture." She laughed and wrinkled her small, perfect nose, and Miller found himself wondering if it was the same nose she'd been born with. "I love the way Arthur says it—the French way, you know," Gina bubbled. "*Om-pier.* Arthur's, well, you-know-what. Which is fine, of course. I mean, I have nothing against that sort of thing. But I've always preferred people of the *opposite* sex." She fluttered a hand in the air. "But there's another attraction. To his apartment, I mean. Arthur has one of those wonderful tented bedrooms that makes you feel as if you were back in the Napoleonic era."

"A tented bedroom?" The powdered headache remedy Gina had brought him was beginning to work, but it had set his heart to pounding and he felt a little dizzy. "Well, Gina, I will admit to you that at the moment, I would rather be any place in time but here in my present life, so if it takes the Napoleonic era to get me out of my predicament, it might be worth looking at."

Gina's laugh at first seemed attractive but went on much too long. She patted Miller's knee, and that went on a little too long as well. "We'll go to Arthur's place first," she said, "but I think the professor's house has much better vibrations."

"Vibrations?"

"It's the color," Gina said. "You know, feng shui." She rounded the corner on two wheels. "Colors have vibrations. It's amazing, but most people don't even know that. I mean they just walk into a paint store and pick out colors without any thought of how they might affect their spiritual and emotional lives. Oh Miller, I could tell you stories. The places I've *seen* in this business. God. For instance, walls. Take walls. How many people know that you need light colors on your walls to keep trouble from accumulating in rooms? My God, I see dark green walls, navy walls. Black. Black, Miller. Oh, don't laugh, it's absolutely true. Do you know anything about feng shui? It's an Oriental thing. You're supposed to arrange furniture and rooms and color to produce positive energy. Like yellow. Now, yellow is very good. Yellow magnifies light, and sunlight is restorative and energizing. So yellow rooms can make you happy. But the real secret of a place is in the vibrations from the foundation. If there's a problem there, you're going to have bad luck, you're going to have illness, you're going to have money problems, you're going to have divorce, the whole shebang. I mean, if you live in a place with bad vibrations, you can bring complete ruin upon yourself and your family." She frowned and put her hand on his knee again. Miller felt the heat of her palm through his rumpled khaki slacks. "Oh dear," she said, "I just now realized that I really ought to go over to Katie's and study the atmosphere. It could very well be the cause of all this instability in your life, Miller."

Miller had to bite his lip to keep from laughing. If he did, he might not be able to stop. It would be the same kind of scene that had occurred in Buckman's office.

As soon as they walked into Arthur dePier's sumptuous apartment, Miller felt claustrophobic, and even before he saw the first cat, he recognized the sharp, distinctive smell of litter boxes. In both the kitchen and the bathroom, they were full to overflowing. Gina deftly guided him away. "Now before you make a hasty decision," she said, "let me show you the rest of the place." She took his arm and led him into the bedroom and waved her hand with a flourish. "*Ta da*," she sang. Miller looked up. What looked to be hundreds of yards of red brocade were draped from a single focal point on the ceiling. With all that fabric, Miller found it difficult to get his bearings. It was like being lost in a Middle Eastern piece goods store.

Gina pointed toward the wall behind the bed. "Now, see, this is exactly the kind of thing I mean. What direction would you say the bed is facing, Miller?"

"East, I think. Yes. Definitely east."

"Exactly," said Gina. "You see? That's why Arthur's business is failing. If only he had asked me. My God, everyone knows the head of the bed should always face north and the foot south."

"Bad vibrations?" Miller said.

Gina squeezed his arm. "You learn fast, Miller. Bad vibrations." With her hand still on his arm, she closed her eyes and drew in her breath, causing her already generous chest to expand even further. "Just let yourself go for a minute, Miller. No, not like that. Breathe here." She placed her hand on his diaphragm. "Try to feel the vibrations in this room. Trust me, Miller. You should never make a real estate decision without testing vibrations."

"I don't need to test vibrations, I already know I hate this place." Miller eased himself out of her grasp. When he turned to leave, he tripped over a Siamese cat that had settled on the rug near his feet. "He went off and left his cats here?" Miller said.

"Well, I promised I'd take care of them," Gina explained. "I'm over this way just about every day."

"So the cats come with the place? No thanks," Miller said.

"Wait," Gina called as Miller headed for the front door. "You haven't tried the bed." She leaned over and pushed a long-haired white cat off one of the pillows.

"The bed?" Miller said. His stomach contracted in a sudden painful cramp.

"Yes, try it. I mean, the bed can easily be moved to correct the vibrations, Miller, and this is such a wonderful bed. Believe me, Arthur has only the best of everything." She sat down on the edge of the mattress and tugged at Miller's hand. "New mattress, too. Just test it," she coaxed. "Oh, come on, spoilsport. Just for a minute."

It wasn't enough that Miller sat down. Next she urged him to lie back against the pillows. To encourage him, she herself lay back on the bed and pulled her feet up, resting her green linen shoes on the bedspread. "Just try it," she said, lifting her red hair off her neck so that it cascaded across the pillow. "Oh, what a heavenly mattress. Arthur told me he had it made to his exact specifications. It's sort of like the baby bear's bed—not too hard, not too soft, but just right. Come on, Miller, try it." She patted the place next to her. "Just lie down for a second and see for yourself."

Before Miller could protest she had pulled him down next to her. For a minute they lay in silence, staring at the wellspring of the red brocade tent above them. Miller was anxious about what Gina might do next, but he was also curious in a perverse sort of way. He wondered how far a woman might go to rent an apartment, even if it *did* have bad vibrations. Gina was still holding the hand she had pulled him down with. "This red color may seem overwhelming to you at first glance, Miller," she said, "but actually sometimes dark colors *are* restful, regardless of the basic rules. They *enclose* vibrations, they act as insulators."

Miller gently extricated his hand. "Can we go now?" He felt in jeopardy, lying there with Gina so close to him.

She propped herself up on one elbow and looked down into his face. Her long red hair fell across his shoulder and tickled his chin. "What about the view?" she asked.

"The view can't compensate for the smell of cats," Miller said. "Or for the cats themselves."

Gina scrunched up her nose. "I was hoping you wouldn't notice that."

Despite himself, Miller laughed and Gina leaned over and kissed him quickly on the mouth. Before he had a chance to react, she jumped off her side of the bed and opened the door to the balcony. "Cats or no cats," she said, "you have to see this."

Miller sat up and wiped his hand across his mouth. When he stepped out onto the balcony, Gina was leaning against the railing as if nothing had happened. She was right about the view, though. You could see for miles up and down the river—the university, the farms, the small tributaries and islands, the fine terraced backyards and docks of the estates along the boulevard. But the cats and the tented bedroom weren't worth it, whatever the price. Nor were the phallic spears and swords carved into the wooden furniture. "I shouldn't have come," Miller said. "I'm sorry I've wasted your time. I guess I'm really not in the market after all."

Gina followed him back inside and frowned as she closed the French doors. "Of course you are, Miller. It's just the vibrations you're reacting to. Negative, I told you. Poor Arthur. He doesn't have a clue. But don't worry, I know you're going to love the professor's apartment. There's not much of a view but there's a lovely little garden." She tilted her head and eyed him seductively. "Anyway, this rental is only temporary, am I right?"

He nodded and allowed her to wind her arm through his again. Her energy was so overwhelming that the best course on his part seemed to be passivity. There was less chance to be physically injured that way. The headache that had seemed to be receding now picked up its tempo again, throbbing unmercifully. Even the brief trip to the next apartment became blurred and interminable. By the time they reached the professor's apartment, he was vaguely nauseated.

"Now this is so much better, don't you think?" Gina said when she opened the apartment door in the Tudor-style building. Ivy covered the cream-colored outside walls, and paint was peeling on the dark brown windowsills. The inside was better. "Take this sofa, for instance, Miller. See how it's placed in front of this big mirror? That way, whenever someone sends you a negative wave, it bounces off the mirror and is automatically sent back to the sender. And all the plants? Positive. Very positive. Healthy. Lots of oxygen in the place." She pinched the fat leaf of a philodendron. "Now these plants look good, don't they? I've agreed to water them until we can find an occupant."

She seized his arm again and led him through the other rooms. "Oh this is it," she said, patting a table. "This is good. Biedermeier."

"Biedermeier?"

"The furniture. It's friendly. See? This light wood, black trim? It's positive and inviting, don't you think?"

In the bedroom she stopped short. "Oh and look at this, Miller. What is the first thing you notice?"

Miller felt obliged to furnish the correct answer. Something—he wasn't sure what—seemed to depend on it. "Uh, light. Lots of light. Cream-colored walls."

"That too, but what about the bed?"

"The bed?"

"Yes. What do you notice about the bed?"

"Oh. The head faces north?"

Gina was obviously pleased with his answer. "Exactly. That's exactly right." She sat down on a bench by the window and faced him seriously. "This place is available for nine months, but, I have to ask you this for business purposes. Would you stay that long? I mean, is it really over with Katie?"

"I don't know," Miller muttered. "I hope not."

"Let me say this, Miller, just so you know. If you ever need a friend, if you ever, ever, *ever*, need to talk, well, my number is on my card." She studied him carefully. "You do have my card, don't you?"

Miller pushed his hand into his pants pocket, where earlier he had deposited her card. "Let me think about this, okay, Gina? Give me until tomorrow." He looked around. "I do like this place better than the last one. I'll let you know."

Gina followed him outside and locked the door behind them. She babbled as they drove back to the motel. Miller didn't even need to talk. When she dropped him off, Gina smiled up at Miller. "The card," she said. "The number, remember? Call me."

Miller nodded and watched her streak off in the convertible. Then he walked to his motel room, went inside, and vomited.

17

Miller didn't know whether he had taken the professor's apartment to escape from Gina's advances or simply because he was so tired. The next day he moved his suitcase and the two cardboard boxes from the motel and walked into the new place, feeling displaced and alienated. Once he had sat down on the flowered sofa, he wished he had stayed in the motel. That was safer—less emotional and less personal. This place had some kind of history. For one thing, it belonged to a man who had a real life. Miller could see it in the accessories—in the silver-framed photos of women, all with blonde hair and Nordic cheekbones and pale, transparent eyes, in the mementos from travels—blue-speckled river rocks, sea glass, a blown glass paperweight, a calendar from Rhodes. And books. Books piled on tables and shelves and windowsills in careless but orderly disorder. After looking through all these possessions, Miller decided that the professor must be an interesting guy who led an interesting life, but sitting in the midst of somebody else's memories made him feel especially lonely.

This was fascinating, though—trading a life. It was a highly marketable idea, he thought, if only it could somehow be pulled off—offering one life for another, memories, old girlfriends or parents. Different children. Maybe you could pick up a forgiving child and trade off an unforgiving one to somebody who had more expertise and patience. Swaps like that sometimes seemed to work with marriages, didn't they? He thought fleetingly of Adra, of what it might be to have her as his wife. She'd probably be happy in a bait shop or on a farm, unless, if she envisioned a future with him, she might be expecting something grander than what she was used to. Then he felt a stab of guilt, because he hadn't gone to see her since their return from the beach—ten days now—but that last parting had been awkward. At night, in bed, he felt himself longing for her, the tiny waist that he could nearly circle with his big hands, the ribs he could count with his fingers, her long hair spread out around her face as he knelt above her. It was thrilling to teach her things and watch her reaction, and it touched him to measure the wonder in her eyes at the simplest of pleasures. He had even loved watching her eat, biting into a tomato the way you would an apple, juice running down her chin, she laughing as he licked it from her face. One night at the beach he had danced with her, holding her as he had held girls in high school, close enough so that the vertical lines of their bodies moved together in the music, in the moment. He willed himself not to think of Adra or what she had given him, said to him, because he was torn between desire and his need for solitude. Now he had this place and he could have brought her there, but for now it was his alone, and he wanted to keep it that way a while longer. He began to worry that renting an apartment might send a message to Katie that he had given up on their marriage. And maybe Adra would think it made him more available. Or what if Gina thought it made him more vulnerable? Of course, Adra didn't know about it yet, but Gina had probably reported it to Katie first thing.

He opened the top of the cardboard box so that he could put some of his clothes in the empty drawers in the bedroom. Right on top was the high school reunion invitation. He and Katie had looked forward to going, and Miller had mailed in his reservation check almost immediately the winter before. Now Katie wouldn't even speak to him. And if he showed up alone, people would ask questions.

He carried the cardboard box into the bedroom and set it on the trunk. The room was tastefully furnished, with a faded Oriental carpet in shades of black and camel and an antique sleigh bed covered in a well-worn but clean white coverlet. He lay down on the bed to test it, thankful that he had not given Gina the opportunity to ask him to try that one, too. The day after she had showed him the place, he called her and told her he was ready to sign the papers. It would do until he knew how things were going to turn out with Katie. He'd been pleased that the bathroom and kitchen were sparsely furnished and utilitarian. No sign of a woman in the place except for a filmy black negligee hanging on the back of the bathroom door. Miller took that down and stuffed it into the clothes hamper. It wouldn't do to have Judd see it, or Katie, if either of them ever decided to visit.

He got up and walked through the other rooms. In the kitchen, the refrigerator was empty except for a half-empty bottle of gin in the freezer and a few condiments in the food keeper. Otherwise it was clean and efficient. There was a microwave oven and a small stove with a two-burner range. The floor was covered in black-and-white tile, and the window, curtainless, looked out into the garden of the next-door apartment.

The dining area was only an extension of the living room, but at the end of it, French doors opened onto what Gina had called "the garden," a ten-by-twelve area now dried up and overtaken with weeds. Miller shook his head, remembering that "the garden" had been one of Gina's selling points. He walked outside and stood knee-deep in the tangle. Beneath the morning glory vines and the invading Johnson grass were a few courageous coral bells and lilies and Shasta daisies. He leaned over and pulled up a few strands of grass and tossed them onto the brick patio. Later, he thought—maybe some cool evening, he would put his hand to the garden, but not now. It was too hot. He walked back inside, out of the sun. The living room was homey, almost too homey, with the flowered chintz sofa and armchair, the Biedermeier end table, and a small cherry chest. He wondered if the professor had inherited this stuff from his mother or an ex-wife.

As if to confirm his fears, the telephone rang. Gina was the only person who knew the number, and he was certain it wouldn't be Katie. He picked up his car keys and hurried outside. On the highway he headed toward Blue Creek. He didn't know how Adra would receive him. Maybe she would refuse to speak to him. He wouldn't blame her if she turned him away. And if she did, maybe that would be the best thing. It would certainly make things simpler. He knew his motive for going to Adra was selfish. He was lonely. It would have been better, he thought, to find a stranger, someone who would demand nothing of him, at least not at first, but that idea seemed too exhausting—the initial effort, pretending to be sociable, playing the role. Like that woman in the bar. If he had thought she were still there, waiting alone at that table, he would go back and claim her. But he laughed at his fantasy. How long ago had that been? Eight days? Nine? Without any kind of routine or schedule, he was losing track of time.

Adra's truck was gone when he got to the house, but when Miller went up onto the porch to look into the windows, he smelled green beans and bacon cooking inside, something slow and savory. He laughed at himself, realizing that in a way he was surprised that Adra had gone on with her life without him. Perhaps he had thought she was incapable of that, yet he had left her—hadn't he?—to make do on her own. He found a piece of paper in his pocket and made a list of repairs still to be made on the house—roof, gutter pipes, foundation, barn door. Then he sat down under the shade of the porch roof and waited. Half an hour later, Adra and the baby pulled up in the truck. She did not even look at him when she drove past the porch, but kept driving up to the turnaround space in front of the barn. Miller thought he noticed her chin lifting a little. It was something women did when they were angry. Katie, in fact, was an expert at it.

Adra jumped down from the cab of the truck and then went around to lift the baby out. Miller didn't move. He waited, watching her the way a criminal who is tired of running watches his captor approach. Waiting to meet his fate.

Adra dropped the hinge on the truck bed, and even when she hoisted the baby over her shoulder and pulled the grocery bag into the crook of her arm, Miller sat still, waiting.

Adra set the first grocery bag down on the bottom step of the porch and then walked past him to carry the baby inside. Sister reached a hand toward Miller. "Dada," she said, but Adra kept going. Her legs were still dark from the sun and Miller noticed a gleaming narrow chain around her ankle that he had never seen her wear before. She wore her Sunday-go-to-meeting dress, and Miller felt a twinge of pity. Maybe he could make things up to her by taking her shopping for some new clothes.

When she came back out, this time without the baby, Miller stood up to help her bring in the rest of the groceries. She shook her head and skirted around him, pushing open the screen door with her elbow.

Miller followed her inside, down the dim hallway. "Where did you get that ankle bracelet?" he asked.

She set the bags down on the table and started taking out cans and boxes. Her mouth was set in a firm, straight line. Miller sat down on one of the orange plastic chairs and watched her. "None of my business?"

She was silent.

"Can you understand my position at all?" Miller asked.

She slammed a jar of baby food down onto the table. "What position is that? I remember you had a royal wealth of positions in that bedroom back at the beach."

Miller groaned. "Can we be civilized here?"

"I thought *you* was supposed to be the civilized one. But we all make mistakes, don't we? Difference is, I can forgive myself *my* mistakes."

"I see. And I can't, and that is the problem."

"Oh, there's lots more problems than that," Adra said. She leaned toward him then, her eyes blazing. "You throw things away, don't you? You get tired of 'em and you throw 'em away. I should have listened to my mama. She told me a man who leaves his wife for another woman will leave that woman, too, give him enough time. Lord Jesus, you must've set a record."

"Wait a minute," he said. "Are you saying I threw you away?" He reached for her wrist, but she snatched her arm back and brushed it off as if his touch were contaminated.

"Yes, I mean me. I mean me, my baby, your job, your family, everything. You ain't the only thing that bleeds, you know. You ain't the only thing that hurts." She leaned on the word *ain't,* as if in some way that reclamation from her old bag of vernacular expressions could injure him more than anything else.

"I know, I know. I've neglected you, but I've been trying to sort things out," Miller said. "I came to tell you that I have my own apartment now, and it's a place you could come and bring the baby, if you want to visit me. I couldn't call you, you know, when you don't have a telephone. Why don't I get you one?"

She held the paper grocery bag against her chest and smoothed the creases down. Her hands were shaking. "Leave me be. Just leave me be, Miller Sharp. I can take care of myself. I was doing fine without you, and I'll do just fine by myself again."

He nodded. "I know that. You might do even better, maybe." He waited for her denial, but, wordlessly, Adra slid the bag between the refrigerator and the wall and slammed the last cabinet shut.

"I think about you a lot," Miller said. "All the time. Every day. Almost every minute. Especially at night, when I go to bed. I think about when we were together, at the beach."

A tight smile played across her mouth. "Oh yeah," she said. "I noticed." She swung around and put her hands on her hips. Her hipbones jutted out under the cotton of her dress. "Just tell me this. Just tell me why in the hell you came here today." Miller reached for her hand again, and this time he caught and held it. He could not remember which declaration women preferred—*I need you* or *I want you.* He picked the wrong one.

"You need me?" She shook free of his grasp. "I am not your play-pretty." She hesitated. "I thought . . ." At last, she burst into tears and covered her face with her hands.

Miller pulled her down into his lap. "Please, Adra honey, please. I'm so sorry I hurt you. I'm bad, aren't I? I'm a bad person." He wrapped her tightly against him and felt her grief so acutely, it seemed to knock up against his chest.

"Ten days," she said. "Ten days and you didn't come. I thought you hated me."

"No, no, honey," he whispered. "No, no, sweetheart. How could I ever hate you? If I thought I couldn't see you, I think I would just dry up and blow away." Her sharp bones felt unfamiliar again. It was as if he had never made love to her, as if she were a stranger. But he held her tight, trying to conjure up the old feeling of intimacy they had shared at the beach. He was drained of desire, wanting only compassion now, some strength that he could lend her against the pain he had inflicted upon her. "Let me buy you a telephone," he said, "so that I can call you. And you can call me any time you need me. See? That's what we need to keep in touch. I would have called if you'd only had a phone. I simply didn't have the strength to come here to see you. Do you understand? I've been sick. I've been trying to sort out my finances so I know how Katie and I will split our property."

"You're divorcing her?"

"It seems that way."

She clutched his shoulders and burrowed deeper against him. Then, just as he was beginning to feel tender, the baby cried out from the bedroom. "I'll check on her," Miller whispered, grateful for an excuse to extricate himself. He left Adra in the kitchen and made his way back to the baby's room. He picked her up and held her over his shoulder so that he would not have to look into her face. Those big pale eyes and the wide hungry mouth. It frightened him—how much she looked like her father. He stood there, holding the child, until Adra appeared in the doorway and wordlessly took her from his arms and carried her back to the kitchen. In the brighter light of that room, Sister seemed innocent and unmarked. The moment had passed. Adra sat the baby in her high chair and then glanced at Miller briefly. "How much would that cost every month—a phone?"

"Don't worry about it. I'll pay for it."

"Why?"

"Why do you always ask *why*?"

"It's my nature." She said it again. "Why?"

"I want to."

"Why do you want to?"

"I care about you."

"That's all? Care?"

"I can't answer that right now."

"What's so wrong about right now? Maybe I need to know."

"Can you wait? Can you wait a little longer?"

"I've spent my life waiting for men to give me answers. My daddy, my granddaddy—oh, there was a nice one, I could tell you stories about my granddaddy and how much he loved me—then Jimmy Duane, and now you. You're all alike, you men, aren't you? It don't matter. Education, money, sweet talk. White hair, old, young. In the end, you're all alike."

"You're comparing me to Jimmy Duane?"

She shrugged.

He stood up. "I'm sorry," he said. He looked at her for a long minute, as if trying to remember who she was. Then, in a whisper, he said, as if he had just noticed, "You're so young."

Something akin to fear flashed across her face. "I'll take the telephone," she said hurriedly. "That's kind of you. Thank you."

"No," he said. "No. Thank *you*. Thank *you,* Adra." He flushed, realizing that his gratitude must seem disproportionate to the occasion. He turned to leave and then he stopped in the doorway. He owed her something, he knew that. "Do you have a party dress?" he asked. "I want to take you to a reunion with me next week."

Her mouth fell open. "A family reunion?"

He remembered then that she had never graduated from high school. "This is a high school reunion," he told her. "My twenty-fifth."

She shook her head.

"Adra. There are no tests, I guarantee it. Can you get a baby sitter? I'll pay."

She hesitated. "I reckon my mamma would keep the baby." And then she brightened. "A party dress? I could borry one from my sister. You sure?" She threw her arms around his neck.

He held her listlessly, suddenly weary. "I'll call the telephone company as soon as I get back to the apartment. Tomorrow I have to try to see Judd."

She gave the baby a cracker and walked with Miller to the car. He could not kiss her, not yet. He embraced her, struggling to get back the emotion he had felt for her at the beach, but it seemed beyond his reach. "I'll order the phone connection, and then I'll call," he said. He saw her disappointment when he left without kissing her, but she would have to wait until he could work things out.

He drove back to the apartment and he dreamed that night of Greek islands and women with Nordic features and pale blue eyes. For one night at least, Jimmy Duane Goodfriend was in somebody else's dreams—maybe Adra's.

18

Miller had never before realized what it really meant when people said they were separated. He had never had to measure the pain, the lonely nights, the bewilderment about when things had first begun to disintegrate. The gossip made it sound so easy—separated, as if whatever had caused the break could be fixed with glue or counseling sessions or a good hot bath. Sometimes people—especially men, he thought—looked wistful and slightly envious when they heard such a piece of news about somebody else. It sounded like freedom. It sounded like possibility. When he told a friend that he and Katie were separated, the man looked at him with an expression close to complicity. "It could have been any of us," he said.

But pulling into the driveway of the house on Sunday morning, two weeks into the separation, Miller knew it meant alienation from the family and home you had known for all the years of the marriage. Sometimes it even seemed like all the years of your life.

Katie's car was parked outside, but when Judd appeared on the porch and closed the door behind him, Miller knew that he was not destined to see Katie that day. He leaned over and unlocked the passenger door, and Judd climbed in, grim-faced and sullen. He didn't look at Miller or speak to him, but slouched in the corner, as far away from his father as possible.

Miller gripped the steering wheel and looked at Judd's profile. "How are you, son?"

Judd stared at the dashboard. "The only reason I'm here is because Mom made me come," he muttered. "She said this is between you and her, that it has nothing to do with me."

Miller nodded. "That's true. She's absolutely right. It has nothing to do with you."

Judd's jaw tightened. "Bull*shit*," he said. He looked at Miller then, glared at him with an impenetrable anger. "What? Do you think I don't live here, too? Like I'm not part of the family or something?" His lower lip trembled, but he pressed his lips together and turned his face away. "Let's go. Let's get this over with."

Miller looked once more at the house and then started the motor and backed out of the driveway. *Let's get this over with*. In a sense he felt that way, too. *Take it easy, be patient, he's a kid.* "This apartment I'm renting—just temporarily—isn't far from here," Miller said. "I thought we could go there first, and I'll cook you an omelet. Remember how you always used to like my omelets on Sunday mornings? I've bought all the fixings. Sausage, cheese, peppers, onions. Hot sauce. The really hot kind that you like."

"I'm not hungry," Judd said. His voice was hoarse and deeper than Miller remembered it. His eighteenth birthday was only a month away. Katie had had him tested when he was five and then decided to get him into first grade just before the deadline. Now Miller wished that they hadn't forced it, not because Judd hadn't done well, but because Miller would have more time to make amends. He sensed, though, that Judd could already smell his own freedom, especially now, with things the way they were at home. He was going to be out there in the world on his own in nine months.

"Let's go to my place anyway," Miller said. "There's a garden." It was the first time he had actually claimed ownership of the apartment. *My place.* "It's only temporary," he said, "just until your mother and I can iron things out."

"Whatever." In Judd's shrug, Miller sensed that the boy was casting off all filial responsibility. Miller felt the same kind of catch in his chest that he had felt that morning at the beach with Adra. His heart raced. He noticed that his knuckles, clutching the steering wheel, were white. The silence that followed was so ominous that Miller in his confusion drove past the apartment and ended up backtracking. He was sweating by the time they pulled into the complex, and, after Judd had climbed out of the car, Miller took a deep breath and held it until his lungs started working again.

He pushed the key into the lock and threw open the door. "Welcome," he said, realizing too late that he must have sounded foolish. Judd stood at the edge of the living room carpet, as if hesitant to step in.

"What do you think?" asked Miller.

Judd shrugged again. Every time he did that, Miller felt a layer of their old relationship fall away, disintegrating like paint flaking from an ancient wall. "Looks kind of feminine to me."

"Feminine?" Miller was a little shocked. "Jesus, I wouldn't describe it that way. A man owns it. A professor at the university. What is it—the flowered sofa? Is that it?"

"Mom would hate it," Judd said.

Miller couldn't figure out why he felt so offended. It wasn't even his own place. "Okay, I'll take the bait. Why would your mother hate it?"

Judd walked around, picking up things—the glass pieces, the silver picture frames. Each time he examined something, he deliberately put it back in a different place. "Mom likes simple things. This all seems"—he waved his hand in the air—"so *precious*. Is he gay?"

"Who?"

"Whoever owns this place. The guy. The girl. Whoever."

"Of course not. Well, even if he *is*, so what? That's his business. Anyway, look. He has all these photos of women around. What's the big deal?"

Judd stared out the glass door at the unruly garden. Okay. If Judd was angry at Miller, all right. He could take it out on the apartment, on the absent professor, the flowered sofa, the silver picture frames, the innocent cloudy sea glass. "Make yourself at home," Miller said. "I'll put some coffee on. Or I'll fix you a Coke. Would you rather have a Coke?"

"Nothing," Judd said, poking his head into the bedroom. "I don't want anything."

"*I* do, though," Miller said. "I haven't eaten any breakfast, remember? That was the plan—to have breakfast together and talk."

"Mom's losing weight," Judd said. "A lot of weight." He pulled back the shower curtain and inspected the tub. "You need a maid," he said. Then he opened the medicine cabinet and surveyed its contents. Miller hoped he wouldn't look in the clothes hamper. But to find the mysterious black negligee, he'd have to dig through all Miller's dirty laundry first.

Judd sauntered down the narrow hallway, looking at the paintings and ever so slightly tilting each one askew. Miller shuffled into the kitchen and spooned coffee grounds into the filter. He realized that he was clenching his teeth. Non sequiturs. They always revealed what people were really worrying about. "So your mom's losing weight. Is she all right?"

Judd opened the door to the garden but didn't bother to walk outside. He pressed the remote control for the television set, flipped through the channels, then turned the power off. "She cries all the time. She doesn't eat. Last weekend she didn't even get dressed. She wore her bathrobe all day. She won't even answer phone calls anymore."

Miller slid the carafe onto the heating element of the coffee maker. "I have no way of knowing these things if she won't talk to me."

"Well, you know now."

Miller took a deep breath. "We could address all these problems," he said, "if she would just talk to me. I'm sorry, Judd. I know you're both angry at me."

Judd put down the remote and walked into the kitchen. He opened all the cabinets, inspecting all the nooks and crannies of Miller's new life, then left each door gaping. "Why should she talk to you?"

Miller's voice came out louder than he had meant it to. "Because, Judd, Jesus Christ. If she would talk to me, maybe we could straighten out some of our problems. And will you please close the damned cabinet doors?"

Slowly, deliberately, Judd put his hand on each door and slammed it shut. Slammed. He wore an enigmatic expression on his face, as if he were pleased to have unfastened Miller's carefully controlled anger. "I don't think Mom wants to talk to you anymore," he said. "I think you've already pretty well fucked things up beyond repair."

Miller was shaking. "Don't you talk to me like that," he ordered.

Judd shook his finger in Miller's face. "Look who's talking. How dare you treat me the way you treated me that day with Cindy while you were fooling around with some poor white trash whore?"

Judd was already swinging when Miller stepped into the arc of his reach, and the blow hit his cheek and knocked him backwards into the counter. The coffee pot came hurtling across the floor, and Miller felt his back scrape against the handle of the dishwasher as his feet went out from under him. Crumpled against the base of the counter, he was still trying to get his breath when he heard the front door slam. He waited for the sound of his car to start up, but then he remembered the keys were in his pocket. There was only silence. Judd was gone and somehow he would find his way home—he'd call Cindy or Katie, get a bus, a taxi, maybe even walk or jog the five miles back. But he was gone, and Miller couldn't imagine how he could have handled things any differently. He touched his cheek tentatively. It was already beginning to swell. When he stood up to get an ice cube, he noticed the searing pain in his back and when he put his hand there, it came away bloody. The dishwasher handle had scraped a long gash along his lower back. He hobbled into the bathroom, took off his shirt, and turned his back to the mirror in order to get a look. "Oh shit," he whispered when he saw the wound. He wiped it with a wet washcloth and then swabbed it with some alcohol he found in the medicine cabinet. The cut wasn't deep enough for stitches, but it was ugly looking. He couldn't remember the last time he'd had a tetanus shot or whether this was the kind of accident that called for one. Katie always kept the records on things like that, but of course he couldn't call Katie. He pulled his shirt down carefully, and when he turned his head he noticed the lump on his cheek swelling and darkening. He limped back into the kitchen and wrapped an ice cube in a towel and held it against his face. This was the second encounter with Judd lately that had resulted in violence.

He covered the chintz sofa with a towel and eased himself down into a position that caused the least amount of stress to the laceration on his back. Holding the ice cube against his cheek, he lay staring into space. At first the tragedy of the situation was alleviated by the irony of it—Judd's getting the best of him again. Miller seemed to have no strength, no direction any more. He was a middle-aged man with a fairly long future ahead of him and none of it looked good. All he could see was loneliness, confusion, economic worries. More doors slamming.

He rolled over slowly, flinching at the pain, and woke a while later with the wet towel on his chest, his shirt soaked and a spot of blood on the sofa. When he limped into the bathroom to change the shirt he caught a glimpse of himself in the mirror, cheek puffy and blue, face haggard, the beard ragged. His appearance kept changing. If it changed enough, he thought, maybe no one would recognize him any more, and he could walk away a free man. He could understand now how men could park their cars on the side of the interstate, hitch a ride to some new city, and start a completely new life. He eased out of his slacks and underwear and stepped into the shower. He let the water run over him for a long time before he remembered to pick up the soap. He had lost Katie and now maybe he had lost Judd. If his own father had done what he had done, he might have stopped loving him, too. He slid down to the floor of the shower and let the water spray over his head, weeping for the first time over the loss of what he had thrown away but was not yet willing to return to.

19

The minute Adra walked out of the house in the white patent leather pumps and the leopard-print dress, Miller knew he had made a mistake. Her smile vanished when she saw the expression on Miller's face. "You hate this dress," she said.

"No, no, it's fine, honey. You look fine, really." He struggled for a compliment that would seem sincere. "Your hair looks pretty. I like it pulled back like that."

She hesitated for a second, then noticed the corsage box he carried. "What's that?" she asked.

Miller held the box behind his back. "I'm told that women don't really wear these anymore," he said. "I shouldn't have bought it." It would be disastrous for her to wear a white gardenia on a leopard-print dress. Anybody would know that.

Adra smiled and reached around him. "Let me see, Miller."

"You don't have to wear it. It's a gesture, that's all."

"What do you mean by that? A gesture? What does that mean?"

"Well, in high school we would bring the girls corsages when we went to a dance. It was sort of a gift. I thought it would be fun. But . . . well, we're not in high school anymore, are we?"

Her face crumpled, and Miller held out the corsage. "Here, go on, take it. Put it on. You look great, Adra, really, you do. Thanks for being my date."

He opened the car door for her, but she hung back. The plastic box with the gardenia in it crackled as her fingers pressed into it. "It's wrong, ain't it? This dress. My sister said it was perfect, but it's wrong. She wore it to the Shriners' dance last year."

"No, no," Miller said. "It *is* perfect. It's good." He nodded toward the car and slowly, hesitantly, she climbed in. When he slid in on the other side, she was opening the plastic box. Now Miller wanted to snatch the flower back and throw it out the window. "Really," he said again, "you don't have to wear it. I just wanted to bring you something."

Adra lifted the gardenia from the box and held it against her shoulder. "I've never had one of these before," she said. "Thank you, Miller."

Of course not, Miller was thinking. *You never even graduated from high school.* But he said nothing. He backed up and turned down the driveway, but when he glanced over at her, it was finally too much for him. "Well, truthfully," he said, "I think maybe it's a little too much with the dress. That pattern, I mean." Tears welled up in her eyes. "Oh, look, Adra, shit, just do what you want. If you want to wear it, wear it. Sure, it looks great."

Her chin quivered. "Well, what?" she said. "Wear it or not? You must've paid a lot for it."

"So wear it. Yes. That's final. Wear it, Adra, please. I bought it for you to wear tonight, and you just go on and wear it. Okay?"

She bit her lip and pinned the flower against her shoulder, then leaned cautiously back against the seat and stared straight ahead at the road. In her leopard-print lap, her hands were clenched into fists.

Her hair at least was okay, Miller thought. It was clean and shiny and pulled back over one ear. She was a pretty girl. Unusual, but pretty. Exotic even. Maybe the dress wouldn't have seemed so bad if it weren't for the shoes. White shoes with a leopard dress? He had never once been ashamed of Katie's appearance. She knew how to dress, what to wear on any given occasion. She was always acceptable and dependable. Was that the trouble? No surprises?

The thick sweet odor of the gardenia permeated the interior of the car. The smell was heavy, almost peppery. Miller tried to engage Adra in conversation. He patted her knee. "Are you up for dancing tonight? There'll be a lot of dancing."

"What else?" Adra asked.

"Oh, talking, drinking, reminiscing about the old days, then drinking some more, talking some more, dancing some more, drinking some more. Oh, and then there's checking to see how your old girlfriends have weathered the twenty-five years since you last saw them." He laughed at her worried expression. "That was a joke—the part about the old girlfriends."

"Were they pretty—your girlfriends?"

"Not as pretty as you," he said. He waited for a reaction, but she looked straight ahead. Her hands were still clenched, and he reached over and separated her stiff fingers. They felt achingly cold. "Anyway," he went on, "it was considered cool in those days to have an intellectual girlfriend, and it was even better if she was politically active. There was a lot going on then. Vietnam, the usual suspects." He realized suddenly that Adra had not even been born then. He glanced away from her anxious face and went on. Maybe he could make her laugh. "But we all still secretly lusted after the cheerleaders, the ones who used hair spray and lipstick."

"And what happened to the cool girls?"

"The same thing that happened to all of us. We traded our impossible dreams and leftist ideals for real estate and bank accounts."

"Who were the usual suspects?"

"Oh God, let me think. The Palestine Liberation Organization, Idi Amin, the IRA." He could tell by looking at her that none of those names was familiar. "Jimmy Carter became president the year I graduated," he added. "And Elvis died."

Adra's face lit up. For a second she looked radiant. "Elvis. I love Elvis. Do you believe that he's still really alive?"

Miller laughed. "I don't think so. That's a fantasy. You know, something people want to believe in." *Did he have to explain everything to her?* "Maybe people like Elvis were popular because there weren't really any political leaders we could admire, and there wasn't that much anymore that college students could protest. Which was too bad, because it was cool to be arrested for a good cause."

"Jimmy Duane got arrested lots of times and it was always awful."

"For what? Not protesting, I gather."

"Possession of stolen property."

Miller remembered the boxes in the barn covered by plastic sheets, the new, unused tractor and rototiller. "My God. How did he get off?"

"His daddy did it somehow. He knew somebody who knew somebody who owed somebody a favor."

Miller felt an insidious premonition of danger. What kind of people did Adra come from, anyway? He could tell she was measuring his reaction. "I'm sorry, Adra. Jimmy Duane must have put you through hell."

"You know what I wish?" she said. "I wish you had been the one I had met instead of him. When we was both younger, I mean."

It seemed important to shoot her sentiment out of the sky. "When I was of marriageable age, Adra, you were only a baby." Even that didn't seem enough to dissuade her. "You probably wouldn't have liked me anyway," he added.

"I would so. Why do you say that?"

"What I remember about being that age is that I went through a lot of self-conscious suffering and posing. No, you definitely would not have liked me."

Adra turned her head and looked out the window. She had taken his assessment as a personal rejection, which, he realized, was exactly what he had intended, but he hadn't really meant to hurt her. "You mean you wouldn't have liked *me,*" she said. "I wouldn't have talked good enough for you. I wouldn't have dressed good enough. You were a college boy. You wouldn't have liked anything about me."

"Adra, that's not true," Miller insisted. "You're beautiful now, and I would have found you beautiful then. I like you now, don't I? And I'm a lot smarter now than I was in high school, believe me." *Or was he?* Back then, he had known what he wanted. He had goals, ambitions, he was in love with the world.

Once they had left the county road and crossed the city line, he was thankful for the street lights and the neon signs, the thickening traffic. It seemed to compensate for their lack of conversation. When they finally pulled into the parking lot of the Hyatt, Miller wasn't sure whether he was relieved or sorry to be there.

He looked up at the hotel, an abstract structure of glass and stone dug into the side of a hill overlooking the city on one side and the Tennessee River on the other. Knoxville's skyline was changing slowly, with a few new buildings sprouting up, older ones coming down. In a sense, he thought, expansion was limited because of the perimeters dictated by the river, the university complex, and the interstate. The only changes in the city were mainly internal ones, mostly in the old factory district where decaying buildings had been renovated and entrepreneurs were still opening shops and restaurants. If he were going to stay, he thought, he'd become more involved in the downtown development, try to save more of the old places and preserve the history of the area, but the idea of moving his life to the beach was still pulling at him. With or without Katie, that was still what he wanted to do. As for Adra, he was conflicted. In her own element, and at the beach, she had seemed right, but now, he wasn't sure about anything. He walked around and helped her out of the car, wincing as her white shoes glistened in the setting sun.

In the hotel lobby, Miller followed the signs that pointed to the reunion banquet room. He stopped for a second and looked at Adra. "Sure you want to do this? We could always go someplace else for dinner. I mean, if you're nervous about meeting so many new people." He had been thinking that maybe he could come back later, alone, and seek out people he wanted to see. But Adra's mouth was firm. "Fine," Miller said, and he walked quickly ahead, so that Adra had to lag behind, struggling to keep up in the borrowed high-heeled shoes. Whenever Miller glanced back, the gardenia on her shoulder, slightly askew, appeared as a large white blur. Here was Miller, voted "Most Likely to Succeed" among his high school classmates, and now having failed at almost everything in his current life.

So many people had gathered at the entrance to the banquet room that Adra took hold of Miller's coattail to keep from being swept away. On a table by the entrance, name tags and programs were spread out. Miller found the laminated card with his name and the high school yearbook photo. He hardly recognized his former self, a boy with long dark sideburns and a young, bony face with a stern and righteous expression, a boy too thin and much too serious. He attached the name card to his breast pocket and plunged into the crowd. Adra was still clinging to his coattail. The band was playing "Both Sides Now," and the female vocalist was using all the same inflections that Joni Mitchell had used when she made the recording. Déjà vu all over again.

Miller left Adra waiting by the doorway while he pushed up to the bar, ordering a whiskey for himself and white wine for her. Whenever he ran into old friends who asked, he said Katie hadn't been able to make it, nothing more. People kept glancing at each other's name tags, then hugging and swearing to each other that they hadn't changed a bit. A former cheerleader who, in high school, had always ignored him ran up and kissed him on the mouth. The band was playing "MacArthur Park," and the woman, already a little drunk, laughed. "What in the hell does that song mean, Miller? I could never figure it out, but I didn't want anybody to know." Miller laughed, too, and together they sang the line about leaving the cake out in the rain. "Maybe we can get together afterwards,"she said, leaning into his shoulder. "I mean, you without your wife and all." The music was deafening. She held up her left hand to show that she wasn't wearing a ring.

Miller nodded vaguely and held out the drinks in his hand to intimate that he needed to deliver them to somebody. She nodded and kissed him again and then disappeared into the throng.

Miller stood alone for a minute and sipped his drink. A trickle of moisture from the glass ran down his wrist, and it was only then that he remembered he had left Adra back by the door. But he finished that whiskey and ordered another and then worked his way through the crowd again. Adra was exactly where he had left her, her eyes brimming with tears.

"Sorry I took so long," Miller said. "I had to wait in line forever." Adra's gardenia was already beginning to turn brown at the edges, and her wine glass felt warm when he handed it to her. The music nudged at Miller again. "Proud Mary." He wished to be young again with all these people, the cheerleader, the football players, the activists, the promiscuous girls. Young enough to do things differently.

He was a little drunk now. His second whiskey had made his classmates that much more lovable. *Miller, Miller, he's our man. If he can't do it, nobody can.*

The crowd was moving into the adjoining room where tables were set up for dinner. He pulled Adra into the long buffet line and stood talking to the man in front of him, a former football teammate who was living in Seattle. Behind him, Adra held onto his elbow. She didn't speak, but he was acutely aware of her presence and the overwhelming odor of the gardenia. In the middle of the buffet line, somewhere between the broccoli and the green bean salad, his former best friend, now a lawyer in Richmond, came up and asked to be introduced to Adra. He looked her up and down and gave Miller a knowing wink. Adra waited until the man walked away, then tugged at Miller's sleeve. "I want to go home," she said. Tears were running down her cheeks.

Miller glanced around to see if anyone had noticed, but everybody was leaning over the food, choosing from various steaming trays. "What's wrong?" he whispered. "For God's sake, Adra, why are you crying?"

"You know why," she said, too loud. "That man thinks I'm your whore." The woman next to them looked up, then quickly turned away again. Miller put his plate down on the nearest table and grabbed Adra's arm. People stared at them as they hurried out of the banquet room. In the hallway Miller faced her. "Look, Adra, I'm really sorry. This is all my fault. It was a mistake for me to bring you here tonight. A lot of people know Katie, and they're surprised to see me with somebody else. I guess I wasn't thinking. Believe me, the last thing I wanted to do was hurt you."

"Did you see him? Did you see the way he looked at me?" She wrenched her arm away from Miller's hold and started running toward the lobby. Miller looked around in embarrassment, then hurried after her, his heart slamming against the wall of his chest. Sometime before they reached the door Adra ripped the corsage from her shoulder and threw it to the floor. When she reached the parking lot, the heel on her white patent leather shoe folded and she went down on her hands and knees. Miller knelt beside her and pulled her into his arms to examine her injuries. Her knees and the palms of her hands were bleeding. She kept trying to slap him away, but he helped her up and looked around for the car. It was dark now, and the lights of the parking lot glanced off the hoods and windshields of all the automobiles in the lot, so that they all looked alike. When he finally found his car in the last row, he helped Adra in and pushed the hair back from her eyes. "Adra, Adra," he said, "I'm so sorry I hurt your feelings." He slid over to her side of the car and pulled her onto his lap. She clung to him, crying, and he pulled her close to his chest so that her legs straddled him. Something wild and painful boiled up in him as he searched for her mouth and held her tight against him. He could taste the salt of her tears and still smell the aura of the gardenia on her dress. He pulled at her skirt and she arched her back to meet him. There was no tenderness in it, no loving. It was pure sex, hunger, loneliness, maybe, he thought, for both of them.

There had been a time—yesterday, it seemed—when he had thought she might be the life preserver that would save him. But now he realized that if Adra continued to cling to him as fiercely as she did now, they would both go down together. Down, like Jimmy Duane Goodfriend. Down to the very bottom.

20

Except for his visits to Adra's house, where he was repairing the shutters, Miller avoided social situations. He didn't answer Gina's calls, and Katie and Judd didn't answer his. Sometimes on weekends he took Adra and the baby to his apartment and cooked for them on the grill in the little garden. But since the night of the high school reunion he had avoided intimacy. Both of them made the baby the center of attention now, as if she were the glue that held their tentative relationship together. They were like preoccupied parents, admiring the baby and the fact that, at ten months, she was taking a few shaky steps on her own. They marveled about her first words—*Dada* (meant, of course, for Miller), *Mama, birdie.* But Adra was constantly watching Miller, and these days, her mood seemed to be governed by his.

He had been away from his real family for almost six weeks, and he grew worried about financial matters he and Katie needed to settle. Besides, autumn was coming, and he would need his winter clothes. The only alternative left to him was to take Katie by surprise, show up at the house sometime when he knew she would be home. Bedtime, for example. She had to sleep there, didn't she? He'd go late and catch her unawares.

The next night he left the apartment about eleven and drove to the house. Judd's car wasn't in the driveway, but there was another vehicle there—a black Porsche Miller recognized as Jim Skinner's. Miller felt as if he'd been punched in the stomach. He sat in his car and tried to rationalize why Jim might be there. Maybe he and Katie were discussing her financial situation, but at this hour?

He stepped onto the porch, keeping his footsteps deliberately light, and looked in the window. Jim and Katie were lying on the sofa together, watching television; Katie was snuggled into the crook of Jim's arm, her head against his chest. Jim's shirt was partly open and Miller could see that Katie's silk blouse was pulled out of her skirt waistband. Her hair looked different, too—longer, softer, blonder even. It was tousled, and she had a new cut, a girlish style with bangs.

Two glasses and a half-empty wine bottle sat on the coffee table and a bowl of popcorn was on the floor next to the sofa. Jim and Katie were laughing at something on the screen, and then Jim leaned forward and kissed Katie's ear. She closed her eyes and smiled.

Standing there on the dark porch, Miller felt alienated from both his past and his future. There is no continuity in life, he thought, no happy endings. Things just go on somehow, and people stumble along, doing the best they can with whatever resources they can scratch up. "There is just one chance," his father used to say. "No rehearsal. You get out there and say your lines and make your moves, and until the reviews come in, you never know how you did."

His father had done all right, though, he had lived a good life. Not Miller. He was screwing everything up, ruining lives, leaving destruction in his wake. A serial killer was less dangerous than he was. He walked softly to the door and turned the knob. Unlocked. He let himself into the hallway, and then, with a great shove, slammed the door behind him.

In the living room there was scuffling, then Katie's voice. "Judd? Is that you?"

Miller stepped into the living room. Jim Skinner was standing now, buttoning his shirt. Katie, her face flushed, was straightening her skirt. "Why didn't you knock?" she demanded. "You don't live here anymore; you should have knocked."

Miller glared at her. "As far as I know, this house still has my name on the deed, or have you somehow changed that, too? But Jim would know, wouldn't he? Let's ask our accountant."

Jim knotted his tie, then put his hand on Katie's shoulder. "I should go," he said, "so you two can talk."

Katie grabbed his hand. "No, stay. I want you here."

Miller advanced a few steps. He enjoyed the rush of energy he got from the apprehension in Jim's eyes. "She wants you here, Jim," he said. "But I don't want you here. I want to talk to my wife alone."

Katie laughed sharply. "Your wife? You actually remembered you have a wife?" Her mouth twisted. "You bastard."

"Let this be a lesson to you, Jim," Miller said. "Women who are ladylike all their lives turn obscene when things start going wrong. Or did that happen with your wife, too, when you left home? Did it happen like this? Was there a night when she turned on you, called you names? Did you come home and find her lying on the sofa with another man? Was her blouse hanging half open? Oh no, forgive me. It was the other way around, wasn't it? Didn't I hear gossip about your sleeping around? Do you remember hearing that gossip, Katie?" He wanted to grab Jim's arm and twist it backward until he could hear bones crack and tendons snap.

"You leave my wife out of this," Jim said. "At least I acted civil to her. At least I took care of her."

"You son of a bitch," Miller said. "You couldn't wait to get at Katie, could you? The minute I left your office, I'll bet you called her. That day. That very minute. You duplicitous son of a bitch." He pushed Katie aside and lunged at Jim, shoving him backwards toward the sofa. Then he let his whole weight fall against him and they went down together. The coffee table toppled and the wine glasses and bottle went sliding off the surface and crashed to the floor. Above the rush of his own pulse Miller heard Katie's screaming and Jim's thick guttural grunts as Miller smashed his fist again and again into his stomach. Jim rolled over, retching, and then he lay there in the broken glass, curled into a ball with his knees pulled up. Katie was shrieking something. She yanked Miller's hair and punched his shoulder the way Adra had done that day at the dock. Finally Miller collapsed beside Jim on the carpet. He turned over on his back and lay staring at the ceiling. *Damn it*, he thought, *I belong here. This is my ceiling. This is my living room. I paid for these things. This is my Oriental rug, these are my sofas, my paintings. That woman who is trying to hurt me is my wife.*

He lay there inert as Katie, weeping, helped Jim to his feet. He was vaguely aware that Jim was still vomiting. Moaning, too. Good. He deserved it, Miller was sure. Whatever was going on with him and Katie, he deserved it. Miller heard the toilet flushing and water running, then the door closing and a car driving away. *Coward,* he thought. If I were Jim I would have stayed to make sure Katie was all right. No, wait, he realized. That's my job. Or was. He didn't know anymore. He didn't move. The floor felt good beneath him, solid and safe, though there was danger all around, obviously. The putrid smell of vomit drifted around him, and when he shifted his feet, glass tinkled, but still, he wouldn't get up.

After a while he felt the presence of somebody in the room and he looked up to see Katie collapsed in a corner of the sofa, her head in her hands. "Why do you always have to destroy everything?" she whis-

pered. Her hand swept the air in front of her, indicating the ruin Miller had caused. It reminded him of that day in the kitchen when Katie had cried, a day that seemed much further in the past than a couple of months. At least tonight he had *felt* something. But he couldn't answer Katie because he didn't *know* the answer. He wished desperately to know the answer because it was something he himself needed to know.

"Answer me," Katie ordered, and when he couldn't reply, she threw herself on top of him with a strangled scream that came from somewhere deep inside her, kicking, scratching, throwing the weight of her pent-up anger behind every blow, and his hands came up to protect his face, but he did not fight back.

Finally, when Katie's hand slammed against his cheek he grabbed her wrist and pulled her down against him and he suddenly recognized the softness of her body and understood how he had been longing for it—that weight, the feel of it, that particular body, that very one, the ample breasts, the soft belly—and he understood how he might have missed it, though he had not known until now that he missed it. As he struggled to quell the violence in her, he had a flash of what it was he had given up—her spirit, her fire, her strength—and he held tight as if riding out a storm. "Katie," he moaned. "Katie, Katie, Katie. No, no, no, no, no." He held her firmly until she had expended all her strength and he felt her muscles relax against him, giving up. She lay prone on top of his body and he loosened his arms but began to rub her back and shoulders, feeling under his hands only surrender now, a physical surrender at least, maybe only a truce, but stillness.

Over and over, he repeated her name. For both of them, it was a soothing song. "Katie. Katie." When he said, "I'm sorry," she began to cry again. But she stayed there. That was a hopeful sign, she stayed there. Miller felt the long intake of her breath against his chest and the heat of her tears against his neck, but other than that, neither of them moved. Miller held his hands against the small of her back. Finally he said, "I think I want to come home." And he was surprised, because he hadn't known he was going to say that.

She pushed away from him and sat up. "No." She was rubbing her eyes, wiping mascara from her cheeks with the collar of her blouse.

He raised himself on his elbows and looked at her. "No? Do you mean that?"

She laughed. "How dare you ask me that after what you've done?"

"Are you sleeping with Jim?"

"Are you sleeping with that girl?" She would never allow herself to say Adra's name.

"Don't blame her. She's not the one to blame. I'm the guilty one. She's just—what do you call it?—the catalyst." He was amazed to find himself on the verge of tears. "Katie, I never meant to hurt you. I couldn't think. Everything has been so crazy. Oh God, honey."

Katie sat back and observed him. "I hate you, Miller Sharp," she said. But her voice was passionless, her expression weary.

Miller pushed himself into a sitting position. "You don't know everything," he said.

Katie's head dropped back against the sofa and she moaned. "You mean there's more?"

"I didn't mean that. I mean what happened at first. The drowning, the reason for all of this—the way I've behaved."

She rocked forward on her knees and whimpered. "I'm too tired to hear any more. We've been over this a hundred times. I want you to go, and I want to go to sleep."

"Not yet," he said. "This is important. I should have told you this at the beginning."

He believed this might be the moment when he could reshape her attitude toward him, make her understand. He pulled her up onto the sofa and she let her head fall back against the pillows and closed her eyes. Miller sat down next to her and took her face in his hands. "Listen to me," he said. "Katie, look at me."

Her eyes were glazed.

"Are you listening?" Miller said. He felt a little afraid for her, for what he had done to her, for what might happen to them both.

She turned her head and looked at him.

"When he drowned—when Jimmy Duane drowned—I didn't tell you everything."

She closed her eyes again.

"No, please, honey. Listen. Stay awake, will you? This is the answer to everything. The first time I found him underwater," Miller said, "he found *me*, he attached himself to me, he climbed onto my back and he nearly drowned me. I had to get him off. I bit him."

Katie was staring at him but he was not sure she understood the import of what he was saying. Miller went on. "I bit him to make him let go. When he jerked back I got out of his reach and swam to the surface."

From the expression on Katie's face, Miller realized that this story was not what she had hoped for. His absolution would have to come at the end of some spectacular revelation and suddenly he realized it was not going to be enough for her. "Are you still with me?" he said.

She turned her head away. "You bit him. So? That was a natural reaction. A spontaneous reflex is what you call it."

"Yes. Except that's not the end of it. When I got up to the surface I lied to them—Adra and the others. His friends. I told him I hadn't been able to find him. And then I waited. I waited until I *knew* he must be dead, so he couldn't hurt me, so he couldn't pull me down. And he *was* dead, when I finally went down. He was dead then or close to it, and if I hadn't waited, he would be alive today. Katie, I *let him die."*

Katie's chest heaved as if an implosion were building inside her. Miller shook her arm and in that second he could sense the metallic taste of the lake in his mouth, the bitter amber water that he could never quite swallow. "Did you hear what I said?" he asked Katie. He shook her arm again.

She turned her face to him and peeled his fingers away from her arm. Her voice shook when she spoke. "So then you felt obligated to make it up to the wife."

He nodded. "But not in that way. Not like that."

"You felt obligated at the expense of losing everything else you had valued in your life. You sacrificed me, you sacrificed Judd, you sacrificed your house and your job."

"Nothing seemed worth it once I had lost my self-respect. Katie, I've lived my life the way my father taught me—respecting and honoring other people, living a correct and honorable life, and suddenly that day, when I became as desperate as Jimmy Duane, I lost it all. I lost all my decency and courage and honor."

When she began to laugh he smiled at first, until he saw where it was leading—to a bitter assessment that had nothing to do with the truth. "You gave us up for that little whore."

"No, no. It wasn't like that. Can't you see why I hated myself? Can't you see why I had to change things?"

"You changed things, all right," Katie said. "You changed things so they can never be the same between us. You slept with another woman and in retribution I slept with another man."

"Oh no, oh Jesus, Katie. Did you have to tell me that?"

"Yes," she said. "Yes, I did have to tell you that. Can you begin to imagine the pain you've caused me?"

Miller nodded. "I think I'm just beginning to."

Katie's expression was unflinching. "Do you love her?"

Miller looked down at his hands. "I don't know. Maybe. No. I guess not. Well, maybe I do, in a certain way. Not the way *we* were, you and I, I mean." His hands opened into the empty air. "But I'm not sleeping with her anymore. I haven't—not since we came back." Then he remembered the night of the reunion. "Well once, maybe. But I've hurt her, too. I've been hurting everybody I touch."

Katie laughed. "Not since you came back. Oh, that's great, Miller. What strength, what fortitude. Oh, what a *great man* you are."

He pushed himself beyond her acrimony. "What about you, Katie? Do you love Jim?"

"Of course I don't love him. Jim Skinner? Are you crazy? I *used* him. He used me, too. But we both knew it. That's the point. We both *knew* it. Okay, maybe he didn't know that *I* knew it, but I did, and maybe he didn't know that I knew that *he* knew it, and that was okay. It was like when you were under the lake. All you could think about was coming up for air. That's what I did with Jim. I needed to know that I was still desirable. But what I did with Jim means nothing to me. The significance is that what *we* had—you and I—is forever ruined because of what you did."

"I never meant . . ."

"Please, Miller. Don't insult my intelligence."

Miller rubbed his forehead. "Tell me what you want me to do."

"If I were to let you come back," she said, "and I'm not promising anything—I have to think about it—it would only be on a trial basis. For Judd's sake. Until he finishes high school next spring. After that, we'll sell the house, split things up. But there are conditions."

"Conditions?"

"Separate bedrooms. I need time, and I need respect. You don't see the girl, you don't talk to her. You don't have any contact with her."

"I told you . . ."

"Let me finish." She squeezed her eyes shut and clenched her fists. "Apologize to Judd, make it right with him again."

"That's it?"

"No. There's more. I want you to go back to counseling. I want you to stop drinking. I want you to get your job back."

He shook his head. "Not the job. I can't promise you that. Besides, they wouldn't give me the job back."

"I talked to Jack. He said they would."

"You talked to Jack?" Had she wanted him back for himself, or only to take care of financial matters?

"Yes, he says you can work it out."

"What if I don't want to?"

She stiffened. "Take it or leave it, Miller. It's one of my conditions. You decide whether it's worth it or not. End of conversation."

"Life is too short to be stuck in a job you hate," Miller told her, "day after day, doing work you consider worthless. Jesus, Katie, I want to live, I want to see the world, I want to have fun."

"Have you been having fun these last six weeks, Miller?"

Miller shook his head. "Touché."

Katie's breath pushed out in a short little puff. "What about the rest of us? Are we having fun? What about Judd?"

"Where *is* Judd, anyway?" Miller asked.

"Out with Cindy. He should be home soon." She glanced at her watch. "God, it's one-thirty."

"I should leave, then. He's not feeling too charitable toward me. I'll help you clean up this mess and then I'll get out of here before we have another confrontation."

"He hates you." Katie reached up and turned Miller's face toward the light. She squinted and examined the green-and-yellow skin around Miller's eye. While she held his face, Miller turned his head and kissed her palm. "Did Judd do that to you?" she asked.

Miller nodded. He laughed. "This is getting to be a pretty tough bunch around here."

Katie wasn't ready, he noticed, for smiles of complicity. "Regardless of what happens between you and me, Miller, I want you to square things with Judd. You're his father. Even if you and I never get back together, you and Judd have to deal with each other for the rest of your lives."

"I guess he's lost all respect for me. I can't imagine my father ever doing a thing like this."

"Your father had his faults, too, Miller. Why do you think your mother left?"

Miller felt his blood heat up. "It wasn't my dad's fault. She ran away with another man."

"Ran? Or was chased? Do you think he was so faultless? Believe me, he wasn't."

"What makes you say that?"

"This isn't the time to go into that, Miller. I loved your dad, but I just don't want you to think he was some kind of a saint when he was as human as the rest of us."

"Christ, Katie. You didn't even know my mother. You never even met her."

"It doesn't matter. I picked up things. From your father. From Mrs. Donaldson. From things I went through after the funeral, when we gave his clothes away."

"Like what?"

"Later. Not tonight. I want you to go now."

"I thought you loved my father."

"Of course I loved him. And I'm sure your mother did, too. But there comes a point, Miller, when a man wounds a woman so badly that she has to leave to save her self-esteem."

"Damn it, Katie," he said, "my father was a good man."

She looked up at him and spoke quietly, evenly. "So were you, Miller," she said. "So were you."

21

When Miller got back to the apartment he put a Vivaldi tape on the stereo, poured himself a whiskey, and sat with his hand on the telephone. Despite the ugly scene at Katie's, he would have stayed if she had asked, but she pushed him out, using Judd as an excuse. Miller was aching with loneliness, longing for comfort. He needed someone to talk to, someone who would listen and comfort him without expecting any kind of allegiance or responsibility. No recriminations, no blame, no anger—a woman who was completely invulnerable and utterly carefree. He took out his wallet and leafed through the business cards that were tucked in an inside pocket. When he found the one he wanted, he lifted the receiver and dialed Gina's number. If Phil answered he would hang up.

But it was Gina who answered. Her voice was thick and slightly slurred.

Miller glanced at the clock. "Hi," he said. "It's Miller. I know it's late. I was just wondering. Is Phil there?"

"Miller?"

He hesitated. "Did I wake you?"

She laughed. "No. I was watching television. Couldn't sleep. It's an old movie with Cary Grant. Isn't he divine? Why don't you come over and watch it with me? I have some booze here."

"Where's Phil?"

"He's in Florida, deep-sea fishing." She waited. "I'm serious, Miller. Why don't you come over? You sound lonely. And so am I."

Miller considered inviting her to his apartment, but then, what if he couldn't get rid of her? It would be easier for him to walk away from her place whenever he wanted to.

He could hear Gina breathing on the other end of the line. "Miller?"

"I just need somebody to talk to. That's all. Just to talk to. Christ, Gina, I'm so lonely, I'm aching."

"I understand completely, sweetie. Remember what I told you? If you ever, ever, ever need anything—to talk, to just *be* with another human being, I told you I'd be here for you."

"You sure it's not too late?"

"You know where I live. I'll be waiting." She hung up.

Miller sat holding the receiver. He took another sip of the whiskey and felt it opening him up like a flower, warm, loosening. He hung up the phone and leaned back in the chair. By the time he had emptied the glass, he felt fortified. He went into the bathroom, washed his face, brushed his teeth, and put on a clean shirt. Clean underwear, too, just in case. When he stepped out into the hot, humid night, he didn't know exactly *what* he wanted from Gina, just somebody to hold him, somebody who didn't hate him or question his motives.

On the way to her house, though, he had second thoughts. His decision was just another mistake in the long line of bad choices he'd made recently. What if Phil should walk in? What if he decided to come home from his fishing trip early? What if a neighbor noticed his car and it got back to Katie?

When Miller turned the car onto Gina's block, he switched off the lights and glided into her driveway, pulling past her sports car and parking close to the house at the end of the tree-shrouded driveway. He had no doubts that he'd made a mistake when Gina answered the door in a purple silk décolleté robe, her plump and appealing feet bare, and her thick red hair flowing over her shoulders. It was the rest of it—her assumption that he had come not for company and comfort, but for something more. And why not? At two-thirty in the morning, what was she supposed to think? As soon as she closed the door behind him, she wound her arms around Miller's neck. "This is okay, Miller. Both of us are separated in a sense. You and Katie. And fishing trips and golf always come between Phil and me. You've heard of golf widows?" She moved closer to him and strengthened her hold on his neck. "Consider me a widow."

She was a little drunk, but so was Miller, though he was certain he could hold his liquor better than Gina could. He leaned down and hugged her, hoping that gesture might pass for an acceptable greeting. She smelled like patchouli and whiskey and cigarettes and a shampoo that had the fragrance of lemons. But everything was wrong, especially after the tentative truce with Katie. "I really just wanted to talk," he said, extricating himself from her arms. "Do you think I could have a drink? Whatever you're having."

She took his hand and led him into the living room. The skirt of her robe was slit in the back and the firm curve of her white calves gleamed through the opening with every step she took. Her flesh was solid and polished, like marble, and smooth, very smooth.

In the living room votive candles burned in glass containers on almost all the surfaces of the room—tables, mantelpiece, windowsills. Billie Holiday's voice drifted out over the room. Below the pleasing slide of the music, the air conditioner hummed steadily. Gina poured him a glass of brandy and then sat back on the white brocade sofa. The candlelight softened her face and reflected in her eyes. Miller dropped to his knees on the white shag carpet and laid his head on her silken knee. He was grateful that, for once, she was quiet. She pulled her long nails gently through his hair, raising goose bumps on his arms. "Ummph," he murmured. Then her fingers played along his cheek, caressing. Miller turned around with his back to the sofa and laid his head against her legs again. He closed his eyes and sipped from his brandy. Somehow when Gina slid closer to the edge of the sofa, the skirt of her robe fell away and he felt the soft flesh of her bare thigh warm against his ear. As she stroked Miller's hair and shoulders, he was too relaxed even to sip his drink. Music faded and swelled and the space around him expanded and contracted, a dark island with a white shag coast and dozens of pale, flickering beacons. Lighthouses. Warnings of danger. Death by drowning. As he floated, he saw Jimmy Duane's hand rising from the water, he passed the rowboat where his father was quietly fishing. He could see the shoreline now. He was close to safety. His eye focused on a single dancing light. It was the bedroom he had shared with Katie. No. It was Adra's window at the beach house. Or was it the bright kitchen door at his childhood home? He let the water caress him and he lay back in its cool dark arms and then he drank of the water and sank in a long slow spiral and he was no longer afraid.

Miller opened his eyes and saw through a painful blur Gina's bright face spinning above him. He sat up so fast his head hurt. "God, what time is it? What happened?"

Gina sat down on the chair facing the sofa and laughed. She was wearing a periwinkle blue suit and heavy gold jewelry. Her shapely legs were covered in sheer luminous stockings, her feet fitted into high-heeled shoes with a linen-like texture. She pushed her sleeve back and looked at her gold watch. "It's nine-thirty, baby, and I'm late for a walk-through on a house I've sold."

Miller looked around—slowly, because it hurt to move his head. He was on the white sofa with a blanket thrown across his legs. The glass votives that had burned so brightly the night before were blackened by smoke. Two empty brandy snifters sat on the coffee table, smudged with fingerprints, and one with Gina's lipstick. There was a fresh cigarette burn on the arm of the sofa. In the daylight everything looked theatrical and sordid. "What happened last night?" he asked.

She laughed again. "Unfortunately, sweetheart, nothing happened. You fell asleep, that's what happened." She patted his knee. "It's okay. You were worn out."

Miller groaned. "Oh God, Gina, I'm sorry. I'm really sorry. You looked so beautiful, and you just made me feel so relaxed, I guess I let go. I remember a lighthouse, water."

"You were dreaming," Gina said. "You kept mumbling something about shoals."

"And then?"

"Then you folded," she offered, still in good humor. "You just plain, flat-out folded on me." She stood up and smoothed her skirt. "And now I have to go to work."

Miller held out his hand, acutely conscious of his sour breath and heavy beard. "Can I make it up to you?"

She glanced at her watch. "Not today, sweetie. Phil's coming back tonight and I have to be at a house out in Farragut"—she glanced at her watch—"right now." When she accepted his outstretched hand, he pulled her down beside him on the sofa. "Don't muss me," she warned, and put her finger against his lips. "We'll try this another time, maybe. Rain check?" She leaned over and kissed his forehead. "There's coffee in the kitchen. Just pull the front door closed when you leave." She blew a kiss and disappeared in a mist of perfume, her plump silken thighs whispering secrets Miller knew he would never learn.

He lay back on the sofa and looked around the room. The silence seemed enormous. This was a house without children, a house without much of a center. He was sorry to have deprived Gina of his temporary affection, but he was thankful things had turned out the way they had. It would be far too complicated to get involved with her, and she was not really his cup of tea. Gina probably knew as well as he that there would be no rain check. And she had been a great sport about what happened—or *hadn't* happened—the night before. Katie had been right about Gina. What was it Katie had said? *Once you got past the hair and makeup.* Miller realized that Gina possessed a substantial amount of humanity and compassion, and that what spilled over was seasoned with a considerable hunger and neediness of her own. He'd been selfish, thinking only of his own needs, not hers.

He got up, folded the blanket, and laid it across the back of the sofa. He plumped up the pillows and carried the brandy snifters and crystal candle holders into the kitchen. He was surprised by the sudden burst of light in that white gleaming room, so glaring it made his head throb—white cabinets, white appliances, a sparkling white floor. He put the glasses in the sink, filled it with sudsy water and washed and dried everything. Katie had always hated dishwashing, but for him it was an exercise that seemed infinitely rewarding. It offered immediate satisfaction and the task itself gave you time to plan whatever came next. When he was finished, curious, he wandered through the rooms. Everything was tasteful but cold, with no mark of individuality. From the accouterments you could never have guessed much about the people who lived there. No plants, no paintings, few accessories or mementos except for photographs of Phil— Phil with his golf partners, Phil with his golf trophies, Phil playing golf with Gerald Ford and some other dignitaries, and three plaques naming Gina as realtor of the year. That was all that might give a clue to the occupants' avocations or passions. And if that was the sum of their lives, Miller felt sorry for them.

He trudged up the curving, white-carpeted stairway to the second floor and looked into the master bedroom suite. It, too, was decorated all in white. He saw Gina's bed, still unmade, a huge inviting bed that he in his drunken state might have enjoyed but not remembered. Thank God he had passed out before anything happened. He went in and sat down on the edge of the mattress and ran his hand across the cream-colored satin sheets. There was a smudge of Gina's lipstick and one of her long curly hairs on the pillow case. Her purple silk robe was tossed carelessly in front of the closet door and a green silk thong was thrown over a white upholstered chair. Miller walked into the bathroom and looked around. Jacuzzi, wall-to-wall mirrors, his and her sinks, bidet. God, a bidet. How decadent. The mirror was framed in lights like a theater dressing room. Miller snapped the light switch on and studied his reflection. He looked awful. He rummaged in the vanity drawer and found a pair of scissors. He had at that moment decided to give up the rebellious beard. He hacked away at it and flushed the evidence down the toilet. Then he found Gina's small silver razor, lathered his face with her expensive French soap, and finished the job. Occasionally the razor would slip and add a cut to his already battle-scarred face.

In the shower he was overcome by fear as he suddenly assessed the danger he had put himself in by coming to Gina's house. If Katie found out, if Phil found out, if Judd found out, everything would be lost. He rinsed off quickly and stepped out onto the fluffy white rug. He dressed again in his rumpled, sweaty clothes, and then he walked down the stairs and out of Gina's house.

Finally, it had begun to rain. Steam rose from the warm asphalt and the air smelled cooler. For the first time, he could sense the approaching fall. When he got back to his apartment he called a florist and ordered peach-colored roses sent to Gina's office. No message. No signature. He thought about having the card say "Thanks" or "Sorry," but in the end he decided on no message. The roses would give Gina their own message, and that might serve to satisfy them both.

22

Judd sat hunched against the door of the car, as far away from Miller as he could manage. He had made it clear when Miller picked him up that he had come along on the fishing trip only because Katie had insisted.

Miller glanced sideways at the boy, studying the changes in him. His profile had hardened. His chin was now more defined, the nose and forehead sculpted firmly into the line that would be his adult face. Miller was nervous. This was supposed to be a day of making amends, deflecting anger—whatever it took to get the two of them back in sync. But it wasn't going to be easy, he could see that already. "The creek might be up a little after all the rain we've had," he ventured.

Judd continued to stare out the window, though he could have seen little in the predawn darkness, only the looming bent shapes of hemlocks along the parkway, their limbs heavy with the rain that had fallen for almost a week now, and whatever sights the sweep of their headlights might pick up on the winding road. Occasionally they could see streams of water illuminated as falls trickled down the rocks where the road was carved through the mountain. Springs splashed from the mountainside onto the roadway and the wild run of water in the streambeds, swollen by the long overdue rains, roared at the bottom of the embankments.

Miller tried to pry a crack in the silence. "My dad used to say he could catch fish in milky streams as well as clear ones, even after rains like these we've had lately." In fact, nothing could have kept his father from fishing, no weather devised by God nor any obstacle presented by the configuration of the mountains. Together they had fished Rough Creek, the Middle Prong of the Little River, Spruce Flats, Meadow Branch, Roaring Fork, and the Horseshoe stretch on Abrams Creek. All of them, and in any and every kind of weather—even snowstorms. Sometimes they fished in the black of night, their ears attuned to the splashes of rising fish toward which they might direct their casts.

Still no comment from Judd. Only the burdensome silence and the swish of tires on the wet road. Suddenly a deer sailed across the road in front of them and Miller smashed his foot down hard on the brakes. The car fishtailed on a wet patch and came to a stop just at the edge of a sharp incline, a straight drop studded with jutting rocks and young hemlocks.

Judd sat forward and peered down the precipice. "Shit," he whispered.

Miller laughed. Nothing like a brush with disaster to bring a body to attention. His own skin was prickling with fear at the close call. They watched as the deer's tail flashed white down the embankment. "That would have been a pretty rough descent," Miller said.

Judd grunted. Already, the connection was lost.

Miller rolled down his window to let in the noise of the rushing streambed. As the light came up, he saw that the water was wilder than he had guessed. In places it boiled far beyond its usual boundaries, and many of the spots he had fished dozens of times were almost unrecognizable. He loved the symphonic rhythm of that sound, but you had to be careful with water like that. It was highly unpredictable. He restarted the stalled motor and backed up with his foot on the brake. After that, he drove more slowly along the winding road. "You forget the wildness of this place sometimes," he said. "Remember that day on the trail when we saw the boar? That was something, wasn't it?"

Judd shrugged. He wore his impenetrable anger like a badge. Miller stopped trying to entice him into conversation and he suddenly remembered something his new therapist—a woman—had said. "Be honest with people. You'll be surprised at how well others respond to a forthright explanation on your part. It allows them to enter part of your fear, or your sadness."

Honesty? He had convinced himself that if he told people *part* of the truth, he could still say he was *telling* the truth, even if it were not the *whole* truth. Now he had admitted to this new therapist—Dr. Sylver—that a lie of omission was comparable to a lie of commission. So for the first time he told the whole truth about that day at the lake. Unlike Buckman's expensive leather furnishings, the pieces in Dr. Sylver's office were simple—an oak desk and swivel chair with a tweed cushion, a plain and practical gray sofa, fresh flowers in a green glass wine bottle. And she had a nice, open face and thick, silver-streaked black hair that curved around her small head like a cap. She was small but energetic, with good timing—knowing when to laugh and when to remain quiet, although Miller thought those reactions were instinctive rather than practiced.

The afternoon of his confession, Miller had slumped back on the sofa and rubbed his forehead. "I feel so damned guilty," he confessed.

"Even when I was doing it—treading water, waiting for him to . . ." He stopped and stared out the window.

"To what?" asked Dr. Sylver. "Say it."

He hesitated.

"*Say* it, Miller. Say it *out loud*."

"Okay, okay, I was waiting for him to fucking *die.* Is this loud enough? I just wanted him to leave me alone or to cooperate. Christ, something. Yes, *die*, okay? I knew even then, at that moment, it was cowardly, and now I can't forgive myself for waiting. I mean, is that my true nature? Do I have some huge, fucking character defect?"

"Think about this, Miller. You know how, on an airplane, they tell you that in the event of an oxygen failure, you put the mask on yourself first, and *then* on your children? You have to save yourself first. That's what you did, that's what your basic instincts ordered you to do. All you did was follow the simple rules of survival."

"Then why is it all so painful? And what about the dreams?" Miller asked. "I keep seeing him—Jimmy Duane—under the water. I'm like fucking Hamlet—afraid to die, afraid to go to sleep for fear I'll have the dream, and if I have the dream and wake up in the middle of the night, I'm afraid to go back to sleep because I might fall right back into the dream. So I get up and watch TV, read, or clean out the refrigerator—which, usually, I already did the night before. And I'm worn out, physically and emotionally."

She nodded. "That will pass, too, as soon as you resolve your role in this tragedy."

This, too, shall pass, thought Miller. Maybe. But when? When?

Driving along the parkway with Judd, Miller played the conversation over in his mind. Up ahead, at Abrams Creek, the rainbow trout would be waiting for them. Both their moods would be improved if one of them—he hoped it would be Judd—could land a nice fish. Neither of them spoke as they parked and unloaded the gear. They trudged silently along the trail, Judd lagging far behind out of sheer obstinacy. Mist was still clinging to the low shrubs and drifting up into the tree branches, but the sun was beginning to generate a little more warmth. They slung their waders over their shoulders and Miller toted the backpack with their lunch. Judd carried the fly box and rod that had belonged to Hollis. Miller was going to let Judd wear Hollis's waders, too. They were wider and bulkier than the more modern ones, but there was tradition in them, maybe even a little bit of luck. Miller had tried to teach Judd the rudiments of fly fishing a couple of years before, but Judd had been impatient back then, and irritable. He was a competitive kid who hated failing at anything, not understanding that expertise took time and practice. He kept catching his line in shrubs and trees behind him or jerking the rod so hard that he twice broke the fly off from the leader. "Easy," Miller kept saying, "don't pull it back any farther than over your head," but then finally he got impatient, too, and Judd gave up in disgust.

Miller was trying to remember how his own father had taught him. There was something spiritual and slightly mystical in the art of fly fishing, and getting angry was antithetical to the whole experience.

They heard the creek roaring even before they were halfway through the woods. Water was galloping over the rocks and in some places was ripping down trees and biting into parts of the bank. Rain rushing down from the higher elevations had swollen the water and changed the configuration of the stream. In some places, deep pockets boiled into whirlpools and cascades. As he pulled on his waders, Miller was seduced by the cool hollow vapors that rose from the water, but he worried about the wildness that the flooding had accelerated. The bank curved sharply where the water in its perpetual downhill journey had struck a huge ancient boulder and then turned back to its natural path. "I don't know about this, Judd," he said. "It looks pretty wild out there. See those pockets where the water is grinding up? People can drown in those."

Judd threw his gear down on the wet ground. "You mean we came all this way for nothing? Shit."

"Can we be civilized today, Judd? Can we forget about the anger for a while? Maybe we should just talk, let the fishing go for another day."

Judd sat down on a rock and started pulling on his grandfather's waders. "What? Are you chicken? We came here to fish, so let's fucking fish."

"Get real, Judd. Do you see that water? The first thing you have to learn is to respect it. It's like an animal. Would you stay here if you saw a bear, or a wild boar? That water has a life of its own, and today it's feeling angry, just like you."

Judd looked up from fastening the buckles on his shoulder straps and grinned. "Would Grandpa stay and fish today?"

Miller laughed. The grin pleased him, and the mention of Hollis was a clever way for Judd to crawl into his good graces. "Okay, your grandfather would have fished this stream today, yes. Hell, he's probably here now—fishing downstream somewhere, we just can't see him. But he's invulnerable now. We're not."

"Come on, Dad, don't be a wuss. We'll be careful. We came all this way, let's do it."

They were talking at last, and Miller didn't want to break their line of communication. Maybe if they stayed close to the bank . . . "Will you promise to stay where I can see you?"

"Promise," Judd said, nodding.

"Okay," Miller said. "Let's review the drill, just in case. There are some deep pockets in this creek. They're always there, but after a heavy rain they're especially dangerous. You could be in thigh-high water one minute, step into a pocket the next, and your waders would fill up with water and take you down."

"Yeah, right," Judd mumbled. "Whatever."

Miller took a deep breath and, remembering Dr. Sylver's advice, secretly shaped his hand into a fist to absorb his anger. "I'm serious, Judd. My dad used to tell me if I ever stepped into one of those holes I'd get turned upside down like I was in a washing machine."

"So?" Judd said.

Keep calm, Miller told himself. *Keep calm.* "So." He breathed deeply. "So the natural tendency in a situation like that is to try to come up straight to the surface, but with your waders filled, that's impossible, and you get disoriented from being knocked around under water, so the best thing to do is let yourself sink to the bottom of the pocket and then push out sideways. That takes real guts and supreme concentration. A lot of people get too panicky to do that."

Now Judd seemed a little more concerned. "And then what?"

Miller felt a chill ripple along his spine. The hair on the back of his neck bristled. It was a primeval instinct. "And then they drown," he said. He imagined Jimmy Duane, tossing in the roiling pocket like a rag doll.

Judd was watching him intently now. He must have realized what Miller might be thinking.

"Okay, give that back to me. Tell me what you'd do if you got stuck in a pocket and went down."

Judd sighed and rolled his eyes. "I've *got* it, Dad."

"Repeat it, dammit."

Judd held up his hands in surrender and repeated the instructions in a singsong voice. "Let yourself sink to the bottom of the pocket and then push out sideways."

"Good." Miller felt better. "But to avoid having to put that method to the test, let's just watch it, okay? That's all I'm asking. Be careful."

Miller accepted Judd's grunt as an agreement. He was still concerned, but if they remained close to the bank, they'd be fine. He tied an Adams fly on Judd's line and an elk hair caddis on his own and stepped into the water. The rush of the stream was so loud, they had to yell at each other to be heard.

He stood behind Judd and directed his arm on the first few casts, resisting the urge to slide his arms around the boy and hold him in an embrace. On the first cast Judd snapped the rod back too fast and the line knotted itself with the leader and fly and plopped into the water in an abysmal mess that took fifteen minutes to straighten out. "Think about the loop," Miller said patiently. "Almost immediately when you set the forward motion of the line, you have to check it, reverse it, in order to keep the fly and the leader ahead of the line at the moment they land on the water. Otherwise, the fish sees the *line*, not the *fly*, and then you're through with that particular fish for the day."

What would Hollis have said? *Slow down, slow down*. Miller took a deep breath and let it out. "Rhythm, rhythm," his father had chanted that first day and many days thereafter, and that is what Miller repeated to Judd. "Even catching them, setting the hook," he said, "you have to be aware of your rhythm. When the fish strikes, jerk the line with your left hand or the barb will tear the fish's mouth. We're returning them to the stream, remember? We want them to survive."

After Judd had accomplished a few competent casts, his expression softened. Even the set of his shoulders seemed kinder. Miller reasoned that once the boy had landed a fish, or even experienced a decent strike, the atmosphere for talking would be more sanguine.

Suddenly Judd yelled, and in the moment the big trout struck his

line he turned to Miller a joyful face devoid of all its recent animosity. "Fish," he screamed. "Fish." In his excitement he set the hook too fast, but the line held and Judd was laughing as he brought the trout in under Miller's direction. They measured it at fourteen inches and then, reluctantly, Judd dipped his hands into the water, passed them lovingly across the iridescent scales, and let the trout slip back into the water. "Give it back to the stream," Miller whispered.

They both laughed as the fish disappeared into a roiling pocket of dark green water and Miller realized that this was as close as he had come to being happy in a long, long time. Judd must have felt better, too. There was a slight smile on his lips as he cast his line again, but in his enthusiasm he cast too far back and when he brought the line forward again, instead of the easy ellipse he should have spun, he wrapped the line around the leader and fly and ended up with another knotted wad that landed a few feet in front of him in the water. Once they had straightened that out, he got some confidence back and told Miller he was aiming for the far side of a rock near the opposite shore. Miller agreed it looked like a good place a lazy fish might hide from the increasing heat of the sun. But Judd overestimated and the fly fell straight into some half-submerged branches. When he tugged on the line the whole limb bent forward. All of his efforts to dislodge the hook only seemed to entrench it more solidly in the undergrowth. "I guess I'll have to wade over there and untangle it," Judd said.

"Wait a minute," Miller yelled. He scanned the breadth of the creek, looking for pockets, but the water rushed along so impatiently it was impossible to read the surface. "I'll go after it," he said.

"No," Judd yelled back. He'd already started across, holding the rod in one hand, the other arm spread out for balance. "I screwed it up, I'll get it."

"Remember . . ." Miller began.

"Yeah, yeah. Dad, it's not going to happen." He stepped carefully on one slippery rock and then another, traversing the effervescent pools.

"Careful," Miller whispered, but when Judd made it safely to the other side and freed his line and Miller concentrated for a minute on tying a new fly, it was almost like a dream when he looked up to discover that Judd had disappeared from sight. All he could see was the turbulent roll of the creek before him and the wild boiling circle of the deepest pocket where someone or something might be thrashing under the water—a big fish or a grown boy whose waders had suddenly and unexpectedly filled with water. All he could see of Judd was the tip of Hollis's rod falling forward into the creek and then that too was gone, claimed, like the boy, by the water, perhaps for something Miller owed it.

Miller screamed Judd's name and dropped his rod and then he scrambled not into the pool, but back to the bank to get out of his waders. Once he had managed to pull them off, he ran stumbling into the water, screaming Judd's name, and suddenly he became disoriented. In the deafening violence of the water he saw before him three pools—no, four—and in his panic he could not be certain which one Judd had disappeared into. He plunged into the water, smashing his elbow against a rock, and then pulled himself up again, sliding along the bottom in his sock feet, skidding on the algae-covered rocks and going under in the first deep pocket he came to, which was all green swirling water and white oxygenated foam, and the momentum of the current would not let him touch bottom. Somehow he realized that the solid forms he felt with his feet and hands were almost certainly rock, and he surfaced, gasping, and was carried mid-stream to the next pocket, where he clung to a boulder to stop his progress and pushed his head down and under the water to look for Judd, but the current thrust him up again and carried him along in its relentless sweep, slamming him against stones and sharp branches. Finally it tumbled him close enough to shore to let him grab a cedar limb that held fast when he grasped it.

He clung to it, screaming Judd's name for what seemed like hours, screaming against the deafening noise of the water, and only when he stopped to catch his breath did he hear over the thundering rush of the creek and the explosive pounding of his heart another sound—a human voice. "Dad, over here, Dad."

Oh God oh God. Thank you, Lord, thank you. Miller held to the branch and wiped water from his eyes, and at last he spotted Judd twenty or thirty yards downstream, clinging to a branch that hung low over the water. When Miller opened his mouth to yell again he tasted blood and felt the punishing icy slap of the water. Now he saw Judd's face with its terrified expression, saw his hands slipping along the length of the branch he held and then frantically secure a hold again.

"Hold on," Miller yelled. "I'm coming, son." He managed to swing one leg up and over the branch he held, and finally he somehow pulled himself up on the bank, sliding back down the muddy edge and then wrenching his way up a second time. When at last he was able to hoist himself onto the bank, his legs collapsed, but he pushed himself up onto his knees and then, holding to the branches, stamped warm blood back through his veins and made his way through the thick brush until he was within a few yards of Judd.

He saw his hand and arm first, clinging to the branch, then the face with its bloody gash. Judd disappeared beneath the water with the rushing whims of the current and then reemerged, choking and coughing. His eyes rolled back. He was fading out, swooning, and then jerking himself back to consciousness. Miller knew that if Judd was swept downstream, he would never see him alive again.

He grabbed the branch above the one Judd clung to and eased himself down the bank, sliding on mud and the long wet grass. Roots and rocks bruised his feet, and the bark of the branch cut into his hand, but he managed to keep one foot on solid ground and to slide the other into the creek far enough so that he could reach out and grab Judd's wrist. When he pulled, though, it was as if the boy was stuck, wedged into the creek bed. For a crazy moment Miller imagined Jimmy Duane Goodfriend holding fast to Judd's ankle under the water, claiming him in retribution for his own life. Miller yelled above the commotion of the water. "Can you move your legs?"

Judd's face stretched in pain and Miller saw now that one eye was swollen almost closed. It was then that Miller, tightening his grasp on Judd's wrist, heard a sharp crack higher up on the branch he held, a crack as ominous and threatening as a gunshot. At that moment he remembered the knife in his pocket, the Swiss Army knife his father had told him to carry at all times. Judd's eyes rolled back momentarily and then focused again. Miller was running out of time.

He yelled above the noise of the water. "Listen, son, I want you to hold onto this branch again, okay? I'm coming in there with you." It was a risk, he knew, having them both in the water, but it was a chance he had to take. He directed Judd's hand to the branch again and when he was sure Judd was secure, he let go of his wrist and reached into his pocket for the knife. Then he grabbed the branch again and leaned out over the water and slid the blade of the knife under the straps of Judd's waders. The straps fell from the boy's shoulders and danced wildly in the raging current. Miller had known it wouldn't be enough to free him. He eased himself into the water and with the knife in one hand and the branch in the other he reached underwater and sliced through the rubber above the knee of the first leg of the wader, pulling the knife away from the leg so as not to cut Judd. On the second leg, though, he slipped and the knife hit flesh and Judd screamed and let go of the branch and they both went tumbling headlong down the stream. Miller held onto Judd's foot and both were tossed among ragged patches of white sunlight, green crashing water, and brown-speckled rocks. Miller's wrist smashed against a rock but he held onto the foot. *At all costs, he thought. At all costs.* When the creek tossed them into a shallow bed, built up by the current with pebbles and sand, Judd was still there, still breathing, and he gathered the boy's crumpled body in his arms and held him and rocked him in the cold water. Delivered. "You didn't get him, did you, you bastard?" Miller howled at the creek, but he knew that he was really talking to Jimmy Duane.

Where they sat in the stream, the water was only knee-high, a virtual bridge of rocks built up from the sediment and detritus that had been swept along in the flooding current. Miller rocked the boy and saw that the cut on his forehead was deep and the eye was cut, too, almost closed now, but Judd smiled up at him. "I did what you said, Dad. I went to the bottom of the pocket and came out sideways. You were right, Dad." He closed his eyes and Miller shook him awake again. "Don't go out on me, Judd, don't go out."

Miller hugged his son to his chest. His fingers were getting numb and he stood up and pulled Judd across his shoulders. Ahead were more dangers—slippery rocks, the raging current, time itself. Time. He stepped carefully, tripping, sometimes falling to his knees, babbling to Judd as he picked his way across the creek. "Keep your eyes open, Judd. That's the important thing. Don't fall asleep. Please, please don't sleep. Think about what you're going to tell Cindy. Think how she'll cry when you tell her."

Judd moaned.

"Talk to me," Miller said, fighting to keep his voice from breaking. "Talk to me. Don't sleep. Talk to me, goddamn it." Judd's weight shifted against his shoulder and the noise from the water hurled itself up around them. "What do you see, Judd? Tell me what you see."

The boy's voice was weak. "Please, Dad, I need to lie down."

"Keep talking." When Miller leaned forward to shift Judd's weight farther up on his shoulders, Judd screamed with some injury he had suffered under the water. "Judd. Tell me. Who do you love?"

"Mom. Cindy."

"Excellent. Keep talking. Who do you hate?"

"You. I hate you, Dad."

"Good. That needed to come out. What day is this?"

"Dunno."

"Who's the president of the United States?"

"Dunno. Can't . . ."

"Come on, who's the president, for Chrissake?"

"Down," said Judd. "Go to sleep."

Then, miraculously, they had reached the bank. Miller leaned forward and let Judd roll off his shoulder and onto solid ground. Once he had dragged himself up onto the bank, he lifted Judd over his shoulder again. "Now we're going to the car," Miller said. "One more little ride over your dad's shoulder. Talk some more." He stumbled along the path with his burden, looking up occasionally to get his bearings. It was hot in the trees now, but they were both shivering, and occasionally a long, drawn-out shudder rolled through Judd's body. Hypothermia, Miller thought. All that time in the water and the shock of his injuries. "Talk to me, boy. Talk."

But then they came into the clearing and saw the car. *The key, the key. It was in his pants pocket. Oh thank you, God. There it is.* Miller stripped Judd's wet clothes off and deposited him in the front seat, sitting him up so he would not go to sleep. Then he ran to the back of the car and opened the trunk to get his father's old army blanket out. He covered Judd with it and then drove like a madman through the mountains, passing on no-pass curves and double lines, praying that a forest ranger or state trooper would see him and give him an escort, but he saw none. Nobody else had been fool enough to come out on a day like this. Judd's teeth were chattering and he was shivering under the blanket, though outside the sun was burning off the remaining morning fog and steaming through the underbrush of the forest. Miller turned the heater to high and rolled down his window for fresh air. Every time Judd closed his eyes Miller yelled him back to consciousness. "Talk," he ordered. "Tell me why you were mad at me."

"You left."

"What else? Tell me. Talk."

"Girlfriend."

"Keep talking."

"You quit."

"Keep going."

"Dad. Let me sleep."

"No." When Miller finally saw the sign for the hospital, he grabbed Judd's arm and shook it. "We made it, Judd. Don't let go, son, don't let go." He leaned on the horn as he skidded into the emergency room entrance.

Judd's head rolled against the seat. He was unconscious.

"No, goddamn it, Judd, no. Not yet. We're here, son. Stay awake."

The rest of it seemed to happen in slow motion. An orderly rushed out with a wheelchair and then other people appeared, shouting instructions while Miller tried to explain what had happened. He ran down the hallway after them, but a door suddenly closed in his face, and a nurse took his arm and led him to a cubicle where he filled out papers. Then there was nothing left to do but to call Katie and wait. When he heard her voice, Miller broke down and Katie was screaming for him to tell her what had happened. "Is it Judd?" she cried. "Oh, God. He's dead, isn't he? Is he dead?" As soon as Miller was able to explain that they were at the hospital in Maryville, she hung up, and thirty minutes later she was there, pacing the floor in the waiting room. She looked at Miller with all the steely hatred and contempt that had built up in her heart over the past three months. "Everything you touch . . . ," she began, and then she turned away and began to weep.

When Miller reached to comfort her, she pushed him away. So he stood as close as she would allow and recited the details of the accident because she would not yield, she would not look at him.

"Is this the truth?" she asked. "Are you still lying?"

"Oh God, Katie," he said, "don't do this to me. You know how much I love that kid."

She sank down into a corner of the green Naugahyde sofa and curled up into a ball. She covered her face with her hands. "He's *my* baby," she cried. "He's my only baby." Her body was a closed circle, complete and discrete and utterly impenetrable.

She did not move until the doctor came in. "Your son has two serious injuries," he said. "A head injury and a cracked pelvis. His left arm is broken, too. The cracked ribs and the cut on the leg are minor."

"How bad is the head injury?" Katie's voice came out shrill and urgent.

"We're not sure yet. He's gone to sleep."

"What do you mean, gone to sleep?" Katie demanded.

"He's lapsed into a coma."

"For how long?" Miller cried.

"We don't know. It could last days or even weeks. We're going to do a CAT scan and an MRI to see if there's any edema—any swelling—on the brain."

"I know what edema means," snapped Miller. "So does my wife."

Katie cast him an imploring look. "Miller, for God's sake . . . "

The doctor waved his hand to dismiss the outburst. "He'll be in intensive care when we get back from x-ray. You can see him when he's settled in there, and then you can visit every four hours."

Katie's face crumpled. "That's all? Every four hours?"

The doctor looked at his chart. "Mrs. . . . Sharp. We have other patients in there who are even sicker than your son. It has to be a controlled atmosphere. I wish I could tell you more, but I won't know the full extent of his injuries until I see the x-rays." He took Katie's hand. "Look, I know how worried you are. I have children of my own. I promise you, we'll do everything we can. I know you're worried. I'll get back to you as soon as I can. We have to take this hour by hour." He reached over and shook Miller's hand. "You look pretty banged up, too. You ought to go down to ER and get somebody to look at your cuts."

Miller's clothes had dried since they left the creek, but he was chilled to the bone. His head hurt and new pains were sending signals to his brain every few minutes. He would have prayed, but in his heart he believed that his prayers would not be heard, he had done too many bad things. That day he had found his father, he had prayed for some sort of divine intervention and it had not been granted. And since then, he had hurt so many people, committed so many transgressions, that his prayers would not even be worth the wasted breath. He didn't know about Katie anymore. Throughout their marriage, she had gone to the Episcopal Church without him. He knew that she prayed. And every night before going to sleep she turned her back to him for a few minutes and whispered some sort of prayer, but they had not discussed God very often in their years together.

He looked over at the woman who had been his wife for twenty years and he felt that he had used up his last chance with her. She had slept with another man, she had prayed secret prayers, and now Miller had injured her only son. She must have felt his penetrating gaze because she looked up at him with a desperate face, fierce eyes. "You were supposed to be talking, for God's sake. You were supposed to be *explaining*, and now . . . " She gestured wildly. "Now *this.*" She was shaking. "Stay away from us, Miller," she cried, "just stay away. You're poison."

"That's not true. Listen, Katie. When this happened, when I pulled him out, it was like old times, like we were close again. I carried him. I had to carry him through the woods and across the creek. And, I don't know, I can't explain, we were close again."

"He was only half conscious."

"Yes, but I could feel this . . . closeness."

She shook her head. "Stop it. Just shut up, will you, Miller? Shut up. I hate you. None of this would have happened if you hadn't done what you've done."

Miller grabbed her arms. "The point is, Katie, I got him back again. I got him back."

"This far," Katie said. "And what now? What if . . . ?" She could not bring herself to say it and he would not listen. You do not say such things about your child, you do not think about the unthinkable. To articulate it might make it come true. Miller remembered the sidewalk game he had played as a child. *Step on a crack, break your mother's back.* He remembered how he professed not to believe, but he never stepped on the cracks. Not once in his entire childhood.

Katie turned away. At the time when they needed each other most, they were like strangers. Miller could never go home again, not now. Yet, it was not Katie who was changed, he realized, it was he. And he could never go back to the way he had been before, even with the job back, even without Adra. Something had shifted inside him, altered him irrevocably. He shuddered and turned his head toward the window. The sun was lowering, it was getting late. He wanted only to rest, to drift into a forgetfulness that would give him peace. He sank down on the sofa of the waiting room, ignoring the stares of the other waiting families. He would have his wounds tended to later, but at that moment he savored the pain. He wanted to feel what Judd was feeling. The last thing he remembered seeing before he sank into sleep was Katie leaning forward on the other end of the sofa, her hands pointed under her chin in an attitude of prayer. As if that could help them now. As if that had ever helped.

23

Four days. Judd had been unconscious for four days. Miller and Katie took turns making brief trips home to change clothes and shower, and then they were back, keeping their vigil in the waiting room of the intensive care unit, making friends with other anxious parents, and renewing their acquaintance with pain. During the times they were allowed in to see Judd, Miller leaned over his bed, whispering anything that came into his head, but most of what was there, he couldn't say. It was like trying to pray after you haven't done it for years. He and Judd hadn't really talked for a long time, not the way they used to, so everything seemed to be about Miller. *Judd, I need you to wake up. Wake up now. This is your dad. I have to talk to you. I have to explain. Don't let go now. Oh God, please come back to us.*

After the dry summer, now it seemed that the rain would never end. It fell unrelentingly, glazing the streets and sidewalks, flattening and fading late summer blooms and flooding the rooftops that Miller could see from the sixth-floor hospital window. But he was glad for the rain. It suited his mood and made the outside world less pleasant for all those who were not forced to share in his suffering. While he and Katie sat in the waiting room, friends came, shaking moisture from their umbrellas and bringing things that were useless but comforting—fruit waxed and polished to a colorful sheen, plants that would have to be taken back home, inspirational books that would never be read, hugs, tentative kisses, hand-holding, tears. It was the tears that Miller received most gratefully. Those were the friends who really understood, he thought. Re-Phil, seeming genuinely concerned, stopped in a couple of times a day when he was making hospital rounds, and Miller felt sorry for all the terrible things he had said about him. Gina came daily, somber and subdued, and Miller saw from the first moment that she would never mention that lost evening they had shared. She sat with her arms around Katie and whispered encouragement. For Miller, there was a light kiss on the cheek and a squeeze of the hand, but Miller could tell it was really for Katie's sake that she visited. All these commiserations were received gratefully, but when Jack walked in and Miller fell against his shoulder, he felt truly protected for the first time since the accident.

The two men walked slowly down the long corridors of the hospital, their footsteps echoing against the marble floor. "He's going to pull through," Jack assured Miller. "You know how you get feelings about things? I just have this feeling about Judd. I have faith in his power to survive. He takes after you. You're a survivor, Miller. So is he. He's gonna make it, buddy."

Miller nodded, unable to speak.

Jack squeezed Miller's shoulder. "Hey," he said, "the office has gone to hell since you left. They've given your staff and your contracts to that asshole Lucas."

"Lucas? Shit. They gave him the California contract? He couldn't find his ass with radar."

Jack laughed, his eyes glistening. "That's what I'm saying, buddy. You've got to come back."

Miller cheered up a little. It was good to talk about other things, worlds other than the one at the hospital, with its antiseptic aura, gleaming floors and cold silver basins, its muted voices and cries, the smell of unerasable suffering and anguish. And he and Katie were now an integral part of it. Insiders. Every time they went into intensive care they wept to see the tubes and needles that connected Judd to his oxygen, IV, and monitors. Occasionally his eyelids would move and sometimes he would moan faintly, but he never responded to their constant attempts to awaken him. Miller had thought of little else, not Adra and her baby, not his lost job or his lost marriage or his past, only Judd's condition and his unpredictable future—when he might move, smile, wake up, say their names.

Miller and Jack stopped at the nursery window and looked in at the newborns. Miller was transfixed, looking at the miniature, perfectly formed little fingers and noses, eyelashes like filament, the steady pulse beneath the thin skin of the tender, unfinished skulls. He remembered looking at Judd for the first time, marveling at his completeness. Katie had cried when they held the baby up for her to see. "Look what we did, Miller," she said. "This is better than all our academic degrees, anything we could buy, build, or imagine. It's the best thing we'll ever do together."

She had been right. It was the best thing they would ever do together. And if they lost this trophy, their life together would be finished. There was no question about that, especially since Miller was culpable. He walked quickly away from the nursery window and Jack didn't catch up with him until he turned the corner of the next corridor. Jack pushed him against the wall. "Okay, talk," he said. "Tell me."

"I shouldn't have let him wade out that far, with the stream swollen from all the rain. I told him about the deep pockets and then I wasn't looking. I was tying a fly. I wasn't even looking, after warning him about it. It was like a dream, Jack. He was gone, just like that."

Jack put his arms around Miller's neck and held him in a rough embrace. "Will you stop torturing yourself, for Christ's sake? Why do you always have to make it so hard on yourself? Shit happens, Miller. There's nothing we can do to change it."

Miller pulled away and started walking back toward the waiting room. "Katie blames me. She acts as if I did it on purpose."

"Come on, Miller. She doesn't mean it. She's mad as hell at you, and she can't articulate it except to blame you for this, because it's so immediate. It's something she can put her finger on, and she's scared, just like you are."

"Yeah," said Miller. "I am scared, Jack. Scared shitless."

"I know, buddy, I know." Jack scratched his head. "How long before the next visiting hours in intensive care?"

Miller glanced at his watch. "Two hours."

"Okay, let's get out of this place for a while. Just coffee. I know you're not drinking any more."

Miller shook his head.

"Why not?" said Jack. "You have two hours. Come on, I'll have you back here in plenty of time. There's a restaurant right down the block. Maybe Katie will come, too."

"No. She won't budge from here. I can't leave her. Even if she's not speaking to me, I can't leave her. Judd either. What if he woke up?"

Jack nodded. "I understand, Miller. It's fine. It's okay."

When they got back to the waiting room Katie was talking to the doctor. Miller's heart raced. "Is something wrong?" he demanded, pushing between Katie and the doctor.

"No, no," the doctor said. "I just wanted to tell you there's been a change, an encouraging change. Judd's very agitated. He's thrashing around a lot, crying in his sleep. It's a good sign. They do this sometimes when they're trying to wake up."

Katie held both hands over her mouth. Her eyes were wide. Jack put his arm around her shoulders and kissed the top of her head.

"Can we see him?" Miller asked.

"Wait a while. Wait for visiting hours. It's pretty disturbing to see him now, but I promise you, it's a good sign. Why don't you go out and get some dinner, get a change of scenery?"

Katie shook her head. "No. I'm staying right here. If Judd wakes up, will you come and tell us right away?"

The doctor took her hand. "Absolutely. I'm due in surgery now. I'll keep you informed about your son's condition." When he turned and walked away, Miller was frightened, as if with the doctor's disappearance they were suddenly left defenseless. He walked over to the window and leaned his palms against the marble sill. Below in the city street he saw people walking in the rainy September night. "Four days," he whispered. "He's been unconscious for four days."

Katie disengaged herself from Jack's arm and sat down on the sofa. "I'm not leaving here," she said, her voice shaking. "If Judd *is* waking up he might call for me. I want to be here when he comes to." She waved a hand in Miller's direction. "*He* can go."

Jack looked at Miller and shrugged, and Miller shook his head and turned back to the window. A few minutes later he saw Jack on the street below, coming out of the hospital entrance, hunched against the rain. It was the way he saw everything now—from a distance, disassociated.

At their next visit Judd was still unconscious, still agitated. Occasionally he would yell something they couldn't understand and then weep as if he were heartbroken.

When they left the unit that night Katie lay down on the sofa in the waiting room and covered herself with the afghan she had brought from home on one of the few excursions she had made to shower and change clothes. She was closing up again. Miller leaned over her. "Katie." She rolled over on her side and shut her eyes.

Miller turned away and walked out of the room. At the end of the hall there was a door marked "Chapel." He hesitated, pushed the door, and then went in. It was a small room with a few chairs lined up in rows and a nondescript altar topped with a vase of spider mums. He was thinking about Pascal's wager. Maybe it was better to take the chance and pray than to do nothing at all. He sat down on the back row and grasped the back of the chair in front of him. He was a sinner. He had failed his family. Would God listen? Would God care about the concerns of a murderer? He closed his eyes and started to talk. Just started to talk. "Listen, I know what you must be thinking. We come when we need you. When we don't need you, we don't communicate. We don't pray. I've never been sure about you, whether you're really up there, whether you really do know how many hairs are on our heads or how many birds fall from the sky. All I know is that somebody, some—being—gave me my boy. It must have been you, it had to be. And I don't want to lose him. Please God I need you to save him. You made him perfectly and I need you to keep him that way. And what I'm telling you—what I'm prepared to do—is promise to make everything right if you'll save him for Katie and me. I swear it." His voice dropped to a whisper. "I swear it on my very soul."

He sat back and opened his eyes. The room was the same, yet he felt relieved somehow, as if he had done his best now, tried every possible way to save his child. When he stood up he sensed the weight of his grief like a hard thing under his heart. He shuffled back to the waiting room and looked in. The lights had been dimmed for the night, and all over the room, in chairs, on sofas, on cots brought from home, families slept, waiting for word about their loved ones. The sleeping bodies breathed off trepidation, resignation, a dull heavy sense of acceptance and a thin vapor of hope.

Miller tiptoed across the room and looked down at Katie. She slept deeply, her mouth open, her forehead creased in an expression of stunned concentration. Miller saw on her cheeks the dried streaks of her earlier tears. It broke his heart to think she had fallen asleep crying. He nudged her over slightly and then stretched out beside her, fitting her back against his chest, her warm rump against his senseless groin. Even in those crowded and desperate conditions, with other families sleeping and tossing around them, it felt good to be lying beside her again. As he rearranged the afghan over them, Katie woke briefly. "Miller?" she whispered. He was afraid she might send him away, but she pulled his hand onto her shoulder. "Tell me about Judd," she murmured. "Tell me something good."

"I only know what you know," Miller whispered. "He's not awake yet."

"I don't mean that. Tell me about Judd's life. Tell me what you love about him."

Miller pulled her closer and whispered against her neck. "I loved Judd even before he was born," he told Katie, and he could sense her smile without seeing her face. "Remember the nights when you were pregnant and we used to lie in bed and wonder about him, what he'd look like, how funny or tall or smart he'd be? I'd put my hand on your belly, and he'd bounce all over the place, rolling around in your stomach. We used to joke that he'd be an athlete. Remember that? And when we played music, and he moved, we thought he might be a musician. You said a dancer, maybe, and of course, I wasn't crazy about that idea. He did somersaults, too, what my grandfather used to call *didos*. And when he was finally, finally, born and the nurse carried him out to show me, I thought he was the most beautiful baby, the most perfectly formed, the most alert child that was ever brought into this world. And the next day, in your room? I don't think I ever told you this, but when I watched you breast feeding, God, Katie, I never loved you so much as I did at that moment. You seemed like an angel, and the baby—the baby seemed to flourish in your aura. You were so beautiful, so serene, and so sure of yourself as a mother. Me, I was all thumbs. I couldn't even open the safety pins for the diapers at first, and I was awkward holding him. But you took to motherhood right away, as if you'd been born for it.

"I was so excited in those days. I couldn't wait to get home from work, to see how Judd had changed or what he'd learned that day. Remember how he'd pound on that little piano he had? And, oh—those sounds he made, the way he tested his lungs, even when it made no sense. Then, when he was old enough to play with blocks, I was convinced he was going to be an architect. And he had such a sweet nature. He'd kiss us with those soft little lips and put his little arms around us and—Katie?" He felt her body relax, and she breathed with soft little snores. Miller pulled her closer to him and wrapped his arms around her waist, treasuring the closeness of her, the soft, round lines of her body.

And then in the middle of the night it happened—the thing Miller had prayed for. A nurse shook his shoulder. "Mr. Sharp," she said in an excited whisper. "Come quickly. Your son is waking up."

24

Miller needed to talk to somebody. He tried Dr. Sylver's office, but her secretary said she was out of town for the weekend. Then, driving along the interstate, he suddenly remembered Mrs. Donaldson. He stopped at a flower shop and bought a bouquet of sunflowers, and then he drove to the old neighborhood.

Every time he visited there, things seemed smaller than they did in memory. The narrow streets were cracked with age and overhung with huge old trees now bare of foliage—sycamores, maples, locusts, and ancient, gnarled dogwoods. Gutters were choked with fallen leaves, streets shiny with rain. In this area there was still a real connection to the past—sidewalks with curbs, small yards, alleyways and gardens, and houses with arches and gables and cupolas and columns and wraparound porches. Trellises supported tangled rose vines, now bare except for a few brown rose hips. Miller passed gazebos, tree houses, ten-foot azaleas, and wisteria with vines as thick as tree trunks. Old trees, old houses, old memories. History. Many of the people who lived in this neighborhood had been born there and would die there, having come full circle among the people they grew up with or outlasted.

Both his father's house and Evelyn Donaldson's were Arts and Crafts bungalows, with heavy, dark woodwork and elaborate staircases. On the landing of Hollis's house was a beautiful stained glass window that, every afternoon, washed the steps in blue, opalescent light. The rain was letting up a little now and occasionally the sun dipped out below the clouds. Miller parked in his father's driveway and then walked up to Mrs. Donaldson's front steps and rang the bell. He could hear her shuffling slowly through the house. When she opened the door she squinted, blinked, and then smiled when she recognized Miller. He extended the sunflowers and she clapped her hands. "How did you know I missed my flowers? Winter's coming, isn't it?" She took the sunflowers in her gnarled white hands and then stepped back to allow Miller entry. "Stay a bit," she said. "You seem like a man with time on his hands these days."

He sat down on the Chippendale sofa, its worn arms covered with clean crocheted doilies. The house was too warm, he thought, but it had a pleasant smell, like lavender, and the fragrance of something like cornbread baking in the oven.

"I'll be right back," Mrs. Donaldson said. "Let me put these in water. And I'll make us some tea."

Miller looked around the room while Mrs. Donaldson moved about the kitchen. Everything seemed exactly as it had been thirty years before. The Seth Thomas clock over the mantel, the orange-and-brown afghan hanging over the back of the wing chair, lace curtains, Oriental carpets. When Mrs. Donaldson came back, Miller took the tea tray from her and patted the sofa cushion beside him.

She looked at him closely, as if reading his mind. "You need someone to talk to. What's the matter, Miller?"

He took her hand. It was so fragile it seemed like a bird's claw, but the skin was soft as old silk. "You're very perceptive," he said. "Always have been."

"You get this old," she said, laughing, "you've pretty much seen everything. And you sense things."

He nodded.

"Does it have anything to do with missing your father? It's nine months now, isn't it?"

"That, too. But so many things have happened." He released her hand and took out a handkerchief from his pocket to dab at his eyes. "Evelyn, I almost lost my son this week."

"No. Oh no, Miller." She squeezed his fingers and edged closer to him. "Tell me. Is he all right now?"

"He will be. We were fishing and he stepped into a deep pocket and the water tossed him around pretty good and he hit his head on a rock. He cracked a pelvis, broke some ribs, got a concussion. He was unconscious for four days. I thought he was going to die. I thought I was being punished for something I had done wrong."

"Some specific thing?"

"Yes."

She held up her hand to deflect his confession. "God doesn't work that way, Miller. If you study the pattern of retribution, you'll see that's it's fairly inequitable. I think hell is something we go through on this earth, but there are periods of heaven thrown in, too." Her voice was soft and melodic, comforting. Miller wanted to lean against the back of the sofa and close his eyes. The warmth of the room made him sleepy. Since Judd's accident, he had not slept more than a few hours at a time.

"Do you remember enough of the old days, Miller, to recall my baby dying, and then my husband passing away shortly after that?"

Miller nodded. "I remember my mother cooking casseroles and bread and Dad carrying things back and forth over here. Everybody was sad. I remember the funeral, too, and the casket. It was so tiny, and that made it sadder. And I remember your laying a bunch of flowers on the casket. They were red. Bright red."

"You remember that? My goodness. Yes. They were poppies. Poppies and baby's breath. The baby only lived for a week. In those days the doctors didn't know as much as they know now. It was some sort of a birth defect, his heart. It was incomplete, they said, as if he wasn't quite finished when he came into this life. On the outside, though, he looked beautiful, just perfect." She moved her hands in the air to shape the image of a child. "It was impossible to believe he was somehow damaged." She looked off into the past and sighed. "We named him Anthony, after my husband, Anthony William Donaldson. I have one photo of him, the one they took in the hospital. They didn't give those bracelets then, you know, the little ones with the beads. Otherwise, I would have had that. And then Anthony having that car accident so soon after that. On his way home from work, something he did every day. And the worse part was that I could never decide whether I had actually been a mother. Or whether I could still be called a 'wife.' So many questions, so much suffering. Your father helped me through that, though, God forgive me."

Miller sat forward. "I don't understand. What do you mean by that?"

Her hand flew to her mouth. "Oh dear, I thought . . . Well, I thought . . ."

"What? What are you trying to tell me?"

"I always thought that you knew. About your father and me, I mean. Remember how he used to come over and help me after

Anthony died? He'd patch the roof, or fix the plumbing. All I had to do was ask, and he was there. It started innocently. It was when your mother got involved in the little theater that it became something more. She'd be gone and your father was lonely and I was lonely, and he'd come over, ask if there was anything that needed fixing. The first time it was a cup of coffee, and the next time, two cups of coffee, and always, always, long conversations. You'd be off with your friends, your mother would be at rehearsal, and we'd talk, and then it was more than talk. It was . . . comfort. Friendship. And then we fell in love. We never intended to do anything about it. Not while Lauralee was alive. And no divorce. I loved your mother, too, you know—as much as she'd let anybody love her. I thought at the time I should move away—but then she left home, and Hollis needed me. And then when we found out that your mother had died, we talked about getting married, but we decided that things were lovely as they were, so we didn't really need that part of it." She patted Miller's knee. "Is it hard for you to imagine either your father or me having those kinds of feelings?"

Miller cheeks grew hot. "I never knew. I never had any idea."

"Oh please don't let this color your memories of your father, Miller. You and Lauralee always came first for Hollis. We both agreed on that. After all, you were his family. It was enough for me, the way things were, because I had my own memories, too." She hesitated, rubbing her hands together as if for warmth. "Are you angry at me, Miller?"

Miller felt stunned. "I'm in no position to judge anyone."

"I don't think I took anything from you, Miller. I never interfered."

Miller leaned over and kissed her hand. "Evelyn, I believe you. It's just that . . . I would never have believed . . ."

She watched his face expectantly. "Believed what? He was the best man I knew. Kinder even than my husband. And that's saying something, because Anthony was a good man. Your father was smarter, too, and I'm not being disloyal when I say that. He just was. He was a fine teacher, I don't have to tell you that. He knew everything, *everything*, and he never stopped learning, never stopped reading."

"I didn't mean," Miller began. He listened to Evelyn's voice, noticing how the modulation changed slightly as she spoke, but there was something inside him that had suddenly dropped away, and he felt inexplicably sad. It was not comforting, as he might have supposed, to know that his father had been as weak and human as he. It was terrifying, because he had always measured everything against his father's example. Everything.

"But we haven't talked about you at all," Mrs. Donaldson said. "Or Judd. We were talking about Judd, and how awful you felt. Oh dear, how did we get onto this subject anyway? You were telling me something." She smoothed her white hair and settled back against the brocaded sofa. "Tell me, now, Miller. Tell me about you and Judd and Katie."

"It's only Judd," he lied. "I needed to tell you about him." He looked at his watch.

"Oh, dear. Now I've embarrassed you," she said.

"No, no, it's just . . . I need some time to absorb this. I'm not judging you, Evelyn. I'm just a little tired."

"Next time, then," she said. "Whenever you want to talk, I hope you'll come back." She looked worried for a second, then held her hands to her face. "Are you thinking of selling your father's place?"

"Not yet, Evelyn. Don't worry. I'll keep it for as long as you . . ." He hesitated. "For as long as you like."

She laughed again. "You were *going* to say, for as long as I *live*."

Miller held up his hands in surrender. "You don't miss anything, do you?"

"But, dear boy. Keep the house? Would you really do that for me?"

"I don't need the money, not if I'm going back to work."

"But you have to pay the property tax, and the utilities, and . . ."

Miller touched his finger to his lips. "Consider it an investment in your happiness. And," he quickly added, "my pleasure."

She put her hands on her cheeks and looked up at him, her eyes glistening. "You're a fine man, Miller. Just like your father."

"And you're a lovely, lovely women, Evelyn," said Miller. He stood up. "Thank you. I'm glad you were there to comfort my father when he needed you, and to love him, too."

He helped her to her feet. "Thank *you*, Miller," she said. "And kiss that sweet boy for me. I shall pray for him. And Katie, too."

Miller pressed her hand, bowed slightly, and let himself out. He glanced over at his father's house but decided not to go in. At the moment, it would have been more than he could bear.

Driving back to the hospital, he felt overcome by loss. Maybe it was the idealization of his father. Maybe it was his own sense of failure. Dr. Sylver had urged him to think of other things when negative thoughts overwhelmed him. He forced himself to count his blessings. *Judd is alive and awake. I have not had a drink in four days.*

When Miller walked into the hospital room, Judd was sitting propped up against his pillows watching cartoons on television. Miller laughed. "And they told me you had no brain damage."

"Okay, so I regressed a little," Judd said. He laughed, too, and that was the thing that made Miller cry. He turned his face to the wall and when the shaking stopped he sat down beside the bed.

Judd turned off the television set. There was a bewildered look on his face. "Are you okay, Dad?"

"I am now," Miller said. "Or I will be. Son, can you ever forgive me? I'm so very very sorry."

"For what? Jesus, Dad, it wasn't your fault, you know. I mean, you *saved* me."

"Maybe so," said Miller, "but I put you at risk."

"Not intentionally, you didn't," Judd said. He sat forward a little and grimaced with pain.

"But if I hadn't insisted . . ."

Judd held up his hand. "Look, Dad, get over it, okay? I'm sick of this poor-me shit you've been dishing out for the past few months. Stop blaming yourself for everything, will you?"

"But did your mother tell you the truth about the drowning? That I waited, and the man drowned?"

"He would have drowned anyhow," Judd said. "If you hadn't jumped in, he would have drowned, but you *did* jump in." He sighed. "Jesus Christ, Dad, give it a rest."

It was the best gift Judd could have given him—shrugging off a monumental event with his flip, righteous anger. Miller took Judd's hand and leaned forward to hold it next to his own cheek. "Judd, I want you to know how much I love you. No, please let me say this. I *have* to say it. I want you to know how sorry I am that I hurt you and your mother. I'm going to come back home if you'll both have me. I'm going to try to get my job back. I've stopped drinking. I'm going . . ." He stopped to catch his breath. "There will be only the three of us—our family. Just us. All together again."

Judd nodded. His eyes were wet.

"You're the most important thing in the world to me, Judd," Miller said.

Judd made a face and nodded toward his intravenous tube. "Please, Dad, don't make me sick. I'm eating."

Miller choked on the laugh that burst from his throat.

"Are you okay, Dad?" Judd said.

"Yeah, I'm fine now," Miller said, coughing. "So we're back on track again, you and I?"

Judd gave him a thumbs-up sign. "And you're coming home?"

"That's up to you and your mother, but it's what I want more than anything."

"All *right*," said Judd. He held up his hand and Miller slapped his palm against Judd's and they both grinned at each other.

"So," Miller said, "where is your mom, anyway?"

"She went home for a change of clothes. I told her I'd be fine, she doesn't have to sleep here tonight, but—you know *her*—she thinks I might need something."

"Tell you what. I'll try to talk her into letting me stay this time, okay?"

"Yeah, that would be cool. We could watch the Tennessee football game tomorrow on TV."

Miller stood up. "Yeah, that *would* be cool," he said. "I'll be back in an hour. Anything you want?"

"Double cheeseburger, no onions, French fries. Chocolate milkshake."

Miller laughed. "You got it."

Outside in the corridor, Miller's spirits plummeted again. He would have to face Katie. And at this point, he didn't know what to expect. When he got to the house she was just coming down the stairs, freshly showered and dressed. She looked pale and weary.

"What are you doing here?" she asked.

Miller shrugged. "I want to come home."

She sat down on the step at the top of the landing. "For how long?"

He leaned against the banister and propped his foot on the first step. "Forever, if you'll let me."

Katie bit her lip and thought for a moment. "What about *her*?"

"Her?"

"That girl."

"Adra," he said. "She has a name, Katie."

"I don't really give a damn what her name is."

"It's over," Miller said. "I was on my way to her house to tell her, but I wanted to see you first. I'm worried about you."

Katie dropped her head and started to cry. "How could you have done this to me, Miller?"

"I'm trying to find the answer to that question, Katie," he said. For some reason her tears made him feel stronger. He climbed the dozen steps between them and handed her his handkerchief. So much crying today, so much crying. "So?" he said finally.

"So, what?"

"So can I come back home?"

"What about the job?"

"I'll go in and talk to them Monday morning. Jack says Lucas is screwing everything up. They'll probably be glad to see me."

"And the drinking?"

"I haven't had a drink in four days. I was hoping you'd noticed."

She bit her lip. "I want everything back the way it used to be."

"Too late," he said. "Everything's changed. We have to go on from here, this moment. This is the jumping-off point. Are you up for it?" He sat down beside her and she let him pull her against his chest.

"I'm so tired, Miller," Katie said. "Why did this have to happen to us?"

"I wish I had an answer for you, Katie. It's life, I guess. It's just life."

Her chin trembled.

Miller kissed her cheek, and this, too, she allowed. "Why don't you go on up to bed, honey?" he said. "I'll go back to the hospital and spend the night with Judd."

Katie got to her feet. "No. I promised him I'd be there."

"I just came from there," Miller said. "He wants me to stay tonight. He said so."

"He said so?"

"He wants to watch the UT game with me tomorrow. Katie, will you please for God's sake go to bed in a real bed for a change instead of trying to sleep in a rocky chair in a hospital room? Get some rest. Take a long hot bath in the whirlpool tub. You can come to the hospital in the morning and I'll be there for the night in case Judd needs anything. He's mending now, Katie. He's going to be fine. The doctor has said so. He ought to be back home in a week."

"And you?" Katie said. "When will you be home?"

His heart pounded. "Day after tomorrow?"

For a minute she said nothing. Then she turned and started up the steps. At the top she looked down. "I'll expect you for brunch around eleven," she said. The glimmer of a smile played around the corners of her mouth. Then she walked the rest of the way upstairs without looking back.

Miller stood at the bottom of the staircase, his hand on the newel post. He would have liked to follow Katie upstairs, to lie down with her in their old familiar bed, to close his eyes and hear her whisper her prayers and then maybe feel her turn toward him and lay her hands on him and bless his body with whatever faith and forgiveness she had left to give him.

But he had promised Judd.

He sighed and walked out the door and down the porch steps. Keeping it alive, he thought, is so much harder than giving it up, but for the first time in a long time, it seemed worth working for. Between them, he and Katie had this life they had made together, this house built from their labors, and a child who was flesh-and-bone testimony to their union, their old love and passion. If Miller had not been given the miracle of Judd's waking up, he would have asked God to give him that passion back. The passion alone—give or take

the love—could sustain him. But with or without it, he had made the bargain, and he believed that with Judd's recovery, he had been allotted the single miracle he would ever be given in his life. But he still wished to find resolution with Adra.

He opened the front door and walked out. At the bottom step of the porch he turned and looked back at his house. A small wind lifted his hair and ruffled the colorful leaves on the trees. Autumn. A new season. A new beginning. When at last he turned away and walked toward his car, he felt what he thought the saints in their martyred ecstasy must have experienced—not happiness, not satisfaction or redemption, but a fine and exquisite pain.

On the way to Adra's house, for one shimmering instant, he understood that there is a universal plan and that he was part of it and he must do his best to accept his role in it. And in that instant he comprehended everything clearly, and then just as suddenly as he had grasped it, he lost the comprehension and saw only the gleaming highway, the stark forms of trees, and the long cold shadows swallowing up the daylight. But for the moment it was enough and he was glad.

25

By the time Miller was on the highway driving toward Adra's house, the rain was sweeping across the black asphalt in great silver sheets and bending the dry wildflowers that lay brown and brittle in the fields. Daylight was fading, but when he pulled up in front of the house, no light showed in the windows. After he had knocked on the door, the image that came to his mind was Adra's face that night at the beach house, looking up at him as she sat on the floor surrounded by her magazines. She had seemed like a child, her eyes reflecting the wonder of all the simple things Miller had opened up for her. What was it she had said? Something about a hummingbird. Something that took flight.

A nightingale sings.

Miller, soaked now by the downpour, hunched his shoulders against the rain. He didn't know how to begin, but by the time Adra opened the door, Miller saw by her expression that what he must put into words, her heart already understood. Something in her face had already closed up. Abruptly, her eyes shuttered against him, too.

"Can we go somewhere else to talk?" Miller asked. "I can't explain it. I'm uncomfortable in the house."

She leaned out of the doorway and nodded toward the barn, then pulled her sweater around her arms and lowered her head. As she began to run toward the barn, Miller remembered her terrible fear of lightning. He was aching to touch her, but he followed behind, clenching his fists to ease his anxiety.

Inside the barn, it was even darker than outside. Rain needled against the tin roof, and old smells that had been born there years before were sharpened by the dampness—the sweet thick fragrance of hay, the sharp acrid smell of horses now long gone, rusting metal machinery, and the earthy fragrance of the dirt floor.

Adra turned to face him. Her nipples showed dark through the front of the soaked cotton dress, and her eyelashes were pearled with drops of water. "You're goin' back to your wife," she said.

"It's not that simple," Miller said. "Something happened"—he struggled to remember when—"a few days ago, last week, I guess."

She waited, her arms crossed beneath her breasts. Her jaw jutted out impatiently.

"There was an accident," Miller said. "I took Judd fishing and the creek was swollen and . . ." When he tried to tell her the story, tears pushed up in his throat and he gestured helplessly. "He almost drowned. He's still in the hospital. He was hurt badly—his head, lacerations. Cuts, I mean. Broken arm. He was unconscious for four days. He just woke up."

She reached out a hand, then pulled it back. "Oh Jesus," she whispered. "Oh, Miller. Your boy? Will he be all right?"

Miller stumbled on, his voice snagging. "It'll take time, but he'll be all right. God, Adra, I was so afraid. I thought he was going to die." His voice sounded small and feeble in the cavernous barn. He wanted more than anything to pull her against him, to lie down with her and forgive himself through her passion. What would it hurt? If it was the last time, what would it hurt? A swift staccato of rain on the tin roof overhead tapered off again into soft, intermittent showers, and a bird that had roosted in the loft above suddenly beat its wings and flew into another corner of the barn. "Adra," he said, his voice trembling, "he almost drowned, and it was my fault."

Adra's eyes burned through the murky atmosphere. "Like Jimmy Duane," she said. Her face was like carved ivory in that light, pale with a yellowish tint. Her bare arms and hands seemed sculpted, she was so still. The sweater hung limp around her shoulders.

"I'm sorry," Miller whispered. "Adra, I'm sorry. I know how much I've hurt you. I wanted to help you, and I only hurt you. I should have left it alone, I should never have come into your life. It was something *I* wanted, not something *you* wanted, but I persisted until it came true."

Adra shook her head. She leaned forward and twisted her hair into a soft dark rope and wrung it out. Water ran down her arms in slow rivulets and dripped down from her elbows.

Miller felt a sense of panic, as if he must spit out his message as quickly as possible, as if he were being pursued by the truth. "Adra," Miller said, "I don't want to lose my son. If I keep seeing you, I'll lose him. I promised God one night in the hospital. I promised him I wouldn't see you anymore if he'd let Judd live. I guess I promised him the thing I wanted most, to make sure Judd would survive. It was the thing that would make me suffer the most. To punish me, I mean. To punish myself."

Adra stared past him into the dark recesses of the barn. "Katie hates me, I guess."

"No, no. It's me she despises."

"No. You're the one she has to live with." She stared up at the loft of the barn and tapped her foot against the straw on the floor.

He didn't know what else to say to her. "Are you cold?" Miller asked.

She shrugged. He could see the flesh rising on her arms. She shuddered almost imperceptibly and pulled the wet sweater tighter around herself and then she seemed all at once to surrender her anger, or maybe to surrender Miller. *Why are we so practiced at being cruel,* he thought, *to the people we love the most*?

Adra's mouth tightened into her old defense mode.

Miller leaned back against a box that was covered with a drop cloth. "These conditions," he began, then choked on the words and started over. "Katie wants me to go back to work, to stop drinking, to stop seeing you. Judd will be in his last year of high school. Katie wants us to make this effort for him. It's sort of a trial separation. We won't even be sleeping in the same room. If it doesn't work, then maybe there could be a future for you and me, but I have to try this. I have to salvage my family. Maybe later, maybe you and I could see each other again."

Adra laughed.

"Adra . . ."

"No," she said, "don't lie to me anymore. Don't lie to yourself neither. It hurts too much."

The rush of emotion in his heart felt like a wave breaking, falling suddenly after the beautifully tempting long slow rise to the crest, and the light that had gathered in it broke and splintered into a million irretrievable drops. "Everything that happened between us was true," Miller said. "Everything."

She backed away. Her face was in shadow now and he saw only the hard glitter of her eyes and the flash of her teeth when she spoke. "I don't think so. Just like I never knew what was true with Jimmy

Duane. He'd hit me and then tell me how much he loved me and how he never meant to do it. But it was different with you—for a while, anyway. You didn't mean to hurt me—in your heart, I mean, in your head, you didn't really mean to." Here her voice broke for the first time. "For a little while," she said, "it was the sweetest thing." She swallowed and then went on. "The difference between you and Jimmy Duane was that he *meant* to hurt me, and you didn't. With you, it just sort of happened, because you were fighting your conscience, I guess. Your heart was in loving me, but I reckon your head wasn't." She observed him with something like kindness. "I know you wanted to do good. You're a good man, Miller Sharp."

"I just wanted to help you," he said. "At first, I mean. Then, then I wanted you. I wanted you in the worst way." He hesitated and looked away from her face. "Adra, there's something else I have to tell you."

"What?"

"It's something I've kept from you. You won't like me very much when I tell you, but I've hurt you so much already, you probably can't hate me any worse."

"What?" she said. "That you let Jimmy Duane drown?"

Miller stepped back as if struck.

"I saw the mark of your teeth that day at the lake," she said. "I knew it wasn't there when Jimmy Duane jumped in the water. I knew it because he'd hit me that morning. Up in my face, on my cheek. He had got up mean because the baby was crying. She was only hungry, that was all. I told you at the beach about him shaking the baby, and I hit him to make him let go of her."

"That bruise on your wrist . . ."

"You remember that, do you? Well, that wasn't all he did. There was plenty more you never saw. Bruises and stripes under my clothes. On my back and my breasts. But at least it was me that got it instead of the baby." She laughed. "What do you call it? Distracted. That's what I done. I distracted him."

"Adra . . ."

She held up her hand to silence him. "So when the law come to the dock after Jimmy Duane drowned, they seen the bite and the coroner did an autopsy. They kept saying it was standard practice, the autopsy. And then the next day they sent a policeman to the house, asking did Jimmy Duane have a fight with somebody, was it foul play. I showed him my bruises and told him I was the one who had bit Jimmy Duane and he seemed to be satisfied with that. I mean the bite couldn't have killed him anyway. They said he had water in his lungs and that's what killed him. Asphyxiation. That's weird, ain't it? They didn't call it drowning, they called it asphyxiation."

"But why? Why did you protect me?"

"Because, Miller. If it had gone on, I would have ended up killin' him with his own shotgun. I'd already took it out and practiced shooting while he was at work. I knew just where he kept the shells and I hid some under the porch so I'd have them when I needed them. So, see? If it wasn't for you, I would've gone to jail and my baby would've come up without me if Jimmy Duane didn't kill her first."

Miller moved toward her, but she backed away. "Look," she said, pulling a tarpaulin from one of the stacks in the corner. "Look at this stuff. Stolen, all of it. Jimmy Duane was the middleman for this stuff. Every time a car drove up I thought it was the law coming for us both. Oh God yes I wanted him dead or just gone or something. Jesus knows I did. So don't you go worrying about me no more, Miller. You fixed things for me. You fixed them good."

Miller looked around. "But what will you do with all this—this stuff? What if the police come now?"

"My daddy knows some people. He'll take it off my hands and give me a little money back for it. Maybe a lot. That's the least Jimmy Duane owed me."

Miller felt a chill run along his arms. *My daddy knows some people.*

Those people are rednecks, Katie had said.

Miller's head was spinning. He leaned against the stack of stolen merchandise and marveled at the danger he had exposed himself to. "Adra," he said, his voice shaking, "I can't leave unless I know that you're going to be all right. You and Sister. I can't just walk away like this."

Her jaw was clenched. "I'm going to go live with my mama and daddy. I'm going to get my high school diploma. I'm going to college after that." She lifted her head and smiled a bright, unnatural smile. "I'm going to make a good life for my baby."

Miller held out his hand again.

"Just go," she whispered. "Just please get the hell out of here before I die of this pain in my heart."

He started toward the door and then looked back at her. "Adra, can you ever forgive me? I need you to forgive me."

She put her hand to her throat and looked into his eyes. "Not yet," she murmured.

He stared at her for a minute and then he turned and walked out of the barn and into the rain. It was too hurtful to look back. Along with his guilt he felt grief that she had relinquished him so easily, without a fight. He passed by the porch and the steps he had made, the wood still new and yellow. He had never repaired the roof, but everything there now was over, finished. There would be no physical or emotional closure.

He climbed into his car and when he turned around in the driveway he saw in his peripheral vision that Adra was standing in the doorway of the barn watching him and he kept driving and he never looked back again because that was what Katie wanted and that was what he knew he had to do.

He bumped down the dirt road, now rutted with mud puddles and covered with wet, fallen leaves. At the highway he turned left toward Knoxville and wherever his life might lead him after that. Only then did he remember to turn on the windshield wipers.